DETECTIVE RITA TRIBLE HAS A LOT TO WORRY ABOUT

She has an ex-husband whom she loathes, and a new boyfriend who seems too good to be trusted.

She has a job in peril as cops under her try to sabotage her career, and superiors come down hard on her case.

She has the Church using all its power to pressure her when she discovers the photo collection of a local priest with a taste for altar boys like the ones turning up savagely slain.

And she has a little boy named Greg she loves with all a mother's love, and fears not even all her cop's savvy can protect him from being the next victim.

Rita has to do more than pray—she has to act fast and gamble big—to stop a vicious killer who makes the wrath of God seem sweet....

A SOUL TO TAKE

A SOUL TO TAKE

C. N. BEAN

AN ONYX BOOK

ONYX
Published by the Penguin Group
Penguin Books USA Inc., 375 Hudson Street,
New York, New York 10014, U.S.A.
Penguin Books Ltd, 27 Wrights Lane,
London W8 5TZ, England
Penguin Books Australia Ltd, Ringwood,
Victoria, Australia
Penguin Books Canada Ltd, 10 Alcorn Avenue,
Toronto, Ontario, Canada M4V 3B2
Penguin Books (N.Z.) Ltd, 182–190 Wairau Road,
Auckland 10, New Zealand

Penguin Books Ltd, Registered Offices:
Harmondsworth, Middlesex, England

First published by Onyx, an imprint of Dutton Signet,
a division of Penguin Books USA Inc.

First Printing, June, 1996
10 9 8 7 6 5 4 3 2 1

  REGISTERED TRADEMARK—MARCA REGISTRADA

Printed in the United States of America

PUBLISHER'S NOTE
This is a work of fiction. Names, characters, places, and incidents either are
the product of the author's imagination or are used fictitiously, and any resemblance to actual persons, living or dead, events, or locales is entirely
coincidental.

BOOKS ARE AVAILABLE AT QUANTITY DISCOUNTS WHEN USED TO PROMOTE
PRODUCTS OR SERVICES. FOR INFORMATION PLEASE WRITE TO PREMIUM MAR-
KETING DIVISION, PENGUIN BOOKS USA INC., 375 HUDSON STREET, NEW YORK,
NEW YORK 10014.

Dedicated to

F.S.H.

and three angels

M.J.
JESSICA MARIE
SARAH ELIZABETH

A special thanks to a team of guides who safely led me through uncharted territory . . .

Matt Bialer
Audrey LaFehr
John Paine
Leah Bassoff

Now I lay me down to sleep,
I pray the Lord
my soul to keep.

If I should die before I wake,
I pray the Lord
my soul to take.

—Child's prayer

1

Wearing an old fishing jacket over her red silk blouse, Rita Trible took an indirect route down to the river. The tall wet grass saturated her navy slacks and leather slip-ons. She flashed a captain's credentials, Wisconsin's Criminal Investigation Division (CID), and told the assembled officers and park officials to move back. When they did, she saw the murdered boy. Despite being a nineteen-year veteran and having seen hundreds of murder victims, this one repulsed her. He reminded her of her son, Greg: same age, build, features, everything. "Get back," she told the crowd. To a trooper: "Get these people back."

As the officers withdrew, she stooped to the body, whose flesh was an orange-red, the color of meat in a market. The boy's neck had been cut ear to ear, after which someone had reconnected the carotid arteries and jugular veins, using crude sutures—like something out of a Frankenstein movie.

Her partner, Charlie Dalton, appeared. A huge black man in his twenties, he stopped at the body. She knew he was sickened by what he saw. Blood drained from his face, leaving it ashen. He looked around, took a couple of breaths through his nose, swallowed, and looked at the boy again. His coffee eyes seemed numb. He was a rookie, so new to CID that even his clothes were new: navy blazer, gray slacks, maroon tie, and cordovan shoes.

She told him, "Mark a perimeter." He didn't move, only stared at the boy. She touched his arm. "Mark a perimeter, Charlie," she repeated.

He began to cordon off an area in textbook fashion, using yellow tape as a marker. He trudged out of sight. She could hear him walking through sticks and leaves in the forest.

He had finished his bachelor's degree the previous summer and had passed the detective exam in September. Had it not been for his three years as a state trooper and three years in the military police, she wouldn't have considered assigning him to her Milwaukee-based unit. But she was new to the position and wanted to build her own staff. That, and during the interview she had discovered they had a common bond. He had a daughter with leukemia in remission just as she had an older brother with leukemia in remission.

From one of her jacket pockets she removed a pair of eyeglasses. The jacket with many pockets had belonged to her father. After he had died and her mother had moved to a nursing home, Rita had inherited the jacket. It had remained in a closet for five years before she brought it out the day she and Steve had separated. She brought it out determined never to be controlled again. She emptied its pockets of lures, hooks, and tangled fishing line, and filled the pockets with her own items. Only then had she fully felt her independence.

As she cleaned her glasses, she became aware of her reflection in the lenses. Though the two images were inverted, she knew the reflection well. Her face, etched with permanent creases, attested to a dark past, a past of abuse by her father and her ex-husband. Her auburn hair also showed signs of age. Despite the fullness of the shoulder-length hair, a premature gray had set in. At least her cinnamon eyes were young, she thought, though she knew that even that was deceptive because she needed the glasses to check the settings on her camera, which she had also found in one of the jacket pockets. By habit she found herself looking through the glasses to read the small lettering on the camera.

From the bank where she stood, she studied the surrounding forest. She ran a hand through her hair. To no one in particular she asked, "Has anyone touched the body?"

One trooper raised his hand. She noticed the disparity between his and her heights. She had a habit of doing that. "I checked for vital signs," he confessed.

She wondered why he had done that. The boy was obviously dead. In an irritated voice she said, "Get the names and addresses of everyone here." She began to take photographs. Stay calm, she told herself. Take your time and don't overlook anything.

It was the Tuesday before Easter, in the south branch of the Kettle Moraine State Forest, an hour west of Milwaukee. An anonymous telephone call had reported a dead body. Apparently someone had seen it while out for a morning jog. Since the body had been found in a state park, the case was referred to the CID.

The spectators talked while the uniformed trooper

collected names and addresses. Normally it wasn't a
river at all, one park official said, little more than a
stream, though there had been so much rain during
February and March that rivers had overflowed their
beds. The boy had probably been caught in the current, pulled downstream, and dumped on a bank, another park official said. Strange how the water had
discolored his skin.

Death made the spectators chatty. Rita didn't know
why, but it was always that way.

The water, brown and turbulent, was up in the
bushes. Tall grass swayed in the current like dishev-
eled hair.

Charlie returned from having taped off a perimeter.
He was composed again. Any reports of missing children? he asked the uniformed trooper. He articulated
each word carefully, as a stroke victim might do, or as
someone who wanted to be precise about everything.

No, none, the state trooper responded. He was still
collecting data.

Rita bent to the blond boy again, a boy somewhat
overweight. Gently, as if he might be sleeping, she
lifted one of his eyelids. Blue eyes. She guessed him
to have been dead eight to ten hours, maybe twelve.
His fingers were interlocked on his chest. There were
ligature marks on his wrists. Probably, she thought
grimly, the murderer had enjoyed watching him struggle. Studying him through her glasses, she made notes
on a pad she carried with her. No, he didn't appear
to have been in the water, though the clothes were
spotted, most likely from an overnight shower: jeans
and a short-sleeve red knit shirt. He wore black chucks
too. Rita could remember when high-top gym shoes
had been popular in her own youth. Funny how styles

returned, generation after generation. Greg wore them too. Without socks, like this boy. She noted the ligature marks above the ankles. She tried not to think about the pain and suffering she knew the child had undergone. In the wind, the hair of the child stirred, somehow looser than that of a living body. The hair reminded her of the grass dancing in the muddy water.

She turned her back to the others, looking up a wooded embankment that led to the road. The slope was overgrown with brush, though the body lay in a clearing. Someone had wanted it to be found, she thought. Since it was a cloudy morning, the sun was in and out. To Charlie she said, "What do you think?"

He knelt to the boy. He seemed to have been waiting for an opportunity to make his observations. Examining the body, he said, "Perhaps poisoning, though I'm unfamiliar with any toxin that turns skin this color."

She ran a hand through her hair. "He's been embalmed," she told him, her eyes roaming the ground as she searched for any trace of evidence.

He studied the incision on the boy's neck. "Is that what it is?" he asked. He massaged his own neck.

Glancing at the trampled brush on the embankment, she said, "It looks like our killer came down from the road." She called to the trooper: "Make sure everyone stays out of the cordoned-off area." To a deputy sheriff she said, "Call in the medical examiner." To Charlie: "Before we let in the lab people, let's run through a search."

She and he did a grid search. Side by side they climbed the embankment.

"Rita," Charlie called.

In the trampled bushes and rocks were a couple of

shoe impressions, one of which was useless because it looked as if whoever had made it had slipped. The other was distinct. A man's foot. It had apparently caught on a rock, tripping him, but not before a shoe impression had been left. Some of the bushes were crushed, apparently from where the body had fallen.

Charlie said, "You want me to order a cast?"

Rita mumbled, "That'll be fine," as she placed a tape measure beside the print and took a photograph. At the same time something else caught her attention: a cigarette butt. From her fishing jacket she removed a plastic container and a small bottle of black dust. With the camel hair brush from the container, she delicately dusted the cigarette butt. "I got one," she told Charlie. She took a photograph of the print on the butt. She didn't try to lift it. She would leave that for someone more skilled in the process. She marked the butt with a yellow cup. Each time she found something, she made a note in a notebook she carried. Charlie did the same with his own notebook. Later they would compare notes. It was standard procedure.

After the preliminary search, she attempted to cover the victim's hands with plastic bags, but discovered that the hands had been sewn together. Odd I didn't notice before, she thought. She took a photograph of the hands, then put a large plastic bag over them. Charlie outlined the boy's body with evidence paint.

Investigators from the crime lab entered the cordoned-off area. As Rita supervised, they began a meticulous processing of the scene, going back over everything. One investigator took soil samples. Another made a plaster cast of the shoe impression on the embankment. The print was lifted from the cigarette butt. For the better part of two hours, lab personnel combed the scene and took additional photographs. They missed nothing: Rita made sure of that.

Meanwhile, the medical examiner confirmed that the orange-red color of the body was indeed because the body had been embalmed. "Definitely a beginner's job," he said. "Perhaps a student."

At least there's a lead, Rita thought.

The medical examiner began to collect evidence from the body. Rita ordered a search of everything within a half mile of the body. She said, "Check any garbage cans you find, check anyplace that indicates fresh activity, and look along the highway for anything that might have been tossed out a car window. Look for cigarette butts. Winston. Don't miss anything." Once the body was moved by the medical examiner, Charlie took soil samples from the outlined image where the body had been.

By that time a group of reporters had converged on the taped-off area. All the Milwaukee stations had sent "live" crews—channels 12, 4, and 6. Reporters converged on a park official and asked for information about the body in the black bag that had been loaded into the back of a car on the highway. Apparently information was circulating because Rita heard the mention of a child, followed by a barrage of questions: A child, how old, who was it, boy or girl . . . ? Rita walked over to address the group. "My name is Captain Trible of Wisconsin's Criminal Investigation Division. We have assumed jurisdiction in this case." Microphones and cameras turned toward her. She was bathed in the intense light of the cameras. "We have discovered the body of a Caucasian boy, slightly overweight, approximately eleven years old. He is blond with blue eyes." She glanced at her notes. "He is wearing jeans, red gym shoes, and a red knit shirt." She looked at the cameras focused on her. "At this point we have no identity on the victim and no reports of any missing children who meet his description. I can advise your viewers that if anyone knows anything about a child fitting this description, that person should contact the nearest law enforcement agency. That's all we have at this point."

"Does this have anything to do with the rash of attacks on children in the Milwaukee area?" someone called out.

The thought had crossed her mind, but she said, "We can't confirm that one way or the other. We're just beginning our investigation." There had been a number of attacks on children, it was true, and city police had issued a composite of a suspect. He was in his late thirties to early forties and seemed to be Hispanic but didn't sound Hispanic. Perhaps someone with a tan. It might be him, she thought, but it was too early to tell.

"Do we know who the boy is?"

"No."

"Any suspects in the case?"

"We are only now collecting evidence."

"Do we know what time he was killed?"

"We can't confirm that yet. The medical examiner will be making that determination. One more question, and then I have to get back to work."

"Someone said the boy was orange."

"We have only begun our investigation."

"Are you denying the body was orange?"

"I'm not confirming or denying anything. We are

only now beginning our investigation. Thank you."
She walked away.

While the lab technicians wrapped up their work,
Rita and Charlie returned to their car. Before she
started it, she drew a deep breath. "How are you?"
she asked.

"It depends," he said. "How many times have you
seen something like this?"

"Never anything like this."

"I guess I'm all right, then," he told her.

She started the car, made a U-turn, and headed
back to I-94. They rode in silence.

They were almost to Brookfield before Charlie said,
"Who could do something like that?"

She kept her eyes on the road. "Prepare for the
worst."

She could feel him looking at her. She knew what
he was thinking. She was thinking it herself. She had
been thinking it from the moment she saw the body.
"What do you mean?" he asked.

"You know what I mean," she told him. She
glanced at him. "Aside from a couple of slip-ups, this
was too organized to be coincidental."

He looked out his window. "Like this is the kind
of person who will kill again?"

She adjusted the police radio, though the adjust-
ment wasn't necessary. The reception was fine. She
needed something to do with her hands. "I could be
wrong," she said. She didn't think so. She had helped
with the Dahmer investigation. People who killed in
such an organized fashion didn't stop until they got
caught.

"You think it's a serial killer?"

She lost her cool. "Charlie, I didn't say that," she

told him. She took a deep breath to calm herself. "All I'm saying is that we have someone who has murdered a child in a calculated manner. In our line of work, that's not good." When he became silent after that, she was glad—because the questions he was asking were troubling questions, questions whose answers she didn't care to face.

2

At the entrance to the morgue, an anxious mother was waiting. She said she had heard reports about a child's body that had been discovered, and when she began to check around, she had discovered her son was not where he was supposed to be. She said she was sure the dead boy wasn't her son, but since she had yet to locate him, the police had asked her to view the body. The medical examiner escorted the mother, Rita, and Charlie into the stainless steel room, where there were a number of stainless steel tables. Each table was equipped with a pan scale—to weigh body parts—and a microphone that was suspended from the ceiling. The moment the medical examiner unzipped the black body bag that had been placed on one of the tables, the mother screamed frantically. Again and again she screamed, barely able to catch her breath each time. No one could control her.

Fighting and screaming, she was dragged from the room by uniformed police. The body had been identified. Matthew Hammond, an eleven-year-old from Brown Deer, a suburb of Milwaukee. The mother, Crystal, was a twenty-nine-year-old divorcee who worked as a secretary for a Milwaukee law firm. She had not reported her son missing because he was supposed to have spent the night with Bobby Ruble, a school friend. It wasn't until she had heard radio reports about a murdered child that she began to be concerned about her own son. She had called her home number and retrieved a message from the answering machine, a message from the school secretary who had called to ask why Matthew hadn't been in school. Crystal had checked with Mrs. Ruble, only to discover no overnight had ever been planned in the first place.

As the mother's screams receded, the autopsy began with a physical examination and description of the murder victim. The pathologist pointed out that the boy's lips had been glued shut. "It looks like Super Glue," he said. He shook his head. "A trick of the trade for morticians." He pulled open the lips, showing blood-stained braces. "As you can see, the glue doesn't work too well," he said. "Note the tongue."

"Bitten?" Charlie said. "Asphyxia?"

"That's what it looks like," the pathologist said. He looked up at Charlie. "I don't recall having seen you around here before," he said. He asked Rita, "New partner?" She introduced them.

The pathologist pointed out that under magnification there was bruising around the boy's lips, as well as facial scratches, indicating he might have been smothered with a cloth or gloved hand held over the nose and mouth. With tweezers the pathologist removed a tiny thread from the boy's braces. Apparently a cloth had snagged on the wires. "Whoever did this knows what he's doing," the pathologist said. "The body's been bathed, then embalmed. Not a very good job of embalming, but talk about a lack of evidence. Someone didn't want us to have much to go on."

With gloved fingers the pathologist raised the body onto its side. On the boy's back were multiple stab wounds, seventeen in all, each well over an inch in length. "Most of these look postmortem," he said.

Rita took photographs. The pathologist snapped his own.

He collected fluid samples and held up some of the fluid. "I bet you money it's red dye number two," he said. "Like they use in meat packing. That's why his skin is the color it is. Standard practice for morticians." He took swabs of the anal area, pubic area, and mouth. "Definite sex crime," he told them.

"So your guess is the dye is typical of that used in the embalming field?" Rita said.

"Oh, sure," the pathologist told her. "It's what they all use."

With the body on its back again, the pathologist took X rays. Then he used a scalpel to clip the thread that held the boy's hands together. He sliced open the chest and abdomen. The strong odor of bowel permeated the room. The pathologist trimmed the flesh.

With a cutting instrument, he clipped out the rib cage. He drew stomach fluids to determine what the boy had eaten and when. In the boy's lungs, water droplets were discovered, indicating he had inhaled water. The pathologist said he ruled out drowning because there wasn't a sufficient amount of water, though the presence of droplets was perplexing. In all probability, the cause of death was asphyxiation, the pathologist said, caused by smothering. He speculated the body had been hung upside down to drain the blood. "Like you do when you butcher a cow or a pig." Rita took additional photographs of the ligature marks on the ankles. She asked why he thought the body had been hung upside down.

The pathologist told her there were traces of blood in the boy's hair despite the body having obviously been cleansed by the murderer.

As he worked, he said, "Do you know where the saying 'kicked the bucket' comes from?"

Neither she nor Charlie did.

"Isn't that strange?" the pathologist said, busy with his work. "Everyone knows what it means—death—but very few people know anything about the true origin of it." He dropped the spleen in the scale. "You see, it comes from the days when they butchered hogs. They would hang the hog by its hind legs, put a bucket under its head, and cut the jugular vein so the blood drained into the bucket. Invariably the hog's front legs would kick the bucket. Hence the association with death."

The pathologist ruled the time of death at between ten and eleven o'clock at night on Monday, April 5, the night before the body's discovery.

He inserted a scalpel above the boy's right ear. He pulled the scalpel around the head to above the right ear. Then he trimmed back the skin and hair, creating a flap that he pulled down over the boy's face. Once the scalp had been brought forward to expose the cranium, the pathologist used an electric saw to open the skull. Charlie left the room.

Rita went out to check on him. "Are you all right?" she asked.

He told her, "The smell. It got to me. How can that guy be so casual about the whole thing?"

"I guess when you cut people open every day, all day long, you eventually grow rather cold about the process." She studied him. "Are you sure you're okay? You've been to autopsies before, haven't you?"

"A couple. But I'll never get used to them," he told her. "It's almost as bad as the murder itself."

"You feel up to seeing the mother?" she asked.

He nodded.

"You sure? If you need a chance to get your head together, I'll understand."

"I'm okay," he told her.

"We've got to see her. The time element is crucial."

"I'm all right," he emphasized.

They went to see the mother, the smell of her son still on them. As Charlie drove, Rita thought about the case. The thing that bothered her most was the mother's strange presence at the county morgue. How could a mother not know where her son was? she wondered. And if she thought she knew where he was, how could so much time pass before she figured out he wasn't there in the first place? She knew her son, Greg, had gone places without getting permission, but there were only brief periods of unaccountability, and the moment she found out he was someplace he wasn't supposed to be, she punished him, so it was rare he did. Never would he go overnight without her knowing exactly where he was. That bothered her about the case. Sure, the mother's reaction upon seeing her son had seemed genuine, but something bothered Rita. Something didn't add up.

She looked out the car window. Crystal lived in an old section of Brown Deer, a suburb on the northwest side of Milwaukee. There was a varied assortment of aging buildings that the affluent suburb had grown up around. The apartments where Crystal lived were dilapidated, an eyesore to the progressive community. Here and there was an open-hooded car on blocks. A crew of painters were changing the color of the apartments from orange to cobalt blue. The building looked as though it had been repainted a number of times already.

"Who could do something like this?" the mother asked the moment a uniformed officer allowed Rita and Charlie into the apartment. "To a child!" It was an old apartment, with gray wood paneling and orange shag carpeting. The room smelled old, like musty books.

Rita reintroduced herself and Charlie. She let the mother study her credentials in their black leather case. "I know this is awful," she said, "but it's crucial we learn as much as we can about your son, as soon as we can." They sat down together in the small living room. The furniture was worn. The place was a dump according to Rita's standards. Where she sat on the sofa with Charlie, she noticed a torn cushion. The sofa wobbled. Its legs were uneven.

Crystal began with an incoherent flurry of talk, giving random facts about her son.

Pretty soon Rita stopped her. "Maybe it would be better if we asked the questions and you answered them."

The short woman with pixie-cut hair nodded. It needed to be recolored, Rita noticed. Though bleach blond, it had a reddish tint to it.

"You say Matthew called to ask if he could spend the night with the Ruble boy?"

Crystal nodded. "Bobby Ruble. That's what he told me." There was a tic at the corner of her left eye.

Rita couldn't tell if Crystal was nervous or if the tic was natural. Crystal put her index finger at the corner of her eye to apply pressure to the twitching skin.

"Are you nervous about something?"

"No, only upset."

"When did Matthew do all this—I mean, set up the trip to his friend's house?"

"He called me at work on Monday at around one o'clock."

"He didn't go to school?" Charlie asked.

"Yes, he went to school." She tore off a strip of toilet paper from a roll on her lap. After wadding it, she blew her nose. He had called from the school office, she said. "They sometimes let the kids do that." Rita and Charlie took notes.

"Did he need permission to call?" Charlie asked.

She shrugged. "I guess so," she said. "You'd need to ask the school that. He often calls. Anytime he forgets something like his house key or his homework, he calls and wants me to bring it to him."

"And that doesn't upset you?" Charlie continued.

Rita thought the rookie's questions were good.

"Sure it upsets me. I tell him I don't like him calling me at work."

"So this day was all right?" Charlie mentioned.

"What are you getting at? What are you suggesting? Are you suggesting I'm lying!"

"How often did Matthew spend the night with his friends?" Rita asked before Charlie could answer. She wanted to cool down the tone of the interview.

"Almost every weekend during the summer," Crystal said, keeping one eye on Charlie. It was a hostile look, as if she had formed an impression about him. "He either went to one of his friend's house, or one of his friends stayed with us. I don't know why I said yes this time." The answer sounded too rehearsed, Rita thought.

"Why do you say that?" Charlie asked.

"I never let him spend the night on a school day," she said. "And for another thing, he hasn't been getting along that well with Bobby." She sighed. "But he told me he and Bobby had to work on a report for a team project at school, and it was the only way they could get together for a couple of hours."

"So you let him go because he and Bobby were doing a homework assignment together?"

"Yes."

"You say they hadn't been getting along?" Rita said.

"You know how kids are. Especially around that age, they're always fighting."

"Did you take him clothes and things for the overnight?" Charlie asked.

She shook her head. "He had his own key—like I said. He told me he and Bobby would run by after school to pick things up."

"Did you try to call him last night?"

Bowing her head, she said, "He never liked me to call. Like other children his age, he thought he was too old to be a mama's boy."

"Where's the boy's father?" Rita asked.

"Alabama."

"What's his name?"

"Ron Calvin Hammond."

She wrote it down. "Does he visit?"

"No. He's remarried and has two children of his own."

"Any chance he might be in town?"

"No, I called him. He was in Japan on business. He's on his way back to the States now."

"What kind of father was he?"

Crystal looked at Rita sharply. "After we got divorced, he didn't have much to do with Matthew. That was the kind of father he was." Then she sighed. "He had a new wife, and new priorities. I can't blame him."

"Did he ever abuse Matthew?"

She shook her head. No."

"Do you have a boyfriend?"

"What's that have to do with this?"

"We're only trying to collect as much information as we can."

"Yes, I have a boyfriend. His name is Barry Dixon. I called him. He said he would get here as soon as he could. He and his brother own an auto-repair garage, and Barry's the only one there today. I expect him at any time."

"Did Matthew and he get along?"

"They didn't see each other that much, but they got along okay."

Charlie asked, "Have there been any suspicious persons or vehicles around the house?"

"No."

"Has anyone threatened you about anything?"

"No."

"Anyone angry at you?"

"No."

"Who has Matthew been spending time with lately?" Rita asked.

"His friends from school. I told you."

"Who in particular?"

"Mostly Bobby Ruble, though they have had a

cooling-off period. I guess he mostly hung around the other boys in his class."

"What about adults? Did he spend any time with adults?"

"No, only friends."

"Bobby, you mean."

Crystal nodded. "Like I told you, he and Bobby had had a cooling-off period, but I guess they were still friends. Yes, Bobby."

They went over Matthew's habits and routines.

Had he ever been to the Kettle-Moraine forest, the south branch—south of I-94? Charlie wanted to know.

No.

Had he been in any kind of trouble? Rita asked.

No.

Had she noticed anything different about the way he was acting?

No.

Any change in habits or routines?

No.

Rita asked if they could look around in Matthew's room.

Crystal showed them the way. It was a small bedroom across from her own. Matthew's bed was not made, his hamster's cage was dirty, and there was hamster food sprinkled about the carpet. An odor emanated from the cage. A typical eleven-year-old's room, Crystal told them, claiming that the boy had been going through a "messy" stage. Under his bed Matthew kept a rock collection in a tin container, comic books, and a box that contained seashells and baseball cards. Rita looked at the box of shells and cards. Greg's room was the same way, she thought as she looked through Matthew's belongings.

From the closet Charlie pulled out a long white dress, hanging with the other clothes. "Is this yours?" he asked Crystal.

"No, that's Matthew's," she said. "He was serving as an altar boy at St. Paul's."

Also in the closet was a box of eight-track music tapes. Rita picked one up and wiped the dust off it. "I haven't seen one of these in a while," she said.

Crystal blew her nose. "They were mine," she said. "I was going to throw them out, but Matthew wanted to keep them. I don't know why. He couldn't listen to them or anything. We don't have an eight-track player, you know. I don't even think they make such things anymore. I guess he wanted them because they belonged to me. He wanted everything that belonged to me." That caused her to lose her composure. She wept loudly. "He loved his mother!"

Charlie asked, "Did you ever hit him?"

"No—I mean, yes." She was confused. "I mean, I hit him if he did something wrong. Why are you asking these questions! Go find the damn killer!"

Silence.

Rita attempted to assuage the animosity. She said, "Look, the more we know, the more we can help. It's as simple as that. You know Matthew because you've taken care of him all of your life—" Crystal nodded. "We're learning about him for the first time this very moment." Crystal nodded again. "We're going to ask questions that are going to upset you, but this is information we have to know. And when we get done"— she tapped her own chest with her fingertips—"we're going to send in another team to ask you more questions, a lot of them the same ones we asked. We have to know everything we can know. That's our only hope of finding your son's killer. You want us to find him, don't you?"

Crystal nodded. Her eye was twitching again. She held it with a fingertip.

"What about friends or relatives? Who has exposure to Matthew?"

Crystal held up her hands. "My parents are in the Chicago area."

Rita and Charlie went through another round of questions, another hour of them.

By the time they left the apartment, it was late in the afternoon and a drizzle was falling, the kind of rain one doesn't mind standing in, especially after a long day. Rita told Charlie, "I want you to research mortuary-science programs. Find out where the schools are. See if you can generate a list of people in the local area who have gone through such a program or are in such a program. There must be a national organization, state licensing, you know the sort of thing." He jotted notes, nodding as he did so. "Call around to the local funeral homes. See what you can learn. I want to know about anyone who might have had exposure to embalming practices. It might be someone who only worked in a funeral home."

The distant chiming of a church bell reminded her of the late hour. She glanced at her watch: 5:02. She set her watch back two minutes. There were still things to do. She knew she had to stop by the office to brief the other detectives and to assign them to various tasks: Background checks of family members would need to be initiated; neighbors, teachers, and friends of the Hammond boy would have to be interviewed; and evidence reports would need review. She also needed to brief officials in Madison. "When we get back to the office, you head home," she told Charlie. "I'll drop you at the parking garage. Go home and give Keisha a kiss and a hug." She knew he was thinking about Keisha; she had been thinking about Greg all day. When one witnessed a child's death, one always thought about one's own child. "I'll run up to the office for a few minutes, and then I'm off to get Greg myself. We'll hit this thing hard in the morning." They had no sooner got into their sedan than news vans and cars began to arrive. It was as though they were hot on the trail.

Charlie mentioned, "We got out of there right on time."

As they drove into Milwaukee on their way to the office on Wisconsin Avenue, a heavy despondency set in. Rita did ask, "Did you believe her?" to which Charlie answered, "No," but that was the extent of their conversation. She didn't say anything more because she herself thought the mother was hiding something. Until she figured things out for herself, she didn't want speculation to let her thoughts run rampant. Could the mother have murdered her own son? she wondered. As badly as she hated to admit it, the answer was yes. Immediate family members were always key suspects for good reason. A high percentage of them turned out to be the murderers.

3

The Wisconsin Justice Department's CID investigators shared offices with the state's Narcotics Division and Arson Division in a building on 633 West Wisconsin Avenue, a major street in downtown Milwaukee. Rita took the elevator to the seventh floor, which was quiet for 5:45. Normally, there were investigators roaming the halls, firearms clearly displayed, case files in hand.

As Rita passed the main door of the Narcotics Division, she heard a struggle from within the reception area. She opened the door to find two undercover narcotic agents wrestling. They had fallen into a row of chairs, but had continued to struggle with each other, rolling around on the floor.

Reclining at the receptionist's desk, which was cluttered with beer cans, feet on the typewriter, was Sergeant Jerry Grier. In one hand was a bottle of scotch whiskey. They called him the Bull. He looked like a bull. He was chewing on the stub of a cigar. She and he had been friends for years. In fact, Bull was one of the reasons she had been promoted to captain and made the chief investigator of the Milwaukee office. One of his agents had been murdered the summer before, and she had been assigned to head the investigation. Within a few days she had gotten a lead about the killer through an informant. The man had been having an affair with the killer's girlfriend, whom Rita had cornered the first chance she got. As it turned out, the girlfriend had been with the killer on a number of break-ins, and in return for immunity from prosecution she supplied information about the whereabouts of certain stolen property, including a .38-caliber pistol. Rita had gotten a search warrant and retrieved the pistol. Fingerprints and ballistics had linked the killer to the murder.

"Boys! Boys!" Bull said. Beside him was a small marijuana plant growing in a silver teapot.

Skinny, blond-haired Greg Mendelson and the bearded, long-haired Alan Wierbicki stopped wrestling. They got to their feet. Both were red-faced and panting.

With a half smile on his face, Bull spoke around the cigar he held with his teeth. "I see you got my message," he said to Rita.

"What message?"

"I've been trying to get a hold of you the last thirty minutes or so."

"I just got in."

He opened a drawer and pulled out a videotape. "Well, I taped it for you." He went to a television on a cart, turned it on, inserted the tape in the player, and stood back. Crystal Hammond appeared with a group of reporters. Leaning against the door frame of her open doorway was a lanky, dark-haired young man. He looked like some kind of mechanic. His hands were blackened with grease, and there were

C.N. Bean

grease smudges on his face and clothes. Oddly enough, it almost seemed as if there were a smile on his face.

Bull touched the screen, putting his finger on the young man. "I've busted him before," he told Rita. "I've been hearing all day about this case, and that's why I called. Barry W. Dixon's his name."

Aside from a nod, Rita didn't say anything. Barry was the boyfriend Crystal had mentioned.

"I bet it wasn't thirty minutes ago it was on. We were sitting here doing some drinking and watching TV, and this special report came on. There was Barry W., plain as day. Is that the mother's boyfriend?"

"Yes."

"Well, for what it's worth, I've busted him before. It's been awhile back, but I remember he's quite the smartass. I busted him for pot."

"Do you mind if I keep the tape?"

He ejected it, handed it to her, and went back to the desk, where he sat down. He took a swig of his scotch. "Check this out, Rita," he said. From the corner of the desk he lifted an evidence bag filled with smaller baggies of marijuana. "Seventeen of these babies," he said. He took the cigar out of his mouth and held its moist end between his index finger and his thumb. "All in a day's work." He was big—pumped weights regularly—with short brown hair and a tan to match. Only his bright blue eyes stood out as being inconsistent with the rest of him. His body said he was an animal. His eyes said he was intelligent, though the eyes were obviously intoxicated at the present moment. "You'll appreciate this, Rita—" he put the evidence bag down and took a swallow from the bottle of scotch. "We go to execute this search warrant this afternoon—you know, we were checking out how reliable this new snitch was—and this asshole here"—he pointed at Greg, who smiled—"tries to kick down the door of the apartment we raided. His foot gets caught in the hole he makes in the door." He laughed. Greg's face, which had resumed some of its normal color, reddened again. "When we finally get inside, we go through the whole place, and this is all we found." He raised the teapot with the single plant growing out of it. "So I say, what the hell, we'll arrest the dude who's standing there in his underwear watching us search. I tell him to get dressed, and we head for the door to take him downtown." He put the cigar back in his teeth and lit it. He puffed dark smoke into the air. "On the way out the door, I'm starting to feel sorry for the guy—you know, he's shaking like a dog trying to shit a peach seed, and for all I know, he's getting busted for a little plant—so I take this army field jacket from the closet and tell him to put it on. You know, I didn't want him to get wet or cold. And"— he raised the evidence bag again—"guess what was in the coat?" He smiled.

Rita listened patiently to the story before asking, "Is there anything else you can tell me about this Barry Dixon?"

"Like I said, I don't know him that well, but he thinks he's a tough guy. Smartass is how I remember him. Say, we've been hearing rumors about the kid you found. Someone said he was red."

She nodded. "An eleven-year-old boy sliced up and embalmed," she told him. "I was just stopping by the office to wrap up some paperwork when I heard the commotion." She nodded at Greg and Allen.

Bull said, "Oh, they're pumped, that's all. You know how it is when something pays off."

She held up the tape. "Listen, thanks a lot for this," she said. "I owe you."

Bull's face became solemn. "You'll never owe me," he said.

She knew he was talking about Bernie Deaton, the agent who had been found shot to death, slumped over the wheel of his car. She waved, pulled the door shut, and went on to the CID office, which was lighted. She entered a large room filled with desks and filing cabinets.

Lieutenant Adam McCabe was in his office working. Second in command of the Milwaukee division, he was the only one around at that time of day. Rita stopped at his door and asked what he was doing still there. Catching up on some of his reading, he said. His office was meticulous, never a thing out of place. She was about to walk on when he asked, "Have you decided what to do with the Hammond case?"

The comment caught her off guard. Why did he care? she wondered. "What do you mean?"

"Who's going to get it?"

She knew then he wanted it. He had built his career on routine cases and keeping a low profile. For years that had worked to his advantage because he had risen to the rank of lieutenant by hanging around until he got promoted, but in recent years he had been passed over for promotion to captain twice. Each time he had been told it was because he hadn't supervised any major investigations. The truth was, even when Gordon Cales had headed the Milwaukee unit, he had never given Adam any major cases because he didn't think Adam was competent to handle them. Before Gordon had retired, he had told Rita that if she had an investigation that merely needed to be worked for investigative leads, she could give the investigation to Adam because he would eventually get the job done. But if the case was important, she should give it to someone else.

"To tell you the truth, I haven't given that part of it much thought yet," she told him. "We're having a briefing in the morning. I'll make assignments then. See you in the morning." She left his office.

He followed her. "I could use this case," he told her. "My career needs a break."

She realized he had worked late so he would be there when she returned. She wished she could tell him she wouldn't give him the Hammond case even if there were no one else in the office. That's how she felt. In her private office she stopped at the window, looking out at the city damp with rain.

Adam persisted. "Look, I don't hold a grudge that you got promoted over me, even though I'm older than you and I have more seniority. I'm only asking that now that you have what you wanted—you were made chief over the office—that you'd give me a break. From what I hear, this is a big case. I'd like to have a shot at it."

Realizing that evening was setting in and she still needed to pick up her son, she said, "Give me the night to think about it."

He smiled. "That's all I ask. That you think about it. See you in the morning. I'll be here first thing." He vanished.

She felt bad for misleading him. At the same time she realized she had no choice. Had she been truthful with him, there would have been a confrontation, and it was too late in the day for that. She knew, however, that she wouldn't be able to assign the Hammond case to anyone else. If she gave the case to anyone, Adam would file a complaint against her. She'd have to keep the case herself. Besides, for some reason she wanted it.

She called her administrative assistant, Bev Smith, at home. She told Bev to call all the chief investigators but Jim O'Donnell and have them at the office at nine o'clock the next morning for a meeting. She called O'Donnell herself. Aside from Charlie, Jim was the investigator with the least seniority, so she usually ended up giving him the less appealing jobs and assignments. When Jim answered the phone, she asked him if he could arrive at the office early enough that he could run out to the crime laboratory on Eleventh Street and collect the evidence reports from the Hammond case. "We have a meeting at nine," she told him, "so I'll need you to get things together before that."

Once she had given Jim instructions, she called the lab. She emphasized that she had to have all the forensic reports first thing the next morning. She put down the phone and looked around at her desk, cluttered with files and paperwork. It seemed that she was never caught up. She knew she was a top-notch investigator, but she didn't think she made a good administrator. Her place was on the street. That's where she felt most comfortable, not in some office processing paperwork. From the beginning she had made that clear to Paul Clowers, her supervisor in Madison. He had told her not to worry. He said if she took the assignment as Milwaukee chief, he would support however she decided to manage the office.

She booted up her computer and began transcribing her written investigative notes from that day. All the while she kept her eyes on the time. She remembered she had yet to call Paul. She dialed his home number and put the call on the speaker phone. While she typed her notes, she briefed Paul on the case. Apparently he heard typing in the background because he asked if someone was there with her.

No, she told him, she was only trying to get as much done as she could before calling it a day.

He reminded her that she was the supervisor of the office. She didn't need to do everything herself.

"Please, Paul," she said, "it's been a long day."

He laughed. "Go home. Keep me informed."

On her way up Milwaukee Avenue, she stopped at the public library to see what she could find out about embalming. There wasn't much. She found one book that discussed embalming practices in America. According to the author, Americans favored embalming because they didn't have the courage to face death. They wanted always to see a dead body that looked alive. She found another book about Egyptian embalming practices. There the Egyptians removed the visceral organs and dehydrated the body by immersing it for seventy days in a salt solution before wrapping the body in clean linen. The Egyptians embalmed so the soul could eventually reinhabit the body.

It wasn't much to go on, no doubt about it, but she was inclined to believe her killer was both driven to kill and repulsed by death at the same time. She remembered a case in which the killer tried to hide his victim under some rubbish in the victim's basement. When the killer was apprehended, he said he did such a sloppy job hiding the body, not because he didn't want anyone to find it, but because he didn't want to look at it himself. Perhaps that was why Matthew's killer had embalmed him—that is, as a sloppy attempt to hide the face of death from himself.

4

Everywhere there were signs of deterioration in her childhood neighborhood of New Berlin, a suburb on the southwest side of Milwaukee. What had begun as an upper-middle-class community was now a section of town where one increasingly saw For Rent signs in yards. Along with the rental property that had squeezed the "upper" out of the middle-class came less attention to maintenance and upkeep. Houses needed paint and repairs. Once well-groomed properties had turned shabby, with weeds and dandelions overrunning the grass. Trash blew from yard to yard. No one seemed to care. Even the olive-green house where she had spent twelve years of her life—from age six to eighteen—was showing age. It especially needed new black trim. One end of the garage had settled. Her brother Sean hadn't done much to the exterior of the house since he and Julie had moved in.

She walked through the drizzle to the open garage, where she entered the house through the kitchen door. Julie was at the sink.

"Hey," Rita said to the dishwater blonde of fifty, who had her hands on the small of her back. "What's wrong?"

"My back is out again," Julie replied.

"Did you call the doctor?"

"I called the chiropractor. I have an appointment tomorrow morning."

"Now you make me feel bad for having Greg come over here after school," Rita said. She looked around, wondering where he was. She realized how badly she wanted to see him. In the back of her mind she had been thinking about him from the moment she had laid eyes on Matthew Hammond. "Where is he?"

"He's across the street playing with Kyle," Julie said. "And don't be silly. He's been no trouble at all. In fact, he's been across the street since he got here." She lit a cigarette, turned on the stove fan, and stood by the door to smoke, holding the cigarette under the hood where the fan was. She stood with her back very erect. "He's the politest boy."

"Who, Kyle?" Rita asked.

Julie nodded.

Rita opened the refrigerator. "Oh, I know. He's a sweetheart. What do you have to snack on?"

"There's celery in that Tupperware bowl."

Rita got herself a piece of celery. "I bet Greg was thrilled about this for an after-school snack," she said. At the same time, she realized what a good influence Sean and Julie were on Greg. They always had been good parents, though their two children, Beth and John, were grown up and on their own now. Rita walked to the living room doorway, where she could see out the front windows. Greg was nowhere in sight.

"That's right. He eats healthy when he's around his Aunt Julie."

Rita returned to the cabinet next to the refrigerator. "Where's the peanut butter?" She found a jar, removed the lid, and dipped the celery stick in the peanut butter. The celery crunched when she chewed it. "So Paul and Chris have been leaving Kyle with Babe while they go through the divorce?"

"Oh, he's over there all the time now." She took a puff of her cigarette and blew the smoke under the fan apron. "So is Chris. I mean, even though she's divorcing their son, Babe and Norb are still close to her, and you know they love their grandson. Say, I saw you on television today." She became solemn; her lime-green eyes were bitter. "That's terrible about what happened to that little boy. Who would ever hurt a child like that?"

Rita commented, "It's sickening." There was a moment of silence. Rita looked at her watch. She wanted to get home to work on the case. "Sean's out late tonight, isn't he? Is he still at work?"

Julie nodded. "He's the only one I know who works more hours than you," she said. "I tell him to slow down, Rita, but he doesn't listen to me. He doesn't look right either. I'm worried about him. He looks pale, and I think he's losing weight again."

She was always worrying about him, Rita thought, which might explain why he had been in the hospital twice in the past year. Both times had been false alarms. "I thought he looked fine," Rita said. "Have you talked to the doctor?"

"Yes, but he doesn't seem too concerned. He says it sometimes takes a year or so for new bone marrow to work right—it's been just a little over a year since the transplant, you know."

Rita put both hands at the back of her hip bones. "Believe me, I know," she said. "I still feel the pain."

Julie laughed. "Oh, you don't either!"

Rita smiled. "Oh, yes I do," she said. "Having a baby didn't hurt that much. I tell you, it felt like I bounced down a whole flight of stairs on one hip and then down another flight of stairs on the other hip."

Julie ground out her cigarette. She stuck the butt under running water and dropped the butt in the trash.

"So what makes you think Sean doesn't look good?" Rita asked, chewing more celery. She thought it would do Julie good to talk about it and get it out of her system.

"I don't know," Julie said. "I do know he's working too hard again. He doesn't know when to stop. You want some coffee?"

"Sure, why not?"

Julie started the coffee maker. "I mean, when you live with someone day in and day out, you notice things—things other people wouldn't see. You won't tell him I said anything, will you?"

"Of course not." Rita got another piece of celery and dipped it in peanut butter. She took a bite.

A car horn honked.

Julie smiled. "Speak of the devil," she said. "I take it you parked in the driveway, so he can't get his car in the garage."

"Poor baby has to walk through the rain all the way from the street."

Sean, a tall, wiry man of fifty, entered grumbling, "Who in the hell blocked the damned driveway!" Then a smile appeared on his face, and he held out his arms to hug Rita. "I should have known it was you," he said, lifting her off the floor. He was strong for being so thin. "You're the only person I know who's mean enough to do such a thing."

They kissed each other on the cheek and patted each other's back.

Rita pushed back her balding, gray-haired brother. He looked fine. "Julie's right," she said, joking, "I believe you do look like a ghost."

Julie slapped Rita's shoulder. "Rita!" she said, laughing. "I told you not to say anything!"

"What, my sister hold something back from me?" he said. He put his hands on her cheeks. "Really, do I look pale?"

"Don't be so paranoid," she told him. "But your hands are cold as ice." She pulled his hands off her face. "Don't you have any blood in those fingers?" After she said it, she thought of Matthew Hammond.

"It's turning cold out there," he said. He got a bottle of Wild Turkey out of the cabinet. "How about a highball to warm things up?"

"Sure," Rita said. "I'll have a short one. Julie, forget the coffee."

As Sean filled two small glasses with ice, he said, "Have you been over to see Babe and Norb?"

"No, why?"

"They ask about you all the time. Norb says you never stop by anymore."

Rita had baby-sat for Paul when he was growing up. She had grown close to the family back then and had kept in touch with them over the years. She had even baby-sat Kyle now and then. It had been several weeks since she had stopped by to visit Babe and Norb. There was never enough time.

He handed her a highball, which, once she took it, he used his index finger to stir. He stuck his finger in his mouth.

"I hope you washed your hands after you used the

bathroom the last time," Rita said, making reference to his finger in her drink.

With a vague smile on his face he said, "Come to think of it, I can't remember if I did or not." He had lackluster eyes, like drops of partially dried mud. "Listen, Sis, follow me. I want to show you something."

As Rita followed him downstairs, Julie yelled after her, "Do I throw more pork chops in the oven or not?"

Sean yelled back, "Yes, she's not feeding that poor Greg fast food again." He turned on lights as he went, lighting the finished basement.

"I've got to get him over to the mall so we can buy him a new pair of shoes," she told Sean. "I'll eat, but we can't stay long afterward."

"Oh, quit your belly aching. You can go to the mall any ol' night. How often do you spend any time with us?" He took her to her old bedroom, which had a new red shag carpet, desk, chair, and filing cabinet in it. Over to one side was a twin bed. He opened the curtains, letting in rain-drenched light. "What do you think?" he asked. "I'm finally setting up that office I've always talked about."

Rita sat on the bed. "It's nice," she said and took a drink of her highball.

He sat in a swivel chair. "This was the room we were going to fix up for Mom, you know, but—well, we both know she's not going to be coming back home. Not with Alzheimer's." He took a sip of his drink. "Anyway, as I was saying about Babe and Norb, they ask about you all the time. You really should stop over and see them."

Rita looked around at the office. "Speaking of visiting, have you been to see Mom lately?"

He shook his head. "Have you?"

She shook her head.

"To tell you the truth, it's been too hectic," he told her. He drained a good portion of his drink. "Furniture market was just over, and I've been out tying up loose ends from sales I made there. You know how it is."

She did. Life was hectic. "Have you been traveling a lot?"

He nodded. "Mainly day trips," he told her. "I drive down around Chicago, over to Madison, and a couple of times up north. I try to get on the road early enough to get back at night, though. I hate to sleep in a strange bed."

"You're not pushing yourself too hard, are you?"

He sat at the desk and leaned back. He didn't think so, he said. "Say, I heard about that little boy you found."

She looked at him, surprised he had heard. Everyone seemed to have heard.

Suddenly he burst out laughing. She looked behind her, in the direction he was looking.

Greg, covered with mud, stood in the doorway. "Hi, Mom," he said, and adjusted his mud-smeared glasses. He smiled broadly, showing an upper incisor that was crowding two other teeth.

She put down her glass. "Hey, buddy!" she said, and grabbed him despite the mud. He was husky for his age. She could feel him breathing; he was warm. He had been sweating.

"Mom!" he said, and tried to pull away.

She put an armlock around his neck so he couldn't escape. "I don't care how big you get, I can still beat your butt," she told him as he struggled to free himself. He giggled. It felt good to have him laughing against her. "Come on, show me how tough you are."

He couldn't get loose. "That's what I thought. You're a wimp, that's what you are, aren't you?"

He finally broke loose, his cheeks red. "Yeah, now who's a wimp!" he said, panting. "Yeah!" He waved his hands at her, as if to get her to chase him. "Come on!"

"How did you get so filthy?" she asked.

"Playing football behind the Wishauses," he told her. His cheeks remained red. "I'm hungry. When's supper?"

She said to Sean, "Does Julie have any of his old clothes upstairs?"

"Oh, Mom—"

"Don't 'oh, Mom' me," she told him "You're hitting the showers this instant. Then maybe someone'll give you something to eat."

"Aunt Julie has dumb clothes. I have my gym clothes in my book bag. I'll wear them."

She held up a fist. "You'll wear this if you don't hit the showers this minute." She pretended to chase him. She could hear him stumbling up the stairs. Eleven was an awkward age. As soon as he was gone, she laughed.

"Say, how's Charlie's little girl? What's her name—"

"Keisha. She's doing fine."

"She's a cute little thing."

"When did you meet her?"

"You remember, at your Christmas party."

"Oh, that's right."

She looked out the window. She wished supper would hurry up and be over so she could get home and work.

"Hey, guess whom I ran into—"

"Who?"

"Steve."

The name of her ex-husband bought a chill to her. "Where did you see him?" she asked, though she pretended not to care.

"I was out having lunch with a client, and we bumped into each other at the restaurant."

"What did he have to say?"

He shrugged. "You know, it was the same old Steve, all talk. He's still an orderly over at the VA hospital. I guess he'll always be that." He laughed. "You remember how he said he wanted to go to medical school?"

She nodded.

He smiled. "He says he's still thinking about it. That or he wants to be a research scientist." He laughed loudly. "You remember Jethro on the *Beverly Hillbillies*?"

She ran a hand through her hair. She didn't find any pleasure in talking about Steve. "Let's go upstairs so I can make sure Greg got in the shower," she said.

By the time Greg was out of the shower, supper was ready.

At supper Rita couldn't keep her eyes off him. He was a beautiful son, she thought. His hair was plastered down with water, and he had cleaned his glasses. They magnified his blue eyes. Even his cowlick was down. He had a thick patch of dark hair, which she kept cropped close to his head because of the cowlick. He shoved food into his mouth. "Slow down before you give yourself ulcers," she told him.

Greg didn't listen to her. He drank all his milk, leaving himself with a milk mustache. "Mom, can I go back over to see Kyle after supper?"

There was a knock at the garage door.

Greg jumped up and ran to the door. It was Kyle. The boys looked a lot alike, though Kyle had darker hair. Kyle said, "Can you come out and play?"

Rita called to him from the table: "Aren't you going to say hi to me?"

"Hi, Rita," he said politely. "Can Greg come over for a while?"

"I'm sorry, hon, but we've got to leave in a few minutes," she told him. To Greg: "Remember, it's a school night."

"Say, I have an idea. How about if we all go to the zoo this Saturday?" Julie suggested, smiling.

Greg's face brightened. "Can we, Mom? Can Kyle go with us?"

"We'll see."

Both boys slapped hands together in a high-five.

"Right now, high on your priorities is that we get you a new pair of shoes."

Sean seemed to have read her mind. "Even if you do get tied up with work, we can take the boys," he told her.

"We'll see," she repeated, although the mention of work reminded her of the Hammond boy. She looked at her watch. There wouldn't be time for shoes that night. Once she got Greg home and in bed, she'd have just enough time to study her notes from the case. "Get your stuff together, Greg, and let's go. Tell Kyle you'll see him tomorrow."

Kyle said good-bye and left.

Greg collected his things.

Outside, it was dark. On their way to the car Rita reached over and pulled Greg close to her, though he pulled away. He began to jabber about the events of the day. They got into the car. The solemnness of her own day returned to her as she listened to Greg's chatter.

At their ranch-style home in Delafield, they played a game of Scrabble together. He won: 238–136. She always let him win, at which point she made a big deal out of it, as if disgusted she could never beat him. That thrilled him.

Only when he had gone to bed could Rita pull out her notes and begin to put the day in perspective. With a pencil she annotated her notes. A fly flew past her ear, bumped against the windowpane, and traced the dark window, as if researching for a way out. She studied her case notes. The images of the murdered Matthew Hammond wouldn't go away. Neither would the smell.

She took a shower, hoping to wash off the smell of the autopsy. As she stood in front of the steamed mirrors after the shower, she had a strange feeling someone was watching her. "Greg?" she said. She looked behind her, sure it was him. No. She looked in the cabinet for a washcloth to wipe off the mirror. There was none. She hadn't done laundry in several days. From the towel rack where the "company" towels hung, she removed a peach washcloth. With it she wiped off a spot on the mirror so she could watch behind her. She dropped the washcloth in a pile of dirty laundry. She looked past her body, bulging here and there. She ran a hand through her damp hair, still watching. She could have sworn someone was there.

A towel wrapped around her, she went to Greg's room, certain it had been him. Carefully she opened the door. The light from the doorway fell across his bed. She watched him. He was sleeping soundly.

5

Once Greg was on the school bus, Rita drove to the Shoney's in Delafield, off Interstate 94. Outside the restaurant she paused to read the headlines on the papers in the vendor boxes. There was a photograph of Matthew Hammond on the front page of the Milwaukee *Sentinel*. She glanced at the pink sky. Not a cloud in it. She felt her pockets for her sunglasses. She hoped they were in the car.

The restaurant was noisy with dishes and talk. Rita nodded to several of the regulars, not anyone she knew by name but faces she encountered every morning as she stopped for coffee. This morning she was hungry. At the counter, a waitress poured her coffee. Before the waitress moved on, Rita ordered scrambled eggs, sausage patties, toast, and orange juice. Sipping coffee, she caught bits and pieces of conversations. Two women were talking about the Hammond murder: "Isn't it terrible about that little boy they found?"

"Yes, every time the radio had an update, I found myself stopping my work to listen. I hear someone grabbed him in broad daylight."

"Oh? I didn't hear that. And Brown Deer is supposed to be one of the safer suburbs of Milwaukee. I guess it goes to show that no place is safe anymore. Didn't you feel sorry for the mother? I saw her on the ten o'clock news last night. She was devastated, but the reporters kept pushing for information. They never know when to stop. . . ."

Two other people walked by talking about the case. They had returned from the breakfast bar. One said he had a friend on the West Allis police department who said it looked like there was a psychotic on the loose. That's all Milwaukee needed—another Jeffrey Dahmer, he said. . . .

Rita lowered her face into her hands. Not psychotic, she thought. Maybe psychopathic. Too organized for a psychotic. She ran her hands through her hair and looked at her watch. As breakfast arrived, a man carrying a plate of food from the breakfast bar sat down beside her.

"Hi," he said. "I know this is going to sound like the oldest line in the book, but don't I know you?"

She had seen him on occasion at Shoney's. She studied his graying brown hair, slicked back with either water or oil, and beard. He was not that much older than she—perhaps forty-five. In good physical shape, too. His muscles bulged against his lemon knit shirt. He smiled as he stared at her with smoky gray eyes through wire-rimmed glasses. Perhaps a detective from one of the local departments, she decided.

He extended his hand, and she shook it. "Mike Squires," he said. The last name sounded familiar. "I saw you on television last night, and that's the first time I associated the face with the name. I see you all the time here, but you're Rita Trible, aren't you?" She nodded. "Didn't you grow up in New Berlin?"

"Yes."

"This is going back at least twenty years, but I grew up there too. I think you lived down the street from us. We were on Rose Lane. Your family lived on Ash." She vaguely remembered the name, but still couldn't place the face. "You probably don't remember me, since I was at least four or five years older than you. You had an older brother, didn't you?"

"Yes."

He rubbed his beard. "This might be what's throwing you off," he said. "I didn't have this when I was a kid." She smiled. "Only a stubble." She continued to smile. "The last I heard you were married and had a family."

How did he know so much about her after twenty years? she wondered. "Divorced," she told him. "I have a son." Why don't you give him your MasterCard number while you're at it? she asked herself.

"That's nice—I mean about having a son." He started to eat. He seemed to be hungry, or at least he wasn't shy about eating while he talked. He poured ketchup on his eggs.

"And what have you been up to?" she asked, pumping for information. It was a habit of hers.

"Me? Let's see." He rested his face on his right hand. "I was married in 1970. Divorced. Too immature. I've grown up a lot since then."

"I can see that."

He smiled broadly, his teeth showing. They were straight, though she could see his age in them. Teeth always showed a person's age.

"Do you work out this way?"

"Yes. I teach at the Arrowhead High School."

"You do? What do you teach?"

He held up his hands. "Would you like to take me in for questioning?" he asked. She laughed. He shoved more food into his mouth. "I teach English, everyone's favorite subject."

She started eating. "I've had worse courses," she mentioned.

His eyebrows raised, creating wrinkles in his forehead. "Like what?"

"You got me there."

He laughed. "I thought so," he said. "Everyone hates English, and we both know it. You'd have to be insane to like it. Are you insane?"

She shook her head. "Are you?"

He shrugged. "Hey, I teach it," he said. "I didn't say I liked it."

She said, "I hear the Arrowhead system is excellent."

He glanced at his watch. "Speaking of Arrowhead, I'm out of here. Got to be there by seven-thirty." He extended his hand as he stood. She shook it. Using his other hand, he wiped his plate clean with a piece of toast. He shoved the toast in his mouth. "Hope to see you around," he said, chewing.

"Sure."

She watched him as he walked away. She liked his easygoing manner. A moment later, he returned. "Say," he said, "I know you don't need my help to plan your social calendar, but I'm the basketball coach for the ninth-grade girls' team at Arrowhead, and we have a game on Saturday. You interested?" She didn't say. "Your son would love it. Actually, the season is over, but this is a scrimmage we had scheduled with a team last winter but never got to play because of the snow. We thought we'd treat it as a regular game and use the money for a class trip. Come on, it's only a buck apiece to get in." He pulled out a wad of money from his pocket and peeled off two ones. "Here, I'll spring for you and your son—what's his name?"

"Greg." She didn't take the money. "I'll think about it." She liked when someone wasn't afraid to include her son for an activity.

He nodded. "Great. Nine o'clock, at Arrowhead." He left.

Rita smiled as she paid her check. I must be lonelier than I thought, she mused, feeling excited that a stranger had talked to her in such a manner. It had been a long time since she had had a potentially romantic encounter like that. There had been other men since Steve, but they had been people she had known, and it had always been for temporary companionship. A curious unease touched her. It was an odd sensation, something that left her feeling that she wasn't in total control. She liked the feeling.

The moment she got to her car, though, she pushed Mike from her thoughts and began to concentrate on the Hammond case. The fact was the first twenty-four hours of a homicide investigation were crucial. She knew that. She started the car and got on the interstate heading for Milwaukee. A killer's trail grew cold quickly, especially the trail of a careful killer, and this killer was meticulous. She remembered Adam's request. She knew she wasn't going to give him the case, but she also thought it would be to her advantage to keep him content. If she out-and-out refused to give him the case, he would rebel. At the very minimum Paul would become involved because Adam would go straight to him—probably tell him she had promised him the case in the first place—and she didn't need any administrative hassles at the present time. She hated politics and administrative games.

The office was alive with activity. That reassured her. Jim O'Donnell, a short, heavyset detective whose bangs were cut straight across his forehead, handed her lab reports. Falling in alongside her, he told her he had fed the lab data into the computer, setting up an evidence profile.

"What happened to your foot?" she asked, noticing he was walking with a limp.

He told her he had twisted his ankle while playing basketball.

She glanced at the profile and told him to distribute copies of it to everyone in the office. "Make sure you get it to people before our nine o'clock meeting." He headed for the copy room. He's on his extra-good behavior this morning, she thought. Probably because Adam had told him to be that way. Jim was Adam's partner and had been a thorn in her side since she had become head of the office. Adam egged him on every chance he got. Anything to give her grief.

Recently she had even had to issue Jim a written reprimand. She had written him up several weeks before because he had missed a meeting she had called. Adam had missed the meeting too, but he was more careful about covering his tracks. Since it was the second meeting Jim had missed in less than two months, and she had talked to him the first time he was absent, she had put the second warning in writing. At first Jim had been upset. He had posted on the bulletin board a copy of the letter. That had caused a stir in the office. A number of people had even stopped talking to her for several days. Nevertheless, she had refused to confront Jim about the letter. What he did with his private correspondence was his business.

Next thing she knew, Paul had asked her about the letter. Apparently Adam had told Jim to complain to Paul. She had explained the circumstances of the letter, and that was the end of it. Of course, she had been furious that Jim had gone over her head, but she held her peace. Apparently Paul had supported her because Jim dropped the issue. This morning he was all enthusiasm. She was sure Adam was behind it.

As she passed Vince Hoffman and Joyce Smoot, she said, "Remember, I need to see you two in the conference room at nine." She looked at her watch. It was a quarter till.

Vince, a tall, skinny, balding detective sergeant, picked up his styrofoam cup of coffee and sports coat and headed for the conference room. Joyce, who had iron gray hair wrapped in a bun, began to gather her belongings.

Rita passed Charlie, who had appeared, folder in hand. "I need to see you in the conference room," she told him. He followed. "Did you get the stuff I asked for?"

He held out the folder. "A hundred thirty possibilities in this area alone," he said. "That doesn't include Chicago, which is in the same proximity. There are twice as many there. All registered as morticians."

She reminded Ray Lunsford, "I need you in the conference room at nine." He was an eccentric sort of man, gray-haired with a goatee, scheduled to retire in December. She knew all he cared about was retiring. He didn't have a regular partner. He was accompanied by whoever happened to be available at the time an assignment was made. For the most part he shuffled paperwork and passed time.

"I heard," he said.

William Lee looked up as she passed his desk. Of Chinese descent, he was a uniformed state police officer on temporary duty with her unit, also on the tactical response team, or SWAT. She motioned a finger to him. He got up and walked with her. A black belt in tae kwon do, he walked as if he were ready to kick anything that got in his way—always balanced. She told him, "I need you to do me a favor. Drive out to"—she snapped her fingers several times—"Walworth County. Charlie, is that part of the park in Walworth or Waukesha?"

Charlie told her, "Walworth."

"Try both," she told William. "Check with the sheriff's departments in those counties and find out what they know. Maybe one of their people saw or heard something. Ask around. Find out who was on duty during the evening and night shifts the day before last. Ask about unusual activity in the area where the body was discovered. Traffic citations, etcetera. If anyone asks who sent you, tell them it was me. Tell them I want to set up a task force between agencies, but I'm on the run and haven't had a chance to stop by."

William withdrew.

At her office door, she said good morning to her administrative aide, Bev Smith, a pockmarked black woman in her fifties. A grandmother with fourteen grandchildren, she had been an activist in earlier days, having once served as a reporter for the famous *Chicago Defender*. She handled the demands of the current job well. "Bev, call St. Paul's in Brown Deer. Tell them we want to stop by and begin talking to people, especially the kids. Is Adam around?"

Bev said yes, she had just seen him.

"Find him and tell him I need him in the conference room in ten minutes."

Two walls of the conference room had large windows that overlooked the buildings of downtown Milwaukee. The room was crowded with a circular conference table, around which there was barely enough room for six chairs. For larger meetings people stood along the walls.

Adam, late, sat down and leaned back in a chair near one of the windows. He didn't say anything, merely looked around the room as if he were somehow the center of attention. He was a short, skinny man whose face turned cherry red when he thought someone was going to talk about him. His face was that color now. Rita noticed that Jim winked at him.

Once everyone was settled in and had exchanged a round of small talk, Rita said, "Effective immediately, I'm assigning everyone but Jim full-time to the Hammond case." She knew she wanted to break up Adam and Jim.

Vince interlocked his fingers behind his head. "What about the Dix case?" he asked. He and Joyce were the principal investigators on a case involving a string of armed robberies along the interstate between Milwaukee and Chicago.

Rita said, "I'm assigning that case to Jim."

"Can we talk about it?" Vince asked. "I mean, I don't see how we can work as hard as we've worked on the Dix case, and then have you reassign the case right when we're getting some of our best leads. It doesn't seem fair."

Before Rita could respond, Joyce chimed in, "I
agree." Rita knew Joyce wasn't being hostile—they
were good friends—but was only supporting her partner. "We've worked hard on this case."

Ray said, "Can we back up for a minute? I'm confused about this flurry of activity in the first place.
Don't you think we're overreacting a little on this
whole Hammond matter?"

Before anyone could say anything else, Rita said,
"An eleven-year-old boy has been murdered. I don't
think I'm overreacting." No one said anything. "I
know I'm new at this job, but I want to emphasize
that when I make a decision, it's not time for people
to open a discussion." Looking directly at Joyce, she
said, "You know this has nothing to do with anyone's
performance on any other case. If that's the impression you got, I apologize." She looked at Ray: "I'm
assigning you to the Hammond case because I know
you're a stickler for details." Everyone smiled. It was
a standing joke that Ray gave so much attention to
details because he didn't want to solve a case too
quickly. He knew the more productive he was, the
more cases he got. He didn't want a heavy caseload.

Adam spoke up: "Who's going to be heading up
the investigation?"

She had been waiting for the question. "I am," she
said. She could see him turning white with anger. "I'm
making you second in charge. As you know when we
talked last night, this crime is too organized to be a
typical homicide." She knew she hadn't told him anything about the case, but she wanted to make it appear
he was informed. "You've had some experience with
serial crimes. You know how demanding they can be.
They need everyone's attention."

Her careful treatment hadn't worked. She could see trouble brewing. "I've had more than a little experience," he said. He had assisted with the Dahmer case. He was proud of that, though she knew his role had been nominal. "But I would hardly classify one body as a serial crime." He smiled, as if he was an authority on serial crimes. Jim was the only other person who smiled.

Rita was annoyed. "As I said, I'm the head of this office, and I'm making a decision about this case. I don't think it's appropriate that we turn all of this into a joke or discussion. I'm making reassignments. It's as simple as that. Does anyone have a problem?"

No one said anything. Charlie said nothing during the entire meeting. She could see him doodling on a yellow pad of paper. She made assignments: Vince and Joyce were to interview Barry Dixon. She gave them an address and Barry's mug shot. Adam and Ray were to return to the crime scene, comb it again. Jim, in addition to the Dix case, was to take Charlie's list of people with ties to funeral homes and begin to check for possible suspects. She and Charlie would head to St. Paul's.

Back in her private office, she told Charlie, "I think that went rather well, don't you?"

He sat in a chair, put a large shoe on the edge of her desk, and began to tie the shoe. "Adam's pissed, you know," he said. "You could see it in his face."

"Get your damned foot off my desk," she told him.

He laughed and dropped his foot. "Be that way," he said, "but he still hates you. We all do"

She smiled. "I know."

"Better watch your back."

Although they had been joking, she knew he was serious.

6

The rest of the morning she and Charlie interviewed people who had known Matthew, people in the boy's neighborhood of Brown Deer, people at St. Paul's school, where Matthew had been in sixth grade, and people in the church. Father Catalpa, the parish priest was out of town, but Rita and Charlie interviewed the assistant priest, a man in his eighties who remembered Matthew as a respectful boy, someone who was "pleased as punch" to be an altar boy. Everyone had liked Matthew. He was a quiet, polite boy, somewhat of a loner, but everyone liked him.

In the afternoon, with the permission of parents, Rita and Charlie began to interview Matthew's class-mates. Some of the children in his sixth-grade class had thought Matthew a bit strange because he spent so much time hanging around the fifth-graders, espe-cially during recess, but the teachers thought that was because the children in Matthew's class were cliquey. According to Mrs. Morris, the sixth-grade teacher, most of the students had known one another since kindergarten, which made Matthew an outsider. Fifth grade had been his first year at St. Paul's. Of course, most of the fifth-grade children thought Matthew was a pest. The consensus seemed to be that he was funny, though—he could roll his eyes back into his head, showing the whites of his eyes, and he had a way of pinching his chin beneath his lower lip to make it look like "someone's butt."

Bobby Ruble was the most interesting child they interviewed. He said Matthew had "weirded out." "He wasn't my best friend anymore," Bobby said. He was a pale boy with long, oily brown hair and pursed lips. There were brown half circles beneath his dark eyes.

"What do you mean he 'weirded out'?" Rita asked.

Bobby shrugged. "He changed."

"So the two of you weren't best friends anymore?" Charlie repeated.

"No, not like we used to be. We were still friends, but we didn't have as much to do with each other. He didn't want to have anything to do with me," Bobby said. The way he stared straight ahead, it was as if he thought the answer said all that needed to be said.

"I'm not sure I understand," Charlie said.

"After school," Bobby said, looking over, "I'd ask him to come to my house, but he didn't want to."

"Why do you think he didn't want to?" Rita asked.

He shrugged. "I think it was because his mother wouldn't let him. His mom wouldn't let him do a lot of things. But she didn't care about him—not until he died."

What struck Rita most about what Bobby said was how he said it. He said it as though he knew something firsthand. Could it be that Crystal was not the woman she seemed to be, but a demanding, strict disciplinarian who turned violent, if her son didn't mind her?

Charlie asked, "Do you think it was because his mom was worried about him? Maybe his mom was worried about his grades. Do you think?"

Bobby shook his head. "He made good grades," he said. "No, she didn't like me." He became fidgety, his feet tapping the floor.

Rita asked, "Bobby, is there something bothering you? You seem upset about something."

He stopped tapping his feet. "No," he told her.

"There's nothing to be afraid of. Is something wrong?" Charlie asked. "Was Matthew in trouble?" No answer. "Did he tell you something you promised not to say anything about?" No answer. "Do you know who hurt him?"

His lips still pursed, Bobby didn't say. It was as if he hadn't heard any of the questions.

Rita said, "Bobby?"

His eyes shifted to her.

"Are you all right," she asked.

He tilted his head. "Can I leave now?"

"We really need to talk for a few more minutes," she said.

"You can't make me talk."

"I know we can't make you talk, but we care about Matthew, and we want to find out who hurt him. Don't you care about him?"

"I don't want to talk anymore right now," he told her.

She said, "Can we talk again later tonight? Maybe we could stop by your house."

"Maybe."

"Can I ask you one more question?"

He waited.

"On Monday, the day Matthew called his mom to tell her he was going to spend the night with you, did you know he was calling?"

He didn't say.

"It's very important that you tell us," she said.

"He told me he was running away."

"Forgive me, but I must ask just a couple more questions," Rita said, persisting.

"Leave me alone!" he said, irritated.

She didn't press. "Maybe this evening we can talk some more?"

He didn't say.

"Okay, Bobby," Charlie said. "And we thank you very, very much." Once Bobby was out of the room, Charlie said, "I wonder what that was all about."

Rita said, "I don't know, but we need to talk to Crystal again. I do know that. Someone's not telling us something."

They continued their interviews. No one else seemed to have known what Matthew had been up to on the day he disappeared. It had been a normal school day. The secretary remembered him telephoning his mother, and she hadn't noticed anything out of the ordinary.

A crisis-management team arrived to work with the children and family members at St. Paul's. It was standard operating procedure during a tragedy. Rita told the leader of the team to give special attention to Bobby. In the car, she called the dispatcher on duty and had her patch a call through to Vince and Joyce. Joyce's voice came over the radio.

"How did the Dixon interview go?" Rita asked.

"You'll like this," Joyce said. "He smokes, and guess what kind of cigarettes he smokes?"

"Winston."

"You bet, and you'll love this next part. Guess what kind of a car he drives?"

"What kind?"

"He and his brother have fixed up an old hearse."

"You're kidding. Did you get a look at it?"

"Only from the outside. It has tinted windows. You can't see inside."

"What all did he say to you?"

"Not much. He's basically a jerk. All the time we talked to him, he stood at his work counter and made fun of us while his brother and one of the mechanics stood nearby and laughed."

"He didn't seem upset that Matthew had been murdered?"

"He could care less. Vince and I have been talking about it. We think we should bring him in for questioning."

"Where are you now?"

"About a block away watching his place."

"Any unusual activity?"

"When we left he went out to the hearse and got something, but we couldn't make out what it was. That's it. We've been sitting here waiting for you to call. We tried to call you when we got done with the interview, but the dispatcher said your radio was out of service."

"We were in the school. I had my pager off."

"Anything on your end?"

"There's one student we need to talk to again, but we need to have a little help from his parents. What little he did say made it clear we need to go back to see Crystal. Can you hold on for a while until we finish with her, and then we'll see what we want to do with Barry?"

"We'll be here."

"Thanks."

On the way to Crystal's apartment, Rita received a call from Jim O'Donnell. The results of the autopsy had been confirmed: Asphyxia was the cause of death. Also, it was confirmed that the boy had been sexually assaulted. There were lab results. And, yes, the body had been embalmed in a crude but textbook fashion.

She told him to begin to search the files of known sex offenders in the area, even old cases. "Find out what sex offenders have been released from prison in recent days," she said, "and what ones might have been working the neighborhood."

Once she had given Jim instructions, she patched a call through to Adam. Anything new on the crime scene? she asked. His voice was cold: No, nothing.

Anything from William?

No.

Rita and Charlie found Crystal despondent. As she stood at the open door, Rita noticed she hadn't showered and she seemed to be wearing the same clothes she had slept in—wrinkled sweatpants and an undershirt.

Rita said, "I know you've already been asked a million questions, but we need to go back over a few things."

Crystal stepped aside and let Rita and Charlie into the apartment, which had fallen into disarray in the twenty-four hours since they had last been there. Rita mentioned their interview with Bobby Ruble. "He said Matthew was running away."

"That's a damned lie!" Crystal said. She became irritable suddenly, as someone who hadn't had any sleep might do. "Matthew would never run away."

"Why?" Charlie asked. "What makes you think he'd never run away?"

"Because I know my son!" she yelled. "That's why." She shook her head. "That's why I never even liked him to play with Bobby. The boy was a bad influence. He's lying."

"What do you mean, 'bad influence'?" Charlie asked.

"He used drugs."

"Drugs?" Rita asked. "Are you sure?"

"Yes. It was something like heroin. Matthew said he had caught him shooting up a couple times."

There was a long silence, the kind of silence that follows a revelation.

"Where do you think he would get drugs?" Charlie asked.

"I don't know."

Rita abruptly asked, "Did you ever physically abuse Matthew?"

Crystal broke down, crying. "I didn't do that to him, if that's what you mean," she said. She seemed to have been waiting for the question.

"But you hit him occasionally?"

"I would never hit him like that!" she cried. "Yes, sometimes I hit him, but never like that." She wept freely.

"Was there a drug problem at St. Paul's?" Charlie asked.

"Anytime an eleven-year-old can get a hold of drugs, I would say that's a problem."

Rita asked, "Do you think Matthew was involved with drugs?"

"No."

"Are you sure?"

"Yes, I'm sure."

"Does your boyfriend use drugs?"

She didn't say.

"He's been busted for drugs, you know."

Crystal remained silent.

"Does Barry use drugs?" Rita repeated.

"He smokes a little pot sometimes."

"Why didn't you tell us this before?" Rita asked, losing her temper. "We're investigating your son's murder, and you're holding things like this back from us?"

"I didn't think it was important."

"Have you been using drugs?"

"I smoke a little pot with Barry sometimes. That's it."

Charlie asked, "Did Barry ever hit your son?"

She was silent for a moment before she said, "Once."

"Once?" Rita said.

"It was my fault," Crystal told them. "He told me he didn't like to be around children, and one time Matthew was here. He kept coming out of his bedroom, and he was whining. Barry lost his temper. It was my fault. But it never happened again."

"What did Barry do?" Rita asked.

She shook her head. "I don't remember. It all happened so fast. All I can remember was Barry hitting him real hard and me screaming."

"Barry wanted you and not your son, was that it?"

She nodded.

"You didn't tell us about changes in his routines or habits. Some people at school said he was withdrawn. Could it be that Barry had access to him?"

Crystal said she didn't think so.

Charlie said, "If you didn't like him around Bobby, why did you agree to let him spend the night there on Monday?"

"I told you, Matthew called and told me he had a project he and Bobby were working on for class. He promised me Bobby's parents would be there at all times."

Rita asked Crystal if she would mind if they went through Matthew's room again. During a second search of the room, Charlie found a half-burned Winston cigarette and a book of matches wrapped in toilet paper behind the bottom drawer in the boy's dresser. He put the items in an evidence bag. Crystal began to cry.

Rita asked, "What type of cigarettes does your boyfriend smoke?"

"Winston," Crystal said, sobbing.

"Did you know Matthew smoked?" Charlie asked.

Through her sobs she said no.

"If Matthew never had any exposure to Barry, where do you think he was getting Winston cigarettes?" Rita asked.

Crystal was silent.

"Would you take a polygraph examination?"

"Yes."

Once in the sedan, Rita asked, "What made you think to pull the drawers out of the dresser?"

He told her he had sneaked cigarettes when he was about the same age.

That was good work, she told him.

He asked, "How badly do you think she beat him?"

"Based upon her reaction, probably worse than she was letting on." Still thinking, she didn't start the car. "But not bad enough to kill him. Barry's another story." She sighed.

"What's wrong?"

She pushed her hair back until her fingers, interlocked, cupped the back of her neck. "I remember when I found out that Steve had been knocking Greg around," she said. She stared straight ahead. "It was one of those times when Steve was in a good mood. He punched Greg playfully, and I told him never even to play like that. Since Steve was still in a jovial mood, Greg blurted out, 'He's always doing that.' The way he said it, it was like I knew it was bothering him, and he was only looking for an opportunity to say something. I asked Steve if he had hit my son. He said no, and Greg blurted out, 'You do too.' All of a sudden everything came clear to me. I realized what those occasional bruises were." It had been three years since she had talked about Steve.

After she had said it, she regretted airing her private life, especially with someone she didn't know that well. She started the car and put it in gear. "Give Joyce and Vince a call," she said. "Have them pick up Barry and bring him to the office."

Once he had radioed Joyce, he asked, "What are you thinking about?"

"That Matthew was running away for some reason," she said. "I'm wondering who it was that offered to help him."

"Do you believe what she said about the Ruble boy?"

"That was a shock, wasn't it?" She glanced at him,

then looked back at the road. "I hate to think it, but I doubt Matthew would make up a story like that. I mean, why would he say he had seen Bobby shooting up if he hadn't?"

"You know, I was going to say that after we had talked to Bobby, I thought he might be on drugs. Didn't you think so—I mean, the way he looked and acted?"

It was frightening for her to think how vulnerable children were in modern society. It wasn't like when she was growing up. Back then children could be children. She worried about Greg. Sooner or later he would be exposed to drugs, cigarettes, alcohol, and guns. Maybe he already had been.

7

A smirk on his face, Barry Dixon pulled off his hat, releasing a headful of greasy black hair, and repositioned the hat toward the back of his head. He brought out a pair of clippers and began to clip his fingernails while he sat in the conference room at CID headquarters. Rita sat down near him. In the room with her were Vince, Joyce, and Charlie. Rita advised Barry of his rights. He didn't seem to care. Slivers of nails flew here and there.

"Put the fingernail clippers away," she told him.

He looked up at her, head cocked. "You can't boss me around," he told her.

"Do you wish to have an attorney present?" she asked him.

"Believe me, when I get my attorney involved, you'll hear about it."

"I've had a long day, and I don't have the patience for this," she told him. "Let me put it this way: You either cooperate, or we'll begin to turn your life inside out. One way or the other, we'll get what we want. In the process, don't be surprised if your customers won't visit your garage for fear of being linked to whatever has drawn all the police to your business. You make the decision: Cooperate or don't cooperate."

He began to clean his fingernails with the clippers' metal cuticle stick.

"Fine," Rita said, standing. She told Joyce, "Take him back to his business and set up a surveillance. I want him watched around the clock."

She made it to the door before Barry spoke up: "All right, I'll talk, but I'll tell you right now I didn't kill that boy."

Rita sat back down. She fixed her eyes on him. "You saw him more than the mother knew about, didn't you?" she asked.

"That boy was all over the place. She didn't know where he was half the time."

Charlie asked, "Did you teach him to smoke?"

"He was picking up cigarette butts off the street and smoking them on his own. When he stopped by the garage, I gave him a couple cigarettes now and then. What's so terrible about that?"

"Did you ever give him drugs?" Joyce asked.

He laughed. "Oh, like I'm going to tell you." Rita figured that to be an affirmative response. "If you think I murdered the boy, ask your questions 'cause I got nothing to hide. But if you're on a fishing trip and want to bust me for anything you can pin on me, forget it."

Vince asked, "Did you ever hit the boy?"

"Yeah, I hit him once or twice. If he was doing something wrong, I smacked him upside the head. I didn't kill him, though, if that's what you're getting at."

"Tell us about your hearse," Rita said.

He smiled. "That's my pride and joy," he said, putting away the clippers. "My brother and I rebuilt it from scratch."

Charlie asked, "Why a hearse?"

"It's cool, that's why."

"You ever work in a funeral home?" Vince asked.

"No."

There came a knock at the door. Bev stuck her head in. "Can I see you for a moment?" she asked Rita.

Perturbed by the interruption, Rita said, "We're in an interview. Can't it wait until we're done?"

Bev held up a slip of paper. "I don't think so."

Rita took the note and opened it in the palm of her hand so only she could see. There were four words on the slip of paper: "Bobby Ruble is dead."

She stepped into the hall with Bev, who told her she had received word that apparently Bobby had been on his way home when he shinned up a telephone phone down by the river in Brown Deer and touched a live wire. He was dead on the scene.

Rita stepped back into the conference room, which had fallen silent. She asked Barry, "Did you know Bobby Ruble?"

"By name. I know Crystal didn't want him around because he was into some heavy drugs. No, I didn't know him."

Leaving Vince and Joyce to finish the interview, Rita and Charlie headed for Brown Deer. On the way Rita told Charlie what had happened. He didn't say anything right away.

There was no way to explain how she felt, so she knew he must be experiencing the same shock and guilt. Had she pressed Bobby for answers, he might not be dead, was what kept coming to mind. She was sure he had committed suicide because he knew something about Matthew's death. Why else would he have killed himself?

It was one of those moments when she tried to tell herself it wasn't her fault, and yet she asked if it was at the same time. She tried to think what she could have done differently. Nothing, she tried to convince herself.

Beside her, Charlie said solemnly, "It could be a coincidence—an accident."

She repressed the urge to say anything.

When they arrived, people were still gathered at the death scene. It was always that way. People loitered around a death scene long after the fatalities were removed.

According to a group of children who had witnessed what had happened, Bobby had climbed the pole despite their protests. One little girl said there was a puff of smoke when Bobby's head hit the wire, a jerk in his body, and he had dropped. She didn't seem to realize Bobby was dead, or what it meant.

Rita and Charlie talked to Detective Scott Frye, a blond-haired lieutenant from the Brown Deer Police Department. He said he had known it was going to be a bad day when his computer went on the blink that morning. He was quite casual. He looked at the scene, a patch of blood and indentation in the grass, and shook his head. "Everything's linked to the computer these days," he said. He looked at Rita. "You know, you hate to see something like this happen. The boy was showing off. Kids do it all the time." He glanced at the blood and indentation. "It's a damned shame. A waste." He looked at Rita and Charlie. "What brings you guys out here anyway?"

"We're working on the Hammond case," Rita told

him. "The little boy we found out in the Kettle-Moraine. This boy knew the Hammond boy. Same age, school—"

"You think it was suicide?" he asked. He glanced a third time at the blood and indentation, as if it gave him something new to think about.

She didn't say. "Has anyone notified the family yet?"

He nodded.

She handed him a business card and shook his hand. "Let me know if you hear anything," she told him.

"Be happy to help," he said.

From the accident scene Rita and Charlie went to see Bobby's parents. Pat Ruble, the mother, owned a beauty shop, which was in the front part of their house. Kim Mueller, an employee, was in the shop talking to several ladies who had apparently gathered to gossip about what had happened. The ladies looked like they had been crying. Kim said that Pat and Jim had gone to the funeral home, where the body had been taken.

Rita and Charlie drove to the funeral home. They found the parents, hands intertwined, sitting together on a sofa in the parlor. St. Paul's assistant priest, Father Garnett, was with them. The old man seemed genuinely touched. His fat nose was red and swollen beneath his thick glasses, and there were tears in his bloodshot eyes.

Rita knelt in front of the red-haired, rough-looking woman. They had talked briefly by telephone that morning, when Rita had initially gotten permission to interview Bobby. Rita expressed how sorry she was for what had happened, and the mother nodded. She said, "We knew something like this was going to hap-

pen sooner or later." She wiped tears from her eyes.
"I think all of us knew."

Rita didn't say anything.

Jim, a sanitation worker, was still in a dirty coverall.
He said, "He was depressed. We were trying to help
him work through it." He patted Father Garnett's
arm. Jim's eyes were also bloodshot. "It was hard for
us all."

Charlie crouched beside Rita. He asked, "What did
you know? What was going on with Bobby? Was he
in some kind of trouble?"

Pat sighed. "It depends upon what you mean by
that," she said.

Rita said, "I hate to ask a question like this, but
was your son involved in drugs?"

Pat's expression was one of shock. "Oh, that's what
you mean. Of course not! Bobby would never use
drugs. He was a good boy. You couldn't find a better boy."

Rita explained what Matthew apparently had
claimed to have seen.

Jim said, "Oh, that."

"What?" Rita asked.

Pat told her, "Last summer our son was diagnosed
with diabetes. He took insulin shots twice a day. Since
he gave himself his own shots, I'm sure Matthew saw
him give himself insulin once or twice. No, Bobby
would never use drugs." She leaned her head against
her husband's shoulder. "He was a good boy, wasn't
he, hon?"

Jim touched her face with a dirty hand, one hard-
ened and callused from labor. He said, "He hated
what had happened to him, and I can't say I blamed
him. As hard as I tried to be supportive, I would have

never been able to go through all the things he went through—constantly checking his urine for sugar, constantly having to check his blood, having to be careful about everything he ate. Being in and out of the hospital." He shook his head. "But he's in a better place now," he said, looking at Father Garnett, who nodded.

Pat asked Rita, "Are you a mother?"

Rita nodded.

"The police earlier were asking questions. If you're a mother, I know you'll understand if I ask you not to make a big deal out of this," she said. "Our son was showing off, he climbed a telephone pole and got electrocuted. It was an accident. There's no need for an autopsy. Please, don't make a big deal. He wasn't using drugs. I promise you."

Rita rose, as did Charlie. She asked, "How much had Bobby and Matthew been seeing each other?"

"Not at all," Pat said. "Imagine how shocked I was to discover he was supposed to be staying with me when he was murdered. We already told all this to some people from your office."

What good would an autopsy do? Rita wondered. It would only cause the family additional grief. "Would you mind if we looked around in Bobby's bedroom back at the house?" she asked.

Jim gave them a house key. "His room is upstairs. You can leave the key on the kitchen table when you're done." He extended a hand. "We appreciate your understanding." They shook hands with him.

They went to the house and entered through the back door. From the kitchen they passed through a dining and living room to get to the stairs. The furnishings were old and worn, but there were a lot of plants and photographs. It looked like a good home.

Bobby's bedroom had a jacket hanging on the door-knob. The walls were cluttered with pictures of sports heroes, not framed pictures but pages torn from magazines. The pages had been taped to the walls. There was a small radio on the dresser and an old television on a desk. A Sega apparatus was attached to the television. The bed was not made.

Rita began to go through the dresser drawers. Three of them were stuffed with clothes. It was apparent that Bobby had pulled clothes out, and then, rather than refold them, had stuffed them back into the drawers. One drawer was chock full of assorted items, everything from marbles to books. The bottom drawer held games and toys.

Charlie said, "Wow, what a mess."

She went to the closet, where Charlie stood. The floor was piled with shoes, dirty laundry, and trash.

"Another good Catholic boy," Charlie mentioned, pointing out an altar boy's robe. "But certainly not very neat."

They searched the room without finding anything unusual, nothing that gave a clue to what had happened to Matthew. Only then did Rita realize how drained she was. She sighed. "Let's go," she said.

In the car, Charlie told her, "I remember the morning Claudia took Keisha to the doctor that first time." He looked over at her. "Keisha had had the flu a couple of weeks, she was rundown and things, but we didn't think much of it." He tapped his thumbs on his knees. "I'll never forget getting a call from dispatch telling me to call Claudia at the doctor's office." He looked at her again. "You hate to get those kinds of calls, you know." He sighed. "When I got in touch with her, Claudia said the doctor needed to see us.

She wouldn't say why. So I drove over there, and I remember sitting in this empty office, waiting for the doctor to arrive. I hate hospitals and doctors' offices. I think they make you wait like that on purpose. The doctor came in, carrying a folder, didn't shake hands with me or anything, only sat down behind his desk and said, 'I think we have a problem.' "

Rita watched him. It was as though he was trying to swallow something but couldn't get it down.

He finally said, "When we were talking with Bobby this afternoon, I got that feeling—the same one I had when I sat in the doctor's office with my wife." He looked at her, and their eyes met. "I knew something was wrong with that boy," he said. "I could feel it." He shook his head. "I could feel it, and I denied it. I jumped to the conclusion it was drugs, but I knew something was wrong."

Rita started the car. "I'm wondering if we're reading too much into this," she told him.

"What do you mean?"

"I had an aunt who had diabetes," she said. "It's a nasty disease. She went blind, got big ulcers on her legs"—she showed the size with her hands. "In fact, they ended up having to amputate one of her legs. She finally died of kidney failure. She was only in her forties." She looked over at Charlie. "We're acting like we could have done something to stop it, but this might have been something we had absolutely no control over."

As they drove back to the city, Charlie said, "So, you think he was only depressed about his diabetes?" He sounded like he wanted to be reassured.

"It's a logical explanation, isn't it?" She was think-

ing about Matthew's autopsy, a process she knew well.
It was an ugly process. "Do me a favor," she said.

"Sure."

"Let's keep this thing about our interview with
Bobby between the two of us."

"What do you mean?"

"I think it's best if we leave all of this as an accident. No sense dragging Bobby's family through the
mud. You know how it is with autopsies and things."

"Oh, that. Sure. I wasn't going to say anything
anyway."

Rita called the office: No one was there. She called
Vince at home. He said the interview with Barry had
ended shortly after she left because Barry had called
his attorney, who had advised him not to answer further questions without conferring with legal counsel
first.

They drove in silence. Her head was throbbing. She
didn't want to think about the investigation anymore.
She wanted to pick up Greg and go somewhere for a
relaxing dinner.

8

Greg and Kyle ran across the street from the Wishauses', where they had been roughhousing in the front yard. It was obvious Kyle had gotten a haircut, and Rita told him how handsome he looked. Greg began to tease him about it. "Don't be mean," Rita told Greg, roughing up his hair, "you'll be getting a haircut too, the first chance I get to tie you down."

Kyle laughed. He had a shirt with cutoff sleeves. She noticed that in it he was less chunky than Greg, who never had outgrown his baby fat. Kyle said, "Guess what, Rita?"

"What?"

"Mr. Gallagher said if Greg didn't get new gym shoes, he couldn't participate in gym."

Rita looked at Greg's shoes. She knew they were in bad shape, but this new revelation caused her to look at them in a new light. They were worn out in several places. The sock of his left foot could be seen in a tear at the toes. Both shoes needed new shoe-strings. Still, she didn't feel like shopping that evening. "Maybe we can go this weekend," she said.

"Mom," Greg whined. "It's embarrassing to have

to wear these. All the kids have been laughing at me.
They think I'm poor."

Rita laughed.

Kyle said, "Mr. Gallagher has been telling him to
get new shoes for like three weeks. He says it's not
safe to be playing sports with shoes like that."

Rita grabbed Kyle by the arm. "I think you two set
all of this up before I got here."

Kyle pulled free, laughing. "It's the truth. I swear."

"Don't swear." She liked Kyle. He was a good kid,
someone she didn't mind Greg being around. "Okay,
I give in. We'll go get you some new shoes."

Greg and Kyle high-fived each other.

"I knew you two set this up." She tried to grab
them, but they shot out through the yard. She chased
after them, first one, then the other, while they giggled. She caught Greg, threw him on the ground, sat
on him, pulled his hands up, and tickled him while he
laughed hysterically. He screamed for Kyle to help,
but Kyle kept his distance. Then she went after him
and did the same, while Greg stood nearby and said,
"See, how does it feel!"

The boys wanted to continue to play. It was always
that way. They never ran out of energy. She told Greg
to get his things together so they could go to the mall,
eat supper, and then go home.

Saying good-bye, Kyle went back across the street,
where he waved before going into Babe and Norb's
house. She waved and smiled. She felt sorry for him.
She knew it was rough for a child to go through a divorce. Greg had done it. She knew how difficult it was
for him.

She went in, talked to Sean and Julie for a few
minutes, and then took Greg to the Brookfield Mall.

They went to the Footlocker. Right away Greg saw a pair of Converse high-tops he wanted. She told him she wouldn't pay a hundred dollars for gym shoes. He was in the process of arguing with her when someone said, "Hi, Rita, how are you?"

She turned around. It was her ex-husband, Steve Devereux. He was standing with his hands in his front pants pockets. As always, he was smiling. He had gained weight, or at least was starting a potbelly. She thought of Greg and his baby fat. She hoped he didn't grow up to look like Steve. "What are you doing here?" she asked.

He ran a hand across his partially bald head. "Believe it or not, I was getting my sides trimmed."

He didn't have his toupee on.

"Good to see you," he said to her. "Hi, Greg."

Greg mumbled an unenthusiastic "Hi."

She wondered what she had ever saw in him in the first place. "I hear you're still at the VA," she said, not knowing what else to say. He never had had any ambition.

"So, you do keep track of me," he said, still smiling. "Yes, I still work at the VA. Some people like job security. And you might be interested to know I'm working closely with Dr. Levey. Myron Levey. You've heard of him, I'm sure." He expanded his chest proudly.

No, she hadn't heard of him, she said. Didn't know him from Adam.

"Oh, surely you've heard of him. Dr. Levey, the renowned heart surgeon."

No, she repeated, she hadn't heard of him.

"Oh, sure, he's quite well-known. He's been working on an artificial heart, and he's asked me to help with his work on the project. . . ."

As she listened to him ramble, she realized he hadn't changed at all. Same old Steve. Still suffering from delusions of grandeur. Still bragging. She wanted to ask him how an orderly at a VA hospital could be working on such an important research project, but she decided it wouldn't be good to engage in conversation with him. Instead, she interrupted, "Listen Steve, I hate to sound rude, but we really are in a hurry."

He had his hands back in his pockets. "Sure, I understand," he said. "Maybe we could get together sometime and talk. You know, just a social chat. To stay on friendly terms."

"I don't think that's a good idea, Steve. I don't think we have anything to talk about. We're divorced, you know."

"I realize that, but that doesn't mean we can't be friends. I've always tried to be agreeable to you. That's why when you said you didn't want me to have visitation rights with Greg, I didn't fight. Isn't that right, Greg?" The boy didn't say.

She was losing her temper. "You gave up your visitation rights so I wouldn't present evidence to the courts, proving you had physically abused him. Don't try to change that." He was still smiling. She hated how he always smiled. She wanted to knock the smile off his face.

"Like I said, no hard feelings." He saluted. "I hope you two have a nice evening. See you later."

"Bye, Steve."

He left the shoe store in no particular hurry. In fact, he paused to look at a pair of gym shoes on a display at the front of the store, even picked up one of the shoes, examined its sole, and put the shoe back on the rack before moving on.

Greg asked if he could buy the Converse shoes. The appearance of his estranged father hadn't fazed him in the least.

"I told you I'm not spending a hundred dollars on gym shoes that'll wear out in two months at the most," she told him, her mood spoiled by the encounter with Steve. "You go through them too fast to spend that kind of money."

"You never buy me anything I want," he said, peeved.

"You start that with me," Rita told him, "and I guarantee you I'll march your butt down to the Kinney shoe store and buy you a pair of $19.95 shoes."

They compromised on sixty-dollar Nikes. He asked if he could wear them home, so the store clerk boxed the old shoes and helped Greg lace up the new ones. His feet squeaked as he walked across the marble floors of the mall. He seemed to enjoy making disruptive sounds with his new shoes.

She let him go to the Arcade, where he played video games. She sat on one of the benches outside and sipped a cup of coffee. At one point she saw Steve pass in the main corridor of the mall, but he didn't look in her direction. At least she didn't think he did. It reminded her of the days when she had been married to him. He had loved to roam the halls of the local mall. If they ever had any spare time together and she asked him what he wanted to do, he said he wanted to go to the mall and walk. That was all he had ever wanted to do. He hadn't changed at all.

She went into the Arcade to get Greg. "Come on," she told him, "it's time to go." She had to wait while he traded in the tickets he had won from the games. He got two pencils, a magnifying glass, a miniature notebook, and a plastic spider ring.

On the way to the car, she commented, "I can't believe you spent five dollars in the Arcade, and all you have to show for it is a handful of crap that I could have bought for less than a dollar down at Woolworth's." She grabbed him by the shirt as a car passed in front of them. "Watch where you're going," she told him.

"Mom, I'm eleven years old," he reminded her. "I think I'm old enough to cross the street by myself."

Eleven-year-olds think they know everything, she thought. "You're turning into a real smartass, you know," she told him.

"A smartass," he said sarcastically.

"Yes, a smartass. Are you hungry?"

Starved, he told her.

They went to Fudruckers for hamburgers. She drank a couple of beers with her food. She felt better after that.

They had a leisurely meal together, then they went home. She looked over some school papers he had brought home. She was pleased he was doing so well in school. They talked while she followed him around to make sure he brushed his teeth and got his clothes ready for school the next day. Then she poured herself a glass of wine. He went to his room and changed into some pajamas. She kissed his forehead and turned off his bedroom light.

The telephone rang at ten. She expected it to be work, but it turned out to be a nurse calling from the St. Camillus Retirement Center. "I'm calling to tell you your mother has had an accident," the nurse said.

"What kind of accident?" she asked. "Is she all right?"

"She fell out of her wheelchair. "Don't worry, she's fine. The doctor put a few sutures in her head, but I just talked to the hospital, and there was no concussion or anything."

"How did she fall?"

"She was sitting up watching television, and apparently she fell asleep. She slipped forward and fell out of her chair, hitting her head."

"Is she still at the hospital?"

"No, she's on her way back. I assure you, she's fine, though she did ask if you would stop by to see her tomorrow."

"Of course." The only chance she would have to stop there was in the morning. It was the day of Matthew's funeral.

"One more thing."

"Yes?"

"I hate to ask this, but it would make it much safer if when she was in her wheelchair or in a chair she had a restraint on."

Rita sighed. "Have you talked to her about that?" she asked.

"Yes, and she's not happy about the idea, but the nursing staff can't watch all of the residents twenty-four hours a day," the nurse said. "At least this way she'd be safe. Your mother is in her seventies. She's not very steady. We just talked to your brother, and he said it was okay with him, but he wanted us to check with you. If you'll authorize a temporary order, we can discuss this again when you get here and see your mother tomorrow."

"You say you talked to my brother?"

"Yes, and he said it was okay with him if it was okay with you."

"Okay, you have my permission for now, but this

is only temporary. It may change after I talk to my mother tomorrow."

"Of course."

"Are you sure she's all right?"

"She's fine."

"Would you tell her I'll stop by to see her in the morning? And call me if anything at all goes wrong tonight."

First thing the next morning, she drove to the St. Camillus Retirement Center. It was across from the Milwaukee County Zoo.

Rita found Eva sitting in a wheelchair in front of her television. A bar held her in the chair. She had a bandage on her head. Rita went in and kissed her. She was a gray-haired woman with a long, crooked nose. "Hello, Mom," she said. "How are you?"

"What? Oh, hi. I'm sore, honey," Eva replied. "Did you hear about my fall? I'm glad someone finally stopped by to see me."

Rita sat in a chair in front of the wheelchair. It was a small room shared by two women. Mrs. Durant was not in the room at the time. "Yes, Mom, I heard you fell."

"What'd you say, hon?" Eva said, rubbing her crooked nose and leaning forward.

"I said, I heard you fell," Rita said louder.

"Yes," she said, straightening slowly. "I've never been so sore, hon."

"Would you like to go for a little ride?" Rita asked.

"Sure," Eva said.

Rita wheeled the chair out into the hall. At the nurses station she told the nurse she was taking Eva out on the patio. Then Rita pushed the wheelchair through the television room, where groaning residents sat slumped in wheelchairs here and there. The room reeked of stale urine and sour breath.

Outside, it was cool, though Eva didn't complain about that. Rita asked how things had been.

"Oh, hon, did I tell you I fell last night?" Eva asked.

"Yes, Mom, I heard," Rita replied loudly. She was never sure whether her mother heard her.

Eva touched the bandage. "I hit my head."

"I know, Mom."

She began to pat herself. "Have you seen my keys?" She laughed. "I hope I didn't lock the house up. We might be in a real mess."

"Mom, you live in a retirement center now."

"It's terrible to live here," Eva said, returning to the present. "You don't know what it's like. It's a prison. They treat you worse than a prisoner."

"Come on, Mom, it's not that bad," Rita said.

"You don't know what it's like to push your call button for a nurse because you have to go to the bathroom, and no one shows up to help you for thirty minutes or so."

"Mom, they don't make you wait that long."

"This morning I wet my pants I waited so long."

Rita didn't say anything.

"They put us in diapers, you know?" When Rita didn't say anything, Eva mentioned Sean. He never visited, Eva said, then added that she didn't blame him because she was sure he was embarrassed after he had cheated her out of the family home.

"Mom," Rita said, "you sold the house to Sean because you couldn't live there any longer. It was too big for you. Too much responsibility. Don't you remember? Besides, you decided it was better for him to have the house than for you to give it to some stranger. You wouldn't want some stranger in our house, would you, Mom? At least that's what you told me before."

"They always say the ones you got to watch out for are your own family members," Eva replied. "The people who know you the best are the ones who can hurt you the most. Like I said, he never comes to see me now. His wife hates me too. Whenever they come to visit, she says hello, then goes back to the car to wait for him."

St. Camillus was spread over two city blocks. Rita bypassed the patio and headed for the Community House. It was turning out to be a typical spring day. Clouds had moved in. It looked like it might rain. A trail of evidence in the Hammond case would be washed away, she knew. She was anxious to get to work.

"Are you cold, Mom?" she asked.

"I'm fine," Eva said. Then she repeated the story about her fall the night before. She added how awful it was to get hurt and have no one around who cared. "You don't know what it's like to live here," she repeated.

Rita admitted that she didn't know what it was like. She admitted it was easy to be "objective," and to look at St. Camillus as a good place for someone who needed extra attention, but at the same time, she pointed out, there weren't many alternatives. "What do you want from me, Mom?" she asked. "I would let you live with me, but I'm never at home. I'd end up hiring a full-time nurse, and you'd hate that because our house is so small there's barely enough room for Greg and me as it is. But what do you want? Tell me what you want, and I'll see what I can do."

"At least I have my car," she said. "The doctors made them take my license away, but if there ever was an emergency, I'd get in that car and drive in a minute." She began to pat herself again. "Only I forgot where I put my keys." She laughed.

"Mom, you're at a retirement center," Rita reminded her. "You don't have a car. What would you like for me to do?"

"Talk to your brother," Eva said. "That's what I want. Talk to him. He was the one who conned me out of my house. He promised he would fix up a room for me so I could live with them as long as I liked, but once I signed the deed over to him, he started dragging his feet. First it was that he needed time to remodel and make room. Then it was that I wasn't strong enough to live at home. Talk to him," she repeated. "You tell him I know what he did. If I die and go to my grave, I'll die remembering what he did to me. Tell him I know. That's all I want you to do. Tell him I know. Let it be on his conscience."

Rita pushed the wheelchair back to St. Camillus. "Okay, Mom, I'll talk to him," she said. She pressed the door button, and waited for the door to open. She wheeled her mother between the residents, who moaned for attention. A number of them called to her, as if she might be the one to give them help.

In the room, Rita planted a kiss on her mother's forehead. "Mom, I hate to run, but I've got to get to work," she said.

Eva held her. "Please, stay a few minutes. I need to tell you some things."

"Mom, I'm running late, but I'll be back." That's why she never liked to visit. She couldn't ever get away—at least not without feeling guilty. "I promise."

While she held Rita, Eva brought out a key to the dresser cabinet. She had found the only key she had. "Unlock it and look in the top drawer. I have something there for you. You're a good girl. Not like your brother."

Rita took the key and unlocked the dresser. The top drawer contained individually wrapped chocolates.

"Take a handful," Eva said.

Rita took some chocolates, locked the cabinet, and returned the key. She kissed her mother again. "Thanks, Mom. Don't worry, I promise to stop back and see you."

"And you'll see Sean?" she said, holding Rita tight.

"Yes."

Eva let go, though she reached out with an open hand. "Did you hear I fell last night, hon?" she asked. "I've never been this sore before," she said.

Rita kissed her mother's forehead. "Yes, Mother, you told me," she said. "I'm sorry." She was almost out the door when she turned to ask, "Say, Mom, do you remember the Squires family in New Berlin?"

"Squires?"

"Yes."

"Why, sure. You remember who they were. What's the matter with your memory? They lived up the street from us. I didn't know them that well—they never came to church or anything—but they're part of the Talbot clan." She touched her head with a shaky hand. "Say, hon, did you hear I fell?"

"Yes, Mom, I know." She slipped out of the room. Walking down the corridor of the retirement center, she was struck by how quickly the Alzheimer's was taking possession of her mother's mind. It was frightening.

9

As Matthew Hammond's funeral ended, Rita happened to glance at Barry Dixon. Their eyes met. She wanted to talk to him, but decided it would be better to wait until after she had talked to Crystal again. Give it a couple of days, she thought. There were questions she still needed to ask Crystal. Routine questions, to check for consistency in her answers. If that panned out, then perhaps Crystal could put pressure on Barry.

The thing that bothered Rita most was the perpetual obnoxious expression that was a part of his demeanor. It was almost a smile, as if he knew she wanted to talk to him and was determined not to say a thing. Watching her, he lit a cigarette. His head tilted back, and he blew smoke into the sky. She was repulsed by his lack of respect for the dead. Why couldn't he wait to smoke until at least after he had left the cemetery? she wondered. He didn't give a damn about anything or anyone. She could see that. He flipped the cigarette and got into a limousine with Crystal.

Charlie must have noticed her watching Barry because he said, "You don't really think he had anything to do with it, do you?"

The limousine drove away. "Why do you say that?" she asked, watching.

"I don't see him as being clever enough to do it."

"I drove by his garage on my way to work this morning," she mentioned, walking in the direction Barry had flipped the cigarette. Charlie followed. "Have you seen the hearse he and his brother fixed up?"

Charlie said, no, he hadn't.

"I'll say this, if he put his car on display in a car show, it'd win first prize." She stopped at the cigarette, put on a disposable glove—she always carried three or four of them in a pocket—and carefully picked up the cigarette. She squeezed the burning tobacco out; then, holding the cigarette in the gloved hand, she pulled the glove off with the other hand, leaving the cigarette inside. She handed it to Charlie. "When we get back, give this to Jim and have him run it by the lab. I want someone to check this against the saliva on the cigarette found at the Hammond scene."

"You're shrewd," Charlie said, smiling.

They headed for the car. The day was a typical spring day, a bit on the cool side but sunny and fresh.

"But why do you think he'd do it?" Charlie asked. "I mean, Crystal already said she understood Barry didn't want Matthew around. If what she said is true, she was keeping Matthew out of the way. Why would Barry want to kill him?"

Rita took her time answering. She thought about it for a moment as they walked. She said, "Maybe Crystal thought she was going to lose Barry if she didn't get rid of Matthew, and she finally gave in to Barry's pressure to kill him. Or it could be that Barry did it on his own. Maybe he could see that even though she was keeping Matthew out of the way, he was still a pest. By murdering Matthew and then standing by her, Barry might be trying to gain her total devotion. When we get back to the office, I want you to check out something for me."

"Sure."

"Find out what kind of life insurance Crystal had on Matthew."

"Will do."

"One other thing," she said, stopping.

"What's that?"

"Never forget that the people you least suspect often commit the most heinous crimes." She began to feel her pockets for her keys. She thought of her mother. She hoped she hadn't locked the keys in the car.

"Some of the people in the office have been talking about you," Charlie said as he produced the keys. He said it as if he had been wanting to say it all along.

She glanced at him, remembering he had driven. "Oh, yeah?"

"Before you got there this morning, Adam and Jim were stirring things up." He unlocked the car doors. "Adam's cold-blooded. I told you you had to watch your back with him." Over the car roof he said, "He's saying the only reason you wanted the Hammond case in the first place was so you could make yourself look good when the case was solved."

She smiled. "He's pissed I didn't give him the case."

"He says the chief of the office has no business taking cases."

"Ask me if I care," she said, still smiling, though

she did care. Already she was tired of Adam. He had
always irritated her, even before she was promoted to
captain and put in charge of the office. She had always
looked at him as someone who didn't deserve to be
where he was at. Now he was getting in her way.

"I hear you," Charlie said. They got in the car.

The trail of the Hammond murderer was growing
cold too quickly, and now she had to worry about
Adam stirring up trouble in the office, especially with
Jim, who could be an obnoxious brat.

They drove to the CID office, where no sooner did
she get in her office than Adam and Jim walked in and
sat down. Jim rested his left ankle on his right knee.

Rita asked him, "How's your foot?" She wanted to
confront Adam, but she was patient.

"It's still a bit sore, but it's all right."

Adam leaned back in his chair. "I believe in telling
someone to her face when I'm upset," he said, "so I'll
let you know right now I talked to Paul today." She
noticed his hands were trembling.

"What's that have to do with me?" Her tone was
even.

"I told him it was my opinion you have no business
taking the Hammond case yourself, and that I should
have it, being second in command, which is what we
originally agreed upon."

"Who agreed?"

"You and I."

She pointed at Jim. "You need to excuse us for a
few minutes, Jim."

Adam said, "It's fine with me if he stays."

She looked Adam straight in the eye. "I said he
needed to be excused."

He straightened.

Without taking her eyes off Adam, she said, "Jim, Charlie has a piece of evidence I want you to run by the lab. Tell them I need something as quickly as possible. This afternoon if they can." Divide and conquer, she thought.

Jim left the office, closing the door behind him.

"All right, let's get something straight," she told Adam. "No one goes to Paul without coming to me first. You violate the chain of command again, and I'll write you up. You have no business consulting Paul on any work-related matter unless I ask you to."

His face became red. "I came to you first."

"And I told you the nature of the case required the entire office to be involved. You're looking for a case to bolster your career. I'm looking to get a killer off the streets. You do anything further to jeopardize the coordination of this investigation again, and I'll make sure you have no part of it. Is that understood?"

He didn't say. Instead he said, "I'd like Jim back as my partner. He and I work well together."

Rita was in no mood to play games. "I've made my assignments," she told him.

Adam stood. "Then you should know that I'm going to file a formal grievance against you," he said. "You can't stop that."

"Fine. You just make sure you file your grievance on your own time and that you send it through proper channels."

He headed for the door.

"That means, it comes to me first."

He walked out the door without stopping or looking back.

She knew he was trouble, but she refused to give in to him. Best thing, she thought, was to keep one step ahead of him. She called Paul Clowers in Madison. She put the call on the speaker phone. While she organized paperwork on her desk, she briefed him about the case. They discussed the evidence. Paul didn't mention anything about the call from Adam. That bothered her. She wondered why he wasn't saying anything. She mentioned it herself: "I heard you had a complaint from Adam."

"Yes, he talked to me. I told him he needed to take things up with you."

"I know. He just left my office a few minutes ago."

"Tell me what's going on with him. I've heard his side. What's yours?"

She gave a forced laugh. "I'm not sure there is 'a side,' " she said. "What did he tell you? We didn't discuss it. I told him if he had anything to say to you, he was to bring it to me first."

"He told me you promised him the Hammond investigation, and that your duties as chief of the office were too much for you also to head an important case."

"One thing's for sure. I wouldn't give him the Hammond case in the first place."

Paul asked why.

She knew he was aware of the reason, but she also knew he had to remain neutral. "Because he doesn't have the experience with a case this big."

Paul mentioned, "Bob Lyons stopped by to talk about Adam. You know Bob, don't you?"

Bob was in charge of the governor's security detail. "Yes, I know him," she said.

"He was very friendly, and said he didn't want to interfere, but he wanted to vouch for Adam. He said he had known Adam for a number of years and thought had it not been for politics, Adam would have been a lot further along than he was. I know this doesn't necessarily make a difference to you, but I thought I'd pass it along to you."

"In other words, Adam called Bob."

"Yes, but I don't think he did it in an adversarial way."

Bullshit, Rita thought.

"I think he was blowing off steam and wasn't very careful about how he did it. Again, I'm not trying to be a judge here. I'm not interfering—it's your office. But if I can help solve a potential problem, I'm more than happy to offer a bit of guidance."

She said, "I may be reading this wrong, but when I talked to Adam two minutes ago, I think we had an understanding."

"Good. Let me know if I can help, and keep me informed."

She turned off the speaker phone and spun in her chair so she was facing the windows. There was her reflection looking at her. The reflection looked as if she had something bitter or rotten in her mouth and wanted to spit it out. She found herself wanting revenge, wanting to put Adam in his place. She knew that one malicious person in an office could spoil the entire environment. Adam was a troublemaker.

She shuffled paperwork on her desk, but she had trouble concentrating. The papers meant nothing to her. All she thought about was Adam. For the better part of an hour she remained like that.

Charlie entered at around four. He informed her that Crystal had $10,000 in life-insurance coverage on Matthew. That wasn't much, barely enough to cover funeral expenses. She had had the policy for three years.

In a way Rita was happy because she didn't want Crystal implicated in her own son's murder. At the same time, however, she was disappointed because leads in the case were drying up.

Charlie was followed by Jim, who reported that the saliva on Barry's cigarette did not match the Hammond evidence. He handed her a report, which she studied. She sighed. Dejected and dismayed, she felt like she was back to square one, no closer to solving the crime than she had been two days before. "How's my list of sex offenders coming?" she mentioned.

He said, "I'm working on it. There's only so much I can do in a given day. I've been running around all day trying to get this thing for you."

"When do you think you'll have the list done?" she asked coldly.

"Maybe early next week—if I get the time to work on it." He looked at his watch. "Is there anything else?" he asked. "My ankle's killing me. I want to go home and soak it."

She leaned back in her chair. "Go ahead."

He left, limping prominently, as if to document he was in pain. She thought he would be a good investigator if she could keep him away from Adam. She was sure Adam was coaching him about the negative tricks of the trade—that is, how to get out of work, how to cause problems and get away with it, and how generally to be disagreeable. That was too bad, she thought. She needed Jim on her side. A computer expert and a stickler for details, he was the one person she turned to when she needed profiles, background checks, lists, or anything that called for research and precise data gathering. He was good at it.

She picked up the Hammond folder and began to turn pages of notes, photographs, and lab reports. A moment before, when the folder was closed, everything had seemed neat and orderly, reassuring. Now, however, with the folder open, the contents seemed disconnected. Without a suspect it was meaningless. Nothing had any relationship to anything else.

10

By three o'clock on Friday, Rita was exhausted. She said she was going home. She had been at the office since six, trying to catch up on her paperwork so she could spend the weekend with Greg. Between the paperwork and Bobby's funeral, she didn't feel she had gotten much accomplished that day. On her way out the door, however, adrenaline shot through her when she received a call from Vince, who said that he and Joyce were bringing in a suspect who had just confessed to having murdered Matthew. The suspect's name was Luther Ashburn.

When she looked at the tall, husky youth with wild dark hair and the beginnings of a mustache, her first impression was that he looked like the suspect in a police composite of a man who had been responsible for multiple attacks on children in the Milwaukee area. She thought that would be ironic because one of the reporters at the Hammond scene had asked her about the composite suspect. Of course, this man looked younger than the man in the composite, but she knew how rough composites could be.

Vince and Joyce took Luther to an interrogation

room. Rita and Charlie went into an adjoining observation booth.

The questions were thorough, beginning with the
other attacks on children around the Milwaukee area,
two of whom had been sexually assaulted. Luther gave
explicit and precise details about the victims and about
his attacks. He confessed to having attacked six children in all—four boys and two girls. One girl and one
boy had been sodomized. The other four children had
escaped during the attacks.

Once Vince and Joyce had finished the initial line
of questioning, they shifted the emphasis of the questions to Luther himself. He was twenty-three, an only
child who still lived at home, and a dishwasher at
China World, a restaurant in Wauwatosa. That would
be within range of the Hammond apartment, Rita
thought.

When it came to the Hammond murder, however,
Luther's answers were vague. He couldn't remember
details. He spoke in only the most general terms.
Joyce asked if he smoked. No, he said, he didn't
smoke. She asked if he would take a polygraph. He
didn't know what that was. A lie-detector test, she told
him. Yes, he said, he would take a lie-detector test.

In relation to the six assaults, the polygraph indicated there was no deception when Luther claimed to
have committed them. In relation to the Hammond
murder, the polygraph results were inconclusive.

There was jubilation throughout the office. While
Vince and Joyce took Luther to a hospital so he could
give blood samples, the rest of the office staff cele-
brated. Someone brought out champagne. Rita even
had a glass. She called Paul, who congratulated her.

Then she gave instructions that she was to be notified the moment Luther's lab results were back.

Pumped with energy, she headed to Sean and Julie's. By that hour most of the traffic had left the city, so she made good time on the interstate.

Greg and Kyle were playing catch in the side yard.

"Catch, Rita!" Kyle said, and he threw the softball to her.

She caught the ball, which stung her hand, but she didn't care. She felt on top of the world. She threw a pop-up, which went higher than the oak tree beside the house. Both boys hustled to catch it. They ran into each other. She laughed.

Greg came to her side. "Mom, can Kyle go to the zoo with us tomorrow?"

"That's up to your Uncle Sean and Aunt Julie," she said.

"They said it was all right with them if it was all right with you."

"I don't care."

They yelled joyously and slapped hands together.

"Can he spent the night?" Greg asked.

"Not tonight," she told him. "I'm expecting a call later, and I may have to do a little work tonight."

"We won't get in your way," Greg told her.

"Not tonight," she said.

"Can you talk to Babe and Norb for us?" Greg asked. "They said they might let Kyle go to the zoo, but they had to talk to you first."

"Sure, I'll talk to them. Let me see my brother and Julie first." She went into the house and had a bourbon and water with Sean. She told them about Luther, surprised at how much she had to say. Too many days had passed in which she had nothing promising to say.

Now it was different. She had good news to tell. Sean and Julie seemed excited.

Greg and Kyle burst into the kitchen. Greg said, "Come on, Mom. Let's go ask about the zoo."

Rita said, "Are we still on for the zoo tomorrow?"

Of course, Julie said.

Rita, Greg, and Kyle went across the street. She pounded on a door. Skinny Norb opened the door, chewing on a cigar. He had a beer can in his hand. "Wehhhhllll," he said smiling. "Babe, look who we got here. Come in, Rita, come in." She went in and gave him a hug. Greg and Kyle slipped by. They stood nearby, waiting.

Rita said, "Give us a chance to talk, boys."

They smiled and disappeared down the hall.

Babe came around the corner, a chunky woman whose brown hair was cut close to her head. She kept it cropped because she worked in a school cafeteria. Her dark complexion was wrinkled. "Hi there, stranger," she said. Rita hugged her.

Norb said, "Can we interest you in a beer?"

She always drank one when she visited, but she liked them to coax her first. It was a ritual they went through.

"Babe, get her a beer," he said.

Babe told him, "Now, Norb, maybe she doesn't want a beer."

"Sure she wants a beer, don't you, Rita?" He chewed his cigar a couple of times, shifting it in his mouth.

Babe said, "I'll drink one if you'll drink one."

Rita gave in. "Sure, I'll drink a beer." She felt like celebrating.

They sat in three rockers in the living room, all

facing one another in a triangle. Norb put aside his cigar stub and lit a fresh cigar. The house reeked of old cigars and stale beer.

Rita asked him, "So, Norb, what project are you guys working on these days?" He was a carpenter who worked for a local contractor.

He said, "We're up at County Stadium. They're tearing out some bleachers and doing some expanding."

"That should keep you busy for a while."

He nodded. "At least until the fall."

Babe smiled. She said, "Rita, the funniest thing happened to me the other day—"

Norb said, "What's that, Babe?"

"About the grandparents—"

"Oh, yeah, tell her about that. You'll love this, Rita."

Babe continued: "You've seen the cafeteria over at St. Dominick's, haven't you?" Rita nodded. "Anyway, they were having Grandparents Day this past week, and all the kids had their grandparents visiting the school. All of a sudden this one little girl came around the lunch line, back where the kids aren't supposed to be, and she was all sad. I asked her what was wrong, and she said her grandparents lived too far away to visit for Grandparents Day. Then she looked up at me and said, 'Mrs. Wishause, would you be my grandmother for today?' I said, 'Sure, hon, I'd be happy to.'" She smiled broadly.

Norb laughed. "Isn't that great, Rita?" he said. She nodded.

Babe asked, "How 'bout you? You had any interesting cases lately?"

She asked if they had heard about the Hammond

boy. Yes, they had heard about it. Babe said she was horrified by what had happened. Rita drank some of her beer. She told them her office might be getting close to solving the case.

Norb smiled. He said, "Well, as long as you're on the case, we're not worried at all. We know you'll get the bastard." He saw Babe's frown. "Well, that's what he is, isn't he?"

Babe said, "Now, Norb, sometimes you can be so crude."

Norb laughed. He told her he was someone who said what was on his mind. He winked at Rita. "Rita knows that. Isn't that right, Rita?"

She smiled.

Babe said, "I agree with Norb. I'm sure you'll get him. I know back when you used to baby-sit, all the parents in the neighborhood trusted you with their kids. I know we did. You'll take care of this little boy too."

Rita set the beer can on a coffee table and stood. "Well, I knew I hadn't been over for a while, so I thought I'd at least stop by to say hello. I suppose you've heard Greg wants Kyle to go to the zoo with us tomorrow."

Babe said, "Yes, and we talked to Paul. He has to work anyway tomorrow, so Kyle was going to be over here. If you don't mind putting up with him, he can go."

Both boys screamed, suddenly appearing from the hallway.

Norb smiled. He lit his cigar again. It kept going out. He smiled. "You know we always like to see you stop by," he said. "And you know we love that son of yours as if he were our own. He and Kyle are great pals."

Babe said, "It gives Kyle something to do. I think he gets bored at his grandma and grandpa's."

Rita gave each of them a hug and went to the door. She told Greg to say good-bye.

They went home, where she made Greg clean his room in return for the trip to the zoo. She cleaned the bathrooms, the kitchen, and vacuumed. Then she and Greg watched television. She sent him to bed at ten.

Vince called. He said he had good news and bad news. The good news was that Luther was definitely linked to the two sexual assaults. Sheriff's detectives wanted to assume jurisdiction. The bad news was that none of the evidence linked him to the Hammond murder.

"Do I have your permission to turn him over?" Vince asked.

"Yes."

The moment she put the phone down, it was like she was experiencing the full impact of the murder all over again. She ran a hand through her hair, almost unable to catch her breath. What now? she wondered. She took a shower to try to wash away some of her depression and exhaustion. In a robe and with a towel wrapped around her hair, she poured herself a glass of wine, picked up the Hammond file, and went into her bedroom. She straightened a pillow against the headboard, dropped the towel on the floor, and leaned back in bed, where she began to pore over the case.

Next thing she knew, she was awakened by the telephone ringing.

"Hello," she said, picking up the phone from where

it had dropped from the bedside table. Surrounded by notes, documents, and photographs, Rita propped herself against the headboard of her bed and looked at the clock: 11:30. Why is someone calling so late? she wondered. More bad news? On the table was a spilled glass of wine, which she had knocked over in the process of getting the phone.

Crystal Hammond asked if everything was all right.

"Fine," Rita said. She massaged her neck. It was sore. "I dropped the phone, that's all." While she talked, she attempted to blot up the wine from the carpet, using the damp towel from her earlier shower.

Crystal apologized for calling so late, then said, "Things have been driving me crazy, so finally I decided to call you. I hope you don't mind."

"You shouldn't ever hesitate to call me," said Rita. "In fact, I've got everything spread out in front of me right now." She pushed aside some of the case notes.

"I guess what's bothering me is why Bobby Ruble killed himself. I didn't go to the funeral today, did you?"

"Yes, I did," she said.

"I couldn't. I mean, I could have gone had I wanted to, but I couldn't force myself."

"I understand."

"No, I don't think you do. I was angry at Bobby. It's like he knew what happened to my son and took it to the grave with him. I can't forgive that."

Rita, eyes closed, explained there was every indication that Bobby Ruble's death was an accident. She was still depressed about Luther.

Crystal said, "Come on. Don't you think it's a bit odd that two people who live in the same neighborhood, that go to the same school, die in the same

week, that they're friends, and that the one who was
murdered was supposed to be with the other one at
the time of the murder? Don't you think that's a bit
too coincidental?"

Rita was silent for a moment. She sighed and said,
"Crystal, we have to be careful not to read too much
into this."

"I don't think I'm reading too much into it at all."

"Let me ask a question."

"Okay."

"You said you thought Bobby was using drugs?"

"Yes. Matthew saw him using them. I'm telling you,
the boy was into all kinds of stuff. He was always
skipping school, Matthew said."

Rita wanted to ask her questions about Matthew's
liberties, but didn't. "Did you know Bobby was diabetic and in and out of the hospital?"

Silence.

"He needed insulin shots to stay alive. That was the
drug Matthew saw him using."

The silence continued on the other end of the line.
Then: "I didn't know that," Crystal said.

In a gentle voice Rita said, "In my work, sometimes
I think all I see are people's problems and tragedies.
When I first came home after visiting with Bobby, I
was convinced he knew something about what had
happened to Matthew. Then when Bobby got killed,
that was my first reaction—he committed suicide because he knew something about Matthew's murder
and felt responsible. Since then a lot of things have
come to light. I met with Bobby's parents and learned
Bobby was diabetic. Not only do I know something
about diabetes from it being in my own family, but I
talked to a friend who's a nurse and she told me about

diabetes in children. It isn't very pleasant, what I heard. In any case, Bobby wasn't a drug addict, and he didn't know anything about Matthew's murder. He was just a boy whose entire life had been turned up-side-down."

To Rita's amazement, Crystal apologized. She asked if they could get together to talk.

"Now?"

Tomorrow, Crystal said. She asked if Rita wanted to go somewhere for lunch.

Rita tried to think. She knew she had planned to go to the zoo. Then there was the basketball game with Mike Squires—if she went. But she had to ask Crystal questions. Crystal had passed a polygraph, but the investigation was at a standstill. She had to ask more about Barry. How about around eleven? she asked.

"Great. You wouldn't mind if we stopped by the cemetery on the way, would you?"

No, she wouldn't mind, Rita told her.

"I'd like to put some flowers out."

"Of course."

Crystal mentioned that she had found some old photographs of Matthew. "Would you like me to bring them along?"

"Sure."

They made arrangements to meet at Crystal's apartment the following morning.

11

Greg shook her. "Mom!" he said.

"What's wrong?" she asked, alarmed. It was light outside. Her first reaction was to jump out of bed, thinking she had overslept and Greg had missed the bus. "What time is it?" she asked, the clock right beside her.

"It's Saturday, Mom," Greg said, giggling at her panic.

She dropped back on the bed. "Don't scare me like that."

"You were talking in your sleep," Greg said, smiling. "What were you dreaming about?"

She had had a vivid nightmare about finding Matthew Hammond's body again, but she didn't tell Greg that. She told him she couldn't remember.

Greg asked if he could eat breakfast in the living room so he could watch Saturday morning cartoons. She said that was fine. Her mouth was dry. She could taste alcohol in it. She tried to remember how much she had had to drink. However much it was, it had been too much, she decided, and knew she had to be more careful.

After she made coffee, she told Greg that if he got dressed, brushed his teeth, and made his bed, she would take him to a basketball game. He ran to his room. She headed for the bathroom.

In the shower she shaved her legs. Afterward, she rubbed body lotion on herself. It struck her as odd that she was going through such an elaborate process. Is it for Mike? she wondered. A stranger. Someone she had met once. So that's it, she thought. You think it's a date. She smiled at herself. It is a date in a way, she thought. She massaged the back of her neck as she looked at herself in the mirror. She wondered if men still found her attractive, despite her having had a child. She touched herself with cologne. Not too much, she thought.

At her closet, she tried to decide what to wear. She chose jeans and a navy blazer over a tan blouse. By the time she had dressed and returned to the bathroom to dry her hair, it was dry. The more she brushed it, the more static electricity that developed. The hair jumped each time the brush approached. Frustrated, she saturated the hair with water and started over. Next thing she knew it was eight-thirty. Greg brushed his teeth, which he still hadn't done, and she and he headed for Arrowhead High School in Hartland.

Mike Squires was on the court with the ninth-grade girls, who had lined up for lay-up drills. He happened to spot Rita and Greg, so he left the court to greet them. He was wearing navy sweats. He had recently trimmed his beard and showered. He looked handsome, not in a youthful and muscular sort of way, but in a distinguished way, as someone who kept active and in shape despite his age. "I was hoping you'd show," he told her, taking her hand. It was more of a tug toward him than it was a shake. "You must be Tom." He shook Greg's hand.

"No, I'm Greg."

"Oops," Mike said, smacking his head with his hand. "Sorry, Greg,"

The boy smiled sheepishly.

Rita pointed at the girls. "They look good," she said, making small talk.

He looked in their direction. "Of course. What do you expect with me as the coach?"

She smiled. "Conceited too, I see."

He studied her. "You look nice."

"Of course. What did you expect?"

He laughed.

A string of girls from the other team ran onto the court. Mike said, "Listen, I'll see you two after the game."

"Yeah. We'll stick around to offer our congratulations."

He patted her shoulder. "I knew I liked you the moment I set eyes on you." He jogged out onto the court.

"He's strange," Greg said.

"We don't talk like that about people," she said.

"Well, he is." He twirled a finger by his right temple. "I think he has googly eyes for you."

She smacked his leg with the back of her hand.

The teams seemed evenly matched. The first two quarters went quickly, and the Hartland girls were up by one point—21–20—forty seconds from halftime. Mike called a time-out. The girls huddled around him. When they left the huddle, one of the guards broke from the other guard, who threw the ball to her. That guard lobbed the ball downcourt to a forward, who threw it to the center, catching the other team by surprise. The center took an easy shot as the halftime horn blared. Score: 23–20. Along with the hometeam fans, Rita found herself on her feet screaming. Greg was embarrassed. He pulled her back into her seat. "Mom," he said. "Get a grip." Mike disappeared into the locker room with the girls.

When the Hartland girls returned to the court, the tide changed. Number 14 of the visiting team, a lanky girl, shot one long shot after another. She hit them all, or so it seemed. The visiting team won 36 to 31. Mike looked across the court, straight at Rita. He shrugged.

"I guess my halftime pep talk didn't work," he said when he had walked across the court to meet her and Greg.

"I forgot how much fun a basketball game can be," she told him.

"Say, Greg, you want something to drink?"

Greg looked at her.

The moment he nodded, Mike handed him a five-dollar bill. "How 'bout if you grab us something from the concession stand? Diet Coke for me." Rita said she would have the same.

Greg started to take the money, but Mike pulled it back. "Don't try to keep the change either," he said.

Greg laughed and snatched the money out of Mike's hands.

"Have you two decided where we're having lunch?" Mike asked once Greg had gone.

"I've got plans," she told him. She tried to keep her eye on Greg. She didn't like him going off by himself in a strange place.

"So, that's how it is. I take you out on a nice date, and this is how you repay me."

She looked at Mike. So, it is a date, she thought, flattered. "It's work," she told him. She looked back in the direction Greg had gone.

Mike said, "He'll be all right. There's only one way out, and I've got guards posted at the door."

She smiled as their eyes met.

They exchanged small talk until Greg returned, sloshing three drinks. They each took one and went outside onto the field next to the school. It was a bright morning, with wisps of clouds here and there in the blue sky, though the air was cool. Walking backward so he could watch them, Greg said, "Mom, can Kyle spend the night after we get back from the zoo?"

"We'll see," she told him. "I'm not sure what all your Uncle Sean and Aunt Julie have planned."

Smiling, Mike asked, "So, what is mean ol' Sean up to these days?"

"You heard he had leukemia, didn't you?" Rita asked.

"No." She nodded. "Don't I feel like a jerk," he said. He seemed genuinely embarrassed. His face even reddened. "Is he all right?"

"He's doing fine—now that I've given him my marrow during a bone-marrow transplant." She smiled. "He complains a lot, but he's doing fine."

Mike smiled back. "I only said what I said because I'm sure you knew Sean was the school bully when he was growing up. You did know that, didn't you?"

"He wasn't the school bully!" she said, laughing.

"Sure he was. Ask him."

It was a side of Sean she had never heard about.

Greg asked, "Mom, can you really die if you have leukemia?"

"Some people do," Rita said, still thinking about what Mike had said. She didn't know whether to believe him.

"Is Uncle Sean going to die?"

It was the first time he had asked such questions. He's picking a fine time to show his curiosity, she thought. "Honey, Uncle Sean is in what they call remission. It's like when disease goes to sleep."

"Does it ever wake up?"

She looked into his intelligent eyes. "I think your uncle has been in remission long enough, he's safe."

Mike told Greg, "When I grow up, I want to be just like you. I want to ask all kinds of questions and learn all kinds of things."

Greg laughed. "Mom, I'm telling you, the guy's crazy!"

Somewhere a lawnmower roared to life. A large riding mower came around the corner of the school, heading in their direction.

Rita nodded toward the parking lot. "I'm not trying to rush you," she said over the sound of the mower, "but we've got to get on the road. I promised someone I'd meet her for lunch."

At her car, he asked, "Can I call you sometime?"

She said, "Sure."

"I didn't see your number in the book."

At least he was curious enough to look, Rita thought. Greg had already gotten the keys from her and was inside the car. He locked the doors so she couldn't get in. When she tapped on the window, he giggled.

"Open the door," she told him. Her voice was seri-

ous. He unlocked the door. She got in her car, opened
the glove box, and brought out a pen and piece of
paper. On it she wrote her home telephone number
and gave it to Mike. She didn't ordinarily give her
home number to strangers, but she decided Mike was
an exception. Besides, she hoped he called.

"Mom, let's go," Greg said.

"Don't be rude," she told him. She gave him a
harsh glance.

"Bye," Mike said. He smiled and took her hand.
Again, it was a gentle tug.

His smile made her feel good. "Good-bye." She left
him standing in the parking lot, where she could see
him in her rearview mirror as she drove away. For
years she had felt like a throwback, someone whose
marriage had failed, even though she knew she had
proved herself many times over. She had raised a son,
established her own credit, and built a career. Mike
didn't make her feel like a failure, though, despite
having only recently met her. He knew enough about
her to be frightened off if he wanted to be. He wasn't.
He didn't make her feel desperate either.

In Hartland, she purchased a bundle of fresh flowers
at Connie's Flowers. Then she dropped Greg at Sean
and Julie's. She told him she would be back by one
so they could go to the zoo. He ran across the street
to find Kyle. Rita visited with Sean and Julie for a
few minutes, then drove to Crystal's apartment.

Coat in hand, Crystal was waiting when Rita got
there. The living room was full of boxes.

"Moving?" Rita asked, suspicious of what she saw.
Why is Crystal packing? she wondered. Is she going
somewhere?

"I've been looking around at new apartments,"

Crystal replied. "This place is too painful." She seemed changed, somehow more rough around the edges, like someone one might meet in a tavern, not a prostitute, but a woman who was not afraid to sit with men and drink. "Look," she said, "let's get something straight right now. I loved my son." She was shorter than Rita; her left eye was twitching, but she didn't appear intimidated. "I may have been strict with him, but I never abused him." Rita didn't interrupt, wanting to let her talk. "If he ran away, it wasn't because I was mean to him, but probably because I couldn't give him all the things he wanted or thought he should have. I bought his clothes at the Salvation Army, and almost every night we ate macaroni and cheese, or a potato to fill us up because a secretary's salary doesn't stretch very far. If it hadn't been for his father paying the way, Matthew wouldn't have even gone to a Catholic school. I'm not Catholic. Ron was. He thought it was his responsibility to at least expose Matthew to Catholics." She sighed. "I even had to borrow money from my parents to bury him. Now, if you want to go to lunch, I'd like to have you along, but I want to make sure we understand each other."

Rita was satisfied. "Let's go," she said.

"I'll drive," Crystal volunteered.

Rita followed her to a battered red Toyota.

"Where would you like to have lunch?" Crystal asked.

"Anywhere."

The car jerked off. Crystal had trouble shifting gears. It suggested she might be nervous to have Rita in the car. "Have you been to Holy Hill?" she asked.

Rita knew of the religious shrine northwest of Milwaukee, had even seen it on a number of occasions—

on a hill, it was visible for miles—but, no, she said, she had never been there.

"Is that okay?"

"Fine." Rita wanted to ask more questions about Barry, but she was cautious not to seem to anxious or suspicious.

On Highway 41, Crystal said she hoped the stop at the cemetery wouldn't be an inconvenience. Rita assured her it was no inconvenience. Crystal confessed that it was Matthew's birthday—he had been born on a hot Sunday twelve Mays earlier. She began to talk about those early years.

She and Ron had been married a little over a year when she discovered she was pregnant, she said. At first he had taken an interest in a family. She had become encouraged too, even excited, until she discovered that his real interest was in making sure the child was raised Catholic. "He was Catholic through and through," Crystal told Rita. "A new student at Marquette University, and everything. Someone who's not Catholic wouldn't understand the way he was."

Rita told her, "Believe me, I know all about it."

"Are you Catholic?" Crystal glanced over.

"My ex is."

"I'm not surprised. It seems everyone in Milwaukee is a Catholic."

Rita smiled to herself.

"So, did your husband try to convert you?"

"He knew better. But, like Ron with Matthew, Steve pushed to raise Greg Catholic." She didn't know why she was sharing so much of her private life with Crystal. "Is Marquette really a good school?" Rita asked, changing the subject.

Ron called it a "C–" school, Crystal said. It wasn't

that great. The only reason it had a good reputation
was because it was a Catholic university in a Catholic
town. The education itself was next to worthless. Anyway, she continued, she and Ron had taken a small
apartment on the south side of the city, near where
he had worked as a clerk in a convenience store. Since
he had been working part-time there during the school
year, once school was out of session, he had been
given a full-time job working days, which had helped
them financially.

Even then, though, they had been so strapped for
money that she, a medical receptionist at the time,
had worked up until the weekend she had delivered
Matthew. She had been resting on the sofa that Sunday when she suddenly went into labor. She walked
to the convenience store, where she told Ron it was
time. Everyone had warned her that a first birth would
be a slow, painful delivery, but by the time Ron's boss
arrived to relieve Ron, and she and Ron drove to St.
Luke's hospital, she had delivered Matthew. Crystal
laughed at her own story. Rita was struck by the mother's laugh. It was hollow, as if she didn't really find
pleasure in the recollection. Why is Crystal telling me
all these things? Rita wondered. Is she still hiding
something?

The cemetery was in a field lined by trees. From
the entrance where Crystal parked, they walked the
gravel road into the field of markers. On her way
Crystal picked up a beer can someone had dropped
in the grass. When they got to the granite stone marking a plot of new sod decorated with an old pair of
red chucks—like the ones Matthew had been wearing
at the time of his death—a baseball glove, and flowers,
Crystal used a tissue to wipe off the marker, as one

would wipe a child's nose. After rearranging the existing flowers that were fresh, Crystal added new flowers. Hers were carnations; Rita produced daisies. Crystal began to weep, and after a few moments Rita helped her up. Supporting her, Rita stood with her at the grave. "I loved that little boy," she said. Rita wondered how much of what Crystal said was genuine. Were the tears real?

They walked back. In the car, Crystal wiped her eyes with a tissue and blew her nose, but instead of putting the tissue away, she kept it out. She blotted her eyes again and again. Tears kept draining from her eyes. She started the car. "I'm okay," she said. "I really am."

Once out of the cemetery, they caught Highway 167 west, a highway that cut through rich farmland and the north branch of the Kettle-Moraine forest. Crystal regained some of her composure. Occasionally Rita caught glimpses of the distant cathedral on a hill, its spires almost in the clouds. So what happened to the relationship once Matthew was born? she asked, attempting to get Crystal to open up again.

"Well, Ron realized the hard way that life with a child was not as simple as he had anticipated," Crystal said. In fact, she explained, from the beginning it had been rough. For several days after his birth, Matthew had been confined to the hospital because of high levels of bilirubin, which had left him jaundiced. Aside from feedings, he had remained naked under ultraviolet lights, with nothing but special glasses to shield him from the light. "That was hard," she said. "I don't know if you know what it's like to see the baby you've lugged around in your belly for nine months all of a sudden be taken from you and placed in isolation, but the first thing you think of is, 'Oh, no, is this what we've waited nine months to have happen?' " Crystal glanced over, but her eyes as quickly returned to the road.

"Anyway, when we finally got to bring Matthew home, he still wasn't well," she went on. "He cried constantly. Colic." A screaming baby didn't help the marriage, Crystal said. "To make things worse, there was the breast-feeding." She explained how repulsive breast-feeding had been to her, which Matthew apparently had sensed because he didn't like breast-feeding either. That antagonized her relationship with Ron, who, coached by his parents, thought all children had to be breast-fed since that was, in their opinion, the "natural" way. "For me, once the doctor told me I had breast-fed enough to build the baby's immunities, I was done. I switched to formula." She and Ron's relationship had gone downhill from there, she said. By the time he had returned to school in late August of his second year, they were all but separated.

Rita's head was throbbing. So much sounded like her and Steve's relationship. She didn't want to hear about that. She wanted to hear about Barry. She wanted to hear the truth about Crystal and her son. She put on her sunglasses. The car was close enough to the monastery that it was in the wooded hills. She could no longer see the cathedral.

The second semester, Crystal said, turning into the entrance of Holy Hill, Ron had moved out. This is driving me crazy, Rita thought. Get to the point. Crystal didn't seem to sense Rita's impatience. Since she couldn't pay the rent for their apartment, she went on, and couldn't work full-time with a baby, she had gone home to live with her parents, who lived in Waukegan, on the north side of Chicago. Her parents had given her the basement of their house, and Crystal's mother had helped baby-sit while Crystal started a new job.

They passed two joggers. Without forewarning, Crystal confessed that the Matthew she had known was not the same child most people in Brown Deer had known. "They knew him as a quiet, polite boy," she said. "I knew him as someone who was sneaky, stubborn, and rebellious. You know, we each know our own child. I had to watch him like a hawk."

"Everyone I've talked to said he was quiet and un-assuming," Rita said. It was the moment she had been waiting for. Yes, tell me the truth about Matthew, she thought. There were too many inconsistencies in what she had heard, despite the polygraph.

Crystal kept her eyes on the road as it wound through the woods. That wasn't him at all, she said. "I had my share of problems with him, from bedwet-ting to lying and stealing. And believe me, we had some hellacious fights—verbal battles, of course." She said she assumed it had had something to do with him not having a father around.

People always try to rationalize such things, Rita thought. What kinds of things did he steal? she asked.

"Little things like other kids' toys. You know the sort of thing." The car came into a clearing, which made visible the cathedral on the hill. Then the cathe-dral was gone again. "I always caught him with money, and I had no idea where he got it."

Once Crystal had parked in a lot at the top of the hill, they walked to the shrine complex of red brick buildings, the cathedral dominating the top of the hill. Crystal asked if Rita wanted to eat first or look around. Look around, Rita said, so they climbed a winding staircase up the outside of the cathedral complex. Each successive landing gave a better view of the surrounding countryside, shrouded in haze, beneath the clouds. It was all part of the Kettle-Moraine forest, which stretched for miles.

At the main cathedral, before they went inside, Crystal said, "It was all I could do to control him." They entered the cathedral. There was a wedding in progress. Crystal and Rita sat down in a pew to watch.

Rita thought it was strange to watch someone else's wedding. She thought about her own. She and Steve had been married in a small campus chapel at the University of Wisconsin in Madison. The wedding she now watched was an impressive ceremony, full of ritual. The bridesmaids were in long cranberry dresses; the groom's party wore black tuxedos.

After the wedding, Rita and Crystal took an elevator down to the cafeteria to eat. In the warm, sunlit cafeteria they sat facing each other over a table by the window. During lunch Crystal brought out an envelope. "That first day you asked me whether we had ever been to the southern Kettle-Moraine forest," she said, "and I told you no. Later, it dawned on me that Matthew had been out that way." She handed some photographs to Rita. "These are from when he took a field trip with his fifth-grade class to Old World, that museum park with all the old houses." Rita nodded. "You pass through Kettle-Moraine to get there."

There was a tanned, dark-haired girl in several of the photographs. Rita asked about her.

"That's Jenny Davis," Crystal said, "a girl Matthew had a crush on. She moved to Colorado last summer."

In one of the photographs Jenny had her hand up so
Matthew couldn't get a picture of her.

"Could Matthew have been wanting to run away
to Colorado?"

"No. They didn't keep in touch. It was more Matthew being in love with her than she being in love
with Matthew." There was also a photograph of
Bobby Ruble. Crystal said, "I called Bobby's mother.
I feel terrible about what happened." Her eyelid
twitched.

Rita came across a photograph of a giggling Matthew, one that was a striking contrast to the still body
she had seen on the stainless steel autopsy table. This
boy with freckles was hysterical about something,
braces showing. Blue eyes were open wide, as if to
drink in everything. Crystal said, "Jenny took that."

I thought she didn't care about him, Rita mused.

Crystal suddenly said, "Can we go outside? This
place is closing in on me. I need some fresh air." Rita
returned the photographs to the envelope and pushed
it across the table.

Outside, from the summit overlooking miles of
countryside in every direction, Rita took a deep breath
and looked up at the sun. Here and there a cloud was
trapped in a pale blue sky. She put on her sunglasses.
Her head was throbbing again.

She and Crystal followed a half-mile paved path
down the hill from the cathedral, a path marked as
the "Way of the Cross" because of periodic life-size
sculptures illustrating the last moments in the life of
Jesus. It was a trail that wound under tall trees. Sunlight penetrated branches of the trees and dappled the
path. The sunlight was warm.

At one of the sculptures, which was contained in an

edifice of unhewn stones, Crystal said, "Have you ever accidentally fallen asleep during the day only to wake up confused?" Rita didn't say. "You sit up and you look around, and for a moment you're fooled, thinking it's the next morning—as if somehow you slept through the entire night and it's the next day." Rita remembered Greg waking her up that morning. "It's been happening to me a lot lately. All I want to do is sleep once I get off work. I drift off, and when I wake up an hour or so later, there's a split second when I panic, thinking I'm late for work and that I've forgotten to get Matthew off to school. I jump up, only to realize he's gone and there's no one to get off. Then I realize there's still a long night ahead of me before I go to work again."

Down the hill, they happened upon a mother whose two blond daughters were collecting items for a collage they could take to school, a collage of Holy Hill. Crystal smiled as she watched the girls hunt for acorns, flowers, pine cones, and rocks.

Rita finally said, "Tell me about Barry. We've talked to him, but he doesn't cooperate."

Crystal glanced at her. She said, "I've stopped seeing him."

"I didn't know that."

She nodded. "After the funeral we broke up. Believe me, he doesn't know anything. After that one time, I wouldn't let him near my son."

"Barry told us Matthew used to go by his garage."

"That's a lie!"

"He told us he gave Matthew cigarettes."

"I don't believe it."

"Crystal, there's something you're not telling us,

and it's pissing me off because I'm getting things a piece at a time. It's like pulling teeth."

She didn't say anything.

"If you're trying to protect Barry, then you're doing it at the expense of your son."

Still Crystal didn't say anything.

On their way back up the hill, they passed a group of older ladies who were looking at a statue of Jesus. One of them said, "The Jesus I remember from the Scriptures was of medium build. He would have been bigger than this."

Another lady said, "You remember that movie they made where they had a blond-haired, blue-eyed Jesus?" No one said anything. The lady continued, "Anyway, my grandson asked me if that was what Jesus looked like, and I told him, no, Jesus had dark hair and dark skin. . . ."

Out of earshot from the ladies, Crystal said, "Okay, Barry beat on Matthew, I knew he did. I swear he didn't kill him, though." Rita looked into Crystal's olive eyes, the whites of which were veined with blood. The left eye twitched. There was a tiny mole on Crystal's left cheek, Rita noticed. The mole looked as if she had tried to cover it with powder. Crystal smiled sadly. "I promise." She said what was important was Matthew, not Barry. Matthew had a good heart. Someone murdered him. "I'll never forget last Christmas." She went on to tell how Matthew had joined an adopt-a-grandparent program at a retirement center. "It's across from the zoo. St. Camillus. Do you know it?"

"My mother is there!"

"She is? We might have run into each other before, then." Crystal told how Matthew had gone to the classes for the program. "It made me feel good he was doing something like that." She shook her head. "During all the time we were in class, he only asked one question—of course, he was the only child. Do you know what the question was?" Rita waited. "He wanted to know what happened if his grandparent died." Rita thought of Greg asking about Sean that morning. Crystal told how the question had caught the director of volunteers off guard—that is, that a child could be so perceptive.

Once a month, Crystal continued, she and Matthew had gone to visit Mr. Wood, a ninety-year-old resident of St. Camillus. "Right before Christmas, Matthew and I went shopping for a present for Mr. Wood," she said. "Matthew picked out a ceramic Christmas house, a sort of decoration. On the way to St. Camillus, Matthew was looking at the Christmas decoration and he said, 'Mom, look, it's a candle holder.' He removed the lid. 'But we don't have a candle,' he told me. We were already running late, and there was no place to stop for a candle, so I told him they probably wouldn't let Mr. Wood have a candle anyway. When we got to St. Camillus, we discovered Mr. Wood's name had been removed from the door of the room we usually visited. On our way back to the desk to ask where he had been moved, we met the director of volunteers. She told Matthew that sometimes patients did get moved around. We said Merry Christmas to her and went to the nurses station. Matthew asked where Mr. Wood had been moved to, and the nurse told him Mr. Wood had passed away." Crystal smiled sadly. "I'll never forget him standing there holding his present for Mr. Wood. It was like he couldn't possibly understand what had happened. He looked at me, and I didn't know what to say. The director of volunteers caught us in the parking lot and apologized. She was extremely embarrassed. All the way back home Matthew never said a word. I still have that Christmas house without a candle."

They came to the last station. The two blond girls whom they had seen earlier on the path were sprinkling holy water on the box of items they had collected. Rita looked at her watch. In tiny moves a thin black hand jumped forward. She knew she was too late to take Greg and Kyle to the zoo. She was sure Sean and Julie had gone ahead without her. She felt guilty.

Crystal and Rita followed the mother and two daughters back to the entrance of the complex, where a priest blessed the items the girls had collected, flipping more holy water at them. Some of the water got in one of the girl's eyes. Blinking, she wiped it away with a finger. The mother smiled pleasantly, as if water in the eyes was a small price to pay for the power of the blessing.

Crystal wouldn't say anything more about Barry. She said he didn't know who murdered Matthew, and she wasn't having anything more to do with him, so it wasn't important. Rita didn't push.

By the time Rita got to New Berlin, Sean and Julie were gone. There was a note on the kitchen counter: "We have the boys and are taking them to lunch and the zoo. See you around five. Love, Julie."

12

Two more weeks had passed since Matthew's body had been found. The trail was cold. Ice cold. No new leads. No developments. Rita arrived at the office Monday morning feeling a depressing emptiness. She was no longer sure she had made the right decision in assigning the entire office to the case. Perhaps she had overreacted, she thought. She began to work on the mountains of paperwork on her desk. The Hammond case had put her behind, especially on her administrative duties. She had been giving it too much attention. She started processing case files, working as quickly as she could, but by nine-fifteen she had already received several calls from Madison about separate cases. That upset her because she became suspicious that someone was nudging Madison about the administrative matters in Milwaukee. She was sure it was Adam.

She was just about to leave for lunch when Adam showed up. He wanted to talk, he said. She invited him in.

He sat down across from her desk. He said he wanted to find out how much longer he was going to be assigned exclusively to the Hammond case.

She told him a homicide case was a key investigation and was given priority among caseloads.

"It's been almost two weeks since we've turned any leads," he said, "and some of the people in the office have been talking about all the attention a case with no leads is getting."

"Let me ask you this," she said. "Who are these 'people' who've been talking?"

"It sounds like you're questioning whether I'm telling the truth," he said, getting defensive. "Are you calling me a liar?"

"Absolutely not," she said, calmly staring him in the eye. "I'm just wondering who all these people are who've been talking." She opened her hands. "I don't see them."

"Then I'm asking about myself," he said. "It seems a waste if I'm sitting here working on this case every day and it's not even producing leads."

"A few weeks ago you wanted this case all to yourself."

He didn't say anything.

"No one's going to budge until we have a solid lead." She stood. "Anything else?"

He left. He almost seemed pleased with himself.

She sat back down, her plans to get lunch spoiled. She was no longer hungry. Adam knew he had her over a barrel. She knew that. Each day that passed without a significant lead made her look bad. She began to review evidence reports from evidence seized during the weekend, not evidence pertaining to the Hammond case but that routinely processed by the Justice Department. She couldn't let him get her down, she thought.

She tried to convince herself that murder investiga-

tions often didn't produce leads for long periods of
time. They dragged out over months, even years. Seldom was a case as simple as the Anderson case, the
textbook crime.

Jessie Anderson had decided to murder his wife for
her insurance and had put together an elaborate
scheme to divert attention from himself as a suspect.
The only problem was, pieces of evidence had fallen
together almost immediately.

Some time before the murder, Anderson had gone
into Milwaukee, where he had purchased a hunting knife
at a pawnshop. Apparently he had thought the clerk
wouldn't remember it. What he failed to realize was that
pawnshops tend to have a regular clientele; so when
a stranger suddenly appears and buys a knife, especially if he is clean-cut and looks relatively well-to-do,
the salesperson is going to remember the transaction.
That's exactly what had happened. Once detectives
had released a description of the murder weapon
found at the crime scene, the clerk at the pawnshop
called the police.

In addition, a week or so before the murder, Anderson had stopped a black youth in the vicinity where
he planned to commit the crime and had bought the
youth's cap. Apparently Anderson's rationalization
was to leave the cap at the crime scene and claim that
two black youths, one wearing the cap, had attempted
to rob him and his wife. Once a photograph of the
cap surfaced in the media, though, the original owner
stepped forward to give his account of how the cap
had been purchased from him by a man meeting Anderson's description.

Finally, Anderson had committed a classic error. He
had stabbed his wife multiple times in the face. A

seasoned homicide detective knows that when a murderer stabs his victim in the face, the victim is probably related to the murderer. The murderer naturally doesn't want the person he is killing to look at him, and so it's not uncommon for a murderer who knows the victim to try to blind her or him.

No, seldom was a case that simple, she thought, closing her eyes.

There came a tap on her door, which brought her back to the present moment. Vince Hoffman and Joyce Smoot entered and sat down. "Guess what," he said. "I think we may have something again. We put the word out on the streets, and we got a call."

"What kind of call?" Rita asked.

"We found a suspect."

Rita studied him. His tie was loose. He looked as if he had had too much to drink the night before. He said that along with arrest records and the profile Jim had put together, they had a list of twenty-five potential suspects, most of them sex offenders in the vicinity of Brown Deer. Rita said she knew—she had seen the list. He shuffled papers. Of those, Joyce had narrowed the list to ten suspects whose previous records indicated some link to children. Rita said she knew that, too. What was the point? she asked. Joyce said they had received an anonymous tip from a caller who claimed to know who had murdered Matthew Hammond.

"I know we've received a ton of these tips, but this one named one of the ten suspects on my short list," Joyce went on to say. His name was Bill Scroggins, she said, reading from her notes, a thirty-seven-year-old man who shared a duplex with his mother in Menomonee Falls. Twice he had been arrested for molesting minors, but in both cases the youths were in their teens and seemed to have been willing participants. Once Scroggins had been arrested, the parents of both youths had dropped their complaints, probably because they knew what would come out in court would be embarrassing to the family. In a third case, Joyce pointed out, the parents of a nine-year-old boy had filed a complaint because Scroggins had been following their son home from school. They lived in Germantown, a middle-class neighborhood, and Scroggins' 1976 rusty pickup had called attention to itself. Germantown detectives had arrested him when he finally asked the boy if he wanted a ride home. Once the arrest had been made, however, the case never made it to court.

Joyce handed Rita a photograph of Scroggins. A white male with thinning hair, he had the face of a carp—protruding lips and eyes that seemed to look to the side instead of straightforward. Rita asked, "And this matches the profile?"

Joyce smiled. "It's one of those rare times when the profile matches exactly an anonymous tip."

"Have you checked him out?"

"It could be him," Jim O'Donnell said, stepping into the doorway. Rita was sure he was there to claim part of the credit. He was holding a sheet of paper. "I've run some quick checks. Scroggins doesn't work. He receives benefits for a mental disability. He could have been in Brown Deer that day. It's within his predatory zone, and he's definitely a predator."

"Bev!" Rita called out.

Bev Smith appeared behind Jim. Rita held out the photograph. "Get prints of this man and give one to Jim." To Jim, "Put together a photo lineup. As soon as you get one, run it by Crystal Hammond and see if she recognizes Scroggins."

Bev took the photograph and disappeared.

By two, Jim had called in. Crystal had not been able to identify Scroggins. Preoccupied with paperwork, Rita put the call on the speaker phone. He said, "She did tell me that even though she couldn't identify Scroggins, that didn't mean anything because, for all she knew, he could have been a regular member of St. Paul's parish. She's not Catholic, she said, so she's seldom around the church."

This news made Rita restless. She called Charlie. "Let's get out of here for a while," she told him.

They drove to St. Paul's School and showed the photograph to both the principal, Sister Mary, and the secretary. Sister Mary, a tall, gray-haired woman wearing a plain brown dress, straightened her glasses and said she might have seen the man in church, but couldn't be sure because she usually went to the early mass, which meant she didn't see many of the parishioners. Charlie asked if the priest was around, but the secretary said he was in confession. The president of the school board, Mike Eschholz, happened to be walking by, so Sister Mary asked him to look at the photograph. Mr. Eschholz recognized Scroggins immediately. "Sure," he said. "That's Joe Pratt. He used to go to—" He snapped his fingers a couple of times, then pointed at the ceiling. "St. Benedict's in Menomonee Falls. I see him at the evening mass sometimes when my wife and I go on Saturday."

"Joe Pratt?" Rita asked.

"Yes, Joe Pratt. He drives over from Menomonee Falls."

"Why would he drive over here to go to church?"

Charlie asked. "Why doesn't he go to church where he's at?"

"Because this is such a friendly place," Mr. Eschholz said, smiling.

The secretary said, "I could call over to the church and see if the secretary has a mailing address if you want me to."

Rita told her, "That would be nice."

It turned out that the church secretary wouldn't give the address listed for Joe Pratt. Instead, she said that Father Catalpa was on his way to the school to explain. A short, gray-haired priest with a goatee appeared directly, his plump face red with anger. He said, "We do not give out confidential information about our parishioners." He took off his glasses and looked at Sister Mary. "I'm surprised at you. This is a house of prayer, not a police department." With that, he replaced his glasses and walked away.

Rita thought, pompous little bastard. She said, "We're sorry if we caused any trouble."

Off to the side, Mr. Eschholz said, "Oh, don't worry about Father Catalpa. He's always like that. Some people say he has a Napoleonic complex and snaps off like that because he's so short."

Rita smiled, though she was irritated. She would have thought a priest would care a little more about the loss of one of his parishioners.

At St. Benedict's in Menomonee Falls, Father De-Falco was not as reticent about giving information regarding Joe Pratt, whom he knew as Bill Scroggins. Father DeFalco, who appeared to have had a stroke, smiled upon seeing the photograph of Scroggins. "Yes, that's him, all right. I had to ask him to leave our parish here."

"Why?"

"You might say he was too friendly with the little boys. Some of the parents were concerned."

"What do you mean?" Charlie asked.

"Don't get me wrong," he said. "He was always pleasant, but he only seemed to show up to see the children—particularly the boys. In fact, one Sunday he asked one of the teenage boys if he wanted to go bowling. That's when I asked him to leave. It just wasn't healthy for the parish. Of course, he was repentant and claimed he hadn't meant any harm by what he had done, but what else could I do? People were talking." He shrugged.

"Then, one day I was talking to Father Catalpa over at St. Paul's," he continued, "and I told him the story. He was upset that I had sent someone like that away from the Church. He said it sounded like Scroggins only needed some nurturing and guidance, and if we sent people like that away from the Church every time there was a problem, we wouldn't have any sheep left in the flock." Father DeFalco smiled. "I told him he was more than welcome to take Mr. Scroggins off my hands. Father Catalpa said that was fine—all Mr. Scroggins needed was a little counseling and extra attention. So we gave him a new name and sent him over to St. Paul's for a second chance. Father Catalpa has sworn there hasn't been a single problem since Mr. Scroggins entered his parish."

Rita said, "I don't understand why you gave him a new name." That was strange, she thought. It was almost as if someone were trying to hide something.

"Oh, that was Father Catalpa's idea," Father DeFalco said. "He's funny that way. He believes in protecting his parishioners no matter what. He thought a new name would give Mr. Scroggins a genuine second chance."

In the car, Charlie asked about the name change.

She shook her head. She said she didn't understand it because the name change only meant that Father Catalpa was hiding something from his parishioners. "It could be that Father Catalpa knew more about Scroggins than others knew."

Charlie laughed. "Don't expect him to tell us anything," he said.

She didn't, but she was determined to find out anyway.

She requisitioned a surveillance van, and early on Tuesday morning she parked it a block from the duplex where Scroggins lived with his mother. She and Charlie took the first watch. She didn't exclude herself from the monotonous duties of surveillance because of something Gordon Cales had taught her when he had been the chief of the Milwaukee office. He had always said he wouldn't ask his investigators to do something he wouldn't do himself. He had always jumped in and done his fair share.

The van included a portable television and a small kitchen, so she and the other detectives could live in it while watching the house around the clock.

It was a well-kept duplex with stucco siding, on a spacious corner lot with two trees in the front yard. All the curtains in both sides of the house were kept drawn.

Around ten o'clock on the first morning, Scroggins appeared. He was a short, potbellied man who wore a white undershirt and blue jean shorts. For a moment or two he stood on the front porch, looking blankly at the world. Then he walked to the side of the house, where there was a shed painted in the same cream and brown colors of the duplex. He unlocked the shed and opened the doors to a riding lawnmower. He got to the mower, backed it out of the shed, and began cutting the lawn. The ground was saturated from the recent rains, so the wheels of the mower left brownish tracks in the grass. After that, Scroggins brought out a push mower and trimmed. Once he was finished, he put away the equipment and went back inside the house.

At three o'clock that afternoon, Scroggins walked to the corner to check his mailbox, going there right after the mail carrier's white truck had passed. His movements were so precise that it was as if he had been watching for the mail. He took the mail back inside the house and didn't appear again until almost five o'clock, when he carried black bags of trash to the corner. He also brought out a blue bin of recyclables. The bin was heaped with beer cans. Scroggins went back inside.

Adam and Ray showed up to relieve Rita and Charlie around five-thirty. It was apparent from Adam's expression that he was still not happy about the late-hours assignment, but he made no comment.

Wednesday, Scroggins didn't come out of the house at all, except to check his mail. The garbage collectors arrived early on Wednesday. When Scroggins appeared right after the mail carrier's truck had passed his house, he also picked up the empty blue bin the garbage collectors had left behind. Thursday, Scroggins only checked his mail.

Friday, the garage door to his duplex opened, and a battered white pickup truck backed out. Rita and Charlie followed Scroggins to Kenosha, where he stopped one time after another at a string of adult bookstores along I-94. At the first stop, Charlie followed Scroggins in the door. Afterward, Charlie told Rita, "Damn. That place stinks in there."

"What's he shopping for?" Rita asked.

"Looked like pictures of men."

Following his tour of the adult bookstores, Scroggins drove through McDonald's and headed back to his duplex in Menomonee Falls. He took Highway 57 to Brown Deer and got on Highway 100, which he took up to Menomonee Falls. He passed within two blocks of the Hammond apartment.

Now that there was a possible suspect in the Hammond case, Rita left Greg at Sean and Julie's on Saturday, so she could help with the surveillance. Charlie joined her.

On Saturday morning, Scroggins was out early. He backed his truck out and began shopping at garage sales, though he didn't seem to be looking for anything in particular. He dug through books and dishes. Finally, at one house he found something that interested him—items in a cardboard box. Rita brought out a pair of binoculars. "Take a look at this," she said and handed the binoculars to Charlie.

Charlie looked also. "Eight-track tapes?" he said. "Matthew had some of those in his room, didn't he? I never knew eight-tracks were so popular."

"I don't think they are."

They broke off their surveillance in order to talk to the man who had sold Scroggins the tapes. He was an affable man who seemed worried when Rita and Charlie flashed their credentials.

He said, "I didn't need a permit for this sale, did I?"

Rita said, "We want to ask a couple of questions."

"Sure."

"The man who just left—the one who bought the eight-track tapes—do you know him?"

"No, I don't. As a matter of fact, I was rather surprised when he picked up the box of tapes and asked me how much I wanted for each tape. I told him they were no good to me, that he could have the whole box of them for a dollar. He was quite happy. Said he had a collection and they were next to impossible to find." He laughed at himself. "I wish I'd have known that before I told him the price. I could have made some money."

Rita telephoned Crystal, told her they were checking out a lead, and wanted to know if it was possible that Matthew had ever gotten rid of any of her eight-track tapes.

Crystal said she didn't know. "To tell you the truth, I never paid that much attention," she said. "I'm not sure if he ever had any of them out or not."

"If you looked through the box, would you know if any were missing?" Rita asked.

"Wow, it's been so long, I'm not sure what all I had, though I can look."

Once Rita got off the phone, Charlie asked her what she thought the prospects were for getting a search warrant to get inside Scroggins' house.

She shook her head. "Even if Crystal could give a statement saying some of her son's tapes are missing, we couldn't get a search warrant. Not based upon that."

"So why can't we pay him a visit?"

Rita shrugged. "It's an idea," she said. They drove by to see Crystal, who wasn't much help. Her apartment had fallen into complete disarray. She still hadn't moved, had even unpacked some boxes.

She had looked through the box of tapes, she said. The most she could say was that at one time she had had many more tapes. Over the years she had gotten rid of quite a few of them and couldn't remember which ones she had actually given to Matthew.

"Is there any way you could identify one of your eight-tracks if it showed up somewhere?" Charlie asked.

Crystal nodded. "Yes, I could. Mine have my initials on them." She took them into Matthew's room, the only room she hadn't packed. She brought out the box of tapes. On each one her initials were printed on the label.

While they were in the room, Rita picked up a box of seashells she hadn't paid much attention to before. There were several conch shells in the box. "Where did Matthew get these?" she asked.

"His father sent him those," Crystal said. "I found them packed away in my closet, so I brought them out. It's kind of sad because it's like Ron was trying to rub it in that he had gone to the ocean and Matthew hadn't been able to go."

Rita put down the box. "Crystal, thanks for your help," she said. "We'll be in touch."

Crystal walked them to the front door, where she asked, "What do you think about this suspect? Has he been seen with Matthew?"

Rita patted her shoulder. "Don't worry, we're looking into everything carefully," she said.

"Keep me informed."

Rita nodded. She was excited once again. There was too much coincidence. Too many things were fitting a pattern. But she cautioned herself not to overreact. Keep calm, she told herself. Think things through.

13

Rita had planned to pay Scroggins a visit on Monday, but first thing that morning, she was called to Lizard Mound State Park, north of Milwaukee, near West Bend. Another body had been discovered. On the way to the park, she and Charlie talked. The preliminary details sounded like the same M.O. That made her wonder whether she had made a mistake by waiting to talk to Scroggins. What if he was the killer? Why didn't I talk to him? she wondered. There was sufficient physical evidence to make Scroggins a suspect, and he had a history of sex crimes. When Charlie didn't mention Scroggins, she did. She asked him, "You thinking about Scroggins?"

He said, "I guess, but we don't even know yet if this new victim is related to the Hammond case."

She took that to mean if the cases were related, then she had made an error in judgment. Sure, he didn't say it directly, but she could tell that was what was implied.

Charlie continued, "The only thing that bothers me is I wish we hadn't broken off surveillance when we followed up on those tapes."

The same thing had been nagging her. By breaking off the surveillance, she had given Scroggins a window of opportunity to strike again—if he was the killer. Something told her she had made a fatal miscalculation.

The park was on an oasis in the middle of rolling farm country. She knew Lizard Mound as the Potter's Field, which was how a farmer had referred to it years earlier when she, Steve, and Greg had visited the park. The Indian burial grounds had been a source of irritation to the farmer, whom they had stopped to ask for directions. He was a Christian, he had said, and believed in helping the poor and downtrodden, but didn't see why good farmland should be thrown away on a slew of strangers who had wandered the earth two thousand years before. "They've been dead for thousands of years, for God's sake," he had said. With that, he had pointed at a road that divided his property, climbed back on his tractor, and resumed plowing.

It was true. Lizard Mound State Park was set in the middle of what appeared to be prime farmland. A narrow road ran between two cornfields, back to a patch of tall shade trees and thick underbrush. The parking lot was already filled with emergency vehicles and news vans when Rita and Charlie arrived.

Despite the time of day, mosquitoes were everywhere. As Rita and Charlie followed a path that had been pointed out to them by a state trooper, Rita asked Charlie, "Have you ever been here?"

He said yes, he and Claudia had brought Keisha to the park on several occasions. It was a great place for a picnic, he said.

Rita and Charlie slipped under the cordon to the

crime scene. They passed a sign that included information about a tribe of Indians that had lived near the park two thousand years before. The oasis had been an Indian burial grounds. Swatting the mosquitoes away, Rita stepped off the path, onto one of the mounds, a thirty- to forty-feet long rise in the earth. Near the mound was a sign that labeled the mound as a PANTHER, and the sign included an outline of the mound:

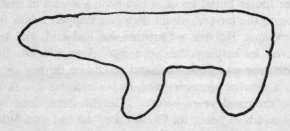

   She came to a standstill over a mutilated boy wearing a white robe, the robe of an altar boy. She turned away, sickened by what she saw. Stay calm, she told herself, swallowing her revulsion. She saw Charlie staring at the boy and was sure he had noticed the same thing. It looked like Greg. The first time, with Matthew Hammond, the resemblance had been a coincidence that she had denied. This time she was certain of the resemblance. She ran a hand through her hair and took a deep breath. She knelt to the boy, approximately eleven years of age. Carefully she raised his robe. The mutilated body was naked underneath.
   The boy had been laid out neatly between the perpendicular offshoots of the mound—the legs of the panther. His skin, like that of Matthew, was an orange-red. He too had had his neck cut from ear to

ear. His carotid arteries and jugular veins had been severed. They had been reconnected with crude sutures. The difference this time, however, was that numerous other incisions had been made in this victim's body and then resewn crudely.

The sheriff of Washington County, Frank Norris, approached her. He was without a coat and had a 9mm in a shoulder holster under his left arm.

"Whoever did this is real sick," he said.

"Hi, Frank." She stood to shake his hand while staring at the husky blond boy, hands sewn together on his chest. "What do we know about him?" she asked. She felt the blood draining from her. She had risen too quickly. For a moment she thought she was going to pass out. A blackness filled her, but when the spell passed, she found herself still standing.

"We think he's Laurence Cassell, who disappeared from Pewaukee on Saturday. We haven't gotten a positive ID on him yet, but everything else adds up. He was out selling magazines as part of a Boy Scout project, and he never returned home. At first the parents thought he might have run away, but—" He looked at the body and shook his head.

Her first thought was that Saturday was when she and Charlie had broken off the surveillance of Scroggins. Why hadn't she made sure someone was watching Scroggins at all times? He was a suspect. She should have treated him like a suspect, she told herself. At the very minimum she knew she should have interviewed him. "Any witnesses?"

"Not yet. But we found the body as a result of an anonymous tip."

She glanced at him. "Were you able to trace the call?" she asked.

"No, apparently not. It came through a Milwaukee hot line, and they passed the information on to us. They said they never trace tips."

Scroggins had been given to them through an anonymous tip, and now a body had been given to them through a tip. It didn't add up. She nodded at the robe. "I'm sure he wasn't wearing that robe when he disappeared," she said.

"Not according to the description we got," Frank said. "The description had him in blue jeans, gym shoes, and a T-shirt."

Rita introduced Charlie to Frank. At the same time she told Charlie, "I want you to go back to the Hammond case and find out exactly how the park rangers happened upon the body in the first place."

Charlie knelt to the body.

One of the sheriff's detectives found a cigarette butt. The cigarette was a Winston. Rita carefully packaged it as evidence. The rest of the area revealed no traces of the crime, though Rita supervised as the crime lab personnel went over everything. Before the medical examiner removed the body, she had him raise the boy so she could see his back. Like the first victim, there were multiple stab wounds.

The parents of Laurence, Ralph and Dorothy Cassell of Pewaukee, identified the body the moment it arrived at the morgue, and Rita assigned Vince and Joyce to interview the family, while she and Charlie stayed for the autopsy.

The preliminary examination indicated that the murders had been committed by the same person, which, given the organized manner of the crimes, now categorized the suspect as a serial killer. As in the Hammond case, the cause of death appeared to be asphyxiation.

There were cloth fibers around the mouth—some type of abrasive cloth. Also, as in the Hammond case, the body had been sexually assaulted and embalmed.

Outside the examination room, Rita slumped back against a wall. Oh, God, she thought. What have I let happen? She put a hand over her mouth. The image of Scroggins haunted her.

Charlie said, "It's as much my fault as it is anyone's," as if he knew exactly what she was thinking. She looked at him. She thought he looked pale. In any case, he was not the same man she had known a number of weeks earlier, when the first body had been discovered. His hair was matted, and he looked like he had just climbed out of bed, half asleep, half disgusted that someone had awakened him too early. His clothes were wrinkled, not because he hadn't ironed them, but because he had worn the newness out of them. He said, "When we broke off the surveillance to check out the guy who sold those tapes, and follow up with all that, I should have suggested we make sure someone kept an eye on Scroggins."

I shouldn't have had to be reminded, she told herself. She pushed herself off the wall and looked around. The corridors were empty, though the smell of the autopsy was near. "Charlie?"

He looked at her.

"Did you notice anything unusual about that boy?"

He seemed to have been waiting for the question. "You mean that he looked like Greg?" he asked.

You know exactly what I mean, she thought, but didn't say it aloud.

"Yes, I noticed. I was going to say something when we found the Hammond boy, but I thought that would be too morbid."

"Then you did notice?"

"Yes."

"Ever since we left Lizard Mound, I've been seeing Greg's face over and over again." She stared at Charlie. "We have a murderer who's preying on boys that look like my son."

He didn't say anything.

"I'm going to nail him."

As they headed to their sedan, he changed the subject, "I've been doing some reading about embalming," he said. "Did you know that in ancient Egypt, the Egyptians embalmed so the soul could return to the body?"

"Yes, I know," she said. "For some reason, I can't imagine this killer trying to save his victims' souls," she added. "How about the list of people who might have training in embalming?"

"So far, it's impossible. Hundreds of people have been licensed by the state, and there are mortuary science schools across the country. But that's not the worst part. The worst part is that just about anyone can work in a funeral home and learn embalming through on-the-job training. If you're talking funeral homes, the list is endless. But I've been going through it a name at a time."

"Good. By any chance is Scroggins on that list?"

"I don't have anything on him."

They headed for the office. Rita told herself she would not make another mistake, no matter what. As Charlie drove, she made notes. At the office building, she and Charlie were rushed by a flood of reporters.

"Is there another serial killer on the loose?" "Have you arrested a suspect yet?" Questions came from all directions. Rita and Charlie pushed through the reporters, entering the building. The lobby guards held back the reporters.

It was noon. Only William Lee and Bev were in the office. Bev told Rita that Paul Clowers was driving in from Madison and wanted to meet with her at one-thirty. Rita wondered who had called him. She said, "I'm going to grab a sandwich. As soon as we get the lab results on that cigarette, I want to know." She went to the YMCA, where she put on her suit, dived into the pool, and began swimming laps. She didn't swim with labored strokes but with slow, even strokes, lap after lap. Each time she got to the end of the pool, she did a somersault, kicked off the wall, and swam in the opposite direction. When she reached the opposite wall, she repeated the process. She swam until her lungs were ready to burst, her eyes burned with chlorine, and her nose felt like it was foaming with ammonia. All the while she kept thinking about Greg. From now on, she decided, she would make sure he was watched like a hawk. He wouldn't go anywhere unless she knew exactly where he was—not even across the street. That made her angry with herself because now that she felt her own son was threatened, she was taking every precaution. She wondered if the death of the Cassell boy was her fault.

In her car, she combed the tangles out of her damp hair. A chill came over her. She turned on the heater, though outside it was warm.

Paul was in her office when she got there. He was standing at the windows, combing his oily black hair, which he always kept neatly trimmed. He had taken off his powder blue suit coat. It hung on a coat rack. "Hi, Rita," he said, putting away his comb. He extended a hand, and she shook it. "Sit down." Instead of sitting behind her desk, she pulled a chair near him and sat down.

She had always known him to be a pleasant, soft-spoken man, and today was no exception. He asked how she had been, how Greg was, and how work was going. He looked right at her with his hazel eyes.

She talked upbeat, though she kept wishing he would leave so she could get to her work. There were things she wanted to do with the Cassell case. She wanted to compare it, detail by detail, with the Hammond case. She wanted to stay on top of it.

From the corner of her desk he picked up a folded letter, which she hadn't noticed before. "Whenever I get any information about one of my people, I routinely check into it," he said. "If it's a letter about one of the people down the line, I pass it on to the supervisors. This letter is about you, so I wanted to stop by and see how things were going." He held out the letter. "You know we've been talking about these matters anyway, what with Adam and all."

She unfolded the paper and read:

Dear Paul,

Normally I never complain, and I try to be as reasonable as I can, but I have attempted to talk to Captain Rita Trible of our office about a problem, and she has refused to listen, so I feel I must take more aggressive measures.

For the past several weeks Captain Trible has reassigned the entire office to a homicide she has taken an interest in. All of the best investigators are assigned to the case, though the case is not producing enough leads to warrant such attention. Mean-

while, other important cases are falling by the
wayside, cases that have produced active leads.

A number of us have talked to Captain Trible
about this, but she refuses to listen. She is even
rude at times. The morale of our office is at an all-
time low.

I would be grateful if you would look into the
matter.

The letter was unsigned. Rita handed it back to
Paul.

He told her, "At first I didn't think anything about
it, but two more people, good investigators, have approached me, and have said that you had access to
information about a key suspect in this case, but you
weren't aggressive enough in following up on it. Now
we have a second victim."

She sighed. She had had no idea there was that
much resentment in the office. She knew the letter
was from Adam, but she assumed the other two people who had complained were Vince and Joyce. The
sad truth was that they were good investigators. She
was sure the only reason they were upset was because
she had not been more aggressive when they had
brought her Scroggins' name. What bothered her,
though, was that neither Vince nor Joyce had come
to her first. The more she thought about it, the angrier
she became.

Paul was congenial, so she didn't think it necessary
to lose her temper, despite how she felt. She said,
"From the beginning I felt the case deserved our full
attention, but all I got was a bunch of feet-dragging.
Now there's every indication that we have a serial killer
on our hands. I think I saw that in the first crime, which

was very organized." She outlined the facts of the two cases to him. "As far as having a suspect," she continued, "we are checking one out, but this is a serious case. I can't just go out and start arresting people because we want them off the streets. We've been watching a suspect, but frankly, I don't want him to know that we know about him until we're ready to move in with a solid charge. Otherwise he might destroy key evidence before we can get to it." She realized what she was telling Paul was little more than an impromptu rationalization, but she felt she had to defend herself.

Even as they were talking, local news sources were reporting that Milwaukee had another serial killer on its hands. Bev interrupted the meeting so Rita could turn on the small television set in her office.

Paul was clearly disturbed by what he saw. He didn't say so, tried to stay unruffled, but she could see disappointment in his eyes. He told her the media attention would exacerbate matters. He stood and shook her hand. "For now I can give you a little room to work, but you can see the pressure's on. I'll watch for a little while, but I might have to shift some things around in order to keep a handle on this." She said she understood. He left.

She spent the rest of the day putting the case in order and coordinating activities. She sent Jim over to South Eleventh Street to pick up lab reports from the crime laboratory. She reviewed the evidence, which substantiated a serial killing. She called the FBI's Behavioral Science Unit to get guidance. They helped her develop a profile.

Finally, at the end of the day, she asked Charlie if he wanted to drive out to Pewaukee to see the Cassells with her.

On their way, she told Charlie about Paul's visit.

"I wouldn't worry about him," Charlie said. "He only wants a piece of the credit when we break the case."

"Cases like this make and break careers," she told him. "I'll tell you right now, there are people who want my head on a platter."

"To hell with them," was all he said.

Silence.

Finally, "You know, there is something that's been bothering me."

"What's that?"

"The altar boy's robe." She shook her head. "The murderer intentionally put that on. What do you make of it?"

"So, he's trying to sensationalize the crimes. What's new about that?"

"But only someone who knew the case would know that Matthew had been an altar boy," she said.

"I think I read something about Matthew being an altar boy in his obituary," Charlie told her.

She glanced at him. "You did?"

"I'm pretty sure I did."

That made sense, Rita thought. She couldn't remember reading that, but the obituary would have included such information. Stop being so paranoid, she told herself.

Pewaukee, despite having grown up along the banks of a large lake west of Milwaukee, was rather impoverished, not what one might expect from a lakefront town so close to a major city. Most of the houses had been built before the upper class of Milwaukee had begun searching for property outside the city, so along the lake there was some new development, but for the most part the properties were monopolized by people who had lived there for years. The homes were generally small, old, and in need of repair and paint.

Rita and Charlie had trouble finding the Cassell home, on a congested hill a couple of blocks from the lake. By the time they got there, darkness had almost settled. It looked as though it might rain at any moment. A storm was moving in.

Every room in the two-story white house was lighted. On the front porch, inside the fence that surrounded the house, was a shadow. The shadow, holding the door half open, watched Rita and Charlie as if to question whether they were at the right place.

It turned out to be a girl of fourteen or fifteen, Julie, Laurence's sister. She had long, wild brown hair with a bleached streak in it. She obviously had been crying.

"Are your mother and father at home?" Rita asked after they had introduced themselves.

Inside the house, there was a musty smell. Ralph Cassell, once he had seen Rita and Charlie's credentials and remembered them from the morgue, turned to his wife, Dorothy, who had short platinum blond hair. "You remember them, don't you?" he said. She nodded. She looked ten to fifteen years younger than he was. She was in her thirties. His thinning black hair, so neatly combed, made him look as if he might have been a CEO of some corporation, though Rita knew he was a tool and dye maker for a Waukesha company. He wore a black suit. Dorothy, also dressed in black, was a waitress at Culver's, a small restaurant in Waukesha.

Also in the family room, off the house proper, were Ralph's parents, Bud and Margaret Cassell. Bud, though he had white hair, had thick brown eyebrows, which he raised as he looked at Rita and Charlie. "I want to know what in the hell you people are doing about my grandson," he said with a pleasant but firm voice.

Ralph looked, face grim, as if he wanted an answer to the same question. Only he said something new: "Those two who were out here earlier—"

"Detectives Hoffman and Smoot," Rita mentioned.

"I guess that's them. Anyway, they were saying you had a suspect but hadn't arrested him yet. How could that be? How could you know you had a suspect and let him kill again?"

Why would Vince and Joyce tell them that? Rita wondered. Why were they being so vindictive? First Paul, now this. It enraged her.

Dorothy spoke up: "My God, my son's been murdered! At least let the people who are going to help us catch his killer do their job. Please, sit down," she said to Rita and Charlie.

Everyone sat down.

Rita told them, "I know you've already been asked a lot of questions, so we're not here to repeat all of that. What we are here for is to ask if you might have seen anyone unusual hanging around this area." She produced a stack of mugshots. "I have some photographs I want you to look at, and I want you to tell us if any of these people look familiar." She lined the photographs on a coffee table in front of the sofa.

Bud leaned forward without getting out of his Lazyboy. He shook his head. "Nope," he said. "Can't say any of them look familiar."

His wife said no, she hadn't seen any of the people in the photos either. Dorothy shook her head, and Ralph, even without saying anything, made it clear by his expression that no one looked familiar to him.

Leaning over the back of the sofa, between her mother and father, Julie said, "I think I've seen one."

Everyone looked at her.

"I saw that one there," she said, pointing. "He was driving around one day."

"Which one?" her father demanded. "Why didn't you say something before?"

She got defensive. "I only saw him once," she said. "He drove down our street and turned around in front of the house. I thought he looked scary. He asked Larry for directions. I pulled Larry back and told him to go in the house. The man drove off. If he'd have come back I would have said something, but he didn't come back. And it's been awhile since I saw him."

"Which one did you see?" Rita asked in a gentle voice.

Everyone was watching Julie. She walked around the sofa and put her finger on Scroggins.

"Are you sure?" Charlie asked.

They watched her, waiting for a response.

"Yes." The tone of her voice was almost one of sarcasm.

Rita said, "It's very important that we don't make any mistakes about this."

Julie was serious. "I don't think anyone would forget a face like that."

Ralph said, "Is this the same one who's your suspect?"

Rita didn't say.

Dorothy began to weep. She said, "It is, isn't it! The one you knew about is the one, isn't he!"

Rita tried to change the subject. She too was sick at the news. She said, "Larry was found dressed in an altar boy's robe. Are you Catholic?"

Ralph said yes, they were Catholic and attended St. Mary's in Pewaukee, but that Larry was not an altar boy.

Rita stood. She knew she needed to get out of the house. She knew she had been responsible for their son's murder. "Mr. and Mrs. Cassell, thank you for your time." Dorothy was still weeping. Rita headed for the door, Charlie behind her, when she stopped abruptly at a small table next to the door and picked up a framed photograph of Julie and Larry together. It had been taken on a windy day, because the children's hair was blowing. Behind them was Lake Michigan. "When was this taken?" Rita asked, staring at the freckle-faced boy who looked like Greg. She thought, no, Larry has longer hair.

Dorothy suddenly spoke. "Last summer," she said. Julie began to weep and ran out of the room. "Excuse me," Dorothy said, and went after her daughter.

Ralph said, "I just don't understand how my son could go out to sell some magazines and end up getting murdered. What the hell is the world coming to?"

No one had an answer.

Rita and Charlie returned to Milwaukee. She couldn't talk to him. She even told him she didn't feel like talking. She was horrified by what had happened. She was horrified it was her fault.

At the office, she called Vince and Joyce back to the office. They had already gone home for the night. Everyone had gone home. There was a skeleton crew working.

Joyce was the first to arrive. She looked as if she suspected what Rita had called her in for, but she didn't say anything, only sat down at her desk and began to work.

When Vince arrived twenty minutes later, Rita excused Charlie and called Vince and Joyce into her office. She confronted them with what she had learned at the Cassells'. She told them, "Ralph Cassell explicitly informed me that the investigators who had talked to the family had told them about a suspect who had not been arrested or questioned at the time of their son's murder."

Rather than to deny it all, Vince spoke up, as if to take the offensive: "We told you about Scroggins," he said, "and I still don't know why you didn't send us out to talk to him. For all we know, the Cassell boy might have been alive had someone been doing something on the Scroggins lead."

Rita told him, "You're talking about a crime when you divulge information about a criminal investigation. How in the hell dare you? What the hell were you two thinking? You've falsely accused someone who hasn't even been formally charged." She was out of her chair. She pounded her desk several times to emphasize her anger. "I could suspend you both! Not only have you falsely accused someone, but you've leaked evidence. Who the hell do you two think you are?" She knew she was losing her temper, but she didn't care. "I have a notion to relieve you both of your duties, and I would be perfectly justified in doing so. Don't you realize you have hurt that family? You don't even know what you're talking about, and you're out there telling people you have a suspect. Who is your suspect?"

Joyce didn't say, but Vince spoke up: "Scroggins. That's our suspect."

"And have you talked to him?"

Vince said, "You know that better than us."

"But you'd like to talk to him, wouldn't you?"

"You're damn right, we would."

"And do you have some physical evidence linking him to the crime?"

Vince didn't say, though he did mention, "We didn't have evidence against Barry Dixon, but you sent us to interview him."

"He's the damned boyfriend of the victim's mother!" she yelled. "What relationship is Scroggins?"

Neither said.

"Did the Cassells identify Scroggins in a photo lineup?"

Again, neither said.

Rita hit the desktop with her hand. "Did they identify Scroggins, yes or no?"

No, Joyce said.

Rita held out her hand. "I want your credentials," she said calmly.

Vince turned pale. Joyce seemed stunned. Neither of them moved.

"Get the hell out of my office," Rita said. They were almost out of her office before she said, "The Cassell girl identified Scroggins." Joyce and Vince looked back at her. "If you'd have done a proper photo lineup, you'd have known that. Instead, you were so busy playing games with human lives and office politics that you didn't give a damn about anyone except yourselves. Get the hell out of here!"

When they left, Rita leaned back in her chair. She could have just as easily exploded at herself the same way. She felt like hell. She knew she was at fault. Only at that moment did she remember that she hadn't picked up Greg. She panicked.

Outside, it was raining. She rushed to Sean and Julie's and got Greg. In the car, he asked why she had come so late. Drenched, she said she was sorry.

"That's all you ever do is work," he complained.

She told him it was true, and she was sorry. By that hour of the day her resilience had worn thin.

"You never do anything with me anymore," he said. "Like the trip to the zoo."

Why should he mention that? she wondered. She tried to think what they could do together, though she didn't feel like doing anything. All she wanted was to get him home and in bed so she could work on the Hammond-Cassell investigation. "How about if we stop by to see your grandmother for a few minutes and then go out to supper?" It had been several weeks since she had seen Eva.

"Oh, Mom," he complained.

"Come on, it'll be fun."

"How come whenever we do something, you get to be the one to choose what it is?"

She felt her anger rising. "Because I'm the mother," she said. "Besides, I don't think it's too much to ask that you do something for me every once in a while." She put the car in gear. The rain was pouring.

He mumbled, "I'd rather stay with Uncle Sean and Aunt Julie."

She slammed on the brakes. "Listen here," she said, jerking a finger at him. "I'm swamped with work, but at least I'm trying to do something with you. I'm not going to let you spoil everything, or I'll take you straight home. I put up with enough of this crap at the office without having to bring it home with me."

"I'd rather go home," he said, looking straight ahead.

"Okay," she said, enraged. "I'll take you home, if

that's how you want it, but don't ask me for anything. Don't ask me to go anywhere, don't ask for any of your friends over, don't ask for anything. Nothing." The car fishtailed on the wet pavement as she gunned the engine.

"Fine," he said.

She drove faster. "Remember, don't ask for anything."

"I won't," he said. His voice sounded sure of itself.

She was on I-94, heading west, before she realized she was out of control. She took the Waukesha exit. "No, I'm not going to let you do this," she said. "I'm not going to let you ruin my night. Now, you're going to see your grandmother, and you're going to be nice to her, like it or not, and then we're going someplace to have a nice dinner together. Do you understand me?"

He didn't say.

"I said, do you understand?"

"Yes," he mumbled.

She took Blue Mound, heading east. Her world had turned upside down.

At St. Camillus, Rita apologized to Greg for being so irritable. She said, "There's just so much going on in your mother's life right now. You wouldn't believe all the pressure." They walked to Eva's room. She had a new roommate, Barbara McGlaughlin, an Irish woman in her eighties. Both women were sitting in wheelchairs.

Greg said he liked how Barbara talked. She was a tall, skinny woman, almost ghostly in complexion. She handed him a stuffed white bear, telling him she used to work in a toy factory. "You know what the bear's name is?" she asked in an Irish accent.

He shook his head. He was obviously too fascinated

with her to tell her that he was a little too old for stuffed animals.

"Shamrock," she said, rolling the r. "You know what a shamrrrock is?"

He nodded.

Barbara asked him, "What is a shamrock?"

"Something that brings you luck," Greg said.

Barbara screamed and clapped with joy. "You're absolutely beautiful!" she said. "Good for you. Now, if you keep Shamrock with you, it will bring you luck and protect you."

All the while, Eva smiled, fascinated by what she was watching.

To Greg, Rita said, "Can you say hello to your grandmother?"

"Hi," Greg said.

Eva didn't know whom he was talking to. It was obvious she was confused. She looked at Barbara, expecting her to introduce Greg. When Barbara didn't say anything, Eva looked at Rita and asked, "Did you hear I fell and hit my head?"

Rita said, "Yes, Mother, I heard. Don't you remember I visited you right after it happened?" How could she be going on about something weeks after it had happened? Rita wondered, then realized her mother had always been that way. She went on and on about things, blowing even the smallest incident out of proportion. Rita wondered if she herself were the same way. Was that why she was running herself into the ground? Had she inherited an obsessive compulsive personality from her mother?

Eva mentioned Greg. "Isn't he a cute boy?" she said.

"Mom, it's Greg, your grandson."

Eva gave a look of surprise. "When did you and John have a child?" she asked. "Why didn't you tell me?"

"It was Steve," she said. "And we're divorced."

"Oh, Steve, that's right," she said. "I'm sorry I forgot his name. I really shouldn't since he comes to see me, but I can't remember anything anymore. At least he's not like Sean, who never comes to see me. I can remember his name."

"Mom, Steve and I are divorced," Rita said. "He doesn't come to see you anymore. He used to come."

"Oh." She was visibly confused. Within the flesh that hung from her facial bones like melted wax, her yellowed eyes darted from here to there, as if the room were closing in on her.

"Greg, why don't you tell your grandmother what you've been doing in school?" Rita said.

"I've been moved to the best readers' group," he said shyly.

"You've been what, hon?" Eva said. She turned her head so an ear was tilted toward him.

Rita said, "You need to talk louder so she can hear."

Greg repeated, "I've been moved to the best readers' group."

"Oh, that's good, hon," she said. She produced a key. "Here, you take this," she told him. "It goes to my cabinet." He took it. "Go ahead, unlock it. There's a treat in there for you."

Greg unlocked the chest and got a handful of chocolates. He relocked the cabinet and gave her back the key.

Outside, under the veranda of St. Camillus, Rita took a few moments to explain to Greg about Alzheimer's. She had mentioned the disease to him before, but now that it was getting worse, she went into more detail. They watched the rain pour. It made a roaring sound. When did she get it? Greg wanted to know. He held Shamrock under his arm so no one could see he had a stuffed bear. "She's had it for a while," Rita told him, "though I haven't really talked about it because it's only gotten bad in recent days."

"Will there come a time when she won't even know who you are?" Greg asked.

Staring at the rain, Rita took a deep breath. "Yes," she said.

"Will you get it when you're old?"

"I hope not." She held out a hand. He took it with his own. "You ready?" she asked. Before he could answer, she jerked him forward and they ran through the rain. Somewhere in the middle of the parking lot, their hands broke from each other. They dashed to separate doors of the car. They jumped inside the car, where they laughed. Greg's laugh turned to a giggle. She liked to hear him giggle.

"I've got an idea," she said. "Rather than run around in this rain, how about if we go home and have a pizza delivered?"

"Mom, you said we could go out to eat."

She didn't feel like going anywhere, but he was right, she had told him she would take him out. "You're right," she conceded. "Where do you want to go?"

"Pizza Hut."

"Greg, we have pizza when we order at home. At least if we're going out, let's have something different." He persisted. She gave in. They went to Pizza Hut.

They didn't get home until almost nine-thirty. The rain had stopped. There was an eerie calm in the air.

She had been thinking about how nice it would be to change into her bathrobe and relax with a glass of wine when she noticed a car in the driveway of their house. It looked like an official car, a blue Plymouth. Mike Squires got out, standing in her headlights. He was tanned, and he had shaved off his beard. He walked up to the window. "Hi," he said, smiling. He held up a bottle of wine. "They were having a sale on this at the store. Can I interest you in a glass of cheap wine and some great company?" She had not seen him for a while, so she gave in.

They went inside, and she brought out a corkscrew and two glasses.

Mike commented, "Who does your housecleaning and interior decorating?" The kitchen was a mess. "I'd love to hire whoever it is."

Greg giggled.

She had meant to clean the kitchen before going to work that morning, but then she had been called to Lizard Mound. She told Greg to take a shower, but Mike asked him to wait, he had a gift to give him. From his jacket pocket Mike brought out a conch. He told Greg, "Hold it up to your ear." Greg took the shell and held its opening to his ear. "Hear the ocean?" Greg nodded. "I picked that up in Florida. It still has the ocean in it."

"I'm sure," Greg said, rolling his eyes.

"You calling me a liar!" He grabbed Greg's hand, keeping the shell upright. "Careful you don't let the water run out."

Greg smiled and rolled his eyes again.

Rita told Greg to go take a shower and get his

things ready for school the next day. She wondered if Mike had really gone to Florida.

Mike opened the bottle of red wine and poured them each a glass. She led him into the living room, where they sat down, she in the rocker, he on the sofa.

"So you went to Florida," she said, studying his tan. "No wonder I hadn't seen you for a while. It must be nice to pick up and go somewhere like that. Where at in Florida?"

"Key West," he told her. He tasted the wine. "Oh, awful. That's what you get when you buy cheap wine." She tasted hers but didn't say anything. "Yeah, this past week we had a teachers' day right at the weekend, and I discovered I had a thousand dollars in the bank. I thought I could either use it to continue my therapy or use it to take a vacation, so I decided on the vacation."

"You should have taken the therapy."

He smiled. "You're a funny lady," he said. He held up the glass of wine. "You got anything to snack on while we drink this?"

She went to the kitchen and brought back a can of cashew halves.

He threw a handful in his mouth. "I should have known—stale."

She laughed. "You know, if you weren't so entertaining, I wouldn't have a damn thing to do with you. You're like a wind-up doll—wind you up and let you bounce around until you run out of energy."

He held out a cashew. "I'm serious, try this." He got up to give it to her, but when she reached for it, he said, "No, open your mouth." She did. He leaned forward and kissed her on the lips. The kiss felt good. It had been a long time since her lips had touched a man's. His kiss felt especially good after the day she had had.

She smiled. "Yeah, you're right," she said. "They're a bit stale, but they're okay."

He put another handful of cashews in his mouth. "Want some more?"

Greg returned from his shower. His hair was dripping water.

Rita said, "You couldn't possibly have taken a shower that quickly."

"Yes, I did."

"And you washed your hair?"

"Yes." He shook his head, flinging water at her.

"Greg!"

He laughed.

"Now, go get your clothes ready for school and"— she glanced at the grandfather clock. It was 9:40— "you can read for twenty minutes before you go to bed."

"Can I watch TV?" he asked.

"I want you to read."

"Please."

"Go."

Once Greg had gone to his room, Mike sat down on the floor in front of her. "Seriously, was it as good for you as it was for me?" he asked.

The room was quiet. She could hear the television playing in Greg's bedroom.

Mike smiled and pulled on her hand.

"What are you doing?" she asked as she slid out of her chair and sat on the floor beside him. He kissed her heavily, the warmth of their mouths uniting. She could taste the wine and cashews in his. He released her mouth but squeezed her hands with his. "I'm forty-five years old," he told her, "and scared to death."

"Is that why you always act like a clown around me?"

"Maybe. Being silly keeps me from having to get serious. In fact, I went to Key West to try to think, to get you off my mind, but you're all I thought about—"

Greg appeared.

"—and him."

She was embarrassed to be caught sitting on the floor with Mike.

"Oooohhhh, viper attack!" Greg said.

"Viper attack?" Rita said.

"Yes. What are you two doing, sucking each other's faces?"

She came off the floor and chased him down the hall. When she came back, she asked, "What do you mean, 'and him'?"

He shrugged. "You know, I never had any kids of my own," he said. "Being a schoolteacher, I realize I like to be around them." He nodded toward the hallway. "I wish I had a son like him."

It was eleven o'clock by the time Mike left. He was still acting somewhat "silly," but she felt better about him. During the course of the evening, when she could get him to be serious, they had pieced together their past lives. She vaguely remembered his family. His father, deceased, had worked for a gas company, and his mother, also deceased, had been a housewife. He was the youngest of six children, one of whom, a brother, had been killed in Vietnam.

He also explained, in an awkward fashion, that most of his insecurity about relationships had to do with the failure of his marriage when he was twenty. He told her, "It was my first real relationship. We were married right out of high school, and after a couple of years she left me for another man. It devastated me. I promised I'd never get close to anyone again." He admitted, though, that his wife had had good reason to leave him because he was still a "kid" at the time.

"And now you've grown up?"

"Oh, sure. A lot."

"I can imagine what your first wife had to put up with."

He smiled.

The one thing she didn't do was talk about work. It was good to put it aside for a couple of hours.

Once Mike had gone, she went to Greg's room to say good night. She found him asleep, the television still on. She turned off the television, pulled a cover over him, and kissed his cheek.

She took a couple of aspirins and crawled into her bed. As she lay there, she thought about Mike. She realized she wanted another relationship with a man, perhaps even with Mike, but at the same time she felt guilty. Where would she find the time? she wondered. As it was, she couldn't keep up. With Greg, Sean, Julie, Eva, and the Hammond-Cassell investigation, there was no time left. She set the alarm for five so she could get up and review her notes before heading for work.

14

The next morning Scroggins, in his undershirt and blue-jean shorts, answered the door, smiling broadly with a mouth too big for his face. His pink, moist lips protruded. Once he had inspected Rita's credentials, he invited the crowd of investigators inside. Charlie, Adam, Vince, Joyce, and Jim were with her. "I thought you might be watching me," he said. He was soft-spoken.

The house was immaculate, not a thing out of place. Even the customary fine coat of dust was absent. There was, however, a permanent odor of cigarette smoke in the air.

"What gave you that impression?" Rita asked once she was inside.

"I've seen you parked down the street. In the white van, right?"

"You must be paranoid," Charlie told him, smiling.

"You guys stick out like sore thumbs."

"Do you know a boy named Matthew Hammond?" Vince asked.

Scroggins lit a cigarette. "Nope," he said, blowing smoke, "I can't say that I do. Why, has someone made a complaint against me?"

"Were you expecting someone to file a complaint?" Charlie asked.

He glanced anxiously at Charlie, as if caught off guard. "Oh," he said, "I know the boy you're talking about. Wasn't he that little boy who was found dead out in a park?"

"Murdered," Joyce said. "What made you think of him?"

Scroggins was visibly troubled, his eyes grew wide, and his voice trembled when he said, "I didn't have anything to do with that! I swear I didn't. Sure, I've seen him around, and everyone in the church I attend knew he got murdered, but that was it. I swear."

"How about Larry Cassell?" Rita asked.

"The boy they found yesterday?"

"You're getting good at this," she told him.

"Come on, that's all they're talking about on TV, and in the newspapers."

"Do you mind if we look around?" Rita asked.

He opened his hands to the house. "Help yourself," he said.

Charlie brought out a Miranda card to advise Scroggins of his rights.

"I'm not being arrested, am I?" he asked.

"No, you're not," Rita said. "You're a possible suspect, and we want to make sure you understand your rights. If you haven't done anything, you have nothing to worry about, right?"

Again, he opened his hands to the rest of the house. "Help yourself," he repeated.

The investigators went in all directions.

Scroggins took Rita on a tour. Upstairs there were three bedrooms. The first was decorated in powder blue—blue curtains, carpet, and bedspread. There was even a black velvet picture with blue leopards on it. Scroggins called the room his "Blue Room." The second room was decorated in a Spanish motif. He called it the "Mexican room." The master bedroom was decorated in black, including black wallpaper with pink roses in it. "This is my room" was all he said.

In the closet of the master bedroom, Charlie picked up a pair of work shoes, which he turned over to look at the soles.

"What are you looking for?" Scroggins asked. "Maybe I can save you some time and trouble."

Rita asked, "What kind of cigarettes do you smoke?"

"Winstons."

Rita's head was swimming with excitement. The evidence was mounting. She felt she might be in the presence of their murderer. Never had she felt closer to catching him.

"You mind if I take a pair of these shoes with us?" Charlie asked. "I'll get them back to you after we take some prints."

"That's fine. I didn't do anything. Take the gym shoes. I don't wear them that much."

Scroggins and Rita went down to the basement.

Joyce had found a collection of eight-track tapes in a small room walled off from the rest of the basement. The room, like the upstairs, was immaculate. Rita took her time examining the tapes. She found several with Crystal's initials on them. "Have you ever met Matthew Hammond?" she asked.

"No," he said, his face draining of blood, so that the stubble of his unshaved face stood out.

Rita said, "Look, I know you met the boy, but if

you want to play this game, I'll get a search warrant
and confiscate the proof I need."

He smiled. "You don't scare me," he said. "You
don't have what's called probable cause, and you
know it."

"You don't know what I have or don't have, do
you?" she said calmly.

He contemplated her. "Okay, so I bought some
eight-tracks. The boy brought some to a church rum-
mage sale. Ask anyone. I happened to buy them, that's
all. I gave him a couple extra dollars to bring me back
more tapes. I tried to get him to sell them all to me,
but he said his mother would get mad because she
had given them to him as a gift."

Vince found a cubby space filled with boxes of pornographic magazines and tapes. Rita joined him.

"Anything illegal about some artistic pictures?"
Scroggins asked, joining them.

They didn't say.

"Is your mother at home?" Rita asked.

"My mother's dead," he said. "She's been dead for
the past two months." His bloodshot eyes were wa-
tery. "I never go into that side of the house now."

Rita pointed at an ashtray where Scroggins had
ground out his cigarette. "Do you mind if I take the
butt with us?" she said.

Scroggins shrugged. "I told you I had nothing to
hide," he said. He held out the ashtray. "But I can
tell you right now, I didn't do anything wrong. And I
didn't have anything to do with that first boy. I bought
some tapes, that's all. The second boy I didn't even
know."

Rita put the cigarette butt in an evidence bag and
marked the bag.

"You say you went to the same church?" Charlie said, appearing.

"Yes, St. Paul's. What's wrong with that? Give me a break, it's a church. Isn't there anyplace where someone can go to get some privacy?" He had lost some of his kindness.

"Can you let us in to see your mother's side of the house?" Rita asked.

No, he said, he would not do that unless they had a search warrant.

"Can I take the tapes you bought from the boy?" she asked.

"If you make sure I get them back. I have a collection, you know. It's my pride and joy."

Outside, the sky was overcast, as if it might rain again, and the humidity made the air thick. In the car, Rita mentioned the dead mother. Charlie didn't say anything. "Someone knew the mother was dead," she said angrily. "Why in the hell didn't anyone tell me?" She looked in her rearview mirror. Behind her car was a sedan with Vince and Joyce in it. Behind that was another sedan with Adam and Jim in it. "Whoever knew and kept this back did it deliberately. I'm tired of this crap."

Charlie told her the shoes were a size too big, as if to change the subject, but he only made matters worse. She had been hoping for a match. Everything else had seemed so promising. If the shoes had been the same size, she would have been truly excited. As it was, she had mixed feelings.

Back at the office, she had Jim take the cigarette butt to the crime laboratory.

She was cheered when she learned the saliva on Scroggins' cigarette matched the saliva on the cigarette butt found at the Hammond crime scene. The cigarette butt from the Cassell scene, though, was not a match. It had not been smoked by Scroggins. Even worse, neither of the people who had smoked the cigarettes seemed to be the ones who sexually assaulted the victims.

"Something is driving me crazy," she told Charlie when she was alone in her office with him. "The same person murdered Matthew and Larry, but the cigarettes seem to be loose evidence."

"Maybe Scroggins watched," Charlie mentioned.

"I've thought about that. I've also thought this might be some kind of a religious cult in which various people help set up the sacrifice of a child, but only the religious leader actually performed the sacrifices and conducted the rituals."

"So what now?"

She sighed. "We have enough for a search warrant," she said. "That's a starting point."

They got a search warrant to look for evidence related to the murder of Matthew Hammond. Another search of the Scroggins house revealed nothing new, though. The side of the house of his deceased mother was as immaculate as his own. They brought Scroggins in for questioning.

He insisted he didn't need an attorney. He had done nothing wrong, he said. He had nothing to hide. He had only bought some eight-track tapes from the boy.

In an interrogation room, Rita told Scroggins, "Look, I don't know exactly what your role was in all of this, but what I do know is that you were there. Now, if you want to play games, we can play games all night long."

"I was where? Where was I supposed to be? I don't even know what you're talking about."

"Kettle-Moraine state park," Charlie said. "You know where we're talking about. Don't play that innocent bullshit with us. We know you were there."

"You're wrong!" Scroggins fired back. "I've never even been to the Kettle-Moraine state park. And, no, I don't know what you're talking about."

Rita outlined the evidence, which turned Scroggins a pasty color. He swore he had never been to the Kettle-Moraine state park.

What had he been doing on Monday, April 5? Charlie wanted to know.

Scroggins said he didn't know. "How am I supposed to know what I was doing that long ago?" When they didn't say anything, he added that he supposed he had been at home since he hadn't worked in over two years. He seldom went out, he said.

Rita told him, "According to our sources, and very good sources they are, you're out prowling all the time. What do you mean, you seldom go out? We can play that game too."

He said he liked to drive around, that was true, but he promised he hadn't done anything wrong.

"You have the tapes belonging to Matthew," Charlie said.

"And your saliva matches that found on a cigarette at the crime scene," Rita added.

Scroggins swore he hadn't been there and would be willing to take a lie-detector test to prove it.

Rita arranged for one to be administered, and they escorted Scroggins to the polygraph room. Rita, Charlie, Vince, Joyce, and Adam all crowded into an adjoining observation room, where they watched the examiner hook Scroggins to the polygraph equipment. The examiner began to ask questions as a scroll of paper passed beneath tiny markers.

"What is your name?" the examiner asked.

"Bill Scroggins."

With a pen the examiner marked the paper where the needles were making marks on the scroll. "Do you smoke?"

"Yes."

"Have you ever been arrested?"

"Yes."

"How many times?"

"Twice."

The needles jumped on the scroll. The examiner made a mark with his pen. "You had some trouble with that question. Do you care to explain?"

"Okay, I've been arrested three times, but I didn't think one was on my record."

"So, how many times have you been arrested?"

"Three times."

The examiner went on with his line of questions: "Is your mother deceased?"

"Yes."

"Have you ever been arrested for a sex crime?"

"Yes."

"Did you know a boy named Matthew Hammond?"

"Not really."

The needles jumped on the scroll. The examiner marked the spot. "You say you didn't know Matthew Hammond?"

"No, I didn't say that," Scroggins said. "What I meant was that I've met him, but that I've never really had anything to do with him."

"You haven't spent time with him?"

"No."

"Do you own a truck?"

"Yes."

"Did you kill Matthew Hammond?"

"No."

"Do you know Laurence Cassell?"

"I may have seen him once."

"Did you murder Laurence Cassell?"

"No."

Several minutes later, the examiner entered the observation room. On a table he spread out the scroll of paper. Using a pen to point, the examiner said, "Here, obviously he was deceptive in how many times he had been arrested." At another scrawl, the examiner said, "Here, there does seem to be deception in his original answer that he didn't really know the deceased, though here"—he moved the pen—"there doesn't seem to be any deception when I directly asked him if he killed Matthew Hammond." The examiner looked up. "I don't think he did it. Do you have any other questions you want me to ask him?"

Rita said, "Yes, ask him if he knows who did murder Matthew Hammond."

In the polygraph room, the examiner sat down again, saying he wanted to ask a few more questions, but Scroggins suddenly became reticent. He said he knew what was going on, knew the scam, and had decided to have an attorney present after all. Rita allowed him to call one.

The attorney, when she arrived, immediately canceled the test and interview.

Once everyone was in Rita's office, Adam angrily said it all made sense to him. There were two suspects, he said, one who committed the murder and the other who watched or helped. Scroggins was the watcher, Adam said. He probably stood on the sidelines and smiled. That's why he was able to answer truthfully that he hadn't murdered Matthew.

"One more question, and we would have had him," Joyce said.

Rita sighed and ran a hand through her hair. "I think we're pushing too hard. I don't like to work that way. We're getting clumsy. We need to slow down a little and let this thing ride until we get some basic facts figured out."

"I say we move ahead full speed," Adam said.

Maybe a prosecutor could strike a bargain with Scroggins, Charlie suggested. Then Scroggins could plead to some lesser offense in return for turning state's evidence about the murderer.

Rita asked Charlie to get the cigarette they had confiscated from Scroggins, plus the cigarettes from the crime scenes.

Charlie went to the evidence safe to get the evidence bags. When he returned, she put the bags on the desk between her and him. "What do you see?" she asked.

"That we have matching cigarette butts in a murder investigation?" Adam said, smiling.

"No. What do you see? Not what the lab tests saw, but what you see."

"There's a motive," Charlie told her. "That's what I see. Scroggins has a history that ties him to the cases at hand."

"Look at the cigarettes!" she said, raising her voice. "Look at the cigarettes, damn it!"

"Why?" Joyce asked. "Let's not play games. What are you looking for? What do you want us to see? Tell us."

"I see something that bothers me about those ciga-rettes," Rita said. "You were a smoker once," she said to Charlie. He nodded. "So was I. Adam, you smoke." He didn't say anything. "Let me ask the smokers and ex-smokers, what did you do when you were outdoors smoking and you finished a cigarette?"

Charlie shrugged. "I gave it a flip." With his thumb he flipped his forefinger.

She nodded. "Exactly. Or you ground it out with your foot."

Adam said, "So?"

"Look at the evidence."

"Oookaaay," he said, drawing out the word.

"One cigarette I took from Scroggins himself, once he had ground it out in an ashtray."

"Okay."

"Damn it, Adam, don't the other two look like they've been ground out the same way?"

He looked at them as if seeing the cigarettes for the first time. "Maybe." He obviously didn't want to agree with her. "But I wouldn't put it past the killers to carry an ashtray and a six-pack of beer with them to be right at home while they were doing their killing."

"Neither would I," she said, looking out her office windows. "But Matthew was murdered and embalmed before he was taken into the forest. Why would some-one carry an ashtray into the forest after the crime had been committed?"

"So you're thinking maybe someone is trying to set Scroggins up," Charlie said. "That's good." His head was bobbing. "Yeah, I see what you're getting at now. Like we got someone who thinks he's real good at what he's doing."

From where she sat, she noticed a partial reflection

of herself in the window, and she pondered the image. "That's one possibility," she said. "I'm also thinking along the lines of a motive. What if it was someone who knows Scroggins and feels threatened by him, someone threatened enough to want to get rid of him?"

Charlie put one of his feet on the edge of her desk and leaned back. He interlocked his fingers behind his head. He filled a large space in her office. He stared at her.

"Go with me on this," she told everyone, realizing what she had said was not clear. "Every crime has a flaw. Every criminal does something that he or she didn't intend to do. Did everyone here see *Silence of the Lambs*?"

There were a couple of nods. Charlie gave her one of those big smiles that stretched his face but didn't show his teeth. "That Anthony Hopkins was cold-blooded, wasn't he?"

"Exactly. And you remember why Jodi Foster went to see him?" Before Charlie could answer, she told him, "Because she knew he would be able to figure out who the killer was. In this case, I'm thinking that Matthew's and Larry's killer knew from the beginning that the only person who might be able to figure out who he was was Scroggins. In desperation the killer decided to lead a trail of evidence to Scroggins so that he would be so busy trying to save his own ass that he'd never have time to think about the real killer."

"Wow, that's deep," Joyce said. "That means Scroggins knows something he's not telling us."

"It's a long shot, but if I'm right, Scroggins knows something and doesn't yet know what he knows, or he knows something and doesn't want to incriminate himself. Does that make sense?"

Adam yawned and stretched out his arms, arching his back. He stood. "Now that he's called an attorney, I doubt we're going to get much cooperation unless we can put some pressure on him. I say we have some evidence, let's hit him upside the head with it and see if that refreshes his memory."

Rita shook her head. "I don't think it'll work," she said. "I think if we put too much pressure on him, he won't be able to think straight, and we'll never figure out what he knows. He doesn't strike me as being the most intelligent of creatures." Sighing, she ran a hand through her hair. "Let's see what we can put together about Scroggins."

Bev transferred in a call from Justice Department headquarters in Madison. Rita put it on the speaker phone. Paul had pulled another twenty investigators from around the state to assist in the investigation. As Rita listened to Paul's instructions, she told Bev to set up an assignment board.

Soon Jim brought in a report about Scroggins. Born in 1945, Scroggins had grown up in a broken home. His father had been an upholsterer, and his mother had been a nurse's aide. Scroggins had an older sister, Sharon, who was a nurse in Kansas City. Rita sent people in different directions to collect other information.

By late afternoon, she had made contact with the sister.

Once she had gotten beyond her initial shock of "Oh, my God, not again," Sharon described her brother as a troubled man. She said she remembered very little about their father because when she was ten and Bill was eight, their parents had divorced. She and Bill had gone to live with grandparents. About all she could remember of her father was that he had been a strict disciplinarian. The Depression had been hard on the family, Sharon said. She remembered one story her father had told about how he had worked two jobs to help keep food on the table, even when he was having trouble with swollen tonsils. One day the tonsils had become so inflamed her father couldn't work, she said. He told how he had taken a couple of hours off work, had his tonsils cut out, and gone back to work afterward. "He was an upholsterer," she said, "and he worked in a furniture factory. All he ever wanted from life was to save enough money to open his own upholstery shop. Anyway, he told how when he got back to work after his surgery, he couldn't slow down for fear of losing his job, so he put a handful of tacks in his mouth as he always did, and he began to spit tacks one at a time between his fingers and hammer the bloody tacks into furniture."

"What was your home life like?" Rita wanted to know.

"What little I remember, my mom and dad were always fighting. All my dad wanted was to open a shop, and my mother had other things in mind. She wanted to take some of the money my dad was saving and use it to go to nursing school. He was absolutely against using his savings that way. That was back in the days when a woman's place was in the home. Next thing I know, Bill and I were sent to live with our grandparents, Mom and Dad got divorced, and Dad opened an upholstery shop. He died a few years later."

"What about your mother?"

"She was determined to do what she said she was going to do. She talked my grandfather into lending her enough money to enroll in nursing school, and she came to Kansas City to pursue her dream. After the first semester she ran out of money and ended up staying on at the hospital as a nurse's aide."

"How did she end up living with Bill?"

"It's the other way around," said Sharon. "He ended up living with her. To tell you the truth, I never heard too much from my mother until I graduated from high school. Sure, she visited Bill and me, but it was like we were distant relatives. She would visit maybe a couple of times a year and bring us presents. Then when I graduated from high school, she suddenly appeared and said she would pay for my nursing school if I wanted to become a nurse. I guess she was determined to fulfill her dream through me, and I can respect that. I didn't have anything else to do at the time, so I applied to nursing school here in Kansas City at the hospital where my mother was working. I've been here ever since."

"But why did your mother move to Wisconsin?"

"It was like she repented for abandoning us. Once she got me through nursing school, it wasn't too many years later that Bill got arrested the first time, and he called her for help. He held one job after another after that—bill collector, one of those guys who do repossessions, you name it, he's done it. The latest thing is I think he's dabbling in computers. Anyway, next thing I know, Mom took her retirement and moved to Wisconsin. She bought a duplex and gave Bill half of it. I guess she felt she had to take care of him—that she was somehow responsible for how he had turned out. He never has amounted to much."

"Did he ever work in a funeral home?" Rita asked.

"How did you know?" she asked.

That took Rita by surprise. She had asked the question as a matter of leaving no stone unturned. She hadn't really expected that the embalmer might be Scroggins.

"Of course, he only helped with the yard work in the summer. That was a long time ago. Yes, what was the name of it—oh, let me think." There was a momentary silence. "Booth. Booth Funeral Home off Twenty-third Street. Burned down years ago."

"Kansas City?"

"Independence."

"Any of the Booths around."

"I'm not sure. But I know the funeral home's been gone for years."

"Did your mother ever tell you what Bill had been arrested for?"

There was another silence on the other end of the line. Then a cold "Yes."

"I know this is hard, but can you remember anything that happened while you guys were growing up that might have been a sign of what was later to happen?"

"What do you mean?"

"I mean, when he was arrested for the first time, were you completely shocked?"

Another momentary silence. "I don't know how old he was," she said, "but it was right after we moved to Granddaddy John's. Granddaddy had a mongrel that had had a litter of puppies. One day Granddaddy caught Billy naked with the puppies in his lap. He was"— she paused and sobbed—"he was letting them lick—you know."

"What did your grandfather do?"

She explained how their grandfather had made Billy put the puppies in an ash can, pour gasoline on them, light a match, and throw it in the can. She wept. "I never will forget those puppies yelping."

Jim burst into her office. He was excited about something, but he froze when Rita held up a hand, signaling him to be quiet. She thanked Sharon for her help and suggested they might talk again at some later time.

"The pathologist just called about something on the Cassell boy," Jim said as soon as Rita had put down the telephone receiver. "This is great! It couldn't be better!"

"Jim, what the hell are you talking about?"

"Larry had been drugged." She stared at him, waiting for him to give her more details. He read from a piece of paper. "Have you ever heard of chlorpromazine hydrochloride?" She shook her head. "It's a powerful tranquillizer"—he glanced at the paper—"an antipsychotic drug. I called a pharmacist at St. Luke's, and he said at one time it was experimented with in surgery patients because it helped keep them sedated. Apparently, it's something new our killer has added." He produced a black notebook. "Guess what else?"

"Yes?"

"When we went through the Scroggins place, I happened upon some bottles of medicine in the kitchen cabinet beside the sink."

She waited.

"I wrote down a few names—" He looked at his list. "One of which was Largactil." He looked at her.

"Yes?"

"Largactil is a trade name for chlorpromazine hydrochloride."

She took a deep breath and nodded. "That's good work," she said, smiling. She called the prosecutor, who agreed to let them hold Scroggins, though he warned her that the evidence was only circumstantial.

Charlie appeared.

Rita passed by him. In the open room, she announced, "Scroggins is ours for now. Keep working. Get me anything you can on him."

She turned to Charley. "I've got to put all this together," she said. "So much is happening at one time." She looked at her watch. She had to get Greg and Kyle, whom she had promised could spend the night. As she went to clear her desktop, she asked Charlie, "Would you mind running by the library and doing some research on religious cults?"

"Will do."

"Let's pick all of this back up in the morning." She packed a briefcase and left the office.

Outside, a drizzle was coming down. Umbrellas were up. Rita didn't have one. As she came around the corner of the entrance, she encountered Adam and Jim standing under a ledge. They were smoking. She hated to see the two men together, but what they did on their own time was their business. She couldn't control that. She said good-bye to them. Jim mumbled a "Bye," but Adam only nodded. "Good work," she told Jim. He didn't show any emotion. In no hurry, she walked to her car. The rain felt good. It had been a good day. She had received her first genuine breaks in the case. Someone raced past her, trying to get to his car without getting wet. She wanted someone to celebrate with. Somewhere a murderer was walking free, but not for long. She was closing in on him.

15

The moment she picked up Greg and Kyle, she noticed how long Greg's hair was. It was as long as Larry's was in the photograph she had seen of him at the Cassell residence. She told him, "Before you guys do anything, Greg, I'm going to trim your hair." She glanced at the two of them bouncing around in the backseat. They were punching and poking each other.

Greg said, "Oh, Mom, not tonight!"

Kyle laughed and punched Greg in the arm. "Does the little boy have to have his mother cut his hair?" he said sarcastically.

Rita smiled.

At home, she saw she had once again fallen behind on her chores. Dirty laundry was piled in front of the washer. On top of the dryer was clean laundry that had been folded but not put away. Dishes filled the kitchen sink.

While she poured toilet cleaner in the toilet, she told Greg to take off his shirt, wet his hair, and set a chair in the kitchen so she could trim his hair. To her surprise, he didn't complain. "Okay, Mom," he said. She thought he was anxious to get it over with.

She poured herself a glass of Chablis from a four-liter bottle, put a frozen dinner in the oven for herself—Greg and Kyle had eaten at Babe and Norb's—and took off her shoes and socks. The cold linoleum felt good on her feet. She began to trim Greg's hair. Clumps of hair fell at her feet.

"Not too much," he told her.

"Don't worry," she said.

Kyle stared at Greg as if horrified. "I'm glad it's not me that has to go to school looking like that," he said.

"Mom!"

"Thanks, Kyle."

"I'm only kidding," Kyle told Greg, and laughed.

"Mom."

"Yes?"

"Can we get a dog?"

"I thought you were being nice for some reason," she told him.

He smiled.

She trimmed his bangs. His eyes looked up at her. With an open hand she brushed a clump of hair off his nose.

"Can we?" he asked.

She began clipping hair again—snip, snip snip.

"You could train him as a guard dog," Kyle said.

Rita stopped cutting. "Have you two been scheming again?" she asked. They both smiled. She took a drink of her wine, pondering Greg. He looked better—not so much like either Matthew or Larry.

"Please Mom."

"I tell you what: If you're good the rest of this week, this weekend we'll go to the humane society and look."

He jumped out of his chair and hugged her. "Thank you, Mom," he said.

"Don't track hair all over the place," she told him. She kissed his soft face. Though he seemed so grown up, he was still her baby.

Then he saw himself in the mirror. "Mom!" he yelled. "You cut off too much! Look at me!"

She joined Greg and Kyle at the mirror. "No, I didn't," she told him. "You look much better."

"I look stupid!"

"Geek!" Kyle said, punched Greg, and took off running.

"Remember, you've got the rest of the week!" she yelled at Greg, who chased after Kyle. She smiled. They were good boys.

She gathered up the laundry and began washing clothes. Nagging her were thoughts of the Hammond-Cassell investigation, of Scroggins, and of the news coverage. She continued to drink her wine. She looked for a peach washcloth to put back on the rack with the matching towels, but couldn't find it. Like socks that inevitably disappeared—there was a stack of matchless socks on the shelf in the laundry room—she eventually decided the washing machine must have eaten the washcloth.

At nine-thirty she sent Greg and Kyle to bed, reminding them it was a school night. At ten, she opened Greg's door, which was closed. The boys were playing Sega. She told them she knew they were being too quiet, and made them turn off the Sega. Fifteen minutes later, she yelled at them because they were still talking. She told Greg it would be his last overnight unless they went to sleep immediately. By ten-thirty the boys were asleep.

The telephone rang the moment she drifted off to sleep herself. She turned on her bedside lamp. "Hello." It was Charlie. He told her to hurry to the television and turn to Channel 6. She hung up and went to the television. On the steps of the Milwaukee courthouse was a crowd of people, at the center of which was the Cassell family. Ralph, wearing an open-necked blue shirt and a navy blazer, had some sheets of paper in his hands, as if he were reading a statement. To her surprise, Rita also saw Crystal with the Cassells, though she stood back from the microphones where Ralph commanded an audience.

Rita turned up the volume of the television. The papers held before him, Ralph had his other hand in the air. "... it's time we put an end to this," he said. "How many children's lives is it going to take before someone does something? We've been doing some checking"—his index finger pointed toward the sky— "and had the law enforcement officials that we give our hard-earned tax dollars to been doing their jobs, it seems our son would not be dead at this time."

That brought a barrage of questions: What did he mean, his son wouldn't be dead? What did the family know that the public didn't—the public had a right to that information? Could he be more specific? Was there some proof for the accusation? The reporters were all talking at once.

Ralph held up his hands for silence. "It seems," he said as the crowd became quiet, "that the police had a prime suspect even before our son was murdered." That brought another flood of questions: Who was it? Was there a name? Why hadn't an arrest been made? Again, Ralph held up his hands. "Excuse me!" he said. The reporters calmed. "I understand there is someone being held for questioning at this time." The television cameras showed reporters scurrying away from the gathering, obviously going in search of answers. Ralph continued: "I've been advised that I can't announce who it is, but I will tell you that the individual was a prime suspect in this case even before our son was murdered"—he shook a finger—"and he hadn't even been questioned!"

Rita took a deep breath and sat down on the edge of the sofa, leaning forward.

He pointed at the people behind him. "The families of the victims have mobilized," Ralph said angrily. "We are determined not to let another Jeffrey Dahmer loose in our community. We are determined that it's not going to take sixteen victims before someone gets this killer off the streets! We are determined to make our law enforcement officials accountable! And I guarantee you, tomorrow we will be on the steps of the state capitol building in Madison, and we're going to make sure the governor and people who run our government hear what we have to say."

The cameras focused on a TV-6 reporter. She said, "As you can see, the victims of the families—"

The telephone rang. Rita used the television remote to mute the sound of the television, then answered the phone. It was Charlie. "Is this bad?" he asked.

She told him, "It isn't good."

There was a moment of silence before Charlie said, "I promise it isn't me that's been talking about the case."

She told him she knew it wasn't him. "I've already confronted part of the problem, but the families are buzzed up. Someone's nudging them along."

"Is there any way I can help?"

"Yes, from now on you and I don't share anything with anyone until we put it in writing," she told him. "I've got to compromise the person who's doing this." She wanted to say Adam's name, but she checked herself. "And if anyone approaches you for information, I want you to pretend I'm giving you the cold shoulder. Tell them so. Tell them I'm not giving you anything. Believe me, in the long run it's going to work out for the best. For one, no one's going to blame you if this thing blows up in our faces."

"I'm not going to put you out on a limb by yourself."

"Don't worry about me. I've been through this kind of thing before. I know how to take care of myself. But I also I know that they always look for a scapegoat in a case like this. If they can't get me, they'll look for someone down the ladder to dump on. They have to have someone. You're a prime target. Right now we have to make sure we protect you. And number two, if our leak thinks you're a safe party, he or she might share something that could ultimately keep us both from walking into a trap."

"You lost me."

"Whoever's doing this wants me, and I hope that person would feel guilty about hurting anyone else in the process," she explained. "He might even approach you to get your support. Then I know you'll let me know what's happening."

He laughed. "I might let him burn your hard ass," he said. "You mean Adam, don't you?"

She didn't confirm or deny it. "See you tomorrow," was all she said.

No sooner had she finished talking with Charlie than Paul called. He asked, "What's going on over there?" He said television crews from Madison had reported a protest at the Milwaukee courthouse. Stories like that get immediate attention, he told her. The governor's office had already contacted the commander of the state police. "Of course, he didn't understand who had jurisdiction here," he said. "It was innocent enough that his office contacted several offices before it finally got to me, but the disadvantage is that things got blown out of proportion in the process."

Rita told him she couldn't control what the families of victims decided to say and do.

"We can control what they know about our investigations," Paul told her. "And someone's obviously giving them an earful. That someone is in your office."

She sighed. "I know," she said. "We both know who it is, and right now I could use some help from you."

"What kind of help?"

"Apparently one or two of my people feel they can run to you or to some other source every time they have a grievance, and someone'll listen. That doesn't help what I'm trying to do over here. It doesn't help in the professional management of a criminal investigation. I could use a little support. When someone calls you, or complains to you, it'd be nice if once in a while you'd say, 'Look, Rita's in charge of that office. Why don't you take things up with her?' "

Paul said, "You're right. Sometimes I try to be a nice guy, and it backfires on me. I'll start sending people back your way, but I'll tell you again you need to get a grip on that office as soon as possible, or I'm going to be forced to do something—not because I want to but because someone upstairs is going to tell me I have to take action."

"I understand all of that," she said. "Right now I only need a little support."

"What I want you to do for now," he told her, "is to prepare a written report of where we're at at this stage of the investigation, one that our liaison office can share with the governor's office so he'll be somewhat advised of the status of this case. You know those family members are going to do like they say and be over here tomorrow morning."

"I know."

"I assume with Scroggins in jail, we can smooth this thing over, but we still have a mess on our hands."

She told him she would prepare something and fax it to him in the morning. She didn't tell him that they might not be able to hold Scroggins if they couldn't gather more evidence. She didn't tell him there might be two murderers working in unison. She, of course, hadn't ruled out that Scroggins might be the murderer, someone who was both a psychopath and a pathological liar, someone who was capable of beating the polygraph. But if that was the case, he'd probably be a genius, and she doubted that.

Rita began composing a report for Paul. At eleven-fifteen, Crystal called. Soft-spoken, she apologized for calling so late and hoped Rita was not in bed. No, Rita said. What was wrong? Crystal told her she had participated in a rally. "I know," Rita told her. "I saw you on television." Silence. "There are no hard feelings."

"I'm not going to Madison with them," she said. "But I want whoever killed my son off the streets."

"We all want that," Rita told her.

That brought a long pause before Crystal finally said, "There is one other thing. This may be nothing, but now that you have a suspect, it might be important. Perhaps it's something you could ask about."

"How'd you know we had a suspect?" Rita asked, fishing.

"I didn't until Ralph told me."

"Do you know how he knew?"

"No, but he said it came from a reliable source."

"Never mind. So, what is this thing you wanted to tell me?"

"I've been bothered by something I noticed tonight, and I thought it was odd, so I knew I should tell someone."

Rita waited.

About a week or so before Matthew had been murdered, Crystal said, she had been talking to him near his bedtime, and he had been watching her comb her hair at her dresser mirror. As they talked, he dug around in a small jewelry box she kept on the corner of the dresser, she said. From the box he removed her engagement ring and asked her why she never wore it. She told him it was because she was divorced, and divorced people didn't wear their wedding rings. How much was it worth? he wanted to know. She told him a thousand dollars or so, maybe fifteen hundred. He was impressed with how much money that was. Yes, she agreed, that was more than she made in an entire month at work. He asked her why she hadn't sold the ring, since it was worth so much money and she didn't wear it anyway. She mentioned that she probably would sell it if she ever needed the money badly enough. It didn't mean anything to her? he wanted to know. No, she told him, it was only a reminder of a painful experience she never wanted to relive. That had been the extent of the conversation, Crystal told Rita.

"So, why does that strike you as being odd?" Rita asked.

"The ring is gone," Crystal said.

It took Rita a moment before she could say anything. She sat forward. She asked, "You think Matthew took it?"

"It had to be him," Crystal said. "It's too much of a coincidence. You know I told you that I caught him stealing every now and then. Anyway, the ring's gone. In fact, a couple of days before he was—" She apparently couldn't bring herself to say that her son had been murdered.

"Yes?"

"Well, I was alone at the time, and I brought out the ring again and thought about what I had said to Matthew. I had seriously considered taking it to a jeweler then and there to see if I could sell it."

"Have you searched his room?"

"I've torn the whole apartment apart looking for it. I thought I might have packed it away, but I know where the ring was, and it's definitely gone."

"Why would he take it?" Rita asked.

Crystal said she didn't know, but she thought if he had planned to run away—she was finally admitting that it was a possibility—he might have tried to sell the ring to get some money, though she still had no idea why he would run away in the first place. She also had no idea whom Matthew might give the ring to. She asked, "Was the ring, by any chance, on him when he was found?"

No, Rita told her.

Crystal said, "Maybe if your suspect has the ring, you can find out more about what happened to Matthew."

Rita cautioned her about getting her hopes too high, though she immediately thought about the Jessie Anderson case. Once investigators had made public the nature of the weapon that had been used to murder Anderson's wife, a pawnshop employee had remembered selling such a weapon to a man meeting Anderson's description. If Scroggins had had the ring, he had either kept it as a trophy of his crime, or he had disposed of it. With something so valuable, she couldn't imagine him throwing it away.

She was cautious about how she worded her response. Even if someone had gotten the ring from the murderer, Rita said, that person would know the ring was probably stolen and wouldn't be anxious to step forward and acknowledge having purchased it. Besides, unless the ring had some distinguishing features, even someone who had seen it as it changed hands probably wouldn't remember anything about it.

It had her and her ex-husband's initials inside the band, Crystal said: "CH-RCH."

Once Rita had taken the description of the ring, she promised to try to get another search warrant for the suspect's house. She also promised to distribute the description of the ring to as many pawnshops and local jewelers as she could, though she again cautioned Crystal that the ring, if indeed it had been taken by Matthew, would probably never surface again.

She put down the telephone receiver, went into the kitchen, and got a glass of milk. Her head was swimming. Everything was happening all at once again. She took the milk back to the living room. Sitting legs crossed in her rocking chair, she closed her eyes in the hope that the dizziness of the earlier events would go away. It didn't. She looked at the book on the lamp table, Dostoyevsky's *The Possessed*. She opened it to the marker and began to read. Soon she became aware of the ticking of the grandfather clock and realized she couldn't remember a thing that she had been reading. The telephone rang. It was Mike.

"I've been trying to call you for over an hour," he said. "Are you all right?"

"Well, I'll put it this way. It's been a long day."

"I saw the news. How are you holding up?"

She sighed. "I'm managing. I knew there was a problem brewing, but I thought it had blown over."

"You know I'm not very good at this, but I was thinking of you, and I wanted you to know I was there if you needed someone to talk to . . ."

"I don't know whether to take you seriously or not."

"Sure you can. Well?"

"Well, what?"

"Aren't you going to say anything?"

"About what?"

"The gift."

"What gift?"

"Wow, I realize I'm not very romantic, but if this is your appreciation for my effort, thanks a lot."

"What the hell are you talking about?"

"Didn't you check your mail when you got home?"

She couldn't remember. She thought she had, but she couldn't remember.

"Go check it," he told her. "I'll wait."

"Mike, it's been a long day. I don't have any shoes on or anything."

"Oh, go check your damn mailbox."

She put down the receiver and, in her bare feet, ran out to the mailbox. She found herself giggling as she danced across the cold pavement, cinders biting her feet. Stuffed inside her box was a bundle of flowers. She ran back to the house and tore open the plastic wrap that contained some wilted snapdragons and chrysanthemums.

"That was a mean trick," she said, picking up the telephone receiver.

"What?"

"I mean, making me run all the way out to the mailbox for nothing."

"They weren't there! I just put them—" He laughed. "Oh, you're a dog!"

"You went to the damned grocery store and bought me flowers, and it hasn't been that long ago. How romantic. And don't act like you were thinking of me. You did just put them in there."

He laughed.

They talked for forty minutes about nothing in particular, but she enjoyed the conversation because she didn't have to be serious with him. He didn't expect it, didn't want it. She felt better after that, more optimistic.

The next morning, at the office, she telephoned the prosecutor and arranged for another search warrant of Scroggins' house. Vince and Joyce led a team of investigators who executed the warrant. When no ring was found, Rita called a friend at the *Milwaukee Journal* and asked her if she would be willing to write a story about the ring as a possible lead in the Hammond murder.

She called Charlie in and was about to talk to him when Vince appeared at the office door. He and Joyce had just returned from the Scroggins house. He said he had been listening to the news, and came to say he and Joyce didn't have anything to do with the new things the Cassell family was saying. "You have to understand, we made some mistakes in what we said, but we didn't say anything more after you talked to us," he said. At the side of his balding head a strand of gray hair stood straight out, apparently from where he had been talking on the telephone. "You also have to understand that we were kind of hurt too," he said. "Joyce and I had spent an entire afternoon with the Cassells. Then it's like you and Charlie ran back out there even before you had read our report of the interview."

"This is not the time to be discussing this," she said calmly.

"Oh, you want this to be private?"

"Yes, I think you could be a bit more professional, rather than discussing these matters in front of others or running off to Madison," she told him.

Charlie excused himself.

"A lot of those things that are coming out on the news are coming from another source," Vince told her.

"You have to admit it's a well-informed source."

"Oh, I don't doubt it's coming from this office, but it's not coming from me, and it's not coming from Joyce. If it was coming from her, I'd know."

In the back of her mind, she kept thinking about

Adam. She knew it was him. Everyone knew it was
him. She was getting sick of it.

She and Vince talked awhile longer. Even though
she knew there was friction between the two of them,
she was satisfied he was not the source of her problem,
only one of the symptoms. It was Adam she had to
stop. She had to find some way to put him in his place.

Charlie returned. The two went to meet with prosecutors, who said they were going to release Scroggins.
They called the evidence circumstantial at best, especially since the second crime scene hadn't produced
enough physical evidence to link Scroggins directly to
the crime. What about if she could produce the ring
and link it to Scroggins? Rita wanted to know. Afterward, she realized how unlikely it was that such a
thing would happen, but the prosecutorial team agreed
to take on at least the Hammond murder if the ring
could be located. Scroggins was released later that
morning.

Rita placed around-the-clock surveillance on Scroggins. During an office briefing she told investigators,
"I want him watched so closely that he'll think he's
the president of the United States and we're the Secret Service."

From the conference room, she went to her telephone and called Julie. She told her not to let Greg
out of her sight when he got home from school—not
under any circumstances.

Of course, Paul was upset when he got the news
about Scroggins, but she assured him they had con-
stant surveillance on him, and that he was still their
prime suspect. She also told him that prosecutors had
agreed to charge Scroggins with the Hammond mur-

der if the ring could be directly tied to him. That seemed to satisfy Paul, at least for the moment.

It didn't satisfy the Cassell family, however. On the front page of that afternoon's *Milwaukee Journal* was a large photograph of the family on the steps of the state capitol in Madison. Being held by Ralph, Dorothy Cassell had succumbed to grief. Her eyes were closed, and her mouth was half open, as if with a gasp. Margaret had also reached out to help support Dorothy, while Bud stood staring at the ground in dismay. The headlines read: "Anguished Mother Collapses After Hearing of Suspect's Release."

No matter how much Rita hated what she saw, no matter how she rationalized that publicity was inevitable and no one would read anything major into the photograph, no matter how she tried to convince herself that she was doing everything she could and everything would turn out all right, she knew the photograph would move everyone who saw it.

16

On Friday afternoon a small story about the ring appeared in the *Milwaukee Journal,* and to everyone's surprise, news of the ring surfaced the next day. It had been found in, of all places, a dry cleaners in Kenosha, south of Milwaukee. Rita and Charlie drove down to interview Myla Dreiser, a seventy-eight-year-old worker who had found the ring. She was a tanned, grandmotherly woman who wore a plaid dress, a string of imitation pearls, and a silver bracelet. Her shoulders were hunched, which caused her to bend forward slightly, and her hands nervously worked each other in front of her. As she relinquished the ring, she said she was ashamed of herself. At first when she had found the ring, she told them, she had said nothing about it.

She insisted she didn't think that by not saying anything she was stealing, because many times over the years she and other workers had found things in customers' clothes—money, pens, jewelry, and so on—and often there was no way to tell which customer the items belonged to because the laundry got mixed up as it was transferred from station to station. Unless a customer specifically reported something missing, she as well as the other employees kept whatever was found, a sort of finders-keepers policy.

In the case of the ring, she went on to explain, she had originally thought she knew where she had found it, but the more she thought about it, the more she wondered if the ring might have ended up there by falling out of someone else's clothes. She had eventually convinced herself she wasn't sure at all whom the ring belonged to. As with other found items, she planned to wait a couple of weeks, after which she would keep the ring if no one claimed it. Sure enough, no one had asked about it—that is, not until the newspaper article. "It's a good thing my son reads the *Milwaukee Journal*," she said, "because I would have never known about the story otherwise. I get the local paper. I did tell my children about the ring. And as soon as my son had read about it in the paper, he wondered if it was the same one. Naturally, once he read me the article, I knew right away it was. See the initials?"

Rita took the ring and examined it. "Where did you find it?" she asked.

Mrs. Dreiser sighed. "That's what's so strange," she said nervously. She knew the ring couldn't belong to the person whose clothes she had found it in, she explained, and since he had not asked about it when he picked up his clothes, she had not said anything about it, thinking that whoever the ring belonged to would eventually make an inquiry about it. After all, it looked like an expensive ring.

Charlie brought out a collection of six photographs, one of which was of Scroggins. He said, "If we show you some pictures, would you be able to recognize the owner of the ring?"

She nodded.

He handed her the photographs, and she went through them. "No," she said, "he's not here."

"Are you sure? Please, look again."

Mrs. Dreiser went through the photographs a second time. "I'm positive," she said. "He's not any of these people."

"Where did you find the ring?" Rita asked, reminding her she had not told them.

Mrs. Dreiser remained silent.

Rita touched her arm. "What is it?" she asked. "What's troubling you?"

Working her hands again, Mrs. Dreiser said, "I know this person could have had nothing to do with the murder of those little boys."

"Who is it?" Rita asked.

"I found the ring in a priest's coat pocket."

There was a moment of silence in which Rita and Charlie exchanged glances. Then Rita asked, "What priest?"

"His name is Father Thaddeus Catalpa," she said, reading from a laundry slip, which shook in her hand. "I've never seen him before, but he said he was on his way to Chicago and would pick up his clothes on the way back. He left a pair of black pants, shirt, and coat, all quite dirty. He said he had fallen."

Could she describe the priest? Charlie wanted to know.

She became flustered. He was a priest, she said. Black clothes, white collar. "He had a . . ." She rubbed her chin with her hand.

"Goatee?" Rita volunteered.

"I guess that's what you call it."

The nature of the allegation against Father Catalpa

didn't give Rita time to think about the implications of what she had learned. All she could do was react out of habit, piece together as much evidence and information as she could without forming any judgments. She worked quickly, flipping through her case notes as Charlie drove her to the law firm where Crystal worked.

Crystal immediately identified the ring. There was a solemn silence after she had identified it.

Rita pulled her into a conference room. She asked, "How could Father Catalpa have gotten hold of your ring?" Crystal said she didn't know, so Rita asked if they could go over the details of the ring again.

When was the last time she had positively seen the ring? Charlie wanted to know.

The Friday before Matthew had called her about spending the night with Bobby Ruble, Crystal said.

How could she be sure it was that particular Friday? Rita asked.

She had left work early to take care of some matters with an insurance claim, Crystal said. Two months before, Matthew had had a tissue graft done on his lower gums, which were receding. When she and Matthew had first gone to the periodontist's, she explained, the receptionist had said that the bill had to be paid in full at the time of the surgery. Crystal described how she had gotten into an argument with the receptionist because she couldn't understand why people had dental insurance if dentists wouldn't accept arrangements for payments by such means. The receptionist had finally agreed to wait for a check from the provider, Blue Cross, as long as the payment was received within sixty days of the procedure. A month and a half after the surgery, Crystal had still been trying to collect from Blue Cross, she said, so on day sixty, she took off work early to go personally to the Blue Cross offices in Milwaukee. She had sat there until they processed a check, which she had then taken to the periodontist. That was the Friday before Matthew called her to spend the night with Bobby Ruble. The day she picked up the check from Blue Cross, Crystal said, was the same day she looked at the ring again and wondered whether it was all worth it—that is, whether she should sell it. She had wondered that, she said, because she was tired of always being poor, and she thought if she sold the ring and opened a savings account—she didn't have one at the time—then she wouldn't have to worry about matters such as waiting for an insurance payment. "But then I didn't do it," she said, "because I decided if I had the money in a savings account, I would spend it."

Rita said, "I want you to listen to this very carefully because I can't overemphasize how important it is for us to make sure there are no mistakes about dates, facts, et cetera." Crystal nodded. "I don't want any speculation at all. I don't want you to tell me anything you think I might want to hear. Are you positive about the time element? Do you have anything to prove the days and events you're talking about?"

Sure, Crystal said, "I've been over everything again and again. I even have proof."

"What proof?"

"It's at the apartment."

"We need it."

Crystal took off work, and they followed her home. She went to the kitchen while they waited in the living room. She returned with a folder of papers. "Working in a lawyer's office, I've learned to keep everything," she said, opening the folder. She handed Rita a yellow sheet. "This is the dentist's bill."

Rita looked at it and handed it to Charlie. "Okay, that shows the date the work was done," she told Crystal. "Now, what about the date you got the check and paid the bill—the Friday before Matthew's death?"

Crystal went all the way through the folder. "Well, I thought it was here," she said. "Maybe it's in the drawer somewhere. Just a minute." She went back into the kitchen.

Rita could hear Crystal rummaging through a drawer. It took a long time, as if she had taken everything out of the drawer. "Oh, come on, damn it, I know it's here," she said. Then: "Here! I found it." She returned with a letter from Blue Cross and Blue Shield dated April 2, the Friday before Matthew's death. The letter indicated a payment had been made on that date. "See, I told you," Crystal said excitedly as Rita and Charlie looked at the letter.

"Do you know if Matthew had seen Father Catalpa at any time during that week?" Charlie asked.

Crystal shook her head. "No, it seems to me he wasn't even in town," she said. "I know he was in Chicago, and didn't perform Matthew's funeral because he still wasn't back. The assistant priest performed the funeral. But I'm not sure how long he was in Chicago."

Rita asked, "What kind of relationship did your son have with Father Catalpa?"

Crystal shrugged. "To tell you the truth, I never had enough to do with the church to know what went on over there," she said. "Matthew was an altar boy. I went occasionally when he was serving. But I tried to have as little to do with the church as I possibly could."

"Had Matthew had any trouble with Father Catalpa?" Charlie asked. "I mean, was there any time your son seemed to be scared, or to have something going on that was bothering him?"

She shook her head. "I thought he and Matthew were the best of friends," she said, "though I didn't think it was right for a grown man to be spending so much time with a group of boys. Of course, I thought it was all innocent. I would have never even suspected a priest would be doing anything to hurt my son. All that stuff you hear about priests, you never think about it happening in your own neighborhood." She waved her hand. "You always think about it as happening out there somewhere."

They asked many questions about Matthew's relationship with Father Catalpa. Then, before they left, Rita said, "Crystal, I want to ask you something, and again I have to emphasize how important it is that we make sure we're precise about this." Crystal nodded. "I think you realize how serious this could be if it involves a Catholic priest." Crystal didn't say anything. "For now at least, we'd like to ask for some time in which we can investigate all of this. We want to check everything and double-check it. The last thing we need is for someone to say there might be a priest involved before our investigation is on solid ground. I'm going to ask that you don't say a word about this to anyone, not even other detectives if they come by asking questions."

Crystal assured Rita she would keep the information to herself.

Rita nodded: "And if anyone questions you about

this case, I want you to call me. I don't care what time of day or night it is. You have my home phone number."

Crystal nodded.

Outside, Rita experienced the full shock of what she had heard during the previous couple of hours. She tried not to say anything. She just wanted to get in the car so she could think. There, her head fell back against the head rest, as if suddenly weighted with cement. Imagine! A priest! It meant they were dealing with more than a murder suspect. They were dealing with an institution, a very powerful institution, the Roman Catholic Church. There was no bright side to her thoughts, not even with the thought of capturing a killer. She asked Charlie if he wanted to go somewhere to have a drink.

He seemed surprised that she would suggest drinks in the middle of the day, but he said he would have something if she wanted something. They went to the Bicycle Club in Brookfield. It was not crowded, so they sat out of the way, where they sipped bourbon and water and talked.

Rita told him, "We don't have very much time before someone's going to find out we're investigating a Catholic priest. And the moment the word gets out, we'll have a mess on our hands. People'll crucify us."

Charlie mentioned, "Can you imagine trying to get a search warrant or an arrest warrant against a Catholic priest? In this town?"

Rita didn't say anything.

"I mean, half the judges who sit on the bench in Milwaukee are Catholic."

She said, "It's all starting to make sense now. Remember the altar boy's gown we saw in Matthew's closet?"

He nodded.

"Then the robe in the Cassell case. And Bobby? There must be a ton of other significant things we've seen but haven't put together yet."

"The thing I don't get is why a priest would draw attention to himself by giving away clues like that."

She shrugged. "It might be that he has some religious statement he's trying to make," she said. "Or maybe he feels he's on a mission of some type."

He gave half a smile. "One thing works to our advantage. You remember back when you were not wanting to rush into the Scroggins connection? At least this proves your intuition was right. This could all work out for the best."

She shook her head. "You need to know right now that I don't see any way this can work out for the best," she said, "which is why I wanted to talk over a couple of drinks." She sipped her bourbon. "I'm talking to you as a friend, not as a boss or a colleague. No matter what we do, this is going to be a mess. It's going to explode in our faces. The moment we corner Catalpa, we're going to have the entire Catholic Church and community breathing down our necks. It doesn't make a damned bit of difference if Catalpa's guilty and the Church knows it. The Church is going to rush to his aid, and it's going to bring pressure to bear on us—huge pressure. Are you ready for that?"

Charlie was staring at his drink. "When I was a kid, I had to pass through this white neighborhood to get to my house. There was always this one place where some kid yelled, 'Nigger!' as loud as he could. I'd hear other kids laughing, but I never did see anybody. All

I wanted was to be big enough that I could go after those kids that were laughing, catch the one who always yelled 'Nigger' and beat the hell out of him. I'm ready."

She smiled and took another swig. "At least part of your wish came true," she said. "You're one big son of a bitch."

He held up an open hand, and she slapped it. They laughed.

She said, "So, let's go see Catalpa."

On their way out the door, Rita said, "For now we'll treat it as a routine interview. You know the sort of thing: Catalpa wasn't in town the last time we were at St. Paul's, so we wanted to make sure we had a chance to talk to him."

"I get the picture," he said.

At St. Paul's, the secretary told Rita and Charlie that Father Catalpa would be pressed for time—a half hour was the most he could spare. They arrived during confession. The secretary let them into Father Catalpa's office, which, once she had closed the door behind them, they quickly scanned, glancing at the walls, the shelves, and the papers. Rita stopped at an opened Bible on a table under the window in the room. The pages to which the Bible was open, 2 Kings 8, were wrinkled, as if they had gotten soiled and had dried. Father Catalpa could be heard talking to the secretary in the outer office, so Rita and Charlie sat down in chairs near the desk.

No sooner had they seated themselves than they rose again to shake the hand of Father Catalpa, all in black except for a white collar. When he shook hands, it was a weak shake, his hand barely making contact. The hand was cold and clammy. Rita was struck by

Father Catalpa's bluish gray eyes. She hadn't paid that much attention to them during their first encounter. Now she noted the eyes were dull, opaque, as if he had cataracts. He tried to keep them looking elsewhere—away from scrutiny.

He said he assumed they were there to talk about the Hammond boy, a most unfortunate incident. He sat down at his desk. Yes, of course he knew Matthew, an occasional altar boy, though his mother seldom came to church, so he didn't know him as well as he knew some of the other children. "He was a quiet boy," Father Catalpa said, leaning back in his chair, "and always polite. I still am sad I was out of town at the time of the funeral." He didn't seem sad. "Listen, I must insist that this is a house of prayer, and while I'm very sorry about what happened to the Hammond boy—"

"Weren't you in Chicago at the time of his death?" Rita interjected.

Father Catalpa appeared to be inconvenienced by the interruption. "Yes, Chicago. I was there doing some research. I'm a scholar, you know. I've written a couple of books. Milton scholar. Have you ever read *Paradise Lost*?" he asked. Rita could tell he loved the sound of his own voice. She let him go the direction he wanted to go. "You know, I have always found it a fascinating question," he said. "If humans were created perfect in the first place, how did they fall? I mean, it would seem to me that a fall implies some type of flaw, and if humans fell out of grace during the creation, there must have been some fundamental flaw in their character to start with." He looked at the ceiling. "Fascinating. Now, where were we?" He looked back at Rita and Charlie, but before either of them could say anything, he went on, "Oh, yes, the Hammond boy ..."

Rita asked, "How long were you in Chicago?"

"Two weeks. A week before and a week after the death."

"Murder."

"Murder, death—" He shrugged. "It's all the same."

Charlie leaned forward in his chair. "No, it's not the same," he said.

Father Catalpa was caught off guard. Then he smiled. "Ah, yes," he said, looking at Charlie. "I see what you're getting at. The question of free will. Death is an involuntary event, and a murder involves the will. It's the same issue in *Paradise Lost*. Humans are perfect, but they have free will. They have the ability to make a choice to fall out of the state of perfection and grace. You can see I've given this quite a bit of thought—"

Rita asked, "Did you see Matthew while you were in Chicago?"

"How could I?" He laughed. "I was in Chicago."

"I know. I'm asking if you might have returned for a day or two."

Father Catalpa's pale complexion turned red. "Why are you asking these questions?" he said. "I told you I was out of town. I thought you wanted information about Matthew. What does all this have to do with me? You make it sound like you're questioning my integrity. Are you doing that? Are you questioning my integrity?"

"Absolutely not," Rita said coldly. Her assurance didn't sound sincere, not even to her. Good, she thought. "We're asking questions. I don't know why you should take offense or get so upset."

"This is a house of prayer. You don't just prance in here acting like you have some authority. I'll call the bishop right now and have your badges if you begin to defile this house and question my integrity."

Rita produced the wedding ring, sealed in an evidence bag. She asked, "By any chance, have you ever seen this ring before?"

He didn't answer right away.

"It belongs to Crystal Hammond."

"Yes," he said, somewhat disconcerted. "One Saturday—I believe it was a Saturday because that's when he usually came to confession and church—when Matthew was serving as an altar boy, he came to confession and gave me the ring—said he wanted me to take it so I would pray for his mother." He shifted in his chair. "I took it because it obviously looked expensive, and I figured he would either lose it, or someone would steal it. I told him I would make sure it got to the right place." He snapped his fingers. "That's right. He gave it to me right before I left for Chicago, and I meant to return it to his mother, but to tell you the truth, I forgot all about it before I left. I can't even remember what I did with it. Where did you find it?"

Neither Rita nor Charlie said.

Rita asked, "Have you ever been to St. Mary's in Pewaukee?"

He nodded. "You're talking about the other boy. Don't worry, I know all about it. Word gets around, you know. One of Father Mario's parishioners, wasn't it? He told me. It's awful what has happened."

"You knew Larry Cassell?" Charlie asked.

"No, I didn't. At least I don't think so. I've been

over to St. Mary's on a number of occasions. I might
have seen him. In fact, when I talked to Mario, and
he was describing the boy to me, I was trying to place
him, but all I could think of was Matthew—they
sounded so much alike."

"So, you had been over to St. Mary's?" Rita
asked again.

"I said I had."

"Why? Did you work over there?" She put up her
hands. "Forgive all these questions, but I don't understand the Church. I'm in the process of trying to figure
things out."

He nodded, obviously not persuaded by her pre-
tenses of innocence. "Of course," he said warily.
"When we hear confessions, a number of us go to
different churches to help out. For example, today
there was a priest here from Milwaukee, and another
from Hartland. I've been over to St. Mary's on a number of occasions to hear confession."

Charlie asked, "Do they still use those confession
booths?"

Father Catalpa smiled. "No, most places don't do
that anymore," he said. "If people want a private confession, we normally do like we do here. There's a
room that's divided by a screen. You can't see through
the screen, but you can see the shadow of the priest.
The priest sits on one side of the screen, and the parishioner sits on the other."

Charlie nodded. "I guess I was really trying to figure
out how Matthew gave you a ring during confession."

"Oh, that," Father Catalpa said. "Most people these
days don't even need a screen. They simply come to
confession, and you sit there and look at each other."

Before he could say anything more about the ring,

Rita asked several more general questions about Matthew as an altar boy, which Father Catalpa answered with ease.

The two detectives stood in unison and headed for the door. Without shaking his hand as they departed, Rita looked straight at Father Catalpa and said, "We may need to talk to you again."

Smiling, Father Catalpa said, "Anytime."

Rita opened the door, encountering a boy about Matthew's age who had come to see Father Catalpa. The boy was let in, and the door was closed after him.

Rita and Charlie didn't speak until they were out of the parish.

In the sedan, Charlie said, "I was hoping we could ask a few more questions."

She shook her head. "If we talk to him again, we need to make sure he's been advised of his rights. We can't make any mistakes on this. He knows something, you can tell. I don't want him to give us something we can't use in the prosecutorial process."

"Did you notice how he looked like one of those devil figures you see on TV?"

Rita gazed into the distance. She said in a quiet voice: "For now we don't say a word about any of this to anyone."

He gave no reply.

The first thing she did once they got downtown was to go in search of a Bible so she could see what was in 2 Kings 8, where Father Catalpa's Bible had been opened. The passage was the story of Hazael, "the son of nobody," who murdered a king in order to take over his throne. He murdered him by soaking a cloth in water and holding the cloth over the king's face so no air could get in. Of course, she thought, a cloth soaked in water! That's how the murderer killed Matthew and Larry. She showed Charlie the passage.

She had him call Mrs. Dreiser to see if she had found any type of cloth with the priest's clothes. There hadn't been. Rita, in turn, telephoned the pathologist, who said there had been some rawness around Matthew's nose, which might have been caused by tissue or cloth, but aside from a string on the braces of the Hammond boy, he had found no significant evidence of cloth fiber. The problem was that the bodies had been bathed and disinfected after they were murdered.

The case of the Cassell boy was less conclusive, though there was more abrasion around the mouth. It might have been the same thing, the pathologist admitted. Probably a heavier cloth, though, he said. Rita mentioned the water droplets. She asked, "What if we find a cloth, soaked in water, had been used to suffocate the boy?" The pathologist said such a method of suffocation was plausible and that if a cloth was found, he would test it against the thread he had found on Matthew's braces.

Rita arranged for a team of investigators to go back to the Kettle-Moraine State Forest once again. She told them to follow the trail of the stream, searching for any cloth that might have been washed away. She arranged to have another team sent to search Lizard Mound State Park. A cloth was the focus of the search.

Late that afternoon, the search teams reported back in. They had found no cloth.

17

Fourteen years earlier, Rita discovered, Father Catalpa had been arrested in St. Charles, Missouri, a suburb of St. Louis, though he had never been prosecuted. The arresting officer, Frank Morley, then a junior-grade detective, was now a retired sergeant of the St. Charles Police Department. Yes, he remembered the case, he told her when she contacted him by telephone. How much could he tell her about it? she wanted to know.

Frank remembered that an irate tax collector with the Internal Revenue Service had contacted him about a Catholic priest he suspected had coaxed his twelve-year-old son to undress. The boy had originally told his parents Father Catalpa had taken some photographs of him naked, though no photographs had ever been found. Morley said he had gone through an elaborate process to identify the priest and get an arrest warrant, but the parents had later refused to prosecute. When Frank had talked to the father of the boy about the decision to drop the charges, the father said the bishop had called them and personally assured them Father Catalpa would be removed from the parish, would be sent to a program for counseling, and would never again be placed in a parish setting. Since the bishop himself had asked the parents to drop the charges, they had. Frank said that without the parents' cooperation, he couldn't make a charge stick.

"That was only the start of it," Frank told Rita once they had sat down together in a bar at the St. Louis airport. Right after she had talked to him on the telephone, she had informed Paul of a potentially sensitive lead, and arranged to fly to St. Louis to interview Frank to see if she could dig up any leads that might help in the Hammond and Cassell investigations. She got there late Tuesday afternoon.

She took a sip of her wine and waited for the retired sergeant to continue.

Guzzling several swallows of beer from a bottle, he looked like he had led a rough life. The blue arteries in his neck stood out like cords from his pockmarked, pale skin. There was still some stubble underneath his chin where he hadn't shaved well, and his bristly hair, cut to an inch in length, had been plastered with grease. "I damn near lost my job," he told her as he raised a finger so the waitress would make sure another beer was on its way. Then he looked at Rita with bloodshot eyes. He said he had never gotten over the case. "It turned out to be the nightmare of my life," he said. "I wanted to try to talk to the Clarks— they were the people whose son it was—but they refused to see me. Then later the boy's father, Jeff Clark, called me at the office and wanted to meet. So we met at a Denny's restaurant." He drank more of his beer.

"Come to find out, Jeff wasn't Catholic," Frank continued. "It was his wife who was Catholic. As far as he was concerned, he wanted to press charges, but she was against it." Frank took another drink of his beer. "Are you Catholic?" he asked.

"No," Rita told him. She sipped her wine, not taking her eyes off him.

Frank shook his head. "I don't mean this in a bad way, but if you know about Catholics, you know how they have this huge thing with guilt." Rita smiled. She knew exactly what Frank was talking about. Her ex-husband being Catholic, she knew all about guilt. "I'm serious," he said. "They make sure they go to church every week not so much because they want to go as because if they don't go, they feel guilty, and they hate feeling guilty." He shrugged. "Anyway, I've seen it again and again, you run a guilt trip on a Catholic, and he or she will do just about anything you want. That, and Catholics are terrified of authority. If a bishop says something, there's not a Catholic alive who'll go against him, even if it means violating an otherwise good conscience."

Rita said, "So Mrs. Clark was a devout Catholic."

He nodded. He saw the waitress approaching, so he guzzled his beer and handed her the empty bottle.

She handed him a fresh beer, asking, "You want me to run a tab?"

That would be fine, he told her. She returned to the bar. "When the bishop called her," Frank said, "Sally got sucked in." He guzzled some of his new beer. Rita wondered if that's how she drank when she lost control. Seeing Frank drink scared her. She drank like that sometimes—drinking as quickly as she could in order to feel the effects of the alcohol. "I guess he told her that Father Catalpa was a bad apple, but if people found out, it would scandalize the entire

Church; then he asked her if she wanted it on her conscience for the whole Catholic Church to be scandalized because of one bad apple. With a promise here and there—that Father Catalpa would be removed from parish duty, et cetera—she gave in. Once that happened, there wasn't a thing Jeff could do because it became a matter of 'I promised a bishop. I could never live with myself if I broke a promise to a bishop.' " His tone was sarcastic. He took a couple of gulps of his beer.

Rita could tell he was an alcoholic. She had seen alcoholism many times before, especially in law enforcement. There was something about the stress of the job. "So, that was it?" she said.

Frank smiled. "Oh, no," he said. "I don't give up that easy. When I had heard what all had happened, I went to see the bishop, the Most Reverend Bernard Lawrence." He said, "Most Reverend" with sarcasm in his voice. "I told him I was outraged by what had happened and asked him how he could let something like that happen to a child and not demand that something be done about it."

"What did the bishop say?" she asked.

"At first he pretended he didn't know what I was talking about. He looked me straight in the eye and lied. So I reminded him I had talked to the boy's parents, who had told me he had talked to them. He told me what he discussed with parishioners was a private matter." The waitress delivered a third beer. It seemed she couldn't deliver them fast enough. She glanced at Rita's glass, but she put a hand over it. "She's getting ahead of me," he said to Rita, though he didn't seem to mind. He went on with his story, "With that, the bishop stared straight at me without

saying anything more. It was like he was dismissing
me with his silence."

"I see."

"Oh, no," he told her. "It gets even better. I put
my butt in the car and drove to see Cardinal Lazarus."

Rita smiled, shaking her head. "Persistent, aren't
you?" she mentioned.

He ignored her comment. "He was a tall, distinguished-
looking man, and the moment I shook hands with
him, I had the feeling he was someone who would
listen and make sure the right thing got done. Sure
enough, I explained everything, and he listened
carefully. He even asked questions and took notes.
Then he said he would check into the matter and
get back to me." Frank smiled and paused long
enough to finish his second beer. "Oh, he was
smooth, all right. He told me it might take as long
as three weeks because he was working on some
other matters and was going to be out of town for
one of those weeks."

Rita sipped her wine.

"At the time I thought that was fine because as I
had been checking around, I had learned that Father
Catalpa might have had some trouble in a St. Louis
parish. The extra time would give me a chance to
check him out. I decided to go to the St. Louis Police
Department to talk to one of the detectives who had
worked on a complaint over there, but this time I got
smart and took Sergeant Faulkner with me. I thought
I better start traveling with some reinforcements.
Faulkner had been around for years, and at one time
had worked for the St. Louis P.D. So we got over
there and were asking questions when the next thing
I know, some lieutenant came up to Faulkner and said

the captain wanted to see him. We went to the captain's office, and Sergeant Faulkner introduced me to the captain, an Irish man, who didn't shake my hand. Instead, the captain looked at Sergeant Faulkner and said, 'Marty, now, you know you and I have been friends for a lot of years.' He spoke in a rich Irish voice. 'You're always welcome over here, Marty.' Then he pointed at me and said, 'But this young man here gets nothing from my department. I don't ever want to see his mug around here again.' " Frank took time to guzzle some of his third beer. He looked visibly shaken, as if reliving the humiliating experience.

"You think it had something to do with seeing the bishop and cardinal?" Rita asked.

Frank motioned to the waitress. When she arrived, he told her, "How about a Johnny Walker Red, double, straight up? Anything for you?" Rita shook her head. The waitress withdrew. Frank went on, "Ol' Sergeant Faulkner was real cool. He didn't say anything. He didn't ask any questions, nothing that might embarrass me. Outside, I remember the sun was shining. We walked along the busy sidewalk. Finally Faulkner told me he had worked a lot of years around the captain and knew him to get moody sometimes. He told me to keep a low profile, and things would eventually blow over. That's what I did."

"Did Cardinal—what's his name—"

"Lazarus."

"Did he get back in touch with you?"

"No."

"No?"

"Never did."

"What happened with the case?"

"That was it. Whatever Father Catalpa had done,

he got away with it, and he vanished." He smiled.
"Come to find out, Father Catalpa was some big-shot
thinker—he had a lot of followers. You know, he had
written some big book, plus he was one of the dio-
cese's top fund-raisers. He could raise more money
than you could shake a stick at. Everywhere he went,
they said, he built a new church." This reminded Rita
of the new wing they were building at St. Paul's. "The
Church likes a priest like that." He stopped to drink
the third beer. The bottle was upside down to his lips
for a long time. When he had finished it, he belched.
"Oh, excuse me," he said. He belched again. This time
he patted his chest. "My gosh." He smiled. The
Johnny Walker Red arrived.

"I was moved to a desk job," he said, "and eventually I went back out on patrol, where I worked my
way back up to the detectives. It ate up three years
of my life."

"Does the department still have the case?" Rita
asked.

"Nope, not anymore," he said. "Probably not much
more than a trace of it anywhere, just as I'm sure
there's not a trace of what happened in St. Louis. I
never did find out if anything really did happen over
there."

Rita finished her wine.

Frank said, "So, our Father Catalpa is up your
way now?"

"Yes."

"What's he done?" Frank asked. "Can you say?"

Rita told him, "If he's done what we're looking into,
it's the worst of crimes."

"Murder?"

She didn't say.

"A boy?"

"Maybe more than one."

Frank shook his head. "I knew it. I could tell from the first time I set eyes on him, he was evil."

The observation caught her by surprise. "It's funny you should say that," she told him. "I've heard a similar thing said about him." She thought about what Charlie had said.

He gulped his Johnny Walker. "You know what gets me?" he said. She waited. "How did that guy ever end up around children again?"

Rita didn't know.

Frank took several more swallows of the Johnny Walker. "I have the case," he said, putting down the glass.

"What?"

"I kept it."

"What?"

"The file. The Catalpa file. I kept it."

"Where is it?"

"At home."

"Can I make copies?"

"You can have it." He shook his head. "It's strange, I've been keeping it hidden away for a long time so no one would destroy it. It's like all along I knew that sooner or later it'd be important." He finished his Johnny Walker. "I knew in my heart things would eventually catch up to him."

"He isn't caught yet."

"Want some advice?"

She waited.

Be careful, he told her. "If you're after Catalpa, you're after the Church."

Rita said she knew.

"Let's get out of here. I'll get you the case."

As it turned out, he didn't have a car. He had taken a bus to the airport, he said. His license had been suspended for driving under the influence. He didn't seem to mind. Rita rented a car, and she drove him to his home, a small ranch house in a St. Charles neighborhood. There were a number of nice cars parked in front and in the driveway. The house and yard were well kept, which surprised her. He left her in the car, went inside the house, and returned with a thick stack of old folders filled with papers. "I'd introduce you to my wife, but she's playing bridge this afternoon," he said. "You never interrupt the ladies while they're playing bridge." He handed her the folders. "This is everything. Remember, be careful with him." She shook his hand and thanked him. He excused himself to go in and take his afternoon nap. He was not at all steady as he returned to the house.

She drove back to the airport, where she got a room for the night. In the hotel room, she spread the folders out on the bed. There were old photographs of Father Catalpa. Though he was younger in the photographs, it was still the same man—goatee and all.

Most of the folders and papers pertained to departmental charges Frank had been brought up on for violating departmental policies and procedures regarding the Catalpa investigation. There was no direct complaint from Father Catalpa, but there were letters to the chief of police from Bishop Lawrence and Cardinal Lazarus. They claimed that Frank had been overzealous in his investigation of a case that had been "unfounded." The letter from the bishop denied any impropriety on the part of Father Catalpa, but the

letter from the cardinal did attempt to explain how
the situation had arisen in the first place.

In his letter, Cardinal Lazarus explained that his
office had reviewed the matter thoroughly and had
concluded that Father Catalpa was not at fault in the
incident. Cardinal Lazarus explained that the alleged
victim, Dennis Clark, was an altar boy at the St.
Charles Church. On the day in question, after services
Father Catalpa had asked Dennis for his robe, so he
could have it cleaned along with the other altar boys'
robes. "Unfortunately," Cardinal Lazarus wrote, "Father Catalpa did not know the Clark boy had no
clothes on underneath the robe, and so when the boy
removed his robe, he was naked. Of course, Father
Catalpa immediately instructed the boy to put on his
robe again. The whole incident was a huge misunder-
standing, though in the interest of all the parties involved, we are having Father Catalpa moved out of
the parish so that any unintentional wounds will heal."

Rita had had so much anticipation in her visit with
Frank and what he would reveal to her about Catalpa
that it left her with mixed feelings. She didn't know
what she had expected, but she had hoped for more,
perhaps a missing child or two in Catalpa's past. What
she got was basically one individual's grievance. Frank
had fought a personal war and lost. He had never
gotten over it. That was obvious enough. She laid out
pages from her own investigation, side by side with
Frank's folders. Am I willing to take on the same
battle? she asked herself. She knew an investigation,
as it had with Frank, could easily shift from a crime
to a career. If she overstepped her boundaries, she
knew the Catholic Church would come after her personally, as it had with Frank. Was it worth it? What

had it gained him? When she got back, Paul would want to know what was so important that it required her to make a trip to St. Louis—instead of one of her investigators. What did she have? She studied the case methodically, going over what she had gone over many times before. She didn't go out for supper but called room service.

From her hotel room Rita telephoned the Clarks the following morning. Mr. Clark answered the phone. She told him she was following some leads in a Wisconsin investigation and mentioned Father Catalpa. Mr. Clark told her he would be happy to be of any help he could. He said that Dennis, now married and with children, was living in Columbia, a city midway between St. Louis and Kansas City. When Rita asked Mr. Clark about the incident, he said he and his wife had later wished they had never dropped charges.

"Why is that?" Rita asked him.

"Because at first when Bishop Lawrence called my wife, he was treating the incident seriously, and he made all of these promises. He promised us Father Catalpa would not only be moved out of the parish, but that he would be placed in a treatment program and would never again be assigned to any duties that involved children. Next thing we know, Cardinal Lazarus is denying everything, calling it all a big mistake— as if nothing had ever happened in the first place."

Rita said, "I know a few of the details of the case. Do you mind if I ask you a couple of questions that might be sensitive?"

"No, go ahead."

"I was thinking it would be better if I could stop by so we could talk."

Mr. Clark checked with his wife. Yes, that would

be fine, he said when he got back on the phone. He
gave Rita directions to the house.

The Clarks lived in a split-level home in Lake St.
Louis, an exclusive suburb of St. Louis. They both
greeted her at the door, and after she showed her
credentials, Mr. Clark invited her in. They went into
the kitchen, which, though the house wasn't directly
on the lake, was set above the other houses enough
that Rita could see the lake from the kitchen patio
door. Mrs. Clark, a quiet woman with short blond hair,
put on coffee. Mr. Clark was an affable man with a
perpetual smile. He looked directly at her once she
sat at the table. "I always wanted to go into law enforcement," he said. "I tried to get on as a Treasury
agent, but it never worked out."

"You were a tax collector, weren't you?" Rita
asked.

"Kind of. I started out as a collector, then I was
promoted to an agent, but I never made it to law
enforcement."

"I've talked to Frank Morley," Rita said.

Mrs. Clark, who was delivering coffee, smiled. "Oh,
he is quite a character, isn't he?" she said, and poured
coffee in three cups. "Probably the only smart one out
of the whole bunch of us."

This got Mr. Clark nodding. "He knew. He knew
the whole truth about Father Catalpa," he said, "and
he wasn't going to let anyone tell him otherwise."

"We should have listened to him," Mrs. Clark
told him.

Mr. Clark continued to nod.

Rita said, "I've heard that the explanation given
was that Dennis—that's your son's name, right?"—
Mr. Clark seemed to like to nod—"that Dennis was

an altar boy and hadn't had any clothes on under his gown, or robe, or whatever it is he had worn on that day."

Mr. Clark said, "We never knew what all happened for sure. At first when Dennis told us about undressing, we thought he was lying. Then when he went over the details of what had happened, we were horrified. We talked it over, and I called Frank. Dennis told us that Father Catalpa had told him not to wear any clothes under the gown when he served as an altar boy. But when Father Catalpa got released, Dennis said it all had been a mistake—that he didn't think Father Catalpa had really been trying to hurt him."

Mrs. Clark nodded. She said, "Part of the problem was me. I refused to believe Dennis. You know, I thought he was making the whole thing up—it sounded so bizarre to start with. You know how kids can be? But the more we heard, the more we knew something was wrong. I didn't know what to do, being Catholic," she said. She nodded at Mr. Clark. "My husband isn't Catholic, you know. I wouldn't be Catholic now if the Church hadn't started taking some real steps in the right direction." She pushed her tongue against her cheek, creating a bulge in it. "To make a long story short," she said, "when Bishop Lawrence called and promised Father Catalpa would get treatment and would never again be around children, I talked Jeff into letting the Church take care of its own problems because we both knew what a scandal something like this would cause, and we didn't want to go through that. Did we?"

Mr. Clark nodded in assent.

"Dennis told you that Father Catalpa had asked

him not to wear any clothes under his gown?" Rita asked.

Mr. Clark said, "That's what he told us at first. Then later he said it might have been his own fault that he hadn't worn any clothes. To this day we don't know for sure. He never talked about it again. It was like he wanted to forget all about it. But I'll never forget the change that took place in him once Father Catalpa had been released. He became withdrawn. You remember it, don't you, Sally?"

She admitted that she had noticed a change in her son, though she didn't give any specifics.

"I would like to get in touch with Dennis if I could," Rita said. "You say he lives in Columbia?"

Mrs. Clark turned her face away.

"We'd prefer if you didn't contact him," Mr. Clark said. "You know how hard this is. We don't want to bring it all up again."

Rita didn't persist. "There was some mention that there might have been photographs taken," she said. "What can you tell me about that?"

Mrs. Clark was staring at the lake.

Mr. Clark said, "No, we're not sure about any of that. At first Dennis said Father Catalpa had taken pictures, then later said he didn't think Father Catalpa had really taken any." He shrugged. "Like my wife said, you know how it is with children. Sometimes it's hard to know what to believe. It's hard to tell what's going on inside their heads."

Mrs. Clark looked at Rita. "It nearly destroyed me, you know," she said. "You heard I left the church for a while, didn't you?"

Rita said she hadn't heard.

"Bishop Lawrence wanted us to believe that Father

Catalpa was one of those people who tended to get in hot water because they were so careless," Mr. Clark said.

Mrs. Clark nodded. "We heard later there might have been some trouble over in St. Louis."

Mr. Clark remarked, "Now, honey, we don't know about that for sure." He looked at Rita. "You know how rumors get going."

Rita asked, "Out of curiosity, what did you hear about St. Louis?"

Mr. and Mrs. Clark looked at each other. Neither said.

Odd, Rita thought. She wondered what they knew but weren't saying. "By any chance was Dennis on the chunky side and blond?"

"Oh, no, he had coal black hair. Still does."

Rita experienced a flush of disappointment. It passed, however, because she thought about Bobby Ruble. He had had a different build from Matthew and Larry, which might explain why Catalpa had let him live—if he had been abusing him also. Maybe the ones who didn't ultimately fit the killer's appetite were the ones who lived.

They drank coffee together and exchanged small talk. At the door, she shook hands with Mr. and Mrs. Clark, and thanked them for inviting her into their home.

Instead of heading back to the airport, though, Rita drove to Columbia, an hour and a half away. Dennis Clark's home was an old house trailer in a rundown trailer park on the outskirts of the city. Mrs. Clark was a dirty, obese woman, who said her husband was downtown playing pool at Booches.

Rita drove downtown. Booches was a pool hall on

Ninth Street. Since she got there right around the lunch hour, the front part of the pool hall was crowded with customers. Rita ordered a cheeseburger and Coke. Next to the wall, she sat at a table that wobbled everytime she touched it. There were a number of men shooting pool, but Rita knew Dennis right away because of his coal black hair. He was nothing like she had expected. Dressed in a black T-shirt and black jeans, he was sitting on the edge of a table, watching his partner take his shots. Dennis was grossly over-weight. His hairy belly hung out from beneath his T-shirt. A stubble of beard left a shadow on his face. The way his right eye was turned, he seemed to be watching her at the same time he watched his partner with his other eye, though when he really did look toward the front of Booches, Rita realized he was probably blind in his right eye.

She nursed her Coke until Dennis had finished his game of pool. Then she approached him, said she had talked to his parents in Lake St. Louis, and asked if they could go outside to talk for a few minutes.

They went out into the bright sunshine, where she introduced herself, showed him her credentials, and asked if she could get some information about Father Catalpa.

Dennis said, "That dirty bastard. He has no business being a priest. He ruined my life."

Rita told him, "When I talked to your parents, they asked me not to bother you, so I know how painful it must be to bring all this up."

He laughed loudly, like someone who was used to laughing, someone who could laugh at a joke that wasn't funny and make you think it was funny. "They didn't want you to talk to me because they're ashamed of me," he said. He pulled on his T-shirt. "I ain't exactly Lake St. Louis material."

"What really happened with you and Father Catalpa?"

From his back pocket he produced a flattened package of cigarettes, in which there couldn't be more than two or three left. He removed one of them, carefully straightened it with his fingers, and lit it. He cocked his head, as if trying to keep the smoke out of his blind eye. "The guy likes little boys," he said.

"Did he ever molest you?" she asked.

"I undressed for him. That was it. He wanted more, but I wouldn't give it to him."

"What about the photographs? There was a mention that he had taken photographs of you naked."

"He sure did. And I wasn't the first one he took pictures of."

"How do you know?"

"He had a great big envelope of pictures he had taken." He held up his hands, at least a foot apart.

"Like one of those large mailing envelopes?"

He nodded. "He had all kinds of pictures of naked boys and men in there. It was like he was keeping track of all he'd been with." He laughed loudly. "Or if someone asked for references, he could open his envelope and let 'em see."

"But he never touched you?"

He shook his head. "Nope. Wouldn't let him. But he let me look at the pictures. I guess he thought they might excite me and that then I might do what he wanted me to do."

"Did he ever threaten you?"

"What do you mean?"

"Threaten to hurt you."

"No, not that. He only said if I ever told anybody, I would go to hell." He laughed. "He was right. If the way I live ain't hell, I don't know what is."

She smiled wanly. At least he had a sense of humor. She told him she had been authorized to pay a reward for any information she could gather, so she held out twenty dollars.

He said he couldn't take it; he couldn't testify.

She told him he didn't have to testify. The reward was for any information she could gather. She said she had heard what she needed to hear.

He smiled, took the money, and said she could come to him for information anytime she wanted.

She asked him, "Did you ever hear about something that happened with Father Catalpa over in St. Louis?"

He puffed his cigarette. "Can't say that I have," he said, blowing out smoke.

"Were there others Catalpa bothered—I mean, ones you knew by name?"

"I guess I wasn't in the circle," he said. "Being fat, I didn't have many friends."

Rita thanked him for his help and drove back to the St. Louis airport to fly back to Milwaukee.

On the plane, she automatically ordered some wine. Then she thought of Frank, and pushed the small bottle of wine aside without opening it.

No sooner did the plane get up through the clouds than the captain announced the descent to Mitchell Field in Milwaukee. Or so it seemed. Whenever she flew, it seemed that it took forever to get up and forever to get back down, but little time to fly the distance. Out the window, the clouds below looked like an endless field of snow, as if she could step out of the jet and journey into a white wilderness. Indeed, it did take a long time for the jet to descend.

She wondered if Catalpa still had the envelope of photographs. The fact that Dennis knew about them and knew he was not the only one who appeared in the photographs was a good indication that Catalpa had shown them to others as his trophies. Somewhere he had them. She was sure he did. She was just as convinced that among the photographs were ones of Matthew. Larry puzzled her, though. She didn't know how he fit in. It didn't seem that Catalpa would have known Larry very intimately, though he had had the opportunity to meet him.

Once the jet cut through the field of snowy clouds, it became suspended above a gray earth, an earth with tiny roads, cars, and houses. So far up, the movement seemed insignificant. Even the occasional air pocket that bounced the jet seemed a temporary inconvenience. Yet as she drew closer to the earth, the objects grew in size and rushed at her. The jet hit the earth, driving her back into her seat. Then music was playing. Passengers were instructed by the captain not to get out of their seats until the jet came to a standstill, but already people were digging around in the baggage compartments above the seats. Rita got up too. The thing to do, she thought, was not to scare Catalpa, not to back him into a corner until she was ready to move. When she was ready, she would hit him with everything she could, all at once.

18

By the time Rita left for the office on Thursday morning, she had set all the details of the investigation straight in her mind. Two cigarette butts, one of which matched Scroggins' saliva and one of which had no match, a footprint, a drug that matched a prescription drug Scroggins took, and a ring that was linked to Father Catalpa. Inconsistent as it was, the evidence implicated both Scroggins and Catalpa. The two men knew each other. Bushes, fields, trash cans, and miles of road and highway had been searched, but no other physical evidence relating to the crimes had been found. There had been no witnesses. Around-the-clock surveillance had turned up nothing on Scroggins. A decision had to be made about him. The Catalpa lead was more sensitive. Aside from Charlie, no one else knew about him. She hadn't even told Paul the specifics.

At the office, all eyes were on her. She wondered why. Unhurriedly, she made her way to her private office, pulling out a set of keys as she went. That's when she noticed Susan Hall sitting with Adam. Susan worked for WITI-TV 6's Contact 6, an investigative reporting team. Rita knew Susan by reputation: She was someone who took only the most sensational stories. Apparently, she thought she had something worth pursuing in the CID offices.

She wore an immaculate navy dress, a thin string of pearls, and gold earrings. There was not a strand out of place in her blond hair. She was ready for the television cameras. Smiling to show her even white teeth, she rose and said, "Captain Trible, I don't know if you remember me, but I'm Susan Hall of WITI-TV 6. I wonder if we might chat for a few minutes."

Rita invited her in.

In the privacy of Rita's office, Susan said, "The reason why I'm here is you're working a case that will certainly have a national impact, what with a Catholic priest now as a suspect in a serial-killer investigation."

Rita was disturbed by what she heard, but she kept her composure. How in the hell did she find that out? she wondered. She said, "I wasn't aware of any involvement of a priest. Where did you hear that?"

"Come on, Rita—do you mind if I call you Rita?" Rita shrugged. "Anyway, I have my sources. I'm good at what I do, and I'm trying to put the best spin on this as I can. The Cassells and others are outraged. They want action. If you'll give me an exclusive, we can run the story however you want. I think you'll be pleased. It'll be professional."

"You put me in an awkward position," Rita said pleasantly. "To tell you the truth, I've seen your work, and I really like your stories"—Susan smiled proudly—"but I guess you're following a lead I haven't heard about yet."

Susan's smile melted. Her voice was quiet, cool, and compelling. "I know my sources," she said. "This is a

story that the public cares about. They'll hear about
it. Freedom of the press and all that. You've heard of
it, I'm sure. When the public is at danger because of
some killer roaming the streets, you have no right to
suppress information that might make the public
safer."

Rita nodded. She said, "I agree, though I also believe in responsible journalism, and there's no sense
creating a panic based upon some rumor you've apparently heard. Now, I'm not saying that you don't
know your sources. I'm simply admitting that this time
you and your sources know more than I do. I can't
help you, but maybe you can help me. Perhaps you
could tell me who your source is, and who this so-
called priest is." She shrugged. "It'd be nice to know."

Susan looked at her in silence, her clear blue eyes
angry. In a quiet voice she said, "I'll get my story,
with or without your cooperation."

Charlie tapped on the door and stuck his head in
the office. "Sorry—" he said, and was withdrawing
when Rita asked, "You ready to work?"

Charlie remained.

Once Rita made sure Susan was completely out of
the main office, she closed her private door, and said
to Charlie, "Look here, I want it straight: Have you
told anyone about Catalpa—anyone at all?"

"You told me not to" was all he said.

"Charlie, you and I were the only ones who knew
about that lead. Channel 6 has gotten information
about a priest as a suspect from somewhere."

"Not from me." He was unruffled. "I don't know
why you'd ask me that. There are leads coming into
the office constantly. Since the cases involve sex
crimes against young boys, I'm sure some of the anon-

ymous tips have mentioned priests. In this day and age, I'd be surprised if a priest hadn't been mentioned as a suspect."

Her voice remained stern. "Don't try to play this off as some kind of coincidence. Contact 6 doesn't chase rumors. They got information from someone."

"Well, if there's a leak, it's your fault."

"My fault?"

"You're the one who ran off on some little spree, not telling anyone anything about what you were doing. Where have you been? I didn't know the specifics." He didn't wait for her to say anything. "I mean, you left me being asked all kinds of questions, you see what I'm saying, and I had no idea what was going on. If there's a leak, I could just as easily say it's your fault."

"Oh, well, yeah, that makes perfect sense. Perhaps you'd like to explain." Since she was being sarcastic, she didn't expect an explanation.

"For one thing, everyone in the office knows you went to St. Louis," he said. "It's like you ran off on some secret trip, but you asked Bev to arrange for your ticket."

Incredulously, she asked, "What does that have to do with anything?"

"It seems to me that's a possible leak."

"She wouldn't say anything—"

"And I would? Don't even try that. You know I wouldn't say anything. And if my memory serves me correctly, you ran a background check on Catalpa yourself. You wanted to see if he had had a prior arrest."

She waited patiently.

"You don't run background checks on someone

without other people knowing. When you run one through the computer, people know right away."

On considering what Charlie said, she ran a hand through her hair, to the back of her head, where she held it. "I need to make a call," she said.

He sat down and put a foot on her desk. "You need to make an apology," he said. "I don't even play this crap."

She smiled. "An apology? For what?" she asked.

"Don't even try it. You know exactly what."

"Okay, I'm sorry. Now get the hell out so I can call Paul before someone else gets to him first."

Charlie pulled the door closed on his way out of her office.

She called Paul and put the call on the speaker phone so she could work while she talked. "What's going on over there?" he said, obviously losing his patience with her. "I've got all kinds of people asking me questions, citizens are protesting, and the media is driving me crazy. The Cassells are up here talking to every member of the legislature that they can find. Rita, you know I like you, but you're putting me in a bad spot. I need to know what's going on, and I need to know what's going on now. Something has to be happening."

She looked around at the stacks of paperwork on her desk. There were files, papers, and books everywhere, not in neat stacks but strewn about. Some of the papers even had notes scribbled on them, notes that were not related to the original correspondence. The notes were either a result of a telephone call, when she couldn't find a piece of scratch paper at the time, or a result of a thought that happened to come into her head at the time of a call, and she didn't want to risk losing the thought while she searched for paper to record it.

"Well? What's happening? And what in the hell are you doing running off to St. Louis? You told me it was some big secret, and you still haven't told me what it was. It didn't pan out, did it?" Before she could answer, he said, "My God, I've sent you extra investigators. You run the office. That's why I have you in there. I don't want you doing all the legwork—what the hell you doing running off? Send someone else."

"I had to, Paul."

"I'm sure you did. I'm all ears. Go ahead, tell me why you had to. Why did it have to be you? Why not someone else?"

She sighed. "We have a new lead in the case, one that's very sensitive. I've told you."

"Okay. So, what's your lead? You need to be more specific."

"Our serial killer may be a Catholic priest."

There was a momentary silence. Then: "Oh, God."

"With something like this, I need to handle as much as I can on my own until I have something substantial to go on."

"What do you have so far?" Paul wanted to know.

She told him what she knew about the Catalpa connection, and what she had learned in St. Louis.

"Rita, I'm going to be honest with you," he said. "You're an excellent investigator and I love you, which is why I have you overseeing that office. If these serial killings involved prostitutes, or someone nobody cared about, that would be one thing, but these are children. Everyone's watching this investigation. The smallest mistake gets a ton of attention. Be careful.

I'm trying to support you—to stand behind you. I want to support you. You know I do. But be careful, very careful. You get the Catholic Church on your ass, and we'll never be able to put this thing to rest."

She didn't ask what he meant.

She sent investigators back to interview school children, and to interview people in the Hammond and Cassell neighborhoods. Then she and Charlie left the office. They requisitioned a surveillance van. A white news van attempted to follow them, but Rita lost them on the interstate. She sped through a radar trap. The news van slowed for it.

She parked the van near St. Paul's parish. It was having some expansion done on the main chapel, so there were trucks and workers moving around the buildings. That made it possible for Rita and Charlie to park their van nearby, though they didn't see much of Father Catalpa. They did learn, however, that he smoked. He sneaked outdoors periodically, carrying an ashtray, and walked to the side of the chapel, where he would stand in the bushes and light up. Sometimes as he smoked, he would pace, as if he couldn't understand why his cigarette took so long to burn. Other than that, he remained inside.

As they sat together, Rita said to Charlie, "Listen, I've been meaning to tell you, I'm really sorry about putting you on the spot these past few days. I didn't want anyone pressing you for information." She outlined what she had learned in St. Louis and Columbia.

Charlie was excited. He said the case would eventually come together.

She said she didn't know about that, but she was encouraged. She got out of her seat and took a cola from the van refrigerator. She popped the top of the soda and took a drink. From the table she picked up a can of cashews, removed the plastic lid, and took a handful.

Toward the end of the afternoon, the winds rose, clouds moved in, and rain began to fall, first in fat drops, then in a roar. Over it Charlie said, "What if we knew it was Catalpa and Scroggins working together but never could prove it?"

"I've heard of such cases, but I'm still not sure they are working together," she told him.

"At one time you seemed convinced of it."

"I know. I think different things at different times. My latest thought is, what if Father Catalpa got Scroggins to open up during one of his 'counseling' sessions? He might have been pressuring Matthew at the same time, and decided he had a way of getting what he wanted from Matthew without getting caught. While Scroggins was spilling his soul, Father Catalpa might have been letting him smoke, maybe he even gave him a beer or two, and afterward he kept the cigarette butts to leave a trail of evidence that pointed to Scroggins."

"But how does the Cassell boy figure in? What about the cigarette there?"

She shrugged. "From the bodies, we have to assume murder is in this man's heart," she said. "He killed once, got away with it, and now he can't stop. Maybe he's decided the crimes will be more perfect if he leaves different evidence each time. You know how it is with some criminals—they start with their crimes and can't stop until they get caught. I mean, we see this all the time."

He said, "It would explain how the murderer managed to pick up the boys so easily. A priest? Most children would trust a priest. But what about the embalming? Scroggins seems to be the one who worked in a funeral home, and even then, according to what little we've been able to learn, he was a custodian and would have seldom been around the bodies."

"Come on, you mean you think that Scroggins worked in a funeral home and didn't have at least some degree of curiosity about the bodies that were being embalmed? You know someone let him watch. You just know someone did."

"So you really think Catalpa did it to make it look like it was Scroggins?" It was more of a statement than a question.

She told him, "Catalpa would have been around dead bodies too. I mean, he's a priest. It wouldn't surprise me to learn that he had seen an embalming or two. The key is that if Catalpa was going to set up Scroggins in order to keep heat away from himself, he'd be looking for ways to tie the crimes to Scroggins."

"It makes sense," he admitted. "But whoever did this would still have to have access to the equipment to embalm. Whatever that machine is that pushes the blood out as it injects the embalming solution is not something the average person would have in a bedroom closet."

Before she could respond to the issue he had raised, Father Catalpa appeared. Hopping across puddles of mud under the overhang of the church roof, he went into the bushes, where he lit a cigarette. There, standing under the overhang of the roof, he smoked.

"So what about the embalming equipment?" Charlie said. "How do you—"

She pointed at the smoking priest. "Wait," she said.

"He doesn't have his ashtray." They watched in silence.

Once Catalpa had flipped the cigarette and gone back inside the church, she looked frantically around the van. She grabbed a handful of evidence bags and jumped out. She ran through the downpour to where Catalpa had been smoking. Charlie was right behind her. She covered with plastic a shoe impression in the mud. Above the sound of the rain and with rain streaming down her face, she told Charlie, "Get someone out here from the lab and let's get a mold of this!" While she searched for the cigarette butt, Charlie ran back to the van.

By the next morning, they had a new lead. They met with Venda Pratt, a black investigator with the crime lab. He clipped two photographs to a display board, as a physician would hang X rays on lighted panels for examination. He pointed at the impression of Father Catalpa's shoe, and then at a nick in the impression found at the Hammond scene. "It's not the same shoe," he said.

"Are you positive it couldn't be?" Rita asked.

Venda said, smiling, "Not the same shoe, but the same size. And—" He produced the cigarette butt in an evidence bag. "This is the cigarette you found yesterday?" She nodded. "It matches the saliva on the butt found at the Cassell scene."

Rita was elated. All of the secrecy and risk taking was paying off.

Rita and Charlie went for an arrest warrant and search warrant. Given the sensitivity of the case, the assistant prosecutor suggested they go to a non-Catholic judge, Judge William Agar, who silently reviewed the evidence about the shoe impression, the cigarette

butt, and the ring. In a deep, distinguished voice he
noted, "You understand all of this is circumstantial."
Rita told him about the Scroggins relationship and the
other evidence they had in the cases. She told him
about what she had learned in St. Louis. He said he
couldn't take that into consideration, though he signed
the search warrant. He said, "I hope you find something during your search because unless you do, you're
going to have a hell of a mess on your hands." He
didn't sign the arrest warrant. "If you find something,
you call me and I'll sign this, but I won't sign it until
I get something solid."

When Rita, Charlie, CID investigators, local police,
county police, and uniformed state troopers executed
the search warrant in the middle of the night, Father
Catalpa yelled at them. She had chosen the middle of
the night so that the search would be less conspicuous.
The less attention drawn to the scene, the better. Also,
she wanted to catch Catalpa off guard.

Father Catalpa insisted on being allowed to make a
telephone call. Rita told one of the detectives to take
Catalpa to a phone while she and others began their
search. The living quarters were attached to the
church.

It was a simple room with polished tile floors, a
desk, a bed, and a metal chair. Along one wall were
built-in bookcases lined with religious books. The
shelves were dusty, as if the books had not seen much
use. In the closet Charlie found two pairs of shoes.
One had a nick in the sole. Carefully he put the shoes
in evidence bags, which he marked with evidence
cards. While he was doing that, Rita removed a cordovan briefcase from the closet. The case was locked, so
she pried the lock open with a screwdriver. Inside was

an old, bulky nine-by-twelve brown clasp envelope. It was filled with photographs of men and male children in compromising positions. Not sure if she recognized Matthew or Larry, she asked Charlie to take a look. Once he began to look, all he said was "Oh, no," after which he sighed and flipped through methodically. Finally he put them back in the envelope. "It's hard to tell," he said at last. Some of the photos didn't include facial shots, which made it impossible to say who the children were.

Rita, who had gone on to search the rest of the sparsely furnished apartment, stopped long enough to cross her arms on her chest and shake her head.

Charlie whispered, "What I wouldn't give to have a few minutes alone with that guy. I'd get some answers from him, even if I had to pound them out of him."

A uniformed state trooper appeared in the doorway. He said, "Father Catalpa says he's chilled and wants to know if he can have his coat hanging on the door." He looked behind the door, where he reached for a coat.

"Stop!" Rita said, surprising everyone. She pointed at the trooper. "Don't touch that coat." She remembered the case her friend from Narcotics, Jerry Grier, had told her about. If a coat could conceal drugs, it could conceal other evidence, she thought. She went to the door, removed the black coat from a hook, and patted it. "Okay," she said, handing the coat to the trooper. On second thought, however, she pulled the coat back. "Wait." She felt through the coat again and stopped. From an inside pocket she removed a soiled handkerchief. "Give him a blanket or something," she said, keeping the coat. She put the handkerchief in an evidence bag.

She called Judge Agar, who said he would sign an arrest warrant based upon the photographs, shoes, and handkerchief. He did remind her, however, that the evidence was extremely circumstantial.

Later, from the car where he was waiting, his hands cuffed behind his back, Father Catalpa called to Rita when he saw her, "You better have put everything right back where you found it!" He shrank back as he noticed people watching from newly lighted houses.

Within a half hour, all was quiet again around the parish. The sounds of police radios had left. Lights in nearby houses had gone out again. Somewhere a dog barked in the darkness.

Rita and Charlie were the last to leave. They drove to the Milwaukee County Jail, where they had Father Catalpa moved from a holding tank to an interrogation room. Charlie advised him of his constitutional rights and offered him an opportunity to have an attorney present, though Father Catalpa said that he didn't need one—that is, he was sure he could clear everything up by answering a few questions. With that, Rita gave him a rights-waiver form to sign, and offered him cigarettes and coffee, which he readily accepted. He lit a cigarette, sat back, and crossed his legs, smiling complacently. "Now, what can I do for you?" he said. He was back in control.

Charlie said, "Let's begin with some basic questions."

"Fine."

"What is your full name?"

"Thaddeus Victor Catalpa."

"Where are you now?"

"You're kidding?"

"Please, answer the question."

"The Milwaukee County Jail."

"What is today's date?"

"May twenty-ninth."

"What is the time?"

He looked for his watch, then smiled. "How should I know?" he asked. "They took my possessions when I checked in."

"What is your occupation?"

"I'm a Roman Catholic priest. A Jesuit."

"Where do you work?"

"I am the priest at St. Paul's parish in Brown Deer, Wisconsin." He puffed his cigarette.

Rita said, "Let's go back to Monday, April 5, the day Matthew Hammond was murdered."

"Yes, I was in Chicago. I've told you that before."

Charlie asked, "When did you go to Chicago?"

"Friday, April second, I left."

"When did you return?"

"The sixteenth."

"You missed both Palm Sunday and Easter Sunday?"

"I took part in them in Chicago."

"But you missed them in your own parish. Isn't that unusual?"

"I'm a world-renowned Milton scholar," he said. "I often travel to conduct my research. I often go to conferences. And so on." He puffed on his cigarette. "No, it is not unusual for me to be away from my parish. The people understand the importance of my work elsewhere."

Rita asked, "Did you return from Chicago at any time during those days?"

"No."

"Never?" Charlie asked.

"Never."

Rita rephrased the question. "You didn't leave the city during those days?"

"Not at all."

She produced a laundry slip from the dry cleaners, saying, "I have a laundry ticket from Kenosha, Wisconsin, indicating that you dropped some clothes off there on Tuesday, April 6."

"There must be some mistake."

"A clerk said you dropped off the clothes."

His pale complexion became red. "She must be mistaken. It's impossible." He stirred in his chair, took a puff of his cigarette, and ground it out.

"Do you want to change your story?" she asked.

"She must have been mistaken."

Charlie said, "Okay, let's move on. We found an envelope of pornographic photographs in your room. You want to explain them?"

"There is nothing illegal about a person possessing pornography."

Rita remembered Scroggins saying the same thing. They must have talked about the subject. "There is if the materials exploit children, which is the case here," she said.

"Tell me, were those photographs listed among the items you were authorized to search for in your warrant?"

Charlie said, "They're related to the nature of the crimes we're investigating, yes."

"It seems to me they're the fruits of an illegal search."

The wording of his statement made her realize he

was versed in the law, not in the sense of someone who respected the law, but in the sense of someone who knew what his rights were and what he could get away with. She mentioned, "For a priest, you seem rather well versed in criminal law."

"No, I am well versed in people who abuse the fruits of temptation. I am also well versed in the state trying to infringe upon the freedoms of the Church. Don't you know I could call the Church right now, and you'd have the fight of your lives on your hands? Don't you know the Church would take my side no matter what? Don't you know the Church would fight to the bitter end? It's used to persecution—"

Rita interrupted him, saying, "You remember the first time we met, we talked about an engagement ring belonging to Crystal Hammond?" Don't let him stray too much, she thought.

He sat silently for a moment. She could see him thinking. "Yes, Matthew wanted to put it in the church collection so it could help poor people," he said. "So I told him I would make sure it got to the right place. I meant to give it back to Crystal, but I never see her in church because she never attends, so it slipped my mind."

"Correct me if I'm wrong," Rita said, "but the first time we talked, I don't remember you telling us that Matthew had wanted to give the ring to help poor people. I thought you gave us a different explanation." Caught you off guard, didn't I? Rita thought to herself. She felt triumphant.

"I did? What did I say? I haven't really thought about it since then."

Rita told him, "You obviously have thought about something because your story has changed. The first time you talked to us, you told us Matthew gave you the ring because he wanted you to pray for his mother."

"Yes, yes, that was it."

"I didn't by any chance tell you where we found the ring, did I?"

Father Catalpa thought for a moment. "No, I don't think we ever got to that point," he said. He said it weakly, as though he might want to change his mind if she refreshed his memory. "I will say this, though, wherever you found it, it doesn't mean anything. Oftentimes people entrust me with money, valuables, and their possessions. Why, does someone think I was trying to steal it? You're wrong. I never did anything with that ring. If that's the best you can do for evidence, you better back up and regroup."

Calmly Rita said, "The clerk at the cleaners in Kenosha found the ring in your clothes, the ones you left with her to be cleaned on Tuesday, April 6, the day after Matthew Hammond was murdered."

Reddening, Father Catalpa lit another cigarette. He stood. "Do you mind if I walk around a bit?" he asked. Neither of them objected, so he paced. "Something's not right here," he said. "Someone's trying to frame me."

Charlie said, "Now, why do you suppose someone would want to do that?"

Without stopping, Father Catalpa said, "Some people hate priests. Some people hate the Church. How should I know why? It's your job to figure that part out. You have a responsibility to protect me."

"There's something that really bothers me about the photographs of yours," Charlie said. "Many of them are graphic scenes of sodomy between older men and young boys. It ties right into the types of cases we're talking about. It suggests a motive."

Father Catalpa stopped at the plate-glass mirror that hid an observation room, looked at himself, and said, "Look, I've been doing a study about homosexuality, and the photographs were part of the evidence I had collected."

Charlie jumped up angrily. "Look, you little sawed-off son of a bitch!" he said. "I've had about all the stinking bullshit lies I can take—"

Rita caught him before he could get to the priest. "I want you out of here now!" she told him.

"He's lying and you know it!"

Holding Charlie with one hand, she pointed at the door. "Out, and don't come back until you've cooled off."

Charlie left the room, slamming the door.

Father Catalpa, who had shrunk back against the plate-glass mirror, regained his composure. "Someone's trying to frame me, I tell you," he said. "It's all lies."

Rita apologized for Charlie. "Sit down, please," she said. "I want to ask you some questions about the murder of Laurence Cassell."

Nodding, he sat down. With a puff on his cigarette, he held the butt straight up so the ashes didn't fall. In that position he let the cigarette burn down instead of grinding it out in the ashtray. "I didn't like what your partner said," he said. "It was insensitive, though I've put up with that same kind of attitude all my life—people making fun of my size." He looked at her with cold eyes. "That's part of the reason I became a scholar. I've got more brains in my pinky"—he held up his little finger—"than that big oaf partner of yours has in his whole body."

Rita sat forward so that she was very close to Father Catalpa. She said, "Earlier you told us you had been to St. Mary's in Pewaukee?"

"Yes," he said. "But I've been to most of the parishes in the area."

Rita sighed. She said to herself, he's catching on to what I'm doing. He knows I'm trying to trip him up. The ring story taught him a lesson. Back up and re-group, she told herself. "You know," she said, smiling, "during our first meeting you said some fascinating things about the poet John Milton."

"You like Milton's work?" he said, straightening. The cigarette butt in his hand had gone out, so he dropped it in the ashtray and lit another cigarette. "I forgot what I said."

"To tell you the truth, I am fascinated by Milton's work, but you are obviously much more versed than I am."

He nodded sheepishly and shrugged. "I've been at it a long time," he said. He puffed the new cigarette, raising a cloud of smoke.

"If you don't mind, I was wondering if we could take a break and talk about Milton for a moment. I'm sure Charlie will be coming back soon, and he wouldn't approve of us talking like this, but—"

Father Catalpa waved a hand. "Oh, don't worry about him," he said, smiling. "He knows you haven't got anything on me. That's what makes him so mad. He knows you've made a big mistake by bringing me here."

"I guess I was curious about this notion of evil in the world. You mentioned it, and said a little about

Milton's *Paradise Lost,* but it was obviously enough to grab my interest. Tell me more."

He looked more relaxed, as if he knew this line of questioning couldn't hurt him. "Oh, Milton is fascinating, all right," he said. "And I've struggled with this question of evil for quite some time. You see, some people think Milton leaves us on the fence, not knowing whether the fall of humans was good or bad, but I know differently because of an important distinction he makes. He makes it clear that evil is no more in an apple that Adam and Eve eat than power was in Samson's hair."

"What?"

He smiled wryly. "It means that if evil wasn't in the fruit, where was it?"

"Where?"

"Inside"—he tapped his right temple—"waiting to be unleashed." He tapped his head again. "And when it's unleashed, this is the only thing that can destroy it."

"Was Matthew Hammond evil?"

He smiled again. "Don't get me wrong; I'm sorry he's dead, and all, but I knew he was going to be trouble someday."

"Why do you say that?"

"You could look at him and tell." His smile stretched into a full grin. "Perhaps because he didn't know the wisdom of the command: Know to know no more, if you know what I mean."

"No, I'm not sure I understand."

"Milton wrote it. It means people should know where to draw the line. Matthew was one of those boys who didn't know where to draw it. He was wild, almost as wild as the Ruble boy, only people didn't know it." Why did he mention the Ruble boy? she wondered. "He was sly. You could tell he was going to end up in trouble. He couldn't control himself. He had no structure in his life. His mother was never around."

There came a tap at the interrogation room door. Rita excused herself. She went next door to the observation room, where, together, she and Charlie watched Father Catalpa get up to pace.

"This guy's full of himself," Charlie said. "Five minutes ago we were grilling him about a murder, and now he's completely oblivious to all that, as if he's giving a college lecture in Milton or something."

Standing close to the observation window, not two feet from Rita and Charlie, Father Catalpa tapped the glass and motioned with his hand for them to rejoin him. It was uncanny, as if he could see them. Then he backed away. "He is evil," she said. Father Catalpa sat down at the table, where he lapsed into a grinning silence.

"You ready for round two?" she asked Charlie.

He nodded.

19

When they reentered the interrogation room, Father Catalpa pointed at Charlie and told Rita, "I don't want him in here."

Charlie said, "You have been arrested on suspicion of first-degree murder. You have no choice." The verbalization of the charge seemed to remind Father Catalpa of why he was in the interrogation room in the first place, because he turned pale and shifted in his seat.

Rita asked, "Tell me about Bobby Ruble."

"What's he got to do with anything?"

"He was an altar boy, wasn't he?"

"Yes."

"Did you know he and Matthew were friends?"

Father Catalpa sank back in his chair.

Rita felt a twinge of excitement. From what Dennis Clark had told her, she knew Catalpa wouldn't want his victims to associate with each other.

Charlie asked, "Is there some reason you don't want to answer the question?"

Father Catalpa stiffened and sat up again. "Like I said, what does this have to do with anything?"

Rita asked, "Were you arrested fourteen years ago for child molestation?"

Father Catalpa reddened. "What's all this got to do with Matthew! That charge was dropped. It never went to trial. It was all a big mistake."

She looked at a pad of notes. "A twelve-year-old boy in St. Charles, Missouri. The same age range."

"The charge was dropped!"

"You took photographs of him naked."

Father Catalpa said, "They never found any photos."

Charlie said, "What about the photographs we found in your apartment? Some of them looked like they might be a number of years old."

Father Catalpa didn't say anything.

"Are there photographs of Matthew Hammond in that collection?" Charlie asked.

Father Catalpa didn't say.

"It's easy enough to find out," Charlie mentioned. "All we have to do is show the photographs to the boy's mother."

"I went to see Dennis Clark," Rita said. Father Catalpa glanced at her. Now he really looked ill. "Ironically, Dennis told me all about the envelope of photographs. Are the photographs we found the ones no one could find fourteen years ago?"

Father Catalpa didn't say, or didn't know what to say. She guessed he was contemplating how to give them a partial explanation, as if the concession would take them off his back. "I bet Dennis would be able to identify a photograph of himself," she said.

Charlie said, "Why don't you run it by us one more time? What were you doing with child pornography?

You said something about a study. Can you be more specific?"

Father Catalpa explained that he had been quite concerned with pedophilia in the Church. He said he had begun collecting child pornography so he could try to figure out what priests saw in young children, especially young males.

"Was your St. Charles arrest part of this famous study of yours?" Charlie asked in a cold voice.

Father Catalpa again fell silent.

"Did Matthew Hammond ever undress for you?" Rita asked.

"No."

"Did you ever ask him to undress for you?"

"No."

"So there aren't going to be any photos of him in your collection?"

"I don't know about that. A lot of people have given me photographs."

Charlie angrily said, "Come on, you expect us to believe someone gave you photos of Matthew?"

"I—" His hands were shaking. "I don't know. I never paid that much attention."

"Have you ever asked any child to undress for you?" Rita asked.

"No."

"Did you sexually abuse Matthew Hammond, murder him, and then embalm him?" Charlie threw in.

"No! No! No! I've told you, no! I've told you no a thousand times!"

"Did you murder Laurence Cassell?" Charlie asked.

"No!"

She asked, "Have you ever been to Lizard Mound State Park?"

"No! I mean, yes. A long time ago. Everyone's been there."

"When were you there?"

He buried his face in his hands. Through them, muffling his voice, he said, "I don't know exactly, but it was at least two or three years ago."

She asked, "Have you been back since?"

"No."

Charlie asked, "Where were you on Tuesday, May the fourth?"

Father Catalpa was becoming short-tempered. "How should I know?" he asked. "I'd have to check my calendar. The church secretary has it. Call her. She'd know where I was. But if it had anything to do with this other little boy, whatever his name is—"

"Laurence Cassell."

"Well, if it has to do with him, I don't even know the boy, I've never met him, and no, I didn't murder, kill, or otherwise harm him or any other boy. No, I didn't kill anybody. What more do you want from me? No, I didn't do it!"

"You need to know when to say no no more," Charlie said calmly.

Father Catalpa shot a glance at him, but before he could make a comment, Rita asked, "Have you ever been to Kettle-Moraine State Forest—the south branch?"

"No. Not really."

"What do you mean, not really?"

"I've been to Old World. You pass through Kettle-Moraine to get to Old World."

"Have you ever stopped at any other place in the Kettle-Moraine State Forest?"

"No."

"And you've never heard of a boy named Laurence Cassell?"

Though the question had already been asked, Father Catalpa didn't seem to mind answering it for her. "No, never heard of him until all this happened and I read and heard about him through the news."

She showed him a photograph of the boy. "You sure you've never seen him?"

Father Catalpa studied the photograph. "I swear I've never seen him, but he does look a lot like Matthew."

"How do you explain the presence of one of your cigarettes where the Cassell boy was found murdered?" Charlie interjected.

Nervously, Father Catalpa got up. He muttered, "Someone's trying to frame me." To Rita: "I promise I didn't even know the boy—never saw him, nothing."

Piece by piece they went through the same evidence again. Father Catalpa, answering questions, chainsmoked. He went to the rest room. Then he was thirsty—said he wanted something cold to drink. Then he wanted coffee. "I know it looks bad," he said, "but I didn't do it. I swear." Yes, he admitted, he had kept the ring. He had meant to contact the boy's mother— he had seen her on occasion but never really met her that he could recall—and return the ring to her, but had forgotten. Yes, he thought something or someone had been bothering the boy. Father Catalpa said he didn't know for sure, but he suspected it might be a parishioner named Joe Pratt.

"Joe Pratt?" Rita said. Bingo, she thought. There's the connection.

"Bill Scroggins is his real name," Father Catalpa said. Now he was calmer. He sighed, took a deep breath through his nose, and lit a cigarette. It was all coming back to him, he said. Yes, it must have been Joe Pratt all along. "The one you picked up earlier." He had been kicked out of St. Benedict's at Menomonee Falls, Father Catalpa said. "Father DeFalco had called me and told me about this parishioner named Scroggins, whom Father DeFalco had asked to leave the parish because he had been bothering little boys. When Father DeFalco told me he was basically a good Catholic, I told him I would take Scroggins in at St. Paul's—that we could give him a second chance."

"Whose decision was it to give Scroggins a new name?" Charlie asked.

"I don't know," Father Catalpa said. "It just came up." He went on to explain that he had done many hours of counseling with Scroggins, who had confessed to molesting little boys. According to Father Catalpa, Scroggins had even claimed to have sodomized a couple of his nephews in the past. "I had seen him around the Hammond boy," he said. "That's it! That's who was bothering Matthew!" He jumped up, leaving a lit cigarette in the ashtray. With a fist he hit his other palm with a loud smack. "If only I had seen it before," he said, red-faced, "I could have saved that boy's life." Tears were in his eyes. "If only I had known." He began to pace again. He snapped his fingers. "I even remember him talking about working in some funeral home when he was younger. That's it! There's your killer!"

Rita thought, he knows everything. Perhaps it was Scroggins and he was trying to take the heat off himself by framing Catalpa.

Charlie said, "Cut the dramatics. You've read about Scroggins in the newspapers and saw it on TV. You knew we picked him up for questioning. But now you expect us to believe all of this evidence we have against you has been the result of some ingenious plan on his part to frame you?"

"I know it looks bad, but, yes, I do." He stopped at the table and stood behind his chair. "I already admitted I knew he had been arrested as a suspect in the Hammond case, but even without that I'd have eventually put everything together anyway. There are too many coincidences."

"So how did one of your cigarettes get out to Lizard Mound?" Rita asked.

"Scroggins could have taken that at any time from an ashtray," Father Catalpa said. He was visibly relieved now. "I used to invite him to my apartment so we could smoke while we talked. At the church I have to go outside to smoke. But when I'm in my apartment, I smoke there. Scroggins and I used to smoke all the time when we talked."

"So you invited him to your apartment?"

"Yes."

"Say what you're telling us is the truth. How do you explain your shoe print at the site of Matthew Hammond's body?"

He was suddenly jubilant. "I didn't take those shoes to Chicago!" he said, excited. "I distinctly remember. I wore these new shoes!" He pointed at his feet. He had put the new shoes on because Charlie had confiscated the other pair from the closet. "That proves I'm telling the truth. Scroggins took my shoes, then put them back. I never keep my apartment locked. Ask my secretary. Ask anyone."

"And what about the clothes in the Kenosha dry cleaners?" Charlie asked.

"I told you! I've never been to a dry cleaners in Kenosha. Never. Scroggins took them there, I lay you money."

"Why would Scroggins want to do something like that to you?" Rita asked. She could understand the logic of Scroggins trying to deflect suspicion from himself once he knew he was a suspect, but for him to attempt to frame Catalpa from the beginning would require some prior motive.

"I can't pretend to know what's going on in his head, but it could be he thought he could make me a believable suspect." When neither Rita nor Charlie said anything, Catalpa continued. "You know what I mean. People are always talking about priests molesting children. It's not true, you know. Most priests would never do anything like that, but let the smallest thing happen, and that's the first thing people think of—they think the priest is some kind of pervert. Maybe Scroggins thought he could make me an obvious suspect."

Rita asked, "Have you heard the story of Hazael?"

Father Catalpa sat down. "Has who? Who's she?"

"Hazael. It's in the Bible," she said, consulting her notes. "Second Kings eight."

"Oh." He shrugged. "I guess I'm not familiar with what story you're talking about. I'm a Milton scholar, not a biblical scholar."

"Hazael murdered a king in order to ascend to the king's throne."

"So, stories like that are all over in the Bible."

"In this story Hazael soaked a cloth in water so no air could get through it, and he held the cloth over the king's face. He smothered the king."

Father Catalpa didn't say anything.

"Does the story ring a bell?"

"Not really."

"You remember the day we met in your office?"

Father Catalpa nodded.

"Your Bible was opened to that story."

"The Bible on the table?"

Rita nodded. "Yes."

"That's for show. I never even use that Bible. I doubt I've ever even looked at it very closely."

She said, "We found the cloth you used to suffocate Matthew with. It was in your coat pocket. The lab indicates you dipped it in water and held it over Matthew's face. Fibers from the cloth match the fibers found around Matthew's nose and mouth." It wasn't true. The lab results from the cloth they had found in his coat were not back yet. But she wanted to see his reaction.

Locked away in each person's psyche is a secluded place, a sanctuary, the gate of which for most people is never opened. Most people don't even realize they have such a place, the place where they unwittingly hide their darkest secrets. Staring at Father Catalpa at that moment, Rita thought she could see him visibly withdrawing. He seemed to be struggling with the gate. Nervously, he ground out one cigarette and lit another. He said, "I want an attorney. Someone's definitely trying to frame me. I want to call my bishop. The Church is going to come down with its full force on this. It'll crush all this evil that someone's trying to do to me."

"You want to call the bishop like you did in St. Charles?" Rita said. "This time you're not going to get off so easy."

"I have a right to an attorney, and I'm not going to

say another word until you honor that right!'' Father
Catalpa yelled, red-faced, jumping to his feet. "I know
my rights!''

Rita and Charlie went into the observation room.
For the first time the plump man seemed depressed
and worried. Breathing heavily, he scratched his neck
absentmindedly. His face had gone livid.

"We had him on the run," Charlie said. With a
raised forefinger and thumb, he said, "We were this
close to snagging him."

"I don't know."

"What?"

Staring at the figure inside the observation room,
she said, "We have two suspects, Scroggins and Catalpa. If one is trying to frame the other, then why
would there be evidence to implicate them both?"

"Neither one of these guys is a genius," Charlie told
her. "Besides, I still don't see why they couldn't both
be involved." She pondered Charlie. Certainly what
he was saying was a possibility. It did make sense, she
thought. "As for Catalpa, there are too many things
he can't explain," Charlie continued. "Like the ring—
sounds like he may even have intended to keep it as
a trophy of his first victim. And the dry cleaners. I
mean, we know he was there. And what about that
child pornography? Come on, did you really buy that
story about his study? I wanted to bust his face. And
what about that arrest down in Missouri? He's dirty,
I tell you, and he knows he is."

"It's true, both Scroggins and Catalpa have their
problems," she said, sitting. "But what we have to
sort out is whether only one was involved or
whether they both were involved. If only one was
involved, which one? If both, how?" She leaned

back, the fingers of one hand pressing in on her eyes. She had trouble imagining Scroggins and Catalpa working together as a pair of killers. It seemed an unlikely combination. "Something doesn't add up," she said, releasing her eyes and sitting forward. "It could be that they did have a plan whereby each of them would incriminate himself partially, just enough to be implicated without being prosecuted, in order to show that they could get away with it, but for some reason they don't seem that smart or coordinated to me." Why would they incriminate themselves to start with? she thought to herself. Because it's a game, she reasoned, and personal risk would make it more exciting. Could it be?

By three in the morning, an attorney retained by the Catholic Church, John Kribble, had arrived at the jail. He was a tall, distinguished man, and he had a soldierly bearing, very erect, even at that time of the morning. His dark, curly hair was well brushed, and he smelled as if he had just climbed out of the shower. The first thing he asked for was a few moments alone with his client.

When Mr. Kribble returned to the hallway, he said, "Naturally, Father Catalpa has indicated to me that he doesn't wish to say anything more. Right now he needs sleep. When is he scheduled to be arraigned?"

Rita said, "The prosecutor mentioned this afternoon."

Mr. Kribble nodded. "The bishop has requested to see him in the morning. We'd appreciate it if you could accommodate it."

Rita said she had no objections.

Just then Father Catalpa said, "I don't want to go

through all this. I want to take a lie-detector test. I'm innocent."

Mr. Kribble told him, "Father Catalpa, we'll have you out of here by the end of the day. For now, be patient and don't say a word. They don't have anything."

"I'm telling you, I'm innocent, and I don't want to stay here."

Charlie commented, "He doesn't want people to find out about his past, that's what he doesn't want."

Father Catalpa cried angrily, "A lie detector test will clear me!"

"I don't advise it," Mr. Kribble said.

"I don't give a damn what you advise! I want a lie detector test."

"There are risks—"

"I want the lie detector!"

"Talk to the bishop first."

"Now!"

The polygraph was arranged, though they had to wait for an examiner to be called in. As was standard protocol, the examiner met with Rita and Charlie, who helped him prepare a list of questions.

Once he had attached Father Catalpa to the polygraph apparatus and had run some preliminary tests, the examiner asked general questions about the father's background. Among those questions were ones that addressed his arrest fourteen years earlier. He admitted to having been arrested, which showed no deception. He denied having photographed Dennis Clark naked. The response indicated deception. When Father Catalpa became angry that the examiner was asking questions that were not related to the Hammond-Cassell murders, the examiner moved to questions regarding the murders themselves:

"Did you murder Matthew Hammond?"

"No, I did not."

"Did you murder Laurence Cassell?"

"No, I did not."

"Do you know who murdered Matthew Hammond and Laurence Cassell?"

"No, I do not."

The needles jumped on the paper. "You had some trouble with that question," the examiner said.

Rita leaned against the observation window, staring at the needles.

"I'll rephrase the question: Are you sure you do not know who murdered Matthew Hammond and Laurence Cassell?"

Father Catalpa cracked. He began to weep. He said, "I was at confession one Friday at St. Mary's in Pewaukee, and someone came in to confess. He was behind the screen. I couldn't see him. I sit under a light. The parishioner can see my shadow, but the light makes it impossible for me to see him. Anyway, this guy told me he knew about my past, and he said some things that made me know he was telling the truth. He told me he wanted to confess to killing two boys. He told me he was sorry for what he had done. He wanted forgiveness. I heard him crying, so I let him get it out of his system. Then he became quiet. I thought he was about to confess the details of his crimes. I waited, and he didn't say anything, so I asked him what else he wanted to confess. I heard someone, so I got up to look behind the screen. There was a little girl sitting there. I asked her if she had seen where the man who had been confessing had gone, but she couldn't remember who had been there. I asked her if she had seen him. She said she had, but couldn't remember him that well."

The examiner resumed his questioning. "Do you think you know who he was?"

"I'm not positive. It didn't sound like him, but the only one who knew about my past was Bill Scroggins. I had told him. I think it was him."

"Are you positive it was Bill Scroggins who made the confession?"

"No."

The needles were steady.

"Did someone make a confession to you at St. Mary's in Pewaukee, claiming to have murdered Matthew Hammond and Laurence Cassell?"

"He didn't mention those names, but he did say he had murdered two boys."

The needles were steady.

"Are you positive you do not know for sure who that confessor was?"

"Yes."

The needles jumped.

"You had some trouble there. Did you have something to do with these crimes, even if you did not commit them yourself?"

"No."

The needles jumped.

"You had some trouble again."

"I told you, I heard a confession. That was my involvement. I feel guilty about that."

Mr. Kribble insisted that he talk to his client. The arrangement was made. Once the conference was finished, Mr. Kribble said, "We're pleased so far with the results of the polygraph, and we've decided to cancel further questions."

Charlie said, "Pleased? How can you be pleased when we're seeing deception at every turn?"

Mr. Kribble told Father Catalpa, "I'm pleased. You got it out of your system, and there's nothing you'll accomplish by saying anything more. You see they don't have anything, don't you?" Father Catalpa nodded. "Then you agree it's over?" The father nodded again. "You get some rest, and I'll have you out of here before you know it." He walked away without saying anything more.

Rita sent Father Catalpa back to a holding cell. Then staring at Charlie, she said, "I remember reading about a case in which a guy climbed up on a table saw and sawed himself in half."

"Yes?" Charlie said, perplexed.

"That's how I feel right now, Charlie," she said. "Like the guy who sawed himself in half."

He smiled. "I love it when you talk dirty to me," he said. "I'm hungry. Can we go somewhere and get something to eat?"

"Only someone big as an ox could want to eat at a time like this," she mentioned.

As they headed for their car, Charlie asked, "What's your read on this?"

"I don't know."

"You think he's telling the truth?"

"He seems to know something, but I can't figure out what it is."

They stepped into the early morning air. The sky was still dark and the streetlights were on.

Susan Hall was among the reporters who had crowded around the entrance of the Milwaukee

County Jail. They all looked tired, as if they had been waiting all night. Susan didn't look happy when she saw Rita. Rita and Charlie pushed by her, through the sea of reporters, past the shouted questions about the Catholic priest who had been arrested.

Over breakfast at Hardee's, Charlie turned pages of a newspaper he had purchased. One story in particular caught his attention, and he told her about it. There had been another report of a leopard on the loose in the vicinity of West Bend. "Up around Lizard Mound," Charlie said. She looked at him askance. Funny he should mention that, she thought. She had been following the story. Ordinarily, she wouldn't have paid any attention, but the sightings were, as Charlie said, in the area of the Potter's Field, and that had struck her as being ironic, though at the time she hadn't known why. There had been several sightings in previous weeks, and what had begun as a rumor of a leopard had taken on various forms. One lady had seen the animal at night and had described it as a panther. She had said it was coal black, so black she couldn't see its spots until the light from her flashlight had caught it. Two different farmers had seen some large cat, but they had said it was probably a cougar. Only the Sunday before, a representative from the Department of Natural Resources had admitted it might be a leopard, though if it were, it was tame. A number of people in Wisconsin had licenses to keep leopards, he had said. Now, according to Charlie, a professor at the University of Wisconsin was confirming that a new sighting indeed sounded like a leopard, which, even if it was tame, was still a wild animal. Charlie put down the newspaper. "What's wrong?" he asked.

She was taking notes on a napkin. Her thoughts had

drifted elsewhere. She said, "It just occurred to me that the mound where they found the Cassell boy was shaped like a panther. You remember?"

He stared at her. "Yeah, I do," he said, as if it were a revelation. "I never even thought about that. You're right."

"Why would a murderer leave a body there?" she asked. "He'd have to be following this story, wouldn't he?" Charlie's eyebrows raised. "What is it about the story that strikes you as being odd?"

Charlie shrugged. "Aside from all the confusion about whether it's a leopard, a panther, a cat, and so on, I don't know," he said.

"Can a leopard change its spots?" she asked, but before he could answer she suddenly stood. "Let's run down to Kenosha."

Charlie began to shovel food into his mouth. "What's up?"

"Catalpa said he couldn't be sure it was Scroggins who made the confession about the murders."

"I don't get it." He followed her out the door.

"Let's make sure we're talking about the same person."

Outside, the first traces of daylight illumined Milwaukee, showing the outline of the city against the horizon. They drove to Kenosha to show Catalpa's photograph to Mrs. Dreiser at the dry cleaners. She was there early—she said she always got there by seven. This time she was even more nervous than the first time they had talked to her. It became apparent to Rita, who was familiar with the symptoms, that the old woman might be suffering from some early stages of Alzheimer's. No, Mrs. Dreiser finally said after she had reviewed a handful of photographs, one of which was Father Catalpa, she didn't recognize any of them. Rita urged her to look again. When that didn't work, Charlie removed Father Catalpa's photograph and held it out. "Isn't this the priest that brought his clothes in to you?"

"Oh, no," she said. "Father Catalpa is bigger. He had a different—" She rubbed her chin.

"Goatee?" Charlie volunteered.

"Or maybe it was a beard. Yes, Father Catalpa had a beard. No, that's not him. You know, there was one other thing I forgot to tell you, something that seemed strange."

"What's that?" Rita asked.

Her head tilted, as if she were confused. "The priest who gave me the clothes—you're going to think this is strange—I would swear he was bigger than the clothes he gave me."

Rita added a photograph of Scroggins, despite the man being approximately the same size as Catalpa.

Mrs. Dreiser looked through the photographs again. She stopped at the Scroggins photograph, which she studied. "No," she said, trembling. She handed the photographs back. "I don't recognize any of them."

Charlie mentioned, "You stopped on one of the photographs. Did you think you recognized someone?" He held out the photographs to see if she could find the one she had stopped on.

She pulled out the photograph of Scroggins. "I thought I recognized this one at first," she said, "but I think it's because it was a new face in the ones you showed me the first round. Didn't you show me this picture the last time you were here?" He didn't say. "Oh, I'm sorry I can't be of more help."

Rita asked if Mrs. Dreiser would help them put to-

gether a police sketch. She hated that no identification
had been made. "You can do it all yourself," Rita
told her, depressed. "No one will bother you with photographs. You tell the artist what you remember."

Mrs. Dreiser said she would try.

Rita and Charlie drove Mrs. Dreiser to the Kenosha
Police Department, where they arranged for her to
meet with a police artist.

It was there that they learned a press conference
had been called about Father Catalpa. Rita and Charlie stopped to watch the coverage on Channel 12. The
bishop himself was on the sidewalk in front of the
county jail. He said he was outraged by what had happened, that attorneys had already reviewed the case
and had determined there wasn't probable cause sufficient to arrest Father Catalpa in the first place, and
that someone would answer for the false arrest. He
urged people not to jump to conclusions—he was certain the charges would be dropped before the day was
over. No, the bishop told one reporter, no priest with
a history of abusing children had ever been placed in
a parish. No, the bishop said, Father Catalpa had no
history of abusing children or any related offense.

Rita thought, he has to know about Catalpa's past.
It angered her to realize the public was being misled.

It was only eight-thirty when Rita and Charlie left
Mrs. Dreiser at the Kenosha Police Department, still
working with the police artist.

The morning sun promised a hot day. Riding into
Milwaukee, Rita noticed the haze that covered the
city, especially the south side. She told Charlie, "When
we get there, you keep your mouth shut. You had
nothing to do with this. When people ask you questions, you tell them that I told you nothing."

"I'm not going to let them hang you out to dry," he said.

"I said, I told you nothing!"

He fell silent.

At her office, she called Julie to make sure she had kept a close eye on Greg when she picked him up from school. Julie told her to quit worrying. "You're getting as bad as your brother." Then Rita called to leave a message for Mike at the Arrowhead High School, but she was told he was out sick that day. She wondered what was wrong. She tried to call him at home, hoping he would answer, but got the answering machine instead. "Hi, sorry to hear you're sick," she said in her message. "I was going to ask if we could get together to talk later, but—well, I hope you get to feeling better."

A printout of Mrs. Dreiser's "Father Catalpa" was coming in, Charlie told her. She went out to the computer terminal. As everyone gathered around the terminal to watch the image appear, it was clear the image was not Father Catalpa. Nor did it bear any resemblance to Scroggins.

Vince joked, "If you took off the beard, it looks like Jim O'Donnell."

Everyone laughed. Jim turned red, though he grinned sheepishly. Rita stared at him, remembering about his sore foot.

The office was not so jovial at one o'clock that afternoon though, when Father Catalpa was taken before Circuit Court Judge William F. Agar, Jr. Judge Agar dismissed the charges against Father Catalpa and released him. That sent a flurry of reporters in all directions.

20

As Rita sat in her office, numbed by the release of Father Catalpa, Paul appeared at the door, escorted by an old acquaintance of hers, Jim Swearingen, who worked at Justice Department headquarters in Madison. She cordially shook the firm hand of her colleague. They had come up through the ranks together, though he had always managed to stay one rank ahead of her.

Paul motioned to her chair. "Why don't we sit down for a minute?" he said. The moment they were seated, he said, "I've asked Jim to take over the Hammond-Cassell investigation."

She sighed. "Oh," was all she said. She barely heard the word herself, but Jim picked up on it right away.

"Look, I don't have to tell you how often this has happened in our department. Some of the people you would least expect have been reassigned from big cases." His voice was cool. Everything about him was refined, from his salt-and-pepper hair, closely cropped, to his mustache, neatly trimmed. She had always known him to be a smart dresser. This afternoon was no exception. He had on a navy pin-striped shirt and red tie under his tan blazer. He sat, one leg crossed over the other. His navy slacks were darker than the stripes in his shirt.

She looked at Paul. "The least you could do is tell me why," she said. "We've known each other for a long time, and I've always known you to be honest."

"The general feeling is that your work on this case just hasn't been that strong," he told her. "I think you've done some positive things, and you've come a long way, but you don't have the respect and cooperation of your investigators in this matter. You've ended up doing the entire investigation yourself. You can't do all the work yourself. You're a manager." He sighed. "Then there's the business with Scroggins and Father Catalpa.

"I can say that I spoke in your behalf. I personally thought you should stay in charge of the case."

"I'm being taken off the case completely?" She experienced a combined sensation of shock, disbelief, and embarrassment all at once. She felt disoriented.

"No," Paul said, "but right now we have a public-relations nightmare on our hands. The Catholic Church is outraged. Not only has the bishop called everyone from the governor on down, but the cardinal has also been calling. They're saying Father Catalpa is a well-respected priest and scholar, and that we've tarnished his reputation. They're demanding a public apology, and they've demanded that you be taken off the case. Now, the Catholic Church doesn't run the state Justice Department, but it's best if I get you out of the limelight. Right at this time it's crucial we restore public confidence in our investigation."

Jim said, "Rita, take it in stride. This happens more often than you realize."

"Am I off the case or not?" Rita wanted to know.

Paul told her, "I want you to take some time off and be back in the office on Monday morning. This is still your office, but it's too much for you to run the office and this investigation. Effective immediately Jim is in charge of the Hammond-Cassell investigation. You're allowed to assist him as he sees fit." He extended his hand. "Go home, Rita. Spend some time with your son. Call me on Monday." She shook his hand, then shook Jim's hand.

Outside, she felt the sunshine pushing her into the earth as she walked to her sedan and got in. For a fleeting moment she thought she would go back in and resign. No, she wouldn't give them the satisfaction of having her do that. That would be a complete triumph for Adam. She started the car but switched off the police radio. She remained composed as she drove out of the lot, got on Wisconsin Avenue, which she took past Marquette University, where she cut over to I-94. Once she was on the interstate, she wept, driving to no place in particular. In the depths of her despair, all she could think was that her life was over. Everything she had worked for was ruined. She could never face her colleagues again.

At home, she dropped into the warm sun brightening her bed, and closed her eyes. She suddenly realized how exhausted she was. She had been working around the clock. It was true. She had been doing all of the work herself because she had gotten to the point that she didn't know whom she could trust. She dozed ... She found herself in a strangely familiar forest, the Potter's Field, illuminated by moonlight. She had been called to help find a wounded leopard. It had been caught in a hunter's trap and had gnawed off a paw to escape. Animal carcasses hung in trees like meat in a slaughterhouse. That meant the leopard was nearby. It was how a leopard fed. It would take its kill up into a tree to eat.

Somewhere a bird chirped. Rita studied the trees. There in the moonlight perched a bird on a branch. Someone said, "Rita." She spun around. It was Mike Squires. He had a beard. "What are you doing here?" he asked. Wearing a hunter's outfit, he held a rifle. She couldn't speak. "We know she's wounded," he said. "She'll probably bleed to death by morning." He smiled so broadly that it stretched his beard. "We'll get her, though." He ran a hand through his hair. "Imagine an animal wanting to live so badly that she chewed off her own paw in order to escape." He laughed.

Once Mike had walked away in search of the leopard, Rita returned to her car and got a flashlight and a first-aid kit. She entered the Potter's Field again. As she walked under the trees, a droplet hit her head. She wiped her head, thinking it had begun to rain, but when she shined the light on her hand, she saw that what she had wiped off was blood. She shined the light up, hitting the leopard in the tree. Blood dripped from where the leopard's front paw had once been. While Rita stood there, shining the light up, the leopard began licking its wound, attempting to stop the flow of blood. Rita climbed to the leopard and began wrapping the wound with gauze. The leopard looked at her with large, frozen eyes. Deep in the center of each silver eye was a slit that glowed like a fire burning on the other side of frosted glass. Rita was drawn to the fire. It was warm. A loud banging startled her. Below, Mike shot wildly at the leopard, the shots barely missing her. She awoke, sweating, in the sunlight. Someone was banging at the door of the house.

At the door she found Mike. There was a day's worth of stubble on his face. "Are you all right?" he asked.

"What are you doing here?" she asked, still groggy. "I thought you were sick."

He stepped into the house. "I am, but I got your message, and I called your office to see what was wrong. They said you were gone. I got worried, so I came to see if you were all right."

"What time is it?" she asked, and stepped back to look at the grandfather clock. It was 2:38. She ran a hand through her hair. She asked, "You want a drink?"

He told her, "My stomach is still queasy—stomach flu—but I'll sit with you while you have one."

They went into the kitchen, where they sat at the table. She sipped a glass of wine while she told him about the strange dream she had had. He said he had heard about the release of Father Catalpa. "That's why I was trying to get a hold of you," he said. "I knew how you must be feeling."

She smiled. "I feel like hell," she commented.

"So what's going on?" he asked.

"I've been put on leave until Monday," she said. "I'm supposed to use that time to get my head together."

He didn't push her for information. "I got an idea. How would you like to spend the weekend on my yacht?"

She smiled again.

"I'm serious, why don't we go somewhere and get away for the weekend—you, me, and Greg?"

"I thought you were sick."

"Hey, I think it's all work and no play that's getting me sick. Nothing could be better for me than to get away."

"I think nothing could be better for you than a shower and a shave."

"Sure, lets go."

"You wish," she said, laughing. She didn't feel like laughing, but it happened anyway. It would be good to get away. She hadn't taken a trip in years. "Okay, how about Door County? Do you realize I've never been up there?"

"You're kidding. All right, let's go."

She looked at her watch. "Go home, take a shower, pack, and get back here," she said. "By that time Greg'll be home from school."

Mike left.

By the time Greg got home, she and Mike were waiting for him, ready to leave. Greg wasn't all that excited, but she didn't give him a chance for a full reaction. She had already packed for him, so she told him to grab a few things he wanted to take, and she hurried him to the car.

They took Highway 42 up Lake Michigan. It was the scenic route. Greg was all right for a while, but then he got restless and began to complain that he would have rather gotten a dog instead of going to "stupid" Door County.

That made her angry because she didn't want anything to spoil the first weekend she had had off in ages. "We'll go look at puppies next weekend," she said.

"Greg, can I come along when you guys get ready to get your dog?" Mike said, looking in the rearview.

"I'll believe it when I see it," Greg mumbled. "She's been promising me for weeks."

"It hasn't been weeks," Rita said.

"Yes, it has."

"No, it hasn't, but in any case, if we had a puppy this weekend, we wouldn't be able to go anywhere. You can't leave a new puppy home alone."

"That's fine with me."

She shifted in her seat so she could glare at him. "That's enough," she said. "You're embarrassing me in front of Mike." She looked at the green countryside sliding past the window. More grief was the last thing she needed. "I bet it makes you happy you invited us along, doesn't it?" she said to Mike.

He ignored the question. Glancing in the rearview, he said, "Greg, you should be glad she's even talking to you about a dog. When I was a boy, my father wanted a watchdog, but we couldn't afford to feed an extra mouth—I had so many brothers and sisters. So whenever we heard a noise at night, we'd bark ourselves."

Greg giggled.

"Say, Greg," Mike said, looking in the rearview again, "how about a game?"

"What kind of game?"

Greg was pushing his knees into the back of her seat, but she didn't say anything.

Mike said, "Let's play pretend. Do you know how to play that?" No, Greg had never heard of it. "What you do is you pretend you could be anyone you want to be, and you tell us who it would be." When Greg didn't say anything, Mike said, "I'll begin. Let me see, if I could be anyone I wanted to be in life, I'd be a comedian."

"You already are one," Greg said. "Look in the mirror—a face like that'd make anybody laugh." Greg giggled at himself.

Rita said, "That was rude. We don't talk like that."

Mike watched him from the rearview. "You think you're real funny, don't you?" To Rita, "Don't worry, we'll make him go last. You take your turn."

She thought for a moment. "You'll think this is real stupid," she said, "but if I had a chance to be whoever I wanted to be, I'd be a philosopher, teaching at some university like Princeton or Yale."

"I didn't know you were interested in philosophy," he told her, glancing over.

"I'm not in the academic sense. I mean, when you start naming off famous philosophers, I lose interest because as far as I'm concerned, philosophy is not about memorizing philosophers and their work, but it's about thinking new thoughts, contemplating life, and solving problems. That's probably why we have so few great philosophers. By the time they get through memorizing everyone else's work, it's like they're burnt out and don't have any energy for their own original thoughts."

Mike nodded. "It's the same in the field of English," he said. "You have all these losers running around, people who couldn't hold a job in the real world, and all they own is a bunch of mental baggage filled with other people's contributions to civilization."

She turned to Greg. "Okay, it's your turn, hon," she said.

"No, not yet," Mike told her. "First, we have to hear some of your philosophy."

She ran a hand through her hair. "Uhmmm, let me think," she said. "Okay, my philosophy has a lot to do with why I went into criminal investigation. It's like I believe there's some kind of a curse or magic spell on the world, and some of us have the ability to break the curse. I feel like I'm one of those with that ability, like I'm locked in a curse, and I have the power to break it. That's why solving crimes is so compelling to me. It breaks a part of the curse each time either I or one of my colleagues solve a case. Each time I solve a case, I come one step closer to solving the big puzzle."

He glanced at her. "Hey, that's pretty good," he said. "I nominate you as a genuine philosopher."

That made her feel better. She raised her hands and began to applaud. "Yeeaaaahhhh!" she said, clapping. "Let's give a big hand for a true philosopher." Afterward she felt embarrassed, somehow immature. She turned to Greg. "Okay, now it's your turn."

Greg said he thought the game was lame. He had a bag of books, magazines, and marking pens she had packed for him, so he picked it up and began digging through it.

They made it to the small community of Fish Creek in Door County in time for a fish boil at Pelletier's, a New England–style restaurant located in Founder's Square. Mike asked Rita if she wanted to stop. She didn't come all the way to Door County to miss a famous fish boil, she told him. Greg said he hated fish.

The streets around Founder's Square were packed with cars, so Mike had to park several blocks from Pelletier's. He, Rita, and Greg walked back to the restaurant, passing a row of specialty shops. It was cool that afternoon, not cold. In the air was the smell of burning wood from the fish boil. Above the sounds of people were sounds of wood popping in a fire.

"I love the smell of burning wood," Mike said.

"I do too," Rita said. "I hope where we stay has a fireplace. Say, didn't you tell me you were an outdoors person?"

"I love the outdoors." To Greg, Mike said, "Greg, you and I'll have to go fishing some time. Would you like that?"

"Sure." Greg seemed more enthusiastic.

Mike asked her, "Did your parents ever take you camping or fishing when you were a kid?"

Rita didn't like to think about her past. "I can't remember us doing that much as a family when I was growing up," she said.

"That's too bad," he said. He asked Greg, "Have you ever been camping?"

"No."

"Surely you've been fishing, though."

"Not really," he said. "I went to summer camp last summer and we fished, but I didn't catch anything."

"I know some places where you're guaranteed to catch something," Mike told him. "I'll take you over to Okauchee Lake. There you throw a piece of bread in the water and a hundred fish come after it."

Greg smiled.

"I'm serious."

Inside the crowded restaurant, Mike bought two tickets for the fish boil while Rita asked for a menu. She gave it to Greg. "See," she said, "there's plenty here for you to eat."

Mike handed her a glass of wine. She told him, "Greg's probably the only one who'll eat well tonight."

Mike nodded.

The waitress told them there would be about a forty-minute wait for dinner.

Mike asked, "You want to go out and watch the boil?"

They went out on the patio, which was filled with people watching an aproned man who was standing near a huge black kettle that had burning wood leaning against it. The wood feebly held in a roaring fire. The fire crackled and popped. The kettle had a layer of steam on it. Drinking glasses of wine, Rita and Mike drew near so they could hear the cook tell a group of senior citizens about the process. The cook picked up a pan of potatoes. "First I pour in the potatoes," he said. "They take about thirty minutes to cook." He poured the potatoes into a basket in the boiling water. "Later, I'll put in the onions—they only take about twelve minutes—then, the fish. It cooks in about ten."

"What kind of wood do you use?" one woman asked.

"Any kind we can get," he said. The crowd laughed.

"What kind of fish?" a gray-haired man asked.

"Any kind they can get," Mike spoke up. The crowd laughed. Rita slapped his arm.

"Whitefish," the cook said. "Our supplier gives us a fresh batch each day."

Greg asked if he could go into one of the shops. She gave him ten dollars and told him not to go anyplace else. He vanished. To her surprise, she realized she was no longer worried about him. It was as if all the danger had been left behind.

Mike said in a low voice, "This is the first time I've seen you where you look like you're having a good time."

"I am having a good time."

"Let's sit down and talk."

They withdrew from the crowd.

A shop caught her attention. "Can we go over here for a minute?" she asked. "I want to get a souvenir. We'll be back by the time the water boils over."

"For some reason I get the feeling you don't want to talk," he said, following her.

"You know what I've heard a lot about is Door County cherry pie," she said, ignoring his comment. No, she didn't want to talk—at least not about anything serious. That was one of the reasons she had agreed to come with him. She knew he was seldom serious about anything, and she could forget her problems for the weekend. When he mentioned they could talk, she became worried he might try to talk about something she wanted to forget. "You can bet I'm going to get a piece of it for dessert."

In the shop, she bought a small soapstone statue of a woman lifting a child. The statue fit conveniently in her purse. Outside on the porch she told Mike that after dinner she wanted to see if she could find a sweatshirt, one with Door County on it. They went back to the fish boil, where the cook was just pouring fuel oil over the fire. Flames jumped up around the kettle; water boiled over into the flames. Greg returned. He had spent the ten dollars she had given him on candy. His mouth was full of bubble gum. She told him not to eat anything else before supper.

They went inside the restaurant and got seats at a table near the windows. Plates of food were delivered to Rita and Mike. Greg's hamburger arrived a few minutes later. The restaurant was noisy with the sound of conversations, dishes rattling, and silverware clinking. Rita tasted her fish, Mike his. "What do you think?" she asked, reserving comment.

He shook his head. "I'm not that crazy about it," he said.

She laughed. "Neither am I," she said. "Maybe the cherry pie will be better."

Greg said the hamburger was great. They laughed at him. Mike tried to steal some of the hamburger, but Greg kept it guarded.

Mike and Rita picked at their food and then ordered cherry pie. It was good but not great.

Later, looking for sweatshirts at a shop near the lake, Mike said, "I think the hype about the fish boils and cherry pie has mostly to do with the ambience."

Rita gave him a signal to leave the shop. Outside she said, "I refuse to pay sixty dollars for a sweatshirt."

They drove to Egg Harbor, where they got a three-bedroom suite for the night. It had a fireplace. Greg claimed the loft bedroom. As they unpacked, Mike asked them if they had brought their swim suits. She said she would look like a beached whale if she put on a suit, but that she would sit with him near the pool if he wanted to swim. He asked if Greg wanted to swim. Greg immediately changed into a pair of cutoffs.

At the pool, Greg and Mike were wild, splashing and yelling. Mike had a chest full of gray hair, but he seemed full of vitality. He and Greg tried to see who could swim the farthest underwater. Rita was proud Greg could swim so well. The years of swimming lessons had paid off. When it came time to get out of the water, Greg didn't want to get out. He wanted to stay and play.

Mike got out. He told Greg there would be other opportunities to swim.

Greg, getting out of the pool, said he wished his mother was as much fun as Mike. She grabbed him and threw him back in the water. He liked that.

How about a walk down to the lake? Mike wanted to know, drying himself with a towel. Rita said that would be fun. He and Greg dressed.

They went outside in the cool air and followed a wooded path. Greg ran ahead. Mike asked her, "Why are you so quiet?"

Why does he keep pushing me to talk? she wondered. Why can't he just look around at the scenery? "Why do you keep grilling me?" she asked.

He led the way on a narrow stretch of path. "I don't want to sound like a shrink," he said, "but it's not good to keep things locked up inside."

"You mean you would actually want to talk about something serious?"

"I can get serious, you know."

She laughed.

"Oh, you're afraid I might laugh at you." She didn't say. "I would never demean someone else when I have such problems of my own."

The path opened to the lake. Mike walked backward, facing her. Greg started throwing rocks into the lake.

Mike took her hand. He didn't seem comfortable walking hand in hand—he didn't strike her as the romantic type—but he at least was making an effort. They went out on a pier. There was a woman battening down the hatches of a sailboat. Rita asked her, "Do you ever spend the night on the lake?"

The woman, about Rita's age, looked up from

where she stooped on the large sailboat. "Sure," she said.

"I bet it's great," Rita added, looking at the boat.

"It's like nothing you've ever experienced," the woman said. She looked out at the bay. The sun had gone down. It would be dark soon. "Of course, it's nothing like the bay here. Lake Michigan is a lot rougher. You have to like that sort of thing." She returned to her work.

Rita and Mike went out to the end of the pier, where they watched Greg skip rocks on the lake. Mike again asked her if she felt like talking.

Irritated, she said, "So what do you want to talk about? About how my father treated me like crap, except when he was about to rape me. Or how my ex-husband was a loser who took out his frustrations on Greg. Or how I've blown an investigation involving a serial killer, and falsely arrested a Roman Catholic priest. Or how I've been relieved as chief investigator. Which of those things would you like me to talk about?"

He raised his hands as if she had aimed a gun at him and whistled. "I didn't mean to push," he said. "Please don't shoot."

She shook her head. "I knew you couldn't be serious for two minutes."

He stared. "Have I told you that I find you incredibly attractive?"

She stared back. "That's just great! Now you want to get serious again. Next thing I know you'll be wanting to go to bed with me."

He smiled. "You like me, don't you?"

She rolled her eyes and gave a .crooked grin. "You're crazy! That's what you are. You make me laugh. That's the only reason I like you if I like you at all."

He laughed and gave her a hug. He had powerful arms.

As they walked back to shore, hand in hand, he said, "So what's the deal with this priest?"

She told him some of the details about Father Catalpa. She said, "I know you'd never say anything about this, but what amazes me is how someone could molest children in the Catholic Church and get away with it. It's like I'm thinking the same thing I've already been told: How did this guy ever end up around children again?"

"You think he murdered those boys?" Mike asked.

"I don't know about that, but it almost seems that he contributed to an environment that allowed something like this to happen."

Greg went to the shore and began to collect shells. He brought some to Mike, who took time to examine each one carefully. That made Rita interested, more than she might otherwise have been. As she watched Mike give his undivided attention to Greg, she had a momentary urge to tell him other things—thought she would feel better if she could get everything out in the open. She found herself trembling. She turned her back to the bay. "I'm getting cold," she said. "You want to head back?"

He pointed at Egg Harbor. "Let's go up and get a drink and something to munch on." They headed up the hill to Jill's Bar & Grill.

For the better part of a half hour, Mike played video games with Greg; then he gave Greg a handful of quarters and went to sit down in the bar with Rita. They sat at a table under a crystal lamp. Once they

had ordered drinks and hors d'oeuvres, Rita began to
tell him more about the case.

Drinks arrived, and he paid for them. She sipped
her wine. She told him everything. It felt good to tell
someone all that was on her mind.

They drank in silence for a couple of moments. A
plate of nachos arrived. She lifted a nacho, whose
cheese stretched from the plate to her mouth. Chewing, she asked, "Do you think I'm right—how I handled things?"

He touched her lip to remove a string of cheese
that had been left there. He said, "We all make mistakes here and there."

"So, you're like the others? You think I haven't
been doing a good job either?"

"No, I didn't say that at all," he told her. "I said
we all make mistakes. The only thing that counts is
that we do the best we can. As serious as you get
about your work, I'd say you've done a damn good
job. Even the best at what he or she does makes mistakes. We're all human. It doesn't make any difference
what anyone else thinks. If it wasn't you that slipped
a place or two, it would have been someone else who
did it. What difference does it make whether it's you
or someone else? No one can accuse you of giving
less than a hundred percent of yourself."

"But why do people have to be so mean and
back-stabbing?"

He shook his head. "You know, the people who
are the supercritical ones are the ones who never do
anything themselves—don't even have the courage to
do it themselves."

She thought that was a good point. Adam was that

way. He could offer plenty of criticism, but he never did much of anything himself.

They would have had more to say on the topic, but Greg returned. He said he was hungry. In a matter of minutes, he had consumed the remaining nachos.

While she watched him eat, Mike pulled her forward and met her lips with his lips, halfway over the table.

"Sick," Greg said.

"You want to dance?" Mike asked. There was a jukebox near the door.

"No, thanks," Greg said.

Rita laughed.

Mike took Greg by the arm. "A real wise guy," he said.

Together Mike and Rita went to the jukebox to look at the selections. "That's what I love about these out-of-the-way places," he told her. "They have the oldies but goodies." He pointed at "Just my Imagination," by The Temptations.

There was no dance floor, but Mike and Rita found a space between two tables in order to hold each other and dance. As they danced, she looked straight into his eyes; he looked at her.

"Mom, you guys are embarrassing me," Greg whispered. He was standing next to them. "Can we get out of here?"

On their way out the door, Mike said, "Greg, I think I saw a basketball hoop at the place we're staying. You want to play?"

"Sure."

"Don't give in to him," she said. "Otherwise, he'll bug the hell out of you."

Mike smiled and pulled her close.

They headed back to the resort. Mike checked out a basketball from the office, and he and Greg went out to the court, which was illuminated by floodlights. As she watched them play, she remembered that at one time it had been the same way with Steve. At one time Steve had been nice too. At one time he had devoted a lot of time and attention to Greg.

At first Mike and Greg played games like Horse and Pig, but then they played one-on-one. Greg, full of energy, had Mike hustling. Then Mike accidentally ran into Greg, which sent him flying. Greg let out a scream as he sprawled across the pavement. Terror-striken, Rita ran to him. Mike was trying to apologize, but she pushed him out of the way. She held her son, who was on the verge of tears. "Are you all right?" she asked.

"My legs" was all he said.

They returned to the room, where she helped him clean the wounds: two skinned knees and scraped palms. It was the first time she realized Mike had the power to hurt her son.

Mike apologized to Greg, who took the apology in stride. He said, "It's all right."

Mike patted his back. "Come on, you cod fish, let's take the basketball back. Say, you're a damned good ball player. . . ."

She watched them head for the office. Mike was limping.

In their room, they rented the movie *Hunt for Red October*. It was an old movie, but none of the three of them had seen it. Greg fell asleep halfway through the movie. Then, the movie playing in the background, Mike and Rita talked in front of the fire.

He said, "You remember how it was when you were

little and you fell down?" She didn't say. "You got right back up. It was like it hurt, but the hurt went away instantly. Greg took a pretty hard fall out there, but he bounced right back. That was really something when he was able to accept my apology like he did. For me, had someone knocked me down, I'd have probably been mad for a couple days or so." Still she didn't say anything. "Tomorrow I'm going to be damned sore from my workout. I can already feel it."

She smiled.

"I don't know about you, but so far this has been a lot of fun," he said.

"Yes, it's beautiful up here," she told him.

"How would you like to live like this year round?"

"Who wouldn't?" She watched the fire.

There was an awkward pause.

He took her hand and stroked the back of it. Then he touched her face. They kissed. Even after the long kiss, their faces remained very close to each other. His fingers outlined her jaw; they went down her neck. His hand softly touched her breast. She could feel her breast rising to his hand. They kissed again. This time her tongue met his. It had been a long time since she had been so attracted to a man.

"Do you want to go to bed?" he whispered.

"Yes."

In the dark bedroom, she undressed and crawled into bed with him. He was warm. He touched her gently. It felt good to be naked with him. They made love.

Later, he said, "You're the first woman I've made love to since my wife left me twenty-five years or so ago."

She laughed. "What? You haven't made love to a woman in twenty-five or so years?"

He laughed too. "Why don't you tell the whole world?" he said. "Sssshhhhhh!" She giggled. He lowered his voice. "What I meant was that I've—well, you know what I've done, but it's not what I call making love."

She was lying in his arm, her head against his shoulder. "I know what you mean." She didn't know why she said it, but she said, "Tell me about your first wife."

"That's a kinky question," he said.

Laughing, she slapped him.

He told how he had married his high school sweetheart, Cheryl Cromer. "Do you know the Cromers?" he asked.

Yes, she knew them, she said, "but I didn't know her personally. Wait! Wait! I know the one you're talking about. You married her?"

"You don't have to get rude about it."

She laughed. "No, I didn't mean it that way," she said. "I remember when the Cromer girl was getting married. Some of my friends and I peeked in the window of her house and saw her when she was modeling her wedding gown. I remember how pretty she was."

"Well, I was the one she married," he continued. He went on to tell about how the relationship had been fun in the beginning. They had laughed at each other's mistakes, had gotten in each other's way, and were generally clumsy at living together. "It's like when you're young, you're proud to be married. You like it when people look at you with envy and see you as having this legitimate relationship." He told how within a short time, a year at most, the novelty of the marriage had worn off. "We began having arguments about housework, et cetera. I was a slob. I admit it. She wanted to grow up. I wanted to remain a kid. I was out getting drunk, raising hell, staying out all hours of the night. Next thing I know, she was talking a lot about an older guy where she worked. I was oblivious to it. I didn't give a damn." He laughed. "You know, when she asked for a divorce, I was as nice as I could be—like her best friend." He gave a hard breath through his nose. "I tried to act mature, told her I understood, and how a divorce was probably the best thing. I was trying to be an adult. Next thing I know, she was living with some other guy, and I'm sitting there like a chump, saying, hey, she really did it. That's when it hit me like a ton of bricks. I went from being proud that I was in an adult relationship to being embarrassed that my wife had moved in with another man."

"Maybe she just wasn't right for you."

"Oh, she was right. You couldn't ask for a better person—yourself excluded, of course—but she wanted something real, and I was stuck in some imaginary world. Marriage to me was a game. Of course, I've grown up a lot since then." He always said it.

She laughed. "You could have fooled me."

He sat up.

"What's wrong?"

"Heartburn."

She wondered if there was another reason. Had she offended him? Maybe he didn't want to be lying by her. "Do you still love her?" she asked.

"You promise you won't get mad if I say this?"

"Promise."

He lay back down again. This time they lay apart.

"What scares me is that I don't think I've ever really been in love with anyone, period," he said. "I mean, I've been infatuated with people, but I've never really felt I've been in love. I think if I had a son or a daughter, that would be different. I think I could love a son or a daughter. That's what bothers me about us."

"That you don't love me?"

"No, I guess what scares me is that I'm afraid I could fall in love with you, but that I wouldn't be able to live up to what you would want in a relationship." He was silent for a long time. She thought he was staring at the ceiling, or maybe he was staring into darkness, no real object in mind. "I'm not very good at serious relationships."

Rita touched his hand. "Don't worry, you're doing fine," she told him.

"Oh, I know I'm good at making love," he told her. "That's not what worries me."

She slapped him again. "Sometimes you're an ass." She got out of bed and began to gather up her clothes.

"Where you going?" he asked.

"Back to my own bed," she told him.

"Rita—"

At the door, she stopped.

"I've been alone for so long that I don't quite know how to say this, but this trip has felt right for me."

"Me too." She said good night and went to her own room.

In the middle of the night, she was awakened by Greg, who cried out in his sleep. She hurried to where he slept on the sofa. In his sleep he cried, "Give it back! I won't tell. No."

She held him. "It's all right," she said.

"Hi, Mom," he said pleasantly.

Mike was right. One could genuinely love one's own child. She laughed. "What were you dreaming?" she asked.

He thought for a moment. "I can't remember." He yawned.

She kissed him on the forehead. "Go back to sleep," she whispered, and put a blanket over him.

In the darkness, she bumped into Mike, startling her.

"Is everything all right?" he asked, holding her until she could regain her balance.

"Yeah, he was having bad dreams. What are you doing up?"

"I heard the commotion and came to see what was the matter."

"Everything's okay." She said good night again and went back to bed. But she couldn't sleep. Greg had not had nightmares for a long time, not since the days when Steve had still haunted their lives. She wondered if the fall had had anything to do with it. She drifted into a turbulent sleep, trying not to feel guilty about going to bed with Mike.

Greg couldn't remember anything in the morning, couldn't even remember her waking him up.

They spent another day visiting the specialty shops before driving to Gills Rock for lunch at a restaurant that overlooked the bay. Mike asked her if she wanted to take the ferry out to Washington Island. She told him, not really, but Greg complained, so she gave in. She said she first needed to call her answering machine to check for messages. She was hoping that Paul had called, perhaps to change his mind about her.

There was a message from Julie. Sean was in the

hospital at St. Luke's. The doctor was running some tests. Rita got the number for St. Luke's and called the hospital. The receptionist connected her to Sean's room. Julie answered. What's wrong? Rita wanted to know. "Is everything all right?"

"Where are you?" Julie asked. "I've been trying to get a hold of you."

She told her.

"Sean was having abdominal pain, so the doctor admitted him to run some tests."

Knowing Sean was near the phone, Rita didn't ask a lot of questions. She said, "We'll start back."

"You don't have to do that," Julie said. "There's no sense running back here until we get the lab results. The doctor says he won't know them until Monday."

"That's okay. I'd like to be there."

As she put down the phone, she knew that Sean's leukemia had returned. It was another sudden disappointment in her life. Only a few days before, she had felt on top of the world. Now it seemed her entire world was collapsing around her. And she had been so encouraged by Sean's year of remission. The doctors had been so encouraging. They had said it was a good sign.

Once Mike had heard about Sean, he suggested immediately that they return to Milwaukee. He put his arm around her and walked her to the car.

In the car, Greg asked a lot of questions about Sean and leukemia. He asked so many questions that Rita finally said, "Greg, Mom needs time to think."

No one said much for a while. For the most part she stared out her window. Now and then she wiped tears from her eyes. She wondered if she was crying about Sean, or whether it was a combination of events that had finally caused her to break down. She didn't care. The tears flowed.

Around Manitowoc, she finally spoke: "Greg, how you doing, hon?" She wiped her eyes with a tissue.

"Fine."

"Hold my hand," she said, reaching out without looking at him.

He took her hand. His fingers were small, warm and soft.

"Do you think it hurts when you have leukemia?" he asked.

She didn't say. In fact, no one said anything for a long time again. That's how the trip back went.

As they were riding through Milwaukee, she felt guilty for having gone away for the weekend. She thought if she hadn't left, maybe Sean wouldn't have ended up in the hospital—as if she were being punished for her selfishness. But she knew that was ridiculous.

In the lobby of St. Luke's Hospital, on the south side of Milwaukee, Rita got the room number for Sean. He was in a general medical wing, on the sixth floor. She asked Mike if he would watch Greg while she went up to see her brother. He nodded.

Julie had been crying. Her face was puffy, her eyes glazed. Rita gave her a hug. Sean was dozing. He looked tired, but he always looked that way. He looked pale too.

Rita produced the soapstone statue from her purse, the statue of a woman lifting a child. "Sean, I brought you something," she said. It was all she could think to say. She knew she hadn't bought the statue for him, but she felt it was only appropriate to give him a gift.

He opened his eyes and looked at the statue. He

smiled. With the switch at the side of the bed, he raised the head of his bed. "What are you doing here? I thought you were up in Door County."

"I know, but I wanted to be here with you."

"Nonsense."

"So, how are you feeling?"

"My belly's hurting a little, but I'm doing all right. The doctor thought I should be here a couple of days while he ran tests."

"How's your blood work look?"

"The doctor said there are a couple of abnormal values, but it's not leukemia."

Rita felt a sense of relief. They talked for a while, then she and Julie went out in the hall. Rita said, "Tell me again what the doctor told you."

"He said he wanted to run some tests and keep him here for a couple of days. I told you not to come back." Tears began streaming down her face. Rita hugged her. "I'm scared," Julie said.

Rita held her tightly. "No sense thinking the worst," she said, though she was thinking the same thing. The way things had been going in her life, the worst was all she could think about.

21

Rita walked along the city's lakefront at the break of day. The morning, heavy with the smell of fish, was extremely quiet. She still had a bad feeling about Sean.

She stopped to study the lake. About twenty feet from where she stood, out in the water, was a large white fish, dead on its back, floating. Even when the waves washed in to shore, the fish didn't seem to move any closer to where she stood. It simply rose and dropped behind each new wave, bobbing, as it were, in front of her eyes.

Rita took off her shoes and socks and rolled up her pant legs. The sand was cold. She could feel its tug, as if trying to pull her into the earth. Walking along the beach, leaving the dead fish behind, she felt small, insignificant compared to the backdrop of the city, a place legend held as "Mahauwaukseepe," home of the Potawatomi Indians. The name was supposed to mean "the gathering place by the river"—presumably referring to the Milwaukee River, though the river was now so polluted that it was hardly a suitable gathering place.

C.N. Bean

She became conscious of the morning traffic along Lincoln Memorial Drive. It brought her back to the present moment. Her feet were numb. She tried to brush off the sand so she could get on her socks, but even when she did, she could feel the sand in them. She looked at her watch: 6:15. She wanted to call Greg, but decided he would think she was checking up on him. He had spent the night with Daniel Christensen, one of his friends at school. Rita had called Daniel's mother, Cheryl, and had asked her if Greg could spend a couple of nights while Sean was in the hospital. As it was, Rita had spent most of Sunday night at Sean's bedside. The nurses had brought Julie a cot to sleep on, but Rita had dozed off and on in a chair.

In the car, she felt like her world was wrecked, all that she had worked so hard to put together. She had been dismissed as lead investigator of the Hammond-Cassell investigation. That was bad enough. But to make matters worse, both Scroggins and Catalpa were walking free because of her. Had I been patient, she thought, I might have discovered the truth. They knew something. She was sure of that. They had somehow been involved. Two cigarette butts proved it. One matched Scroggins' saliva and the other matched Catalpa's. Catalpa's shoe print had been found at the Hammond scene. Scroggins' drug had been found in Larry Cassell. There was an engagement ring. Yet it was all circumstantial. The planner of the crimes was careful. No direct evidence. Nothing directly linking either Scroggins or Catalpa to Hammond or Cassell.

Not only did she feel she had failed Matthew Hammond and Larry Cassell, but she now felt she had

failed Sean. Her bone marrow was being rejected—
she was sure it was. During the night Julie had told
her, "Don't worry, Rita, I'm starting to have a good
feeling about this," but Rita didn't think it would be
that way, not the way things were going in her life at
the present time. What was happening to Sean was a
bad sign.

She drove to St. Camillus to see her mother, to tell
her the news. Eva was restrained in a wheelchair beside her bed. Rita knelt before her. "Mom."

Eva groaned.

"It's me. Do you know who I am?"

Eva didn't say. She only groaned. Next thing Rita
knew, Eva began to cry, as a child would. Then she
stopped crying as quickly as she had started. She
stared at Rita.

Rita said, "Mom, Sean's in the hospital."

Eva began to cry again. Then she stopped crying.

Rita presumed one of the nurses had told her the
news about Sean.

Mrs. McGlaughlin spoke up: "Child, she doesn't
know who you are. She's like that all the time now."

Rita rose. Her mother's eyes followed her. Rita
kissed her forehead. Eva began to cry again. Before
Rita had gotten out of the room, her mother had
fallen silent.

From St. Camillus, she drove to the office, where
she had to pass through a crowd of protesters, including the Cassell family and new relatives, in order to
get inside the building. Rather than saying anything,
they all stared at her in silence, as if she herself had
killed their son. That made her angry. What had she
done to hurt them, or to harm the investigation?
Hadn't she done everything to solve the case? They

parted to let her through, and she might have made it safely inside had not Susan Hall appeared, holding a microphone. Behind her was a TV-6 camera. Susan said, "Captain Trible, is it true you've been fired from the Hammond-Cassell investigation?"

Rita tried to push her way into the building.

Susan blocked her way. She persisted with her questions: "Is it true the Catholic Church of Milwaukee has filed a complaint against you in the matter of the false arrest of the Catholic priest Father Thaddeus Catalpa?"

Larry's grandfather, Bud Cassell, grabbed Rita's arm. He said, "Why don't you answer the lady? Why don't you tell her how you weren't doing your job and got our grandson killed? Why don't you tell her?"

Rita stared at the old man's hand that held her. Ralph pulled Bud away, saying, "No, no, don't get yourself in trouble over her. She's got plenty enough problems on her hands as it is." Bud released her.

She made it inside the building, where she immediately glared at the guard who was stationed in the lobby. He seemed to sense her rage because he said, "Is everything all right, Captain?" She walked past him, heading for the elevators. "I was going to give you a couple more seconds, and if they were still blocking your way I was going to be out there—"

She got on the elevator. The doors closed. Never had she felt so humiliated.

All eyes were on her as she walked through the CID main office. She went straight to her private office without saying anything to anyone, not even to Bev, who said, "Hello, Rita," and shook her head solemnly.

While she was in her office, pondering the solitude,

there came a tap at the door. "What is it?" she called out.

Charlie entered and closed the door behind him. He didn't sit down. "How you holding up?" he asked.

She told him, "It's best if you're not seen hanging around me. You stick with Jim Swearingen. He's a good person. He'll take care of you."

"For what it's worth, he has nothing but good things to say about you and how you've handled this case."

She looked at him.

"I heard Paul ask him if you'd done anything improper on the case, and he told Paul you'd done things strictly by the book."

She felt better.

He sat down and leaned forward in his chair. "How's Sean?" he asked.

"We'll know today," she said. "The doctor's supposed to see him in a little while."

"Can Claudia and I help in any way—taking care of Greg, or anything?"

She gave half a smile. "That's kind of you," she said softly. "I'll let you know—"

There came another tap on the door. Jim Swearingen stuck his head in. He was smiling. "Hi," he said. "Got a moment?"

She motioned him in.

Charlie stood and said, "I'll talk to you later." He left the office.

Jim sat down. "I heard about Sean," he said. "How's he doing?"

She shrugged. "As I was telling Charlie, we're not sure yet. The doctor will be in to see him this morning."

"What are you doing here, then?"

"I had to get away from the hospital for a while," she told him. "I was there all night. It was closing in on me." She looked at him, knowing their small talk was preliminary to his giving her more bad news. Perhaps he had come to tell her privately how she had bungled the case, but that he had stood up for her.

Sure enough, he came right to the point: "I've been reviewing this investigation all weekend." She knew that was why he was in her office. "Isn't this the damnest case you've ever seen?"

She ran a hand through her hair.

"We must be overlooking something."

Was he using "we" in such a manner as to imply she had overlooked something? she wondered.

"What's your theory?"

She studied him. He seemed sincere. She decided to tell him what was bothering her, what she had been thinking about all weekend. "Would you do me a favor?" she asked. The most he could do was say no, she thought.

"What's up?"

"Do you think you could get another search warrant for Scroggins' place?"

"What are we looking for?"

"A drug. Largactil."

"We already know it's been prescribed to him in the past."

"O'Donnell says he saw a medicine bottle of it at the house, though we never picked it up. I want you to confiscate the bottle."

"Why?"

"For fingerprints."

Jim smiled. "If someone's framing him, you think there might be prints on the bottle?"

She hadn't mentioned a frame, but she was glad he had picked up on it. At least it told her she wasn't being paranoid. "It's worth a try."

"Who do you think it is—Catalpa?"

She shook her head. "We already know he's a suspect," she told him. "Even if his prints were on the bottle, it wouldn't advance your case very far."

"What's this 'your' case? Our case. We wouldn't be this far if it hadn't been for you."

"I thought I was out of the picture."

He shook his head. "Paul made me chief investigator as an administrative shift to satisfy critics, not because you had done anything wrong. He didn't say we couldn't work together on the investigation."

She didn't say anything. She was still embarrassed that she had been replaced as chief investigator, but at least the person who had replaced her was still treating her with respect.

He asked, "So, who do you think it is?"

She didn't say. Instead she asked him the same question. "Who do you think it is?"

He stared at her. "I think it's someone in this office," he said in a low voice.

She smiled. They were thinking along the same lines.

"Someone's trying to set you up. Whoever's doing this knows police procedure to a T."

Excited, she said, "I know, I've been thinking the same thing, but I was afraid to say anything. It seems like it's someone who knows this case inside out and is leaving a whole trail of leads for us. The question is, how do we get him?" She wanted to say O'Donnell's name, but she refrained from doing so.

"I like your suggestion about the medicine bottle,"

he told her. "My idea is to check the bottle for prints, and then run it against everyone in the office."

She nodded. She liked the idea.

"Anyone else you want me to run?"

She wrote a list of names on a slip of paper and handed it to him.

As he looked at it, he asked, "Who's Michael Squires?"

She hated to put the name on the list, but she had to check everyone. She couldn't afford to make any more mistakes, not with a killer on the loose and Greg possibly in danger. "Call him a placebo," she said.

"Come on, who is he?"

"Someone who introduced himself to me the morning after Matthew was found. An old friend of the family. I swear, don't ever let anyone know his name's on that list unless you come up with a set of prints you can't account for."

Jim stood. "Stop worrying," he said. At the door, he asked, "How did we find out Scroggins was taking Largactil?"

"Jim O'Donnell noticed the bottle during our first search," she said. "He and Adam."

"Then I'm assuming his fingerprints are probably on the bottle."

"We all had plastic gloves on," she said. "I made sure of that. His prints better not be on the bottle."

He smiled. "By the book," he said. "That's what I like about you. Rita, get the hell out of here. Go be with your brother."

"One other thing," she said.

He waited at the door.

She motioned for him to move closer. He did. She said, "I don't want to sound paranoid, but now that you mention it, maybe we should be extra careful with this."

"What are you thinking?"

"You know Jerry Grier down in Narcotics?"

"Sure."

"He's been a friend for a long time. When you get the bottle, take it to him and ask him to run the prints. I think it'd be better if no one in our office has access to it. Ask him as a favor to me, and have him keep it strictly confidential."

"I'll be the only one who touches it, and I'll personally turn it over to him." Jim left the office.

She tried to catch up on some paperwork, but she couldn't concentrate, so she went back to St. Luke's and sat with Sean while Julie went to the hospital coffee shop and then to have her hair done. Rita knew what it was like to sit for too long in a hospital room.

In the afternoon, Julie called the doctor's nurse and asked when the doctor would be visiting Sean. The nurse told her the doctor was running behind in his rounds and would be there as soon as he could.

Rita said she was going to run by the school to meet Greg, who would be spending another night at the Christensen house. She also needed to pack him a bag of clothes, she said.

At home, she threw some things in an overnight bag for Greg. She drove to his school. She was waiting at the door when he came to get on the bus. "I'm sorry you have to spend another night with the Christensens," she said. She looked around. "Where's Daniel?"

"He was getting things out of his locker. He's coming. I thought you said we were going to look for a dog," he said, disappointment in his eyes.

"Your Uncle Sean's still in the hospital."

"Mom, you promised!"

She grabbed him by the arm. "Listen, I said your uncle is still in the hospital. I don't have time to argue." She looked around. She noticed others were looking at her. "Here's a bag I packed for you."

Dejected, he took it and said, "You lied."

She found herself pulling him to the car.

"Mom, I'm going to miss the bus!" he said.

"Listen here," she told him as she opened the car door and shoved him inside. "You do not act that way in public, do you understand me?"

When she was beside him and had closed the door, he said, "I hate you."

She slapped his face. The moment she saw her red hand print on his cheek, she was terrified and hugged him. "I'm sorry," she said. "Oh, God, I'm so sorry. I didn't mean to do that." He had begun to cry, which he seldom did, not an audible cry but the kind of crying that leaves a steady stream of tears running down one's face. What's happening to me? she wondered. She told herself she would rather lose all that she had than to hurt her own son.

"I hate my whole life," he told her.

"Don't ever say that," she said, still holding him. All she could think of was Bobby Ruble.

"Well, I do." Now his crying was audible. "You never let me do anything, you're never home, and then when you promise me stuff, you never keep your promises. It's like you care about everything but me."

She could feel his warm, damp face against her chest.

"Here." She pushed him away and scribbled out a note. She held it out. She looked over at the buses. Daniel Christensen was at the doors to one of them, looking in her direction. "Hurry," she said, "the bus is waiting."

"What's that?" he asked, wiping his tears and taking the note.

"A note for your bus driver tomorrow. It says I'll be picking you up after school tomorrow, so you won't be on the bus."

"What does that mean?"

"You know exactly what it means."

"We can go get a dog?"

"Yes. It means that if I don't pick you up, you won't have a ride home, and you know I'd never leave you standing at school without a ride."

He put the note in his shirt pocket.

"Now go get on the bus before it leaves without you," she said. She used a tissue to wipe the tears from his face. She kissed his cheek. He got out of the car and ran to the bus.

Once Greg was on the bus, she drove by Mike's house, a small house in a neighborhood on a hill in Hartland. Her conscience was bothering her. Common sense told her that Mike would never know she had put his name on a list, and that it would be better if she didn't tell him. Yet she knew the investigation was of such a nature that everyone close to it had to be eliminated as a suspect, herself included. She was certain that Mike would take it all in stride. It would be as if a health professional contracted some type of contagious disease from her work environment. Her entire family, and probably anyone she came into close contact with, would be tested for contamination. He was not a suspect, and he would laugh it off, she was sure.

At she drove up to the house, she realized she had never been inside. Once they had stopped briefly there, but she had waited in the car while he ran in to get his checkbook. They were in a hurry on that occasion, because they were trying to get to the theater before the movie started. Why hasn't he ever invited me in? she wondered, suddenly troubled at how little she really knew about Mike.

The house looked deserted. She made a U-turn in the cul-de-sac. She drove slowly by the house again, almost convinced it would be better not to say anything. There was a small sailboat beside the house, but other than that the yard and house were nondescript, except that there was no porch for the front door. What if I hurt his feelings? she wondered.

It was too late. Mike happened to open the front door and step out at that moment, carrying a large black athletic bag, the kind coaches carry equipment in. She stopped the car. Out of curiosity she dug through the case on the seat beside her, finding the composite drawing Mrs. Dreiser had helped produce. The individual in the drawing had a fuller face than Mike's, but there was a slight resemblance. She hated herself for thinking so because she knew that composite drawings tended to be extremely rough and vague. They were often more of a psychological tool than an identification aid. Psychologically the public was reassured of a productive investigation when the police issued a composite drawing, which was why police often distribute such drawings, no matter how unreliable they are. She got out of the car.

When he saw her, he was visibly surprised, as if to say "what are you doing here?" "Hi," he said. "This is a pleasant surprise. I'd invite you in, but I have to run this equipment over to school." He raised the bag. It looked heavy.

"That's okay, I was just stopping by to say hello."
She joined him.

"How's Sean?"

"We're still waiting for the doctor to get by," she
said. She nodded at the bag he was holding. "I thought
the basketball season was over."

"What? Oh, yes. Yes, that season's over." He
smiled. "Now it's baseball. It's one thing after another
for a world-famous coach."

She asked, "How was your day?"

He gave a slight laugh. "Are you serious? The kids
about drove me crazy today. Listen, I really do have
to get some equipment over to the school. The team
needs things for practice."

She stepped back. "I'm sorry," she said clumsily.

"I have an idea," he volunteered. "How about if
you and Greg stop back in a little while? It'll give me
a chance to pick the place up a little. I'll rent a couple
videos while I'm out, and we can watch a video, sip
some wine, and eat sandwiches. It'll get your mind off
Sean. I know you're going through some rough times."

"I can make it, but Greg is staying all night with a
friend," she told him. "You know, what with Sean
and all."

"I meant to tell you, I could help out with Greg if
you wanted me to," he volunteered.

"That's okay, he's doing fine. I'll see you in a bit."
She looked at her watch. "Say around six?"

"Fine."

She drove home, where she called Julie at the hospital. She was buoyant. She said the doctor had just
left, and the news was wonderful. "The leukemia's not
back," she said. "You'll never guess what it is."

"What?"

"Sean has an ulcer." She laughed. "He worries so much that he's given himself an ulcer." She went on to explain that the doctor had ordered some blood for Sean and wanted to keep him in the hospital several more days to get the bleeding stopped. "Then it's some medication, a proper diet, and he's fine."

Rita also talked to Sean, who was in good spirits.

She brought out a bottle of Wild Turkey and poured herself a shot. She added water, a couple of ice cubes, and stirred it with her finger. As she drank, she felt as if a huge burden had been lifted from her.

She went back to Mike's at around six. He had freshly showered and changed clothes.

Inside was small, though cozy. The rooms were immaculate, with highly polished hardwood floors. There were Persian rugs here and there. "I can't believe how nice you keep the place," she commented. "I thought you told me you were a slob, and that's one of the reasons your first wife divorced you." The Wild Turkey had made her light-headed, perhaps because she had drunk it on an empty stomach. She realized she hadn't eaten all day. She felt numb.

"I told you I'd grown up."

She told him about Sean.

He hugged her. It was great news, he said.

"I'm starved. Do you have anything to snack on?"

On their way to the kitchen to make a snack tray, she glanced down a stairway. He seemed to have noticed. "That's the 'dungeon,' " he told her, where he kept the washer and dryer. "It occurred to me earlier that you've never really been here. That's strange."

As she cut chunks of cheese on the kitchen counter, it was hard for her to concentrate. He cleaned some fresh broccoli and cauliflower for a vegetable dip.

"What movies did you get?" she asked, hoping that the talk would keep her oriented.

"One is *Sleepless in Seattle*. I know it's old—have you seen it?"

She nodded.

"Oh. Well, the other—do you like classics?"

"Sure."

"I got *Frankenstein*."

She felt her heart skip a beat. She thought of Matthew and Larry.

"Did you know that in the original novel by Mary Shelley that the monster was not named Frankenstein?" he asked.

No, she hadn't known that, she told him.

"It's true. The doctor's name was Frankenstein, but the monster never had a name. Some movie versions leave you with a different impression. They make you think that Frankenstein is what the monster was called. But in reality, a monster without a name is much more frightening, don't you think?" She didn't say. "A sort of fear of the unknown type of thing," he went on.

She was close to him, could feel his smoky gray eyes watching her, though she continued to cut chunks of cheese. She remembered the conch he had given Greg. Matthew had had shells that his mother had found packed away. "Do you ever think about trying to get back to Florida?" she asked him.

He continued to watch her. "Why do you ask that?"

Her eyes wandered away from him, which angered her because she was having trouble keeping her attention on him. She mustered as much concentration as she could manage, looked directly at him again, and said, "What?" She tried to remember what he had asked her, what they had been specifically talking about.

He folded his arms over his chest. He smiled. "Are you drunk?" he asked, studying her.

"No, I'm not drunk." She thought her words were slurred, and that frightened her. She awkwardly dumped too many crackers on the tray with the cheese.

He laughed and helped put some back in the box. "If you're not drunk, I'd say you'd had one too many."

She carried the cheese and cracker tray into the living room while he carried wine, glasses, a corkscrew, and the vegetable tray. The room was sparsely furnished with a sofa, two armchairs, and a coffee table. They sat at the table. He picked up the corkscrew to open the wine.

She got up to go to the kitchen. "I'll get the napkins," she said.

She was unsteady, and he tried to help her, but she pushed into the kitchen. "They're over here," he told her as she opened and closed cabinets, but as he reached for a cabinet door, he hesitated. He slapped the side of his head. "Oh, I forgot," he said. "I meant to buy some while I was at the store." Under the sink he found paper towels. "These all right?" he asked. He pointed at the living room. "Go sit down before you fall down."

She felt unsteady on her feet. It was impossible, she thought. She had not had that much to drink—at least she didn't think she had.

"You should see your cheeks," he told her. "They're beet red."

She dipped a branch of cauliflower in the vegetable dip. A glob of dip dropped on the table. He wiped it up with a paper towel. "I'm not drunk," she told him, and bit into the cauliflower.

He was staring at her again. "I'm sure." He laughed.

She stopped chewing and tried to stare at him. "I think I know who killed those boys."

His voice was subdued. "The priest? Or was it that other guy you arrested?" It sounded like he was mocking her, she thought, as if to say, "who are you going to arrest next?" He was about to open the bottle of wine when he said, "Listen, you sure you want this?" She shrugged. He smiled. "To tell you the truth, I don't think you'll be drinking that much. Rather than opening a new bottle, how about if I use one I already have open?"

"That's fine."

He took the corked bottle into the kitchen. She could hear him in the refrigerator. "You don't mind if it's chilled, do you?" he called out.

"No."

Glasses rattled. He returned with glasses of white wine. "So, you were saying you think you know who killed the boys?" He set a glass in front of her and raised his glass for a toast.

She moved her tongue around in her mouth, across her teeth. "This dip needs something," she said. She made smacking sounds with her mouth. "Hot sauce," she told him. "Have you got any hot sauce?"

He put down his glass and returned to the kitchen. While he was gone, she switched glasses with him. She didn't know why she did it, didn't know why she was doing anything. He returned with a bottle of red pepper sauce and a spoon. She shook a few drops of sauce in the dip. He stirred it in. "Try it," he said.

She dipped her broccoli. "Uhmmm, that's better," she said, chewing.

He raised his glass. They touched glasses and drank.

He asked, "So, are you going to tell me or not?"

She watched him, wondering what he was talking about.

His eyebrows rose.

She drank more wine. Then she was angry with herself because she didn't want to drink more. Already she had had too much to drink. She knew it. What she needed was some food in her stomach. She ate a piece of cheese. She tried to remember how much she had had to drink at home. She thought it was two drinks, but she wondered if it had been three. She had been so relieved to hear the news of Sean that she might have lost track of her celebration.

"Oh, you can't talk about it," he said. "That's it. Well, why in the hell did you dangle something like that out in the open if you weren't willing to talk about it?"

She smiled. "What are you talking about?" she asked stupidly.

He laughed, his hands rising in the air, as if she had a gun pointing at him. It was his new habit. "Okay, I can wait to find out who did it until it comes out in the papers—just like everyone else does. The only thing that counts to me is that you seem to be in a better mood, and I like that."

She ate a cracker. She was feeling better. They talked and ate. Before she realized what had happened, he opened the second bottle of wine, the one he had brought out to open in the first place.

"I will say this," he said, refilling the glasses, "I believe I know you well enough to realize you wouldn't have arrested that priest if he wasn't dirty for something."

Had they been talking about the case again? she

wondered. She was confused. She talked about Father
Catalpa, trying to listen carefully to everything she
said.

Mike brought out a bottle of Jim Beam. They continued to drink and talk. Eventually he kissed her.
They kissed again. The room was swimming. She
laughed. "I think I am drunk," she confessed.

"Me too."

She tried to get to her feet but fell backward. She
giggled but couldn't get up. She shut her eyes. Blackness closed in on her.

About four o'clock in the morning, she awakened
from a dead sleep for no apparent reason. It was raining. Her head was still swimming. She tried to sit up
but couldn't. There was a light in the hallway. She
could hear water running. Apparently Mike was taking
a shower. Why would he be taking a shower at four
in the morning? she wondered.

She was in his bedroom, in his bed, naked. She
couldn't remember making love to him, though she
was sore, as if he had been too rough with her. The
shower fell silent. Mike appeared in the doorway,
naked, drying his hair with a towel. Water was dripping from him. "Hi," he said, smiling.

She drifted back asleep as she watched him. She
saw the Cassell boy. He was standing in a shower,
stuffing toilet paper into his mouth. Then he opened
his mouth full of toilet paper under the water shooting
from the shower. Shreds of toilet paper were going
everywhere. He looked at her with panic in his eyes,
choking on the toilet paper.

Again she awakened from a dead sleep. It was 6:12.
She felt as though she hadn't been sleeping for more

than a few minutes. Outside, it was raining. She wondered why she had had such a terrible dream, and
then she recalled a videotape she had seen of Larry
Cassell. The videotape had been taken the previous
summer when the family had gone to the Wisconsin
Dells. At one point in the film Larry had been about
to embark upon a water slide, and he had stood under
a shower in order to get wet first. The father had
filmed Larry in the shower, where he had stood with
his mouth open to catch water.

She glanced at Mike, who was in bed next to her.
He was snoring lightly. She got out of bed and began
to dress. He didn't stir. As she went out to find her
purse and car keys, she passed the stairway down to
the "dungeon." She turned on the hall light and went
down the stairs. Every time they creaked, she looked
behind her to make sure Mike was not there. Just as
she was opening the door, there came a loud "Oh,
shit!" and Mike came tumbling down the stairs,
knocking her into the dark room. He immediately
helped her up. "Are you all right?" he asked. He
turned on the light. The basement was a cement junk
room. Then: "What in the world are you doing
down here?"

She pretended to be confused. She was still half-
drunk. "I'm not sure. I must have taken a wrong
turn."

He laughed loudly. "Don't you know a big elephant
like me could have killed you!" he said. He hugged
her. Only then did she feel the electricity in her chin
from where it had hit the cement floor.

She massaged her chin. It hurt. "I have to go," she
told him. She wanted to cry, could feel tears in her
eyes.

"You can't drive in this condition. At least have a couple cups of coffee."

"I'll be okay."

She insisted on driving herself home, where there were a number of messages on her answering machine. No sooner did she push the button to listen to them than the telephone rang. She stopped the answering machine and picked up the receiver. Another body had been found, Jim Swearingen told her. It was in the state park on the east shore of Nagawicka Lake. That was only a couple of miles form Mike's house, Rita thought. "You're kidding" was her reaction. When he didn't say anything, she knew what she had said was inappropriate. "Where at in the park?" she asked.

"The boat launch."

She immediately called Cheryl Christensen to make sure Greg was all right. He was fine, Cheryl told her. "The boys are eating breakfast right now."

Rita ran out the door, jumped in her car, and drove to the east side of the lake, where there was a parking lot filled with police vehicles, lights flashing. More cars were arriving, one after another.

The rain had stopped, all but at drizzle, but everywhere there was evidence of a heavy rain: puddles and mud.

Jim met her to show her the way to the body. "You got here in a flash," he said as they walked.

She asked about the medicine bottle.

There were prints, he told her. "Jerry Grier is running them."

They walked along a dock, following a passageway to the lake, up a small, muddy hill, from the top of which they could see a body, as if it had been heaved down the hill. This crime scene was disorganized, not careful and planned like the first two murders. Before she went down to the body, which was near the water, Jim said, "One thing we do know is that Catalpa and Scroggins couldn't have done this. They're both under surveillance."

She took an indirect route down the embankment.

She clasped her hands together and began to weep the moment she saw the mutilated body that was draped in a white robe. It was Kyle Wishause. Weeping, she bent down and put her hands on the boy's chest, as if to comfort him. He was dirty but not completely muddy, which suggested that he had been tossed down the embankment before the rain had started.

Kyle did not look peaceful, not like the other victims. His eyes were crudely sewn shut, so she couldn't see his eyes, but he, like the first two victims, had an orange hue from his embalming. An appearance of a scream was frozen upon his badly beaten face. It seemed that someone had hit him so hard that his jaw had been dislocated, leaving the scream locked there. Beneath his robe he was naked, but he had been mutilated. He was partially eviscerated, from where the murderer had not sewn him up completely.

Jim helped her up. "What's wrong?" he asked. She told him who it was, where he lived. Beginning to cry again, she felt angry. Someone had killed Kyle on purpose—to get to her. She wanted to kill that person, whoever it was. Then she was depressed because she knew she had to face the Wishauses. How can I tell them? she wondered. I have to be the one.

"Does this Squires guy know this boy?" Jim asked.

Why is he asking about Mike? Rita wondered. Did

Jim know something she didn't? She thought it was rude he would even mention the name, especially since she had asked him to keep it in strict confidence. "No," she said. She kept staring at Kyle, tears flowing. "I mean, he could have seen him before, but what's he have to do with anything?"

Jim said, "I was just wondering why the eyes are sewn shut."

She thought of the Anderson case. He had stabbed his wife in the eyes.

"No, he didn't do it," she said. "I have to go," she told Jim, and stumbled as she tried to get up the embankment. Jim helped her.

At the top of the hill, she looked back at Kyle. It seemed like only yesterday that he had been a baby in her arms and she had loved him like her own child. It seemed like only yesterday that she had hugged him and lifted him high in the air, pretending he was an airplane. He had liked that, smiling in excitement. She wept as she returned to her car. Nothing seemed real.

Accompanied by uniformed officers, she went to Paul Wishause's house. He was not there. No one was there. She went to Babe and Norb's. Paul was there. She had not seen him in months, not since he had been going through his divorce. He had kept hidden away.

He was a skinny red-haired man in his thirties. He smiled the moment he saw Rita. She could remember the time he had had a crush on her, and she had had to explain to him about infatuation.

Babe immediately asked Rita if she knew where Kyle was. "Paul thought he was over here, and we thought he was at home, and we can't find him."

Rita watched the room of calamity without moving.

Paul was smiling, as if Rita would take care of everything. Norb was flipping pages in the telephone book.

"Another body's been found," Rita said bluntly.
Once she spoke, she realized how loud she had said
it because every activity in the room stopped. She
could hear her heart beating. She could hear her own
breath. She could hear a clock ticking somewhere.

Babe collapsed, as if she had been hit in the head
with an iron bar. "God, I knew it," she said, and
began to weep, her body on the floor. "I knew something horrible was wrong. I knew it! It's him, isn't it!"
She was screaming.

"Yes." It was over. She had told them. Norb covered his face. He didn't want anyone to see he was
crying, though Rita could hear him. Paul stepped forward. "What are you talking about?" he asked, the
smile vanishing. "For God's sake, has something happened to my son?"

"He's dead, Paul," she told him. "I just came—"

"Stop it! Don't ever say something like that!" He
grabbed her in a rage. She didn't resist.

Uniformed officers held Paul. She said, "You'll
need to go and identify him." They suddenly knew
what she had told them was the truth. She could tell.
As the uniformed officers confirmed what she had told
them, Rita had to look them full in the face, with
nothing but a shadow of their previous relationship
still alive. Paul let out a cry and started throwing
things. He broke a plate, knocked over a lamp, and
tore a picture off the wall before Babe and Norb could
restrain him. Rita held the officers back. Then there
were the soft sobs of a family together, suffering a
devastating loss. Oh, God, was all Rita thought, watching them. Oh, God.

22

At home, she brought out the bottle of Wild Turkey, sat down at the kitchen table, and began to drink. All she could think about was Kyle. All her life people had entrusted her with their children. She had baby-sat Paul Wishause when he was a child; then he had grown up and had a son of his own. She had cared for that new child. And now Kyle was dead. It was her fault. The more she drank, the worse she felt. She could never face the Wishauses again. She wept bitterly. Then as quickly as the tears had arrived, they left.

She was stupefied. She felt like she was going to pass out, which concerned her because she hadn't consumed more than three or four shots of bourbon. Surely that wasn't enough to make her so drunk. Something was wrong. Everything about her took on a shade of black, a blackness that expanded and contracted with each breath she took.

"Boy, are you predictable" came a familiar voice.

She looked up. There standing in the kitchen doorway was Steve, her ex-husband. Dressed all in black except for a small white square on a clerical collar, he stood with his hands in his pants pockets, smiling smugly. He wore glasses, like Mike, though she couldn't tell if that was part of his disguise, because she knew he wasn't a priest. His belly pushed against his black shirt. "Hello, Rita," he said.

She tried to get up, staggering and dazed, but knew she would pass out if she didn't sit back down. She returned to her seat.

His hands still in his pockets, the smug smile still on his face, he said, "I wouldn't move around too much." From his pocket he produced a small baggy of pills. "Largactil," he said. "Billy Scroggins had enough of these to drug an army. It's amazing what you can learn about a person when you sleep with him a time or two."

The revelation sobered her somewhat.

Smiling, he said, "Does it surprise you that I can sleep with a man or a woman and feel the same satisfaction from either relationship?" He leaned against a kitchen counter. "As I was saying, you can learn a lot by sleeping with someone. Billy told me his entire life, from his fantasies to his medications." He held up the plastic bag and looked at the pills as if he were a child looking at new goldfish he had just bought. "It really is an amazing drug," he said. "To tell you the truth, I had never even heard of it until Scroggins told me all about it." The smile on his face would not go away. "When I tried to figure out how to make sure you would take some of it, I thought of one of two places to put it. I said, 'Put it either in a wine bottle, or put it in her Wild Turkey.'" He shook his head. "I put it in both. As usual, you're quite predictable."

No wonder, she thought. I've been drugged. "How'd

you get in here, Steve?" she asked angrily, though the
anger seemed to potentiate the drug's effect.

"Albert," he said. "I go by my middle name now.
Albert Devereux." From his other pocket he produced
a key on a chain. He held the chain between his
thumb and index finger so that the gold key dangled.
"It's still my house, you know," he said. "Being the
predictable person you are, I knew you would never
get around to changing the locks after I moved out,
just as Greg knew you'd never get around to getting
the puppy you had promised him."

"How'd you know about that?" she asked, terrified.
The terror helped activate the drug even further, perhaps because the fear caused her heart to beat faster.

"The attic," he said. He pointed at one of the vents.
"Having installed the extra insulation up there, I know
it like the back of my hand. Now, there's a job I
hate—you remember how I itched for a week afterward?" She didn't say. "Anyway, I bet it's a hundred
degrees up there on a normal day. The nice thing is
that toward night, it cools down. Did you know you
can look down around the cracks in the duct work
and see everything that goes on down here? I've been
watching you off and on since we broke up two years
ago. I've been waiting patiently to destroy you like
you destroyed me, watching your every move and
planning for this moment."

She lunged at him, but fell into a pool of blackness.

She found herself in a small, well-lighted room
whose cement walls had been painted white. The room
looked like a laboratory. There were beakers and test
tubes and bottles of chemicals. The cement bled
through here and there, and there was the smell of

human flesh in the room, as when she went to an
autopsy. A steel support pole was positioned in the
center of the room. Rita, her hands handcuffed behind
the pole, woke up at eleven-thirty, sitting on the cold
floor. She knew it was eleven-thirty because there was
a large clock on the wall directly in front of her, above
a white porcelain table. At the head of the table was
a sink, and there was a machine that included a large
glass jar with tubes running from it.

Steve entered the room carrying a second large jar,
this one containing an orange-red fluid. A smile still
on his face, he said, "I see we're awake again." He
held up the jar. "Red dye number two." He set the
jar on the floor near the machine. "Isn't this great?"
he said, turning to her. "You've seen these people
who drive around old hearses"—she remembered
Barry Dixon—"I've always been fascinated by someone who would want to buy an old hearse, fix it up,
and drive it. Like Barry. Anyway, I managed to find
a great buy on an old funeral home. Of course, I've
fixed it up a bit, but the setting is wonderful, don't
you think? I'd take you on a tour of the upstairs—a
couple of the rooms are as old and gloomy as if the
caskets were still in them—but unfortunately that isn't
possible right now."

"What do you want from me?" she asked.

"It's not you I want at all," he told her. He walked
over to a refrigerator, which he opened. In the lighted
compartment was a container of blood. "It's the soul
of the flesh," he said, lifting the Mason jar.

"What are you talking about? Steve, you've gone
mad." It was terrifying to see him with the jar of
blood. She knew it was either the blood of Matthew,
Larry, or Kyle.

"Albert. I go by Albert now. No, I'm not mad at all." He unscrewed the lid of the jar and drank some of the blood. The sight repulsed her, made her want to throw up. There was blood on his lips when he said, "You've heard the story about the man in the tombs, haven't you?"

She didn't know what he was talking about. He seemed to be rambling, talking to himself.

"There's this ancient story about a man who buries bodies, and each time a new body comes to him, the soul of that body cries out for a new home. So the gravedigger takes the soul as his own." He held up the jar of blood. "It's like the little prayer we teach our children: Now I lay me down to sleep, I pray the Lord my soul to keep. If I should die before I wake, I pray the Lord my soul to take."

"Steve, you're trapped in a fantasy world," she said. She saw the glaze in his eyes and knew she was getting to him.

He got angry, pointing a finger at her. "Albert. And don't you talk to me that way!" he said. "I'm very much in this world. You think I'm stupid. You always have. But I'm smart enough to be doing your job better than you can do it." He smiled. "Yes, you taught me well. You said I never listened to you. I listened to you, I watched you, I read your books, I read your reports, I knew everything about you and your work. I even knew how to make sure you got a case. I knew the body had to be found on state property, or you wouldn't have jurisdiction. I left you clues so you would find them, so you would solve this case. What about the Bible? I even turned the pages to that story about Hazael and sprinkled holy water on them so it'd look like someone had been crying over the story.

I know the real world better than you think I know it. That's what makes you scared of me, because you know I'm very much in touch with reality. You wish I was crazy, but I'm just as sane as you are. You destroyed my life. You took away all I loved, and now I'm going to take it back."

"You're crazy!"

"Stop saying that!" he screamed. His face was red. "I hate it when you say that!"

"So, what are you going to do to me?" she said sarcastically.

"It's early still," he said. "Don't be in a hurry." He pointed at the clock. "We still have a few hours until Greg gets out of school." He produced the key again. "I'll pick him up for you."

She could not tell whether he was still smiling or not. His face expressed a strange mixture of arrogance and determination. "Please, don't do this," she said. She suddenly understood what he had in mind. "Do whatever you want to me, but please don't do anything to harm Greg. He hasn't done anything to you. Don't hurt him."

His eyes became dreamy as he stared into space. "It doesn't hurt," he said. "That's what people don't understand. If it hurt, I wouldn't do it. You don't know what it's like to be able to bring such pleasure to someone." He looked at her. His eyes were still dreamy. "That's why they fight so much. That's why they scream. They want more. They like what I do. They want me to overpower them, to control them. They scream for me because they know I can bring them a pleasure they've never experienced before. Don't you see, if they didn't want it, they wouldn't fight, they wouldn't struggle, they wouldn't scream for more attention."

Desperate, she tried to reason with him. "How could you care so little about human life, especially a child's life?"

His eyebrows furrowed as if he was in deep thought. "I do care," he told her. "I keep telling you that. That's why I've been planning this since our divorce—back when you took my son from me. He's a part of me. Don't you understand that? You stole a part of my soul, and now I'm going to take it back. I want my soul back."

"But why did you murder three other children?"

"So I could live!" he screamed. "You stole a part of my soul, and I had to survive until I could get it back. You act like it's such a crime. If I need a heart, and someone gets killed in an accident out on the highway, you wouldn't think twice about taking that person's heart and transplanting it to me. You took a part of my soul, and until I could get it back, I had to have transplanted souls to keep me alive."

"You hurt others so you can live?"

"You hurt me. What was that for? It was for yourself. And, no, I don't hurt others. I bring them pleasure. If they have to die, that's part of it. I don't like that part." The smile vanished. "Don't you know I think about that? I mean, sure, I feel great relief each time I do this because I can experience such pleasure myself—I know I'm one step closer to having my soul back—but I know what happens to those kids. I care about them. I pray for them afterward. I go to church regularly, and I pray—" He shook his head. "Oh, you don't know how much I pray for them. I even went to confession." Now he was smiling again.

So, that had been the confession Father Catalpa had heard, she thought.

"You'll see," he continued. "You'll see what an intense experience it is, so intense you won't even be able to stand it. I bet you'll pass out as you watch."

"Please, don't do this," she told him. "I'll help you. We'll work something out."

He stood with his hands in his pockets again. "Rita, you should have thought about this a long time ago." Smiling broadly, he raised his chin and stuck a finger down beneath the white square at the base of his Adam's apple. "You want to work something out now? What about two years ago when you said there was nothing to work out? What about when you said you didn't care? You weren't sensitive to me at all. You never understood that once I was Greg. I was once eleven. I remember the man who lived in a house down the road. Mr. Carnes. Never forget him. I remember how he took me swimming in a nearby stream one day, and afterward he took me into the woods. He touched me here and there, and then he knocked me on the ground and raped me. He did that off and on for several years. It was something in me that brought it on. Greg has it in him too."

It made her sick to listen to him, but she had to know as much as she could. As long as he was talking, she felt there was hope to stop him. "How did you find Matthew and Larry?" she asked. "Why did you choose them?"

His eyebrows furrowed again. He rubbed his chin. "It's a long story," he said. "You see, at first I didn't even know Catalpa was a priest. I saw him and Scroggins down at one of the bookstores along the interstate around Kenosha. They seemed to have an

understanding with one of the people at the book-
store, who gave them some special magazines, you
know, the kind they don't normally sell over the
counter, and I could see right away they were books
of children, so I followed them. Soon I was a part of
their group. That's when I learned Thaddeus was a
priest. He would talk about the little boys he had mo-
lested over the years. He let me see his envelope of
pictures. He talked about a couple of the boys he was
molesting at St. Paul's—Matthew and Bobby. I guess
that was the first time in my life that I realized it was
okay, that these urges I had were not wrong. I mean,
after all, if a priest had them and could act on them,
then I was as holy and as important as a priest. The
Church knew what he was doing. He said he had been
caught before. He said if he got in an embarrassing
situation, the Church would always stand behind him.
They would move him on to someplace where no one
knew him." He smiled. "That's because there aren't
enough priests to pass around. They have to recycle
them. Yes, ol' Thaddeus. He was as predictable as
everyone else. Never locked the door of his apartment, not even when he went on a trip. I stopped
seeing Thaddeus and Billy.

"That's because the first time I saw Matthew, I
saw the resemblance to Greg right away." His dreamy
eyes cleared. "You saw it too, didn't you?" She didn't
say. With his right hand he massaged his ring finger,
where his wedding band had once been. "I was careful," he said. "I wanted to make sure everything was
perfect."

"Then you meant to murder him?"

"Oh, sure. Remember, I've been planning this for
two years. I had even written out a list of everything

I was going to do to him once I got him." He smiled
and started itemizing the list on his fingers. "First, I
was going to smother him." His eyes were dreamy
again. "Not all the way. Then when he came back, I
was going to choke him. Then we'd get undressed together. Then we'd take a bath together—my father
and I used to take a bath together. Then I'd beat him
and rape him. Then I'd stab him to make sure he
was all the way dead. Then I'd embalm him—can you
believe I learned the basics from Scroggins? He's quite
a talker. I think I'm getting rather good at it—embalming. Don't you think? Where was I?" He looked
at the three fingers he had not used. "Oh, I forgot.
I'd practice sticking needles in his neck to find his
veins and arteries—that was before I'd embalm him.
I'd glue his lips shut so he couldn't cry out, and then
I'd sew his hands together so he couldn't reach out to
get his soul back as I drank it." With that, he rubbed
his hands together, as if warming them. "Listen, I'd
like to stay and chat, but I've got some business to
take care of. You make yourself comfortable." He left
the room, closing the door behind him. She could hear
him locking it; then she heard his footsteps climbing
wood stairs. The stairs creaked under his weight.

Using the pole as support, she got to her feet. Then
she stooped as far as she could, given that her hands
were cuffed on the other side of the pole behind her
back, and managed to get one foot through her arms.
She got the other foot through, so she was partially
turned around. She stood. She was not sure what advantage that gave her, but it did allow her to see her
wrists, chained together by handcuffs. As she stared
at her wrists, she thought of the nightmare about the

leopard. In the nightmare the leopard had chewed off
one of its paws in order to escape a hunter's trap.

She wondered how she could escape, whether she
should scream. Without any windows in the room, she
doubted anyone outside the house would hear her.
Besides, Steve might return and drug her, which would
destroy any window of opportunity she might have for
an escape.

Of course, she knew something Steve did not know.
She had given Greg a note the day before to excuse
him from the bus. Since she had given Greg that note
while he had been in the car, she assumed Steve
wouldn't know about it. What worried her, though,
was that if she wasn't there to pick up Greg, the
teacher might make him get on the bus. Would he go,
or would he insist that he was supposed to wait for
his mother? All she could do was wait and see.

In the meantime, her only hope rested on the possibility of getting Steve close enough to her that she
could kick him, though she was not even sure he
would be returning. As far as she knew, no one knew
where she was.

She looked at the clock: 12:16. The thin second hand
traced the numbers of the clock face.

Now that she knew she could change positions
somewhat, she returned to the position she had originally been in, with her hands behind her back. She
called for Steve. There were no sounds on the stairs.
She screamed. Still no sounds. She screamed and
screamed, but could hear only the sound of her own
voice, the breaths of her own desperation. The more
she screamed, the angrier she became. She wanted to
kill him, thought that if she could get him close
enough, she could kick him so hard she would kill

him. She would kick him in the throat, use the small white square beneath his Adam's apple as a target. That's what she would do. But he didn't appear.

At 12:28, he returned. She had no illusions about persuading him not to do what he had planned; all she was looking for was an opportunity to stop him. She knew she had one chance only, if she had that. He stood at the porcelain table and unloaded a sack he had, one from Bergner's. The sack contained cosmetics of the Clinique brand. It was the brand she wore because it seemed to be more hypoallergenic than other brands of makeup. Other brands made her face break out. It angered her that he had bought that brand. In fact, his very presence she found disgusting, especially since she could see in his face an expression of power, a certain satisfaction with himself. Perhaps it was only the same expression that had always been there, she reasoned.

What bothered her the most was how he presently ignored her, said nothing to her, though she knew by the expression on his face that he was well aware of her presence, that she was chained to a pole just beyond his reach. That he was giving the cosmetics serious attention was a facade. She knew it, could sense it. Yet, taking his time, he opened one box after another of facial creams, lipsticks, and mascaras.

He finally said, "You wouldn't believe how expensive this stuff is." He had finished opening packages. He put the wrappers and empty boxes back in the Bergner's bag. He smiled. "But then again, you would believe it, wouldn't you? This is what you wear. Of course, I didn't want to spare any expense on such a special occasion."

"Why do you have to do this?" she said, hoping to draw him into conversation again.

He looked at her. "Maybe it's to show you I am in control," he said. "You always thought I'd never amount to anything. I'm showing you, I can do anything I set my heart to doing. I'm in full control. It was like when I was upstairs, I heard you calling, heard your screams, but I let you carry on. I knew exactly what you had begun to think. Like I said, you're too predictable—you thought I wasn't around, and that's what I wanted you to think." He laughed.

"You make me sick," she told him. "You've turned into a fat, ugly pig." She laughed. "You've got the face of a pig, you know that?" He reddened. She wanted him to lose his temper, wanted him to attack her. "You look like Porky Pig. Did anyone ever tell you that?" She laughed loudly.

He put his hand in one pocket, then in another of his coat. "I had something I wanted to show you," he said, regaining his composure. He checked his pants pockets. "You wouldn't laugh if you could see what I have."

"See what I mean?" she said. "You're losing it. You think you're in control, but you're losing it. Like with Kyle." His face showed signs of confusion. "You were real clumsy with him."

That seemed to strike a nerve. He stopped what he was doing. "I may have been a little careless, but I accomplished my objective. I've shown you that you can make mistakes too. You got pulled from the case. That was humiliating, wasn't it? Falsely arresting a priest. Your reputation is ruined." He rubbed his hands together, as if warming them. "Of course, no one gives a damn about Scroggins, but people'll put

it all together. They'll see how sloppy you were."
Then his hands were still, held in a praying fashion.
"Where did I put that?"

It was terrifying to see how callous he was.

Steve was smiling through it all. He said, "I can tell
by your eyes that you're finally putting things together
yourself." He searched his pockets again, the same
ones he had already searched. "That's good." It was
as if there was something there, but he simply couldn't
find it, despite there being so few possibilities. "I was
sure I had it." Taking the Bergner's trash bag with
him, he said, "I must have left it upstairs." He left
the room, closing the door behind him.

At first she wondered why he kept closing the door,
and then she remembered it was one of his neurotic
habits. When she had lived with him, if she or Greg
left a door open, he had thrown a fit, claiming that it
made heating and air-conditioning the house impossible. It was why he had put extra insulation in the attic.
He couldn't stand to let any air in or out of the house.
He wanted to control everything.

He returned holding a wrinkled peach washcloth,
the one she hadn't been able to find. "Here it is," he
said. "I used it for the Cassell boy. It still has his
slobber on it. It really is exciting to watch someone
die," he told her. "All of a sudden you see all of the
human dignity go out of a person, and you see someone slobbering and pissing his pants." He laughed.
"You remember that time Greg crapped in the bath-
tub?" She hadn't heard about that experience. She
wondered what else had happened between him and
Greg that she didn't know about. "It was the first time
I ever saw him that scared. He was such a whiny boy,
always wanting his mother. Sometimes I couldn't stand

it. I literally shook the shit out of him." He had that smug smile on his face. "His Mama ain't going to be able to help him this time, is she?"

Her mouth was dry, probably from the drug he had given her. She was having trouble swallowing. She said, "That isn't the cloth. We have the cloth."

"No, you don't."

"Yes, we do. Father Catalpa had it. We confiscated it in a search."

"Then you would have been able to hold him. You don't have anything. You have only what I've given you. Trust me, this is the one I used on the Cassell boy." He sniffed the cloth. "You can even smell him on here." He held out the cloth and approached her from the side, avoiding her feet, which were stretched out where she was sitting.

The moment he was close enough, she kicked him as hard as she could in the testicles. When he dropped, her foot aimed for his throat but grazed his shoulder instead, which spun him, bringing him down on her left leg.

He flew into a rage, pounding her with fists. Just as quickly he jerked away from her. He rubbed his bloody knuckle that had been cut when he had hit her mouth. She realized that, like a wild animal, she had been trying to bite him. With a foot he kicked the washcloth away from her, so he could pick it up without getting within her reach.

"You know I'm telling the truth," he told her, panting. "They always say the people who know you the best can hurt you the most. And that's what I'm doing to you. I'm hurting you like you've hurt me." He left the room, closing the door behind him.

She had ruined any chance she might have had to

save her son. She was trapped. She closed her eyes and tried to think. It seemed her entire life had been like that, one trap after another. She could feel herself slipping into a state of blackness, withdrawing from the pain.

The next moment, she awakened to a commotion on the stairs beyond the closed door. She could feel the swollenness of her face. Panic-stricken, she looked at the clock: 4:30. Steve was back with Greg, she knew. For a fraction of a second all hope went out of her, but suddenly there was an explosion as the door burst open and Steve, Greg, and Charlie flew into the room, sprawling onto the cement floor. The impact knocked the breath out of all three of them. Then Greg let out a terrifying scream, half human, half animal, and crawled across the cement to get away from the two men as they renewed their struggle.

Charlie managed to stagger to his feet, but Steve grabbed him from behind, clamping an arm around his neck. Charlie drove himself backward, throwing Steve into the wall, which broke the hold. Charlie spun and hit Steve squarely between the eyes. At the moment a burst of blood appeared on Steve's face, his head slammed into the wall, and he collapsed. Charlie kicked viciously at him.

Jim Swearingen and Jerry Grier ran into the room. They grabbed Charlie to restrain him. "That's enough, Charlie!" Jim said.

Charlie stopped kicking. Panting, his clothes twisted about him, he turned to Rita, who had Greg's head in her lap. "Are you all right?" he asked.

"Get these cuffs off me," she said.

Jim unlocked her, while Charlie and Jerry dragged Steve to the pole, to which they chained him.

Still in shock, she asked, "How did you know?"

"Jerry called me the moment he had a match, and we stopped by the house to tell you the prints from the medicine bottle came back," Jim said. "We came to tell you they weren't Mike's, but that you had another name on the list that matched. We saw Steve driving away at the same time we arrived."

Charlie flexed his fist. "Damn, I think I jammed my finger." He pulled his middle finger, trying to get it to pop.

Jim smiled. "We didn't know at the time that Greg was in the car with him, so we swung around and followed."

Sirens approached.

"What happened up there?" she asked, motioning toward the stairs.

"I tried to stop him upstairs," Charlie told her. "He's wild."

Jerry brought out a cigar and lit it. Puffing, he asked Greg, "You all right, son?"

Before Greg could answer, Steve moaned to consciousness. No one spoke, no one moved. They watched him, as if paralyzed by the sight of some vicious animal rising from the depths of evil.

23

The Fourth of July guests congregated under the trees of Rita's backyard and drank wine and beer as they laughed and talked. Mike stood at the Weber grill, the lid of which puffed smoke. He removed the lid. Flames jumped up through the hamburgers and hot dogs. With a spray bottle he sprayed water at the flames, which receded. He replaced the lid.

Preoccupied by her thoughts, Rita studied the smoke pouring from the lid. Earlier that day she had learned that Thaddeus Catalpa had been dismissed from the priesthood. Crystal Hammond had identified a photograph of Matthew among Catalpa's collection. All Rita could think was that Catalpa should have been in jail—he should have been in jail years before.

Jim Swearingen, carrying a Coors Lite, stopped at the grill. He said, "It smells good."

"I love food cooked on the grill," Mike replied. A slight hissing came from the grill. "When are you heading back to Madison?" he asked.

"Tomorrow morning," he said. "And not a moment too soon."

"Why do you say that?"

"Milwaukee's a fine place to vis᾿: for a while, but I wouldn't want to live here."

"I'm glad you supported Rita through all this," Mike mentioned, putting an arm around her shoulder.

"What was I supposed to do, condemn her? She's a damned good investigator—the best I've seen."

"I don't feel like the best," she said.

Jim shook his head. "You were reminded the hard way of something a lot of us forget," he said. She looked at him. "We look at crime and think it's out there somewhere"—he gave a sweep with his hand—"not really a part of us. The truth is, child abusers, wife abusers, thieves, murderers—you name it—are living right next door. Sometimes they're in our own homes. They're part of everyday people. They have friends, relatives, and so on. Your ex-husband happened to be a killer. I'd say that early on you used good judgment by getting away from him. You didn't make him a killer. It was in him to start with. He'd have killed no matter what." He smiled slightly. "The other thing is that if it wasn't for you and the VA giving us a name and fingerprints, he would have kept killing. We wouldn't have him yet."

She took Jim's hand and smiled. "I think I'll keep you around to build up my ego," she said.

He laughed, which is something she rarely saw him do. To Mike, Jim said, "Speaking of standing by Rita, you haven't been so bad yourself."

Mike stared into her eyes. "She's a special woman—I've known that from the start." To her, he said, "I'd have done the same things you did if it had been my son. You've got to protect the children. I don't want you down in the dumps about all of this. It's time to move on."

She smiled. "Are you kidding? Now that Adam has announced his retirement, I think things are looking nothing but up."

A group of screaming children appeared from the side of the house. They were chasing Greg, the oldest of them, who was right behind a seven-week-old German shepherd. The shepherd, tail wagging, was bounding through the grass, as a puppy does. Greg whistled and said, "Here, K!" K turned to Greg and jumped into his lowered hands. Greg hugged him.

Rita patted Mike's back. She said, "I'm starved. How long?"

"Five minutes," Mike told her.

At the monkey bars of Greg's old swing set, Keisha Dalton jumped up and grabbed a bar. "Mom, Dad," she called, "watch!" Charlie and Claudia went over to where their six-year-old daughter was hanging. Claudia stood on one end of the monkey bars, and Charlie stood behind his daughter. "That's good!" they coaxed her as she swung unsteadily from bar to bar. At the last bar she called out, "Dad, help me!" She was too short to reach the foot rest.

Charlie said, "Drop to the ground. You won't hurt yourself."

"No, Dad, it's too far. Help me!" She was getting frantic. She clung to the last bar until Charlie reached up and helped her down.

Rita walked over to them. She told Charlie and Claudia, "She looks like she's doing great."

With a large hand Charlie pulled Keisha against his leg and patted her back. "She's fine," he said.

"How's Sean getting along?" Claudia asked.

"Aside from worrying to much, there's not a thing wrong with him."

Mike was trying to get everyone's attention. With the Weber lid in one hand and a metal spatula in the other, he pounded on the lid. "Excuse me for a minute," he said. Eyes turned toward him. Rita was expecting him to announce that the burgers and hot dogs were ready. He said, "I'd like to take this opportunity to recognize a very special person, a good friend, Captain Rita Trible."

The guests applauded.

"Come on, everybody gather up here. Rita, come up here by me." She went to him. Vince, Joyce, Jerry, Jim, Charlie, Claudia, Greg, and others all gathered around. From his pocket he produced a diamond ring encased in rubies. There were a number of expressions of surprise.

Rita was the most shocked. She knew what was about to happen, but she still asked herself, What's he doing?

"Rita," he said, looking at her, "I love you." He held out the ring. "And you know I'm almost never serious—" There was a roar of laughter. He held up his hand for silence. "But this time no one could be more serious than I am." He looked straight at her, as if he had blocked out the rest of the visitors. "Would you marry me?"

Her life had been stung by mistakes. There had been times when she had felt that life could take her no lower, but the words she heard were new and refreshing, coming from someone who wouldn't dare say them unless he meant what he said.

"Yes," she answered. She would give it a chance.

There came another round of applause. Putting one arm on Mike's back and the other around Greg, who was holding K, Rita stood before the crowd, as if posing for a family portrait.

1

Wainwright Heights was so buried in fog that thirteen-year-old Angela Robles couldn't see the woods between her street and where she normally caught the school bus. She wasn't supposed to take a shortcut through the woods—her mother and father had told her to never go that way—but she always did. Everyone did. Most of the time she had someone to walk with, but this morning she was late and alone. She had fallen back to sleep after her brother and sisters had left for school, and had panicked when she saw the time. Before she knew it, she was in the "swamp," a marshy section of the woods where someone had made a bridge by throwing boards in the muck. Most of her friends ran across the boards. That's because everyone said the Boogeyman hid in the swamp and would get anyone who lingered on the boards.

As she reached the end of the boards, he jumped out of the bushes and grabbed her with powerful hands. She screamed too late, barely hearing her own sound. She fought frantically. He hit her so hard that everything went black for several moments. Then she began to cry. He cut off her breath. Through clenched teeth, he whispered, "Shut up." She could hear the bus and the distant voices of her friends. Then the voices were enclosed by the bus. The sound of the bus moved on. The Boogeyman let her breathe. "Now, do everything I say, and you won't get hurt. You understand?" She nodded, trembling. "Not a sound."

An arm locked around her neck so that his hand cupped her mouth, he trudged through the fog. She could smell nicotine between his fingers. She did her best to keep her feet on the ground as she ran alongside him, but occasionally her feet dropped out from under her. He dragged her when she did that. He had blue tattoos on his arms. One human figure had horns.

As they neared a battered car, out jumped a large tanned man with black greasy hair and a shadow of whiskers. "Did you get the right one, Wild Bill?" he asked.

"What do you think?"

"Are you sure? J.G.'ll kill us if we get the wrong one."

Wild Bill jerked back her hair and face. She tried not to cry, though she could feel herself trembling under the pressure of his grip. "Tell me, Flash, does it look like the right one?" he asked.

Flash nodded. "That's her all right," he said. He opened the back door of the car and jumped in as Wild Bill hoisted Angela in feet first. Flash wound rope around her feet as if he were hog-tying a calf; then he pulled a long piece of brown tape from a roll and slapped it across her mouth. She began to cry again. "Please, no," she tried to mumble, though she thought she was the only one who could distinguish her words. They were going to rape her and kill her, she knew.

Wild Bill said, "I told you to shut up," and raised a hand while he held both her hands behind her back. To Flash he said, "Tie these."

Flash tied her hands behind her. Then he pulled down the backseat, where a huge hole had been cut into the trunk. Wild Bill heaved her in. He said, "I'm going to put this seat up, but if you make a sound, I swear I'll stop the car and cut your throat. You understand?" She didn't answer. He raised a hand. "You understand?" She nodded.

He shoved up the seat, leaving her without light. She was scared she wouldn't be able to breathe, but she dared not make a sound. She told herself to try to be calm. She wondered if being locked in a trunk was like being locked in an old refrigerator. People died in refrigerators. The tape over her mouth resisted her efforts to free her lips. She cried silently, tears streaming freely. She didn't care what the Boogeyman did to her, as long as he didn't kill her. All she wanted was for him to do whatever he was going to do and get it over with. She didn't want to go anywhere to do it, didn't want to wait. She wanted to get it over with and go home. She would always do what her parents told her from now on.

The car started. Then she could hear her own crying muffled by the tape. She could feel movement, not abrupt movement, as if the car were racing away, but cautious movement. It was a long, bumpy ride. She could smell dust in the trunk. She sneezed twice. She could tell the car was on a dirt road.

The car stopped. Car doors slammed. The trunk was opened, splashing sunlight on her.

While Flash yanked her up by the arm, Wild Bill ripped the tape off her mouth. She screamed because she thought her skin had been torn off. Wild Bill slapped her. "Shut up!" he said angrily. "I told you I don't like screaming!"

She cried soundlessly, the salty taste of blood in her mouth. She could feel where she had bitten the inside of her cheek when he hit her. She didn't want him to hit her anymore. All she could think about was her mother and father. She wondered where they were.

The run-down house in front of her had a front porch that was about to collapse. The porch swing was broken. There was a barn nearby, also about to collapse. There were no curtains in the windows. She looked around. She didn't see any other houses or farms. Nothing looked familiar.

Wild Bill seemed to know what she was thinking because as he untied her hands and feet he said, "The closest house is seven miles." Digging his fingers into her arm, he pulled her inside the house, which had been swept, though not very well. "Come on," he said. He walked too fast. She could see broom marks in the dust. There was no furniture.

He yanked her up a squeaky staircase and stopped at an upstairs door. There was a shiny brass lock on it. Shavings from where the lock had been installed littered the floor. He fumbled with a ring of keys, unlocked the door, and opened it to a small room that had a pink blanket thrown in a heap on the floor. "Welcome to your new home," he said.

She took her first good look at him. Through a thick mustache he said, "J.G. told me that when it's all over I get you." He wasn't facing her straight on, though his eyes managed to be staring at her. The words terrified her because she could look at his eyes and tell what he meant. He was going to rape her. She knew it. The eyes were hard and shiny black, like a bird's eyes. His face remained turned slightly, somehow unable to face her, and he smiled eerily. He had thick black eyebrows. His hair was a bush of salt-and-pepper wildness. She looked again at his bulging arms, both covered with blue tattoos. The horned figure drew her attention.

He shoved her headlong into the room and slammed the door. From where she sprawled on the floor, she could hear a key in the lock. As soon as his footsteps went away, she got up and inspected her left arm, which had been scraped when she hit the floor. Hundreds of tiny beads of blood had appeared on her forearm.

She tried the door. It was locked.

In the small room was a dirty window and a second door. She went to the window and pressed her face against it, looking in every possible direction. Outside was a two-story drop to a dump of broken bottles and rusty cans. For as far as she could see there was nothing but dying trees, brush, and dust.

She opened the second door, an empty closet. In the ceiling was a panel. She studied it. Probably a door to an attic, she thought, excited. In her closet at home there was a door to the attic. Sometimes she hid things up there. She went to the pink blanket and sat down without bothering to spread it out.

The more she thought about the attic panel, the more convinced she became that it was her passageway to freedom. She decided that as soon as it got dark, she would climb up through the panel and escape by crawling off the roof and finding a way down. What if it didn't work? she wondered. She found herself crying out, not a loud, uncontrollable cry, but one which released continuous tears. She felt small and powerless, and tried to imagine what she had done to deserve what was happening to her. She couldn't understand where her mother and father were. They had always been there when she needed them. Surely they were looking for her. It was her only hope. She knew what Wild Bill and Flash were going to do to her. She knew what they wanted. Other boys and even men had looked at her the same way. All they saw was her body. Already a couple of high school boys had asked her to go to bed with them.

She planned her entire escape, even imagining herself running to the nearest highway, where she would flag down a car.

Eventually, she got up and went to the window. For a long time she watched the road that led to the house. There was no sign of activity. The road itself didn't look like it was used very often.

She heard footsteps. She hurried to the blanket and sat down. Wild Bill appeared with a paper plate of food. His presence made her tremble. She could feel him staring as he held out the plate. He didn't stare directly at her, but stared from the corner of his eye. There was a smile on his face. She tried to avoid looking at him. She didn't want him to think she was paying attention to him.

The plate of food wasn't much: a piece of cold ham, potato salad—like her mother bought at the deli when the family went on picnics—and a slice of bread, along with a cup of water. There were no eating utensils. She looked at the food. It didn't look appetizing. She wasn't hungry anyway.

Out of the side of his mouth, Wild Bill said, "I know what you want."

She didn't know what he was talking about, but he said it in such a way as to suggest he thought he could read her mind.

"You better keep yourself fed until it's time," he told her, and winked with his left eye.

She tried not to act afraid. "What do I use to eat with?" she asked.

He wiggled his fingers. "These," he told her. He laughed. It was a sickening sound. "If you're nice to me, maybe next time I'll remember to get you a fork or *something.*" His eyes made a couple of provocative jumps.

When he locked the room, she didn't eat, afraid the food was drugged. She was sure they wanted her to eat so she would pass out. Then they both would rape her.

While she sat there knowing he would eventually return, she realized she had to pee. She didn't want to say anything, though, because she was afraid he would want to watch her while she went. She couldn't stand the thought of him watching her pee.

When he returned for the plate, Wild Bill didn't seem to care that she hadn't eaten. He didn't offer to take her to the bathroom either. He only smiled. "Like I said," he told her, "I know what you want, and don't worry, you'll get it soon enough." He took away the plate, pulled shut the door and relocked it. She sat down and began to plan her escape again. She must have drifted off as she planned because she had a nightmare in which she was trying to escape through a sand tunnel. The sand slid down around her, filling in the open space with the light at the end of it.

She awakened drenched in sweat. The room was orange. She had to pee in the worst way. Her belly felt like it was about to burst. She couldn't sit still, so she went to the closet and, using a foot against the opposite wall, clambered up toward the attic panel. She had to get out—if for no other reason than to find someplace to pee. A couple of times she slipped as she struggled up to the attic, but eventually she made it. The panel was easy to shift aside. Straining under her weight, she pulled herself through the opening.

It was oppressively hot in the near darkness, so hot it was hard to breathe, though once she put the panel back in place, she experienced a sense of relief, as if Wild Bill and Flash would never find her. There was a window, partially open, in the opposite wall, where wasps had made a nest in the corner. One flew around her head. She hit the air, knocking the wasp to the floor. She stepped on the disoriented insect before it could fly again. She looked out the window.

There was a short stretch of roof, from which there ran a gutter. She saw she would have to crawl out on the roof, hang from the gutter, and lower herself from one of the gutter drains.

She tried the window. It wouldn't budge. She leaned against it, and pushed and tugged. She thought the glass was going to break. That frustrated her because there was no lock on the window, though it was partially open. She studied the window frame. The only problem was that the frame had swollen.

She shook the window. Nothing was going right. She became angry and rattled the window. The frame broke loose and the window slid up. The wasp nest dropped out of the corner, breaking like a dirt clod on the sill. Two angry wasps flew around the window. She jerked it down. One of the wasps flew away. The other continued to hover near the window, apparently searching for whoever had disturbed its nest. The second wasp returned, flew close to the window, then left again. She wished the wasp that was lingering would leave. It did, but no sooner did she get the window raised again than the wasp returned, flying straight through the opening before she could get it closed.

The wasp flew near her. She swatted at it, which disturbed the air enough to throw the wasp off course. Not for long, though. The wasp returned, flying straight at her. She heard herself make a sound of panic. She hit at the wasp again and again until she knocked it down. She crushed it with her foot.

She squeezed out the window and was heading to the gutter when she heard activity in the room below. Flash yelled for Wild Bill. She knew she was trapped, left with no time to climb down. She returned to the attic and looked around. Most of it had a crude floor, but there was a floorless dark space where the rafters met the structure of the walls. She crawled into that space, careful to keep her weight on the rafters.

It didn't take long for the attic panel to burst open. Wild Bill's head appeared. "Hold still," he said, his head jerking around. "She's out; get me down!" His head disappeared, and she could hear footsteps running down the stairs. Then there were voices from outside the house. Wild Bill said, "She can't be far. You go that way. I'll wring her neck when I catch her."

The house was quiet. The attic smelled like old lumber and was stuffy. She was sweating again. It was hard to breathe and she wondered whether she should slip down through the attic panel and hide in the house, but she was too terrified to move. Besides, she remembered a game she and her father had sometimes played. He would chase after her, she outrunning him.

368   Excerpt from "THE LAKE OF FIRE"

The next moment she would look behind her, only to realize that he was gone. At that point she would know he was going in another direction to head her off, so she would hide. The thing she had learned was that if she kept hidden in one spot, he had more difficulty finding her. It was only when she came out of hiding to run that he caught her.

She was thinking about the game when Wild Bill's head appeared through the trapdoor again. This time he pulled himself up into the attic. "She must be here somewhere," he said. He walked right past her as he went to the window to look out. She noticed he was too tall to stand upright, so he had to walk bent forward.

He knelt at the window and looked out. For several moments he remained in that position. Then he looked behind him, his eyes scanning the attic. "I know you're here," he said. It was eerie. She knew he couldn't see her yet, but it was like he could feel her presence. He said, "It'll be easier if you come out on your own."

She felt herself trembling. The awkward position she was in made the trembling more pronounced. She couldn't stop it.

There was a struggling sound, and she heard Flash say, "There she is!"

She saw his head in the attic opening. He had pulled himself up.

"She's hiding right there," he said. He was looking directly at her.

"Please help me," she found herself saying. She didn't know whom she was talking to. "Please, no." She couldn't withdraw any farther into the rafters, though she tried to pull away. "Help!" she screamed. She began peeing. She screamed and screamed as Wild Bill slapped her with his stinging hands.